I0788199

Whispers

Between Worlds

Whispers
Between Worlds

Shiloh's Secret

L. M. Gabriel

CONTENTS

Chapter One

Carmen

April 15th, 1998

"**C**an you turn the music down, please, sweetheart?" Mom asked, rummaging through her purse as she tried to locate her ringing phone.

I reached over and twisted the volume knob down a few notches. The beat softened, fading into the background.

"Thank you." She pressed the green button and lifted the phone to her ear. "Hello? Yes?"

Her smile slipped away almost instantly. Her grip on the phone tightened, and her gaze remained locked on the road. Her face was shadowed by a disappointment she didn't voice.

"Oh no... How late should we expect you?" A pause. Then a soft gasp, barely audible. "Huh. Okay, well... we can make do for one night. Thanks for letting us know. Bye."

She ended the call and tossed the phone into the cup holder with a dull clack. "Perfect. Just perfect," she muttered, her voice dripping with sarcasm.

"What's wrong?" I asked.

"The moving truck broke down. The movers won't be here until tomorrow."

I looked around the packed car. "Well, good thing we've got pillows and blankets, right?"

We drove for nearly three hours, headed to a new house in a new town called Riverbend Heights. Mom had landed a job offer she couldn't turn down, and honestly, we all needed a fresh start after the divorce. It had been a long and ugly process, months of fights and tension, before Dad finally gave in and signed the papers.

We'd all drifted from him. Or maybe he let us go. Either way, I didn't miss him. I just wanted Mom to smile again. I wanted something that felt new. Something that didn't feel like we were always waiting for the subsequent explosion.

To outsiders, Dad was the picture of charm, warm, funny, and full of life. However, he was quick-tempered and critical at home, often just one comment away from yelling. I used to admire him when I was little, and I believed in him then.

But that was before.

Five Years Ago

I was in the waiting area outside the doctor's office. I sit with my hands tightly folded in my lap, staring at the plaque on the wall that says "Dr. Frederick Wilson, Psychiatry," the letters feeling like they're burning into me. My stomach twists as I try to understand what's happening, scared that my parents will be mad or disappointed, and I don't know how to explain any of it to them. I was sent to the hall after speaking with the doctor for the third time this week, so he could speak with my parents. I knew something was wrong with me since I was eight years old. I tried to keep it a secret, but here I am, three years later, with a doctor telling my parents I have something called schizophrenia. I don't know what that is, but he says it's why I sometimes hear voices in my head and see shadowy figures.

The door opened, and my parents walked out. Mom was crying, and Dad looked mad. He shook the doctor's hand, said thank you, and started walking towards the exit. "Let's go," he demanded.

The first half of the drive home was an awkward silence. Aside from the voices in my head every so often.

...Look at me...I'm right here... it's not safe...

"Am I in trouble?" I asked when I couldn't take the silence anymore.

"No! Of course not, sweetheart," Mom said in a soft, caring voice. "This is not your fault. It's just-"

"Bullshit, Diana," my dad interrupted.

"Thomas, she's-"

"She's just looking for attention, that's all this is," he snaps, gripping the steering wheel so tightly his knuckles turned white. "I don't believe for a second that she has schizophrenia, she's fine, she's just acting out, and I'm not going to let this ruin our family."

"Thomas, my mother-"

"Your mother is crazy! Carmen is not crazy."

Mom tried to defend me, but she knew it was pointless. Whenever Dad was adamant about something, there was no hope in making him see sense.

I wasn't making it up. I didn't even want them to know. They only found out because they overheard me having an audible conversation with the voices in my head. Of course, they only heard my side of the conversation, but it was cause for concern, so they made an appointment with the doctor.

~~~~~~~~~~

"Carmen, honey?" Mom's voice pulled me out of my thoughts.

"Yeah?"

"Are you okay?"

"I'm fine."

She gave me a quick glance. "You sure? You know you can talk to me about anything."

"I know, Mom. Really, I'm okay. I was just daydreaming."
~~~~~~~~~~

There was no point in telling her what was actually on my mind. I think, deep down, she already knew how I felt about Dad. And maybe, deep down, part of her still loved him too.

This move, this whole fresh start, was something we all needed. The divorce left cracks in everything, and we did our best to patch them up. Mom's new job was a blessing, steady, well-paying, and enough for her to care for us independently. That counted for something.

"Okay," she said, her voice softening. "Can you read the directions again? What's the name of the next street we're turning onto?"

I looked down at the folded paper in my lap, her neat handwriting listing step-by-step turns. "Hill Road," I said.

As if on cue, the road appeared ahead, and we turned.

"Alright, we'll be there in about fifteen minutes. Can you call your sister and see how far out they are? Ask if she can grab something for dinner, and let her know the movers won't get here until tomorrow."

I nodded, picked up her phone from the console, and clicked through her contacts. My sister's name popped up, and I tapped it, listening to the line ring while watching the trees blur past the window.

Chapter Two

Karina

I watched as my older sister answered the phone. Her long, golden-blonde hair, with dark roots showing, fell effortlessly over her shoulders. Her pale skin seemed to catch the light, almost glowing, and her blue eyes narrowed slightly as she spoke, her tone calm and collected.

"Hello?" she said. Then she looked at me and mouthed, *It's Carmen.*

"Oh, okay. Yeah, I can do that," she said into the phone. "We just got off the highway, maybe thirty minutes out. Alright, see you soon. Bye."

"What did she say?" I asked.

Liv sighed. "The movers won't be there until tomorrow."

"Great," I muttered. "Guess we're sleeping on the floor."

She pulled into a parking lot, the red neon glow of a "PIZZA" sign lighting up the windshield.

"Mom said to grab dinner," she said as we parked.

We got out and crossed the lot. The bell above the door jingled as I pushed it open. A guy behind the counter looked up from the prep area and walked over. He was tall, with tousled brown hair and sharp blue eyes. A name tag on his shirt read *BRETT*.

"Hey, welcome to Joey's Pizza. How can I help you?" he said with a polite smile.

"Hi," Liv replied. "Can we place a to-go order?"

"Absolutely. What can I get you?"

"Can we do one large pizza, half pepperoni and mushroom, and the other half with green pepper and sausage? And another large, half-Hawaiian and half-supreme?"

He repeated the order back to us, then asked, "Would you like to add any drinks or sides?"

We walked over to the cooler and grabbed a mix of sodas and water bottles—enough for everyone.

"Okay," Brett said, ringing it all up. "That'll be $36.25."

Liv handed him two twenties. "Keep the change."

"Do you have paper plates and napkins?" I asked.

"Yep," he said, reaching for a shelf behind him. He packed them into a plastic bag and slid it across the counter. "Alright, give me about 25 minutes and I'll have everything ready."

"Thanks," we both said, returning to the car to wait.

~~~~~~~~~~

We sat in the car, the engine off, and the windows cracked just enough to let in the warm evening air while we waited for our pizza. Our conversation drifted to the new house.

Liv had seen it a month ago when she went with Mom, but Carmen and I hadn't. It still felt like an abstract idea for me, some distant place we were headed toward, not quite real yet.

"—and our bedrooms share a bathroom," Liv said, "but Carmen gets her own down the hall."

I nodded, trying to picture it after years of sharing a room with Liv; the thought of having my own space again felt like a luxury. I love both of my sisters; I'd do anything for them. However, sometimes, privacy feels like air you didn't know you were missing until you finally get to breathe it again.

It was no secret that Liv and I were closer to each other than either of us was to Carmen. It had always been that way, and we were all okay with it. Carmen kept more to herself, and Liv and I just... clicked.

If we hadn't shared a room all those years, though, I never would've found out Liv's secret.

And if I hadn't... would we still be moving?
~~~~~~~~~~

Three Months Ago

I woke up to the soft creak of the floorboards and blinked into the dark, barely making out my sister's silhouette by the window. She paused for a second, glancing back like she wasn't sure whether to go, then quietly pushed the window open and slipped outside. Curiosity got the better of me, so I crept to the edge and peeked out, just in time to see her meet another girl under the streetlight— tall, confident, waiting. They didn't say much, just smiled like they'd been waiting for this moment forever, and then my sister leaned in and kissed her. My heart thudded, not from shock, but from the quiet realization that I was seeing a part of her I'd never known, something secret, something beautiful. As much as I tried to stay awake, I couldn't; I fell back asleep.

When I woke the next morning, my sister was back in her bed as if nothing had happened. I took that as my opportunity to talk to her. I walked over and sat on the edge of her bed. I softly nudged her arm to wake her. "Liv,?"

She rubbed the sleep from her eyes and propped herself on her elbows. "What's up?" she asked, yawning.

"I uh- where did you go last night?" Her eyes widened in surprise, and she sat up more.

"Please tell me, I won't tell Mom or Dad. But I saw you and that girl, you were..." I trailed off.

She was silent for a moment.

"Nina," my sister finally said, "her name is Nina."

"Is she your girlfriend?" I asked. Liv nodded in response, "Why didn't you tell me? I thought we told each other everything."

"I'm sorry, I didn't know how to tell you. This hasn't exactly been easy."

"So, are you... gay?" she nodded again. A smile grew on my face, and I hugged her. "I'm so happy for you, I won't tell them, I promise."

"Thank you, Karina, for understanding."

"Hey, I'm proud of you for being yourself," I say, smiling widely as I hug her. "It doesn't matter to me who you love; you're still my sister, and I love you just the same."

"I've been so scared to tell Mom, and especially Dad. They're going to freak out," she paused. Pondering her next thought. "I need to tell them. They deserve to know. Will you come with me?"

"You don't have to tell them now. You can wait. I promise I won't say anything."

"I know you won't, but it's time. I've been keeping her a secret for a while, and I'm almost 19 years old. I have to do it eventually. Why not now? Will you come with me?

"Absolutely." I hugged my sister again, so happy she trusted me.

Later that day, after we all had breakfast—it was Sunday, and Mom always made a big breakfast on Sundays since it was the only morning she didn't work the night before—we gathered in the living room. I was sitting on the love seat with Liv, Mom, and Dad were on the sofa, and Carmen was in the chair to the right.

'Mom, Dad," Liv started, "there is something I've been keeping from you. Something I need to tell you," I grabbed her hand and held it in mine for comfort.

"What is it, honey?" Mom asked

Liv took a deep breath. "I've been seeing someone for a few months now. We are really happy and I-"

"You have a boyfriend?" Mom asked with a smile growing on her face. "Why didn't you say anything. Honey, that is great news. I-"

"You better not be pregnant!!" Dad interrupted.

"No," Liv said, "I don't have a boyfriend. I- I have a girlfriend."

Silence fell through the room. Mom stood up, and Dad stayed sitting with an angry look. "Liv, are you saying you are gay?" Mom asked.

"Yes, Mom. I'm sorry." Liv apologized.

Mom stepped forward and wrapped her arms around Liv. "Liv, you are my child, and I love you so much. Nothing will ever change that. You do not have to be sorry; you never have to be sorry. If this is who you are, I support you, and you never have to apologize for being yourself. I'm so happy you told me." Mom stepped back and took Liv's hands in her own. "What's her name? When can we meet her? Will she come for dinner?"

"Stop it!" Dad shouted. The room fell silent once more. Mom turned around to face her husband. "This is sick! This is wrong!" Dad shouted.

"Thomas, it's not a big deal. If she's happy, then why aren't-"

"I will not have it!" His face hardens, eyes filled with anger and hurt, and he shakes his head, "I can't believe this... you're not my daughter anymore." With a cold voice, he orders, "I want you out of my house, now, before you destroy everything we've built."

Dad stood with clenched fists. I stood up and walked in front of my mom and sister, standing my ground. How dare he yell at her for something that is not her fault? How dare he not love his child for who she is?

"You will move out!" Dad said, "I will not support this lifestyle!"

"We are not kicking her out, Thomas!" Mom said back.

"Diana, this is wrong! It is not right. I will not have it under my roof."

Mom stood silent for a moment. A tear escaped from her eye, and she said, "Then you leave."

~~~~~~~~~~

After picking up the pizza, we got back on the road to drive to the new house. We pulled onto Maple Creek Lane. "Wow, these houses are all so old," I said. As we drove down the quiet road, the crumbling Victorian houses loomed on either side, their once grand facades worn and faded by time. The cracked windows and overgrown yards give the whole place an eerie, forgotten feel, as if the houses are waiting for someone to remember them.
~~~~~~~~~~

"Most of them are abandoned," Liv told me. Abandoned or not, they were beautiful. We drove up the gravel road for a few minutes until we reached our new driveway. When we pulled in, I saw Carmen sitting on the front steps, her long, dark hair falling over her shoulders like a curtain. Her fair skin seemed to glow in the afternoon light, and her brown eyes met mine with a quiet, steady gaze. As I got out of the car, I spotted Mom bent over in the front seat of her car, rummaging frantically through the vehicle with a furrowed brow and muttering under her breath.

"What are you looking for?" I asked.

"I can't find the key. I thought I put it in my pocket, but now I can't find it anywhere."

"I have it!" Liv said, holding it up. "You dropped it when you were packing up the car. I forgot to tell you."

Relief spread across Mom's face. "Oh, thank god."

Liv walked over to the front door and unlocked it. I rushed in past her, excited to see the inside. The interior felt cavernous and quiet, with high ceilings, arched doorways, and intricate crown molding that framed each empty room like a forgotten stage. Dust-mottled sunlight filtered through the stained-glass windows, casting muted colors across the faded hardwood floors and emphasizing the elegance that still clung to the home's worn bones.

Chapter Three

Carmen

The moment I stepped inside, a sour wave of dread hit me, thick and choking, bile burning its way up my throat, all while the voices in my head got increasingly louder...*let me out...you're worthless... I'm scared...* Gagging, I bolted back outside and collapsed by the bushes, retching until my stomach was empty. Mom ran out and rubbed her hand on my back as I threw up. "Oh, sweetheart. Are you okay?" Mom said softly and caringly, "I told you not to eat that whole bag of candy on the drive over. Oh, I'm sorry." I didn't think it was the candy, but I wouldn't tell her that. When I was done, I stood back up and walked into the house. I didn't like it. There was something about the place that felt ominous, like there was an invisible veil separating something inside the house from the outside. The air was thick, and I felt weird. Like I was being watched. Like, when you're watching a horror movie, the music is building up in the background, and you know something is about to jump out on the screen to scare you.

I pushed my feelings aside, knowing my mom would just say it's because my mind tricks me. If I told her, it would just mean another trip to the doctor, and I was already on three different medications, and they didn't help at all. All they did was make me feel like a zombie. I was always tired and felt like the world moved in slow motion. It never took the voices away or anything.

My sisters looked around the house, while I stayed on the first floor. Dust blanketed every surface, muting the once-elegant details of carved woodwork and faded floral wallpaper. Cobwebs clung to the corners, and the air smelled faintly of mildew and forgotten time.

We went back outside and began to bring in all the boxes we had brought in our cars. The moving truck carried all our furniture and heavier items, but we packed our cars with delicate items, some of our clothes, personal belongings, and cleaning supplies. By the time we finished getting everything inside, it was already eight in the evening, so we decided to eat the pizza that my older sister, Liv, had picked up on the way. Since we had no table or anywhere to sit, we all sat on the living room floor, talking and eating. It was nice.

I ate my Hawaiian pizza and listened to everyone's conversation.

"We will have a lot to do tomorrow," Mom said before taking a bite of her supreme pizza. "First thing, before the movers get here, I want you girls to sweep and mop your bedroom floors so we can get the beds and everything in after," Mom said to my sisters.

"I'll sweep them all if you mop," Liv said to Karina.

"Yeah, I can do that. But only if you carry the mop bucket up the stairs. You know I'll spill it everywhere."

"Deal," Liv said.

"And Carmen, can you help me wash all the windows and countertops?" Mom asked me.

I nodded in response as my mouth was full of pizza.

Liv and Karina were closer to each other than I was to everyone else. I didn't mind. We all got along and did things for each other. But sometimes, I did wish I could confide in them. When I got my diagnosis, everyone walked on eggshells around me. They always asked if I was okay and if the medication was working. It didn't. It never did, but I never wanted them to worry, so I just said I was fine.

After eating, we threw our trash in a garbage bag in the kitchen since we didn't have our trash can yet. We grabbed all the blankets and pillows from our cars and made makeshift beds on the library room floor, as it was the only room in the house with carpeting instead of hardwood. It was a cool room, lined floor to ceiling with shelves, a window seat, and sliding French doors in the entryway.

It had been a long day, and we were all tired from packing up the cars and the long drive, so we decided to call it an early night. We all fell asleep before ten.

Chapter Four

Karina

April 16th, 1998

I slowly woke up, my back sore from sleeping on the hard carpet, and blinked at the morning light spilling through the window. I could hear my mom finishing up in the kitchen, the scent of cleaning supplies lingering in the air. She'd already swept and mopped the whole main floor. Groaning, I pulled myself up and stretched before heading to the bathroom to prepare for the day. Once dressed, I grabbed a slice of cold pizza from the fridge and bit into it without thinking twice. It wasn't the healthiest breakfast, but it was all we had. After eating, I got straight to helping with the cleaning. It was only half past seven in the morning, and the moving truck was expected to arrive within a couple of hours. Carmen stayed downstairs and helped Mom clean while Liv and I swept and mopped the upstairs floor.

I dipped the mop into the bucket and dragged it across the dusty hardwood, the wood creaking softly beneath my feet. My sister swept beside me, the broom's bristles brushing the floor with a rhythm I'd grown used to. As I moved, my eyes wandered over the details of the house: the tall, arched windows, the ornate baseboards, and the faint remnants of old wallpaper peeking through the layers of dust. It was a beautiful house, even though it was empty.

Shortly after ten, the moving truck rumbled up the driveway, its engine loud and steady like a warning bell on the quiet street. Two large men climbed out and started hauling boxes and furniture up the walkway, their heavy boots thudding against the steps. Liv and I stood in the doorway, pointing out rooms and trying not to get in the way as our entire lives got carried inside piece by piece. We directed them to the appropriate rooms as they unloaded bedframes, dressers, tables, and couches.

I sat cross-legged on the floor of my new room, pulling books from a box and stacking them on the wooden shelf the movers just hauled upstairs earlier. The shelf creaked under the weight, but it held steady as I slid in a hardcover copy of *Jane Eyre*. My window was open, letting in the scent of cut grass and the sounds of the movers outside as they finished up.

One of them said, "This place is old, real old. Been empty for years."

The other guy laughed, adding, "No one ever stays here long. A year or two, tops, and then they're gone."

I paused, a book still in my hands, and stared at the window, a strange chill crawling up my spine despite the warm afternoon air. Although this house wasn't up to standard, it was okay. I did wonder if what they were saying was true or just gossip.

I continued to carefully stack the unread books on my shelf, arranging them in the order I planned to read them, each cover staring up at me like a promise. For the books I'd already read, I lined them up alphabetically by author, the spines neatly aligned in perfect rows. It was small, but I liked how it made the shelf feel organized, like I had control over at least this little part of my life. I didn't have many, maybe around a hundred. I usually check books out at the library, but I occasionally buy some, and I have received a few as gifts, and some were books I've read for school. That's when Liv walked into my room carrying another one of my boxes.

"This was accidentally put in my room," she said.

"Thanks," I told her. She set it down in the corner next to half a dozen other boxes. "I overheard the movers talking about the house. One said this house has had several people move in and out fairly quickly, like every year or two. Don't you think that's strange?"

"Yeah, that is a bit strange. Maybe it was a rental property for a while. Who knows?"

She walked out.

~~~~~~~~~~

The moving truck was finally unpacked two hours later, and the movers had driven off, leaving the driveway empty and quiet. Liv was in the living room, helping Mom arrange the furniture; her voice drifted in now and then with a question about where something should go. I was in the kitchen, surrounded by half-empty boxes, putting dishes away one by one and trying to make sense of the unfamiliar cabinets. Carmen was already unpacking her room upstairs, blasting music loud enough to shake the ceiling. The whole house felt like chaos, but weirdly, it also felt like we were starting to settle in.
~~~~~~~~~~

Chapter Five

Carmen

I smoothed out the last corner of the blanket and stepped back from the bed, satisfied with how it looked; simple, but finally starting to feel like mine. The walls were bare, and boxes were stacked in the corner, but at least the bed was done. I glanced around the room, trying to decide what to tackle next. My eyes landed on the duffle bag slumped by the chair, full of clothes I hadn't seen since we packed up the old house. With a sigh, I hoisted it onto the seat and wheeled the chair across the floor to the closet. As I rolled it into place, the wheels squeaked faintly on the wooden boards. I reached for the doorknob and pulled it open, expecting the usual blank space, just shelves and hangers, but still feeling a weird twinge in my chest as the hinges creaked. I was lucky to have a walk-in closet. It wasn't huge, but it had enough space for all my clothes plus more. My bedroom was the smallest compared to Liv and

Karina's rooms, which were about the same size, except Karina's room had a huge bay window. I was slightly jealous.

But they both had smaller closets, so I felt like I won that battle. I grabbed a few shirts from the bag and walked into the closet. The voices got louder. It sounded like a little girl. *...Let me out... help me... I'm scared...*

As I hung another shirt on the rod, a faint, sing-song voice echoed behind me, high and childish, impossible to make out but unmistakably authentic. I froze briefly, exhaled slowly, and kept working, brushing it off like always. It wasn't the first time I'd heard things like that, and I'd learned not to let it get to me. But then the closet door slammed shut violently, trapping me in the dark so fast my breath caught in my throat. I assumed it was the wind because the window was open, but when I went to open the door, it wouldn't budge. It was stuck. An overwhelming feeling came over me, and I started to panic. The little girl's voice got louder and louder... *help me... daddy please... let me out...*

I heard another voice, a deeper voice like a man ... *you're worthless...*

I tried opening the door. Turning the door handle, but it still wouldn't open. Everyone else was downstairs, so I banged on the door, hoping that someone would hear me, but it felt useless. I felt panic rising inside me. I started to cry. I felt trapped. Like, I would never get out of here. I suddenly felt a tightness in my chest, as if the air had thickened and I was breathing through glass. My heart pounded against my ribs, too fast, too loud, and the edges of everything around me started to blur. I backed up and slid my back down the wall to the floor. I pulled my knees to my chest and wrapped my arms around myself. I couldn't control my breathing, and my hands were shaking. All the while, the voices grew louder and louder. My vision blurred from tears, and I couldn't find my breath. I shut my eyes in defeat.

Chapter Six

Liv

I gripped the end of the couch, carefully lifting it as Mom unrolled the large rug beneath us, her hands steady and precise. The hardwood floor creaked under our feet as we shifted the furniture into place, the room slowly starting to come together. I couldn't help but smile at the thought of how different this old house was, but somehow, it already felt like home. Karina was in the kitchen, putting dishes away in the cabinets. I walked over to the living room entryway, picked up an end table, and placed it next to the couch.

"It's looking great," Mom said,

"It's looking functional," I said with a laugh.

Karina walked into the room, her medium-length brown hair falling messily around her face as she glanced at Mom and me. Her light skin seemed to glow in the soft light, and her bright blue eyes were sharp as always, scanning the room for something to do. "The dishes are put away," she said with a half-smile, as if it were the only thing she could think of to say.

"Great. Thanks, honey," Mom said. Mom glanced at her watch. "Wow, it's nearly three. I'm getting pretty hungry, are you?" Mom asked us.

"Starving," Karina and I said in unison.

"Jinx," we said again with a laugh.

Sometimes, Karina and I seemed like twins because of our striking similarities. However, we were also very different. Karina was sweet, kind, and generous. She was always thinking of others and doing anything she could to help.

"Why don't you go get Carmen and tell her to get ready. We'll go out to get something to eat," Mom said to Karina.

Karina turned on her heel and made it up the stairs. The music playing from Carmen's room was turned off, and not a minute later, Karina shouted. "MOM!" We both sprinted up the stairs to see what was wrong. We ran into Carmen's room, and Karina crouched in front of Carmen's closet.

"What's wrong?" I asked.

Karina stood and pointed. Mom and I peered around the door to find Carmen crying in a ball in the corner.

Mom rushed in, her medium-length blonde hair slightly messy from the day, her light skin pale with worry, and her brown eyes wide as they landed on Carmen. My little sister was curled into a ball in the closet, trembling, breathing shallow and fast like she couldn't get enough air. Tears streamed down her face, but she didn't seem to see us—just stared at nothing, completely lost in whatever had shaken her. Mom dropped to her knees beside her, gently touching Carmen's back, "Carmen? Sweetie?" Her voice was low but urgent as she tried to reach her. Then she looked up at me, eyes sharp, and said, "Liv, go get my phone, now."

I spun around and bolted down the stairs, my footsteps pounding against the wood as I rushed to the kitchen. The phone was sitting on the counter where Mom had left it, and I snatched it up before turning back toward the stairs. Halfway up, I tripped and stumbled hard, but I pushed myself up without thinking; getting the phone to Mom was all that mattered. I went back into the room and handed Mom her cellphone.

She took it in her hand and dialed 9-1-1.

"9-1-1, what's your emergency?" a lady said over the phone.

"Hi—yes, my daughter is having what looks like a panic attack, but she has schizophrenia, so I'm not sure if this is something more serious."

"Okay, ma'am, I understand. Is she conscious and breathing?"

"Yes, she's breathing, but it's fast and shallow. She's curled up in a ball and crying—she won't respond to me."

"Thank you. How old is she?" the lady asked.

"She's sixteen," Mom said.

"What is your address, ma'am?"

"27 Maple Creek Lane, Riverbend Heights."

"Alright, help is on the way. Stay with her, speak calmly, and don't try to move her. If anything changes, let me know immediately. Please stay on the line until the paramedics arrive."

"Okay, thank you. Please hurry."

Mom stayed on the line but didn't pay attention. She was trying to get through to Carmen, who wasn't moving.

Nine minutes later, I stood frozen in the hallway as the paramedics filed into Carmen's room, calm and focused, their voices low and steady. One of them knelt beside her, while the other unpacked a small kit; their movements were practiced, as if they'd done this a hundred times. They tried talking to her gently, asking her name, telling her she was safe, but she didn't answer or even blink. She kept breathing fast, her eyes wide and empty, like she wasn't there. My chest ached watching her like that, so small and scared and unreachable. After a glance between them, one of the paramedics prepared a sedative, explaining quietly what they were doing before giving her the injection. Within minutes, her body began to relax, and they carefully lifted her onto the stretcher. I followed behind silently as they carried her down the stairs and out into the cool air, the ambulance doors swung open like something out of a dream I couldn't wake up from. Mom got into the back of the ambulance with Carmen and the lady paramedic, and Karina and I got into my car to follow.

~~~~~~~~~~

After a tense twenty-minute drive, I'd sat in this chair against the wall for over thirty minutes, staring at the same pale hospital tile and listening to the quiet hum of machines. Mom sat close to the bed, gently brushing Carmen's hair back as she began to stir, her fingers never letting go of hers. I leaned forward as Carmen's eyes opened, the weight in my chest lifting just a little as I finally saw her coming back to us.

"Mom?" Camren said in a groggy voice.

Mom leaned in closer, gripping Carmen's hand in hers. "Sweetheart, I'm right here."

"I feel sleepy," Carmen mumbled. Her eyes barely opened as she stirred from the sedation.

"They had to give you a sedative, Carmen," Mom said. "Do you remember what happened?"

"I was in my closet. The door shut, and I couldn't get out."
~~~~~~~~~~

"Oh, honey, your window was open, the wind probably blew the door shut."

"It wasn't the wind. The door locked. I couldn't get out. I tried," Camren said as a fresh tear fell from her eye.

"Carmen, it's an old house, it must have gotten stuck," Mom said, trying to console her.

Carmen had disbelief in her eyes, but just said, "You're probably right."

A nurse walked into the room. "You're awake," she said. The nurse looked down at the clipboard before saying, "Carmen, how are you feeling?"

"I'm okay," she said.

"You gave everyone quite a scare." She walked over to the monitor, which had wires coming from it and were stuck to Carmen's chest, and pressed a few buttons. "Your vitals look good." She turned back towards the door. "The doctor will be in shortly."

A few minutes later, a man in a white coat came in. He was a psychiatrist.

"Hi Carmen, I'm Dr. Horowitz. I see you've had a hard day. Can you tell me what happened?"

"I don't know. I was in my closet, and the door shut, I couldn't get out," Carmen told the doctor.

"The wind blew the door shut," Mom cut in.

"I see," he said to Mom. "Carmen, can you tell me how you felt when that happened?"

"I felt scared. I felt like I couldn't breathe."

"I see you were diagnosed with schizophrenia about five years ago. Is that right?" Carmen nodded. "And you're currently taking haloperidol and risperidone?" the doctor asked.

Carmen nodded again.

"Were you hearing or seeing anything while this was happening?"

"Um," Carmen quickly glanced at Mom but didn't make eye contact. "I heard two voices. But that's not what happened. It wasn't the wind. Something shut it."

"Carmen, I need you to understand that while it may seem like that, your mind tricks you. Have you been taking your medication every day?"

"Yes," Carmen said quietly.

"Okay, well, maybe we just need to adjust them again. Do you have a doctor you see regularly?"

"We just moved here from Pennsylvania yesterday. I have a couple of referrals from her last doctor, we still need to make an appointment," Mom said to the doctor.

"I see. Well, I would make an appointment as soon as possible. In the meantime, just keep taking your medication."

"Doctor, what happened? She's never been like this before," Mom said with worry.

"It's hard to say, but my best guess is that she had a panic attack," the doctor wrote something down on his clipboard. "They can be caused by stress or anxiety. Sometimes, life changes can trigger a panic attack." He ripped a piece of paper off his notepad. "You said you just moved, which can be stressful and trigger emotions." He reached out his hand, holding the paper, and handed it to Mom. "I prescribed an antianxiety. Give her one a day with food. It should help ease her anxiety."

Mom took the paper. "Thank you."

"I think you'll be fine to go home. Take it easy for a few days, limit your stress, and you'll be okay." He reached out and shook Mom's hand. "I'll have the nurse get your discharge paperwork started, and we'll get you out of here shortly," he said as he exited the room.

~~~~~~~~~~

I watched as Mom hovered over Carmen, making sure she was as comfortable as possible on the couch, fussing over every little thing like she always does when she's worried. Carmen sat there, arms crossed, trying to look unbothered, but I could see the tension in her shoulders. The way she held herself, like she was itching to get up and do something. She hated it when Mom worried about her, always acting like she could handle it alone, like she didn't need anyone to make things easier. But that wasn't
~~~~~~~~~~

Carmen; she always looked out for everyone else, putting herself last. She shot me a quick look that said she didn't want to be treated like she was fragile. I could tell she was putting on a front, trying to be strong, but it didn't stop Mom from doting on her every moment. The house was filled with the sound of Mom's gentle instructions and Carmen's quiet protests, and all I could do was sit back and watch, knowing neither of them would admit what was going on.

Mom hesitated momentarily, glancing over at Carmen, curled up on the couch, before turning to me. "Liv, can you run to the store for me? I don't want to leave her side right now," she said, handing me a crumpled list. I took it from her, my fingers brushing hers as I nodded, already knowing what she needed.

"Yeah, I'll go now," I said, feeling the weight of the responsibility on my shoulders as I turned to head out the door.

Chapter Seven

Karina

I slid into the passenger seat of Liv's car, the engine humming to life as we pulled out of the driveway. The gravel crunched beneath the tires as we turned onto the narrow road, and I glanced out the window, watching the old, abandoned Victorian houses pass by. Some were falling apart, with boarded-up windows and overgrown yards, while others seemed barely standing, the paint peeling as if they were giving up on time. It felt like we were driving through a ghost town, the kind of place where no one had lived for years. As we approached the end of the road, I saw something different: a house, standing proudly, the white trim gleaming against the deep green of its ivy-covered walls. The lawn was perfectly manicured, and a lovely front garden bloomed with colorful flowers, like something out of a storybook. A woman was bent over in the garden, wearing white capris and a blue jacket, pulling weeds or planting something new. Her movements were slow but purposeful, and she seemed so at peace and at home in this place. I couldn't help but stare, feeling as though we had crossed into a completely different world.

~~~~~~~~~~

We drove the twenty minutes to get into town and found the local market. Liv and I talked as we moseyed through the aisles, grabbing what we needed off the shelves.

I trailed behind Liv as we walked through the grocery store, pushing the cart half-heartedly down the cereal aisle. "I still don't think Carmen had a panic attack," I said casually, grabbing a box of granola I didn't want.

Liv stopped and turned to look at me, brows raised. "What do you mean? We saw her; she was curled up in the closet, crying and breathing like she couldn't catch her breath."

"I know," I said, shifting my weight. "She looked scared, but I don't know... it just didn't feel real."

Liv sighed, grabbing a box off the shelf. "Panic attacks are scary, Karina. That's the whole point."

I stared at the cart and mumbled, "Okay, I see your point," before continuing to walk. I didn't feel like continuing that conversation. I understood where she was coming from, but I wasn't convinced. I believed Carmen
~~~~~~~~~~

when she said it wasn't the wind that blew the door shut. She was sure of that. There had to be another explanation.

We finished getting all that we needed at the store. Plus a few extra things that weren't on the list, like ice cream and other snacks. And some drinks besides the OJ and iced tea that Mom wrote on the list.

When we got home, Liv and I carried the grocery bags inside and started putting everything away; the kitchen still smelled faintly of cleaning spray. Carmen was in the living room, curled up on the couch with her Discman, the headphones snug over her ears like always. She didn't even look up when we walked in; she just stared at the ceiling. The music was probably turned up so loud she couldn't hear us anyway. Carmen was always listening to something—rock, classical, even weird ambient stuff— because the noise helped drown out the voices in her head.

I sat on the couch next to Carmen, close enough that Mom would be satisfied I was keeping an eye on her, but not so close that it felt like I was hovering over her. She had her headphones on again, staring off into space, and I wasn't sure if she was listening to music or just trying to block everything out. Mom had made it clear; Carmen shouldn't be alone right now, just in case. While she started dinner in the kitchen, Liv finally disappeared upstairs to unpack her room. I curled up with the new book Aunt Maggie had brought me from her trip to London, *Harry*

Potter and the Philosopher's Stone, the cover already worn from the flight over. I didn't expect to get into it, but when the smell of dinner drifted in from the kitchen, I was five chapters deep and completely hooked. I didn't notice how much time had passed until Mom called us to the table.

We ate dinner, and everyone was quiet at first. It felt awkward. After a few minutes of silence, I started a conversation.

"Can I shop for new clothes before we start school next week?" I asked Mom.

"Of course, but go over the weekend. We still have a lot to do in the next two days before I start my new job," Mom said. "Liv, can you take her?"

"Yes. I need to go too. I need to buy a new pair of black pants for my new job." Liv responded.

"You found a new job already?" I asked her.

"Yeah, it's a coffee shop on campus. It's only part-time, but it's a start. It's easier to get a job when you have one," Liv explained.

"Carmen, you should go too. Get some new things. How does that sound, honey?" Mom asked Carmen.

"That sounds good," Carmen replied.

We moved into the new house over spring break, and now there are only four days left until the new school quarter starts on April 20th. I've been counting down, not because I'm nervous, but because I'm excited. Most people say they love school because they get to see their friends, hang out, and socialize between classes. That was never the case for me. I didn't have any friends at my old school; instead, I had a lot of awkward lunches and quiet walks between periods with my head down. But I loved school anyway. I loved the structure, the smell of books, and the feeling of understanding something new for the first time. Learning made me feel like I had control over something, like my mind had a place to stretch and breathe. I know it's kind of nerdy, but I don't care. This new school feels like a chance to start over, and maybe things will be different this time.

~~~~~~~~~~

April 18th, 1998

The day before was a blur of cleaning, organizing, decorating, and pure exhaustion. We all pushed ourselves to get the house in order before Mom started her new job. She's a nurse and got offered a big promotion here in New York, so we moved to a new state. It was a little after three in the afternoon, and the house was quiet except for the soft hum of the dishwasher. Mom had been gone since seven this morning, so Liv made breakfast for Carmen and me. And by "made," I mean she grabbed three bowls from the cabinet and tossed us a cereal box from the pantry like
~~~~~~~~~~

a gourmet meal. After that, I spent a few more hours organizing my bedroom, lining up my books just right, and setting up my desk exactly how I like it. I took a shower and let the hot water melt away some of the stress from the past few days. Then I wandered into the library, where Mom had helped me set up my favorite reading chair. I curled up in it with a blanket and a book, finally feeling like this place could start to feel like home.

Carmen was in the living room watching TV, and I knew Liv was still in the shower, so I'd been enjoying the quiet while I read. After a few hours, my stomach started growling, so I finally climbed out of my chair and headed into the kitchen. Liv was just coming down the stairs as I stepped through the doorway, towel-drying her hair. But what caught my attention wasn't her, it was the kitchen itself. Several cabinet doors were hanging wide open, as if someone had been searching for something and had forgotten to close them.

"Seriously? Is it that hard to close the cabinet?" I shouted as I proceeded to shut them. "Did you leave these open?" I said to Liv as she walked into the kitchen.

"No, why would I do that?"

I shrugged." Can you make us dinner?" I said to Liv. "I'm starving."

"It's only five o'clock," Liv responded. "Mom's going to be home in a couple of hours, I'll make dinner then so she can eat with us. Just grab some chips or something to tie you over."

"Fine," I said. I walked over to the pantry, grabbed a bag of potato chips, and took them into the living room. I sat on the couch opposite Carmen, back to the armrest, facing her. After a minute, I nudged Carmen's side with my foot.

"Hey," I said, "why did you leave all the cabinets open?"

She turned to me, "I haven't been in the kitchen. It wasn't me."

Okay, the wind did it.

I ate half a bag of chips before I got tired of them.

Carmen was in the living room, watching reruns of *My So-Called Life...* I didn't particularly like the show; the pacing felt slow, and the drama was somewhat overdone, but it wasn't the worst thing to have on in the background. It was okay to pass the time, especially when neither of us felt like talking. I sat on the edge of the couch, flipping through a magazine, half-watching and half-zoning out.

Mom got home from her nursing shift a little after seven, looking tired but still managing to smile when she walked through the door. Her blonde hair was pulled back in a messy bun, and she dropped her bag by the front door with a sigh. Liv was already in the kitchen, plating dinner perfectly like she'd been timing it. The smell of roasted chicken and garlic mashed potatoes filled the house, and everything felt warm and normal for a moment. I sat at the table, watching them both, thinking how nice it was.

"It smells great in here," Mom exclaimed. "Liv, thank you. You didn't have to. I would have cooked."

"Don't be silly, it was your first day. Plus, I wanted to." Liv said back.

We all sat around the table, and the food smelled great. Liv prepared baked chicken breast with garlic mashed potatoes, one of my favorites, and asparagus, which is not my favorite, but I still ate them.

"So, Mom, how was your first day?" I asked shortly after we sat down, breaking the silence.

"It was great. Everyone is so nice and welcoming. I work with a girl named Julie. We got along so great."

We were all sitting around the table, Mom, Liv, Carmen, and me, eating dinner, when we suddenly heard a creaking sound, like a door slowly opening somewhere in the house. I froze briefly, then pushed my chair back and stood up, scanning the room. Nothing looked out of place at first, but something felt off. I walked through the foyer into the kitchen, and that's when I saw two cabinet doors hanging wide open, ones I knew had been closed earlier. My face went pale, and I turned and ran straight back into the dining room, heart pounding in my chest.

"What is it?" Liv asked

"The cabinets. They're open again."

"So?" Liv said.

"How did they open all by themselves?" *Why wasn't she freaking out?*

"Karina, it's an old house, and the screws are probably loose. They just need to be tightened."

I sat back in my seat, my mind racing as I tried to calm my breathing. After the cabinet doors opened by themselves, I felt this weird frustration bubbling up inside me. I didn't believe it was just because the house was old; people always used that excuse, but it didn't explain everything. I didn't think the wind had blown Carmen's door shut the other day. Something was going on, something out of the ordinary, and I wasn't sure if I was just imagining it, but I couldn't shake the feeling that it was real.

Chapter Eight

Carmen

April 19th, 1998

After breakfast, we all got ready to go to the mall to shop for clothes. As much as I liked clothes, I hated shopping. I hated malls, but not as much as doctors' offices; they were noisy, crowded, and my least favorite place. We all piled into Liv's car and drove the thirty minutes to the mall, and I was already dreading it. On the way, I put my headphones on and let the music drown out the chatter from Liv and Karina, who were talking excitedly about what they'd buy.

When we arrived at the mall, we parked and walked inside; the familiar, overwhelming noise and chaos instantly hit me. Right away, I felt that familiar urge to turn around and leave. The flashing lights, the chatter, the hangers clanging, it was all too much. But, of course, I stayed. We stopped in nearly every store, and Karina grabbed item after item, her arms practically piling up with clothes. Liv also got a couple of things, always picking out things that seemed to suit her perfectly, while I trailed behind, silently wishing we could be anywhere else. While Karina and Liv were deep inside Abercrombie & Fitch, I wandered towards Hollister, hoping for a quieter mall corner.

"Hi, welcome in, can I help you find anything today?" a lady with dark curly hair asked as I walked in.

"No, thank you," I said.

I wandered around the store, my fingers lightly grazing the fabric of the clothes as I tried to find something I might like to wear. The bright lights and the endless racks of clothes made me feel a little dizzy, but I kept going, grabbing two pairs of jeans that seemed comfortable, three tops I could wear for a casual day, a belt that caught my eye, and a zip-up hoodie that looked soft enough to live in. I wasn't sure why I was picking up so much. I suppose I just wanted to put the whole experience behind me. When I finally stepped out of the store, the noise and bustle of the mall seemed to be turning down a notch. Liv and Karina were standing by the entrance, already waiting for me. Karina had four bags of clothing, her arms nearly bursting, while Liv had two, looking way more collected than I felt.

"We're going to get something to eat," Liv said.

I followed them to the mall's food court, where the clatter of trays and the hum of chatter filled the air. There were five restaurants to choose from: pizza, Chinese, sandwiches, a smoothie stand, and an ice cream place. We all decided on Chinese, mainly because Karina couldn't resist the fried rice, and Liv insisted on the sesame chicken. Karina and I squeezed through the crowded food court, searching for a table while Liv stayed behind to pay and grab our food. The chaos of people moving in every direction made me feel dizzy, but we saw an empty table in the corner. We hurried toward it without thinking twice, eager to claim it before anyone else could. But just as we were about to sit down, Karina accidentally bumped into a girl, causing her to spill her drink all over herself. The blonde girl gasped in surprise, and before I knew it, her face twisted with anger.

"Ugh!" the blonde girl screeched, her drink splattering all over her clothes. "You did that on purpose!

"What? No." Karina stammered; her hands raised slightly as if trying to understand what had happened. "I'm so sorry, it was an accident."

The girl's lips curled into a sneer. "Yeah, right. You clumsy bitch."

Karina's face fell, her eyes dropping to the floor, and I could see the tears forming at the edges of her lashes.

"Hey!" I snapped, stepping in front of Karina. "We don't even know you, why would she do it on purpose? It was an accident. Just let it go."

The blonde girl raised an eyebrow, her smug smile growing wider. "Why don't I know you?" she asked, her tone condescending. "I know everyone. Right, Leah?" She shot a glance at the girl beside her, who barely nodded.

Ignoring her, I wrapped my arm around Karina and pulled her away. "You okay?" I asked softly as we settled into the nearest available seat.

Karina nodded quickly, wiping her eyes. "I'm fine," she muttered, though I could hear the tremor in her voice.

I squeezed her shoulder gently, trying to reassure her. "Don't let it get to you. Some people are just cruel. That girl is probably insecure and needs to put others down to make herself feel better."

"I know," Karina said quietly, her voice steadier now. "I'm fine. Seriously." But I wasn't so sure.

A few minutes later, Liv walked over with a food tray in her hands and three water bottles tucked under her arm. She set everything down, and we dug into the Chinese food while Karina and Liv picked up right where they left off— chatting about outfits, shoes, and which stores we still had to hit. I mostly listened, nodding along, not adding much. After eating, we cleaned up our table, tossed our trash in the garbage, and headed back into the maze of stores. I didn't want anything else; I was already tired of the crowds and the noise, so I trailed behind Liv and Karina as they browsed through four more stores. When we finally decided to head home, my feet ached, and all I could think about was crashing on my bed and listening to music.

~~~~~~~~~~

When we pulled into the driveway, the sky was already fading into that dusky blue that comes just after six in the evening. Mom had left for her night shift an hour earlier, so the house felt quieter than usual, like it knew she was gone. Karina and Liv headed for the living room, debating which movie to watch, but I didn't feel like joining them. Instead, I went upstairs to my room, craving silence and space.

I stretched out on my stomach across my bed, my sketchbook in front of me and a pencil in hand. My radio played softly from the desk, filling the room with just enough background noise to keep my thoughts from spiraling. I was working on a drawing I'd started a few weeks before we moved, one I couldn't quite bring myself to finish until now. It was a close-up of a girl's face, but one of her eyes was shattered like broken glass. Inside the cracks of the glass, I was drawing another world; darker, stranger, and eerily peaceful. I liked sketching things that
~~~~~~~~~~

made people uneasy, and felt like there was more beneath the surface than you first saw.

All of a sudden, my closet door started to open. The creaking sound sliced through the soft hum of the music playing from my radio, making my hand freeze mid-sketch. I looked up slowly from my sketchbook, the hairs on the back of my neck already standing on end. The door moved inch by inch, groaning on its old hinges like it hadn't been opened in years, even though I'd been there just yesterday. The light from my desk lamp didn't reach the inside; it was swallowed up by shadows that felt far too deep for such a small space.

I stared, heart thudding louder each second, waiting for anything to explain why the door was opening on its own. And then I heard it, that voice. I'd listened to that same little girl's voice the other day, soft and sing-song, but somehow wrong, like it was echoing from a place it shouldn't be.

...Can I come out now? The voice whispered. *...Can I play...?*

My blood ran cold. I didn't move. Didn't speak. I just stared into the closet's darkness, every part of me screaming to run, but somehow, I couldn't.

On impulse, before I could talk myself out of it, I did something I hadn't dared to do in five years, not since my parents caught me and Dad had told me never to do it again: I responded to the voice.

"You can come out," I said, "it's safe."

A pale white arm slipped out of the darkness like it had been waiting, just waiting, for me to look away. It moved slowly, deliberately, with bony fingers curling around the edge of the door handle, creaking as it made my blood run cold. My heart skipped a beat, maybe two, as the rest of her began to emerge. The little girl crawled out of my closet on all fours, her limbs moving with a jerky, unnatural rhythm like a broken puppet. Her skin was paper-white, almost translucent, and her face was a smooth, blank mask except for two dark, sunken eyes that stared straight through me.

My breath caught in my throat as I sat frozen, unable to blink or move. My mind screamed that it was just another hallucination. Just a trick, just my brain lying to me again. But this felt different. Too detailed. Too real. I tried to convince myself it wasn't happening, that I was still in control, but my body betrayed me, my hands trembled violently, and a cold sweat broke out across my back. My lungs felt tight, like the air in the room had been sucked out.

I've had visual hallucinations before; fleeting shapes in the corner of my eye, the shadow of someone standing behind me that vanished when I turned around, but never like this. Never something so vivid I could hear her fingernails dragging softly across the wooden floor. Never something that made me feel like I wasn't alone in my room... or my mind.

...Can I play now?... the little girl asked, her voice soft and lilting, like a nursery rhyme sung in reverse.

"You can go play," I told her, barely recognizing my voice, but calm on the outside, hollow and shaking underneath.

A smile crept across her face, slow and eerie, like her mouth wasn't used to the motion. Without a word, she turned on her heel and skipped out of my room, her footsteps unnaturally light on the wooden floor. I sat there for half a second, stunned, before instinct took over. I bolted out of bed, my sketchbook falling to the floor with a thud, and rushed after her.

I bounded down the stairs two at a time, the house oddly silent except for the pounding of my footsteps. At the bottom, I abruptly stopped, the hair on my arms standing straight up.

Something felt wrong. Off. I turned to my right, heart hammering in my chest, and there she was.

The little girl stood motionless, her back to me, staring out the large back window. Her head tilted slightly, almost like she was listening to something just outside. The light from the porch cast her silhouette in sharp relief, making her seem more shadow than flesh. Then, without warning, she took two small steps forward and passed straight through the glass without a sound. No shatter. No ripple. Just gone.

"Wait!" I called out, stepping forward, my hand reaching toward where she'd vanished.

But it was pointless. She was already gone, like she'd never been there at all.

Still, I didn't move. I stood there, rooted to the spot, my chest rising and falling in short, rapid breaths. Part of me wanted her to come back. Not because I wasn't afraid, but because I had to know. Why did I see her? Why now? I never saw people. Never faces. Just shadowy figures, vague and faceless, flickering at the edges of my sight. This was different, clear, vivid, and undeniable.

Something had changed. I just didn't know what.

Chapter Nine

Liv

"Did you hear that?" Karina asked, her voice low, almost hesitant.

"Hear what?" I said, glancing over at her. She looked uneasy, eyes flicking toward the hallway like she expected something to come out.

"Carmen," she whispered. "I thought I heard her... talking. To someone." I paused, listening. The TV was still playing in the background, some rom-com Karina had picked, but aside from that, nothing. "I didn't hear anything," I told her. "Just the movie."

Karina pulled her knees up to her chest. "Well... can you go check on her? Please?" Her voice was pleading now, the kind that made it hard to say no.

I sighed, defeated, and pushed myself off the couch. "Fine, but I'm telling you, it's probably nothing."

As I exited the living room, the air felt heavier and cooler, as if the temperature had dropped by a few degrees. I turned to my right and froze. Carmen was standing in the hallway, completely still, her back to me, facing the rear of the house. Her posture was too straight, too tense, as if she were holding her breath.

"Carmen?" I called out, but she didn't move. No reaction at all. I took a few cautious steps toward her, my heart beginning to pick up its pace. "Carmen," I said again, this time softer, almost afraid to startle her.

I reached out and gently touched her shoulder. She jolted, like she'd been snapped out of some trance, and spun around to face me.

"You okay?" I asked, keeping my voice low.

"I'm okay," she said, taking a deep breath like she was trying to convince herself.

"What's wrong?" I asked, even though I felt she wouldn't tell me.

"It's nothing," she mumbled, brushing past me and heading for the stairs. Her movements were stiff, distant, and almost mechanical. She didn't even look back as she climbed up, disappearing around the corner without another word.

I stood there for a moment, watching the empty hallway, unsettled. I didn't believe for a second that it was "nothing." But I knew better than to push. Carmen kept things locked up tight, and when she didn't want to talk, no one could make her.

I returned to the living room and dropped onto the couch with a quiet exhale.

"What happened?" Karina asked, eyes wide.

"It was nothing," I said, forcing a casual tone. No use freaking her out too. I grabbed the remote, pressed play on the paused movie, and leaned back against the cushions, though the chill in my spine still hadn't gone away.

~~~~~~~~~~

April 20th, 1998

I was up before the sun in the morning, my alarm blaring at exactly five a.m. Excitement buzzed in my chest, mixing with nerves. I started my new job today and was determined to make a great first impression by arriving early. I slipped out of bed and tiptoed into the bathroom, careful not to wake Karina through the adjoining door. She and Carmen had their first day of school today, and the last thing they needed was me crashing around at dawn. I gently shut the connecting door and turned on the shower. As steam began to fill the room, I tied my hair into a quick bun, slipped out of my pajamas, and stepped under the hot water. The warmth helped ease the tension in my shoulders, though my mind was already racing ahead to
~~~~~~~~~~

everything I needed to do. When I finished, I wrapped a towel around myself and stood in front of the mirror. The glass was fogged, so I wiped it clear with the side of my hand, revealing my sleepy reflection.

I brushed my teeth, then applied some makeup, not much, just enough to feel put together. I usually skip it entirely, but today felt like it deserved something extra. A bit of mascara, brow gel to tame the chaos, and a swipe of tinted lip balm did the trick.

Back in my room, I opened the closet and let my towel drop before pulling on my new uniform, black pants, and a fitted black T-shirt. Nothing fancy, but clean, professional, and exactly what they asked for. Once dressed, I returned to the bathroom and quickly styled my hair into a French braid, pinning back the grown-outside bangs that always escaped no matter what I did. I twisted and tucked them behind my ears with a few stubborn bobby pins until they stayed in place.

At a quarter to six, I was ready to go. I walked downstairs, my footsteps soft on the creaky steps, and reached the bottom just as the front door opened. Mom stepped inside, looking exhausted but smiling.

"Morning, honey," she said, her voice thick with fatigue. Night shifts always wore her down.

"Hi, Mom," I said, hugging her as she kicked off her shoes.

We both made our way into the kitchen. I opened the pantry, grabbed a granola bar, and reached for a coffee mug from the cabinet. Mom sank into the chair at the table with a long exhale, rubbing her temples while I quietly moved around the kitchen, trying to stay upbeat without being obnoxious.

"Coffee?" I asked my mom, reaching for the pot.

She shook her head gently, her eyes already heavy with sleep. "Oh, no, thank you. I'm going straight to bed after the girls leave for the bus. Just leave the pot on. I'll have some later."

I poured myself a cup and joined her at the table, sitting across from her in the quiet kitchen. The only sound was the soft hum of the refrigerator and the occasional creak of the old house settling. We sat silently while I sipped my coffee, the warmth doing little to ease the heaviness growing in my chest. I debated whether to tell her what had happened with Carmen the night before. Part of me didn't want to worry her; she was already stretched so thin. But another part knew she deserved to know. She was Carmen's mother.

"Something happened with Carmen last night," I said finally, my voice low.

Mom straightened, her tired eyes sharpening with concern. "What do you mean?"

"Karina said she heard her talking, but I didn't hear anything, but when I checked on her, Carmen was standing in the hallway, just... staring at the wall. I called her name twice, and she didn't even flinch."

Mom's face paled slightly. "Did she say anything to you?"

"She snapped out of it when I touched her shoulder," I said, remembering how Carmen jolted like she'd been awakened from a dream. "She told me she was fine, that it was nothing. But I don't think she was telling the truth."

Mom leaned back in her chair with a quiet sigh, worry etched in every line of her face. "I need to get her in for another appointment. After last week's episode, and now this... I'm scared it's getting worse."

"She'll be okay, Mom," I said gently. "She's strong." I drained the last of my coffee and glanced at the clock. "I'm sorry, but I need to go. It's almost six."

I stood, rinsed my mug in the sink, and left it on the drying rack. Grabbing my bag off the table, I leaned down to give Mom a quick hug.

"Call me when you get there," she said quietly, brushing a hand over my arm.

"I will," I promised, then turned and stepped out the door, the cool morning air brushing against my face as I headed into the still-dark morning.

I landed a job at a cozy little coffee shop tucked into the edge of the local college campus. Riverbend College wasn't huge, just under 4,000 students, but it had a charm I liked, with old brick buildings and winding footpaths lined with trees. The thirty-minute drive didn't bother me; it gave me time to wake up, listen to music, and clear my head before the day began.

When I pulled into the lot, I spotted two people walking toward the coffee shop's front entrance, a girl and a boy around my age. They looked casual but confident, like they'd been doing this a while. I parked, turned off the engine, and stepped out, crossing the sidewalk just as they reached the door.

"Hi! Are you Liv? You start today, right?" the girl called out with a friendly smile.

"Hi, yes, that's me," I said, returning the smile as I brushed a stray hair from my face.

"I'm Zara, and this is Trenton," she introduced, gesturing to the guy beside her.

"Trent," he corrected smoothly, shooting a playful look her way. "Only Zara calls me by my full name."

We all laughed lightly before stepping inside together. The scent of fresh coffee and baked goods hit me immediately; it smelled like warmth and routine. They led me through the café and showed me how to clock in. Then, we headed to a tiny break room in the back, where they pointed out the lockers and hooks for personal items.

Zara pulled a brand-new apron and a hat from a shelf and handed them to me. "Here you go," she said, quickly knocking on the nearby office door before cracking it open.

"Come on in," a woman's voice called from inside.

Zara stepped in briefly while Trent read something on the corkboard on the wall. A minute later, she reappeared.

"Okay," she said brightly, clapping her hands once. "We're your trainers for the next two hours while Anna, our manager, does inventory."

"Great," I said, slipping the apron over my head and tying it behind my back, suddenly feeling more official. I clapped my hands together, matching her energy. "So where do we start?"

Chapter Ten

Carmen

When I came downstairs, Karina was already at the kitchen table, dressed and halfway through her breakfast. She's always been an early bird, organized, punctual, and enjoys mornings. Me? I sleep until the last possible second and can be out the door in under ten minutes if necessary.

"Morning, sweetheart," Mom said, glancing up from the stove as I stepped into the kitchen, still groggy.

I sat down in the chair next to Karina. "Morning."

"Would you like some breakfast?" she asked, already sliding a plate in front of me before I could answer.

"Sure," I said with a shrug. The smell of blueberry pancakes made me perk up a little. Mom always made them on the first day of school. It was cereal or scrambled eggs on a good morning every other day, but this was tradition.

"Thanks," I muttered, and wasted no time digging in.

"You'll have to eat fast," Mom reminded me gently, pouring herself some coffee. "The bus will be here in twenty-five minutes."

At our old house, the bus came right to the end of our driveway. Here, we had to walk nearly a mile to the start of the road where it picked us up, something none of us were thrilled about.

I polished off the last few bites, rinsed my plate, and left it in the sink. Karina was already at the door with her backpack slung over one shoulder, zipping up her jacket.

We stepped outside, the morning air cool and quiet, and started walking. At first, we didn't say anything, just the sound of our footsteps on gravel and the occasional rustle of leaves in the trees.

"You're nervous," I said after a moment, glancing sideways at Karina. "No, I'm not," she replied quickly.

"It wasn't a question," I said, giving her a look. "I know you're nervous about starting at a new school. You had a rough time at the last one."

"Who told you that?" she asked defensively.

"No one had to tell me," I said softly. "It was kind of obvious. You didn't have any close friends, and I know some kids gave you a hard time."

She was quiet for a moment. "I'll be fine."

"I know you will," I said, nudging her arm gently. "I've got your back." She gave me a small smile, genuine, but still uncertain, and we kept walking.

A few minutes later, we passed the only house on the road that wasn't abandoned. The garden out front was neat and full of early spring blooms. A woman with grayish-brown curly hair was getting into her car, and through the window, I could see two others inside, probably her kids.

She politely waved at us before climbing in and backing out of the driveway. We waved back, then watched her car disappear onto the main road.

Two minutes later, the bus rumbled around the corner, its headlights cutting through the early morning haze.

"Ready?" I asked Karina.

She nodded. "Yeah. I think so." We climbed aboard.

Karina and I sat together near the middle of the school bus, surrounded by the low murmur of sleepy voices and the occasional thud of a backpack hitting the floor. About seven other students were scattered throughout the seats, staring out the windows. The bus jolted forward, and I glanced over at Karina. She was fidgeting with the zipper of her backpack, pretending not to be nervous, but I knew better.

The ride to school took around thirty-five minutes, winding through quiet neighborhoods and into town. When we finally pulled up to the front of the building, students began filing off the bus in a blur of noise and color. We had been instructed to go straight to the guidance counselor's office instead of homeroom, so we went through the unfamiliar halls together, schedules not yet in hand, and nerves tightening with every step.

A friendly blonde woman stood waiting inside the office, her smile soft and reassuring. "Hello! You must be Carmen and Karina. How are you two doing this morning?"

Karina spoke up first. "Hi, I'm Karina, and this is my sister, Carmen."

"It's so nice to meet you both. I'm Miss Meijer, I'm one of the guidance counselors here." She motioned us inside with a warm gesture. "Come on in and have a seat." We each took one of the chairs in front of her desk, while she settled in behind it and pulled out two color-coded folders, one green, one yellow.

"I won't keep you long," she said, flipping open the green folder. "I just want to confirm a few things and get your schedules sorted."

She looked at Karina first. "Okay, so Karina, you're joining our freshman class. It says here you're fifteen, is that correct?"

"Yes," Karina replied. "My birthday's in October."

"Great. And at your last school, you were enrolled in Algebra I, World History, English I, and Physical Science, right?" Karina gave a quick nod.

"Perfect. We've got room in all those classes." Miss Meijer turned to her computer and began typing. "Now, for your electives, you can choose one language: Spanish, French, or Latin. And you'll also have a choice between art class and study hall."

Karina thought for a second. "Can I take Spanish and a study hall?"

"Absolutely," Miss Meijer said with a smile. She clicked a few more times, then turned toward the printer as it hummed to life. "All set." She handed Karina a freshly printed schedule and then turned her attention to me.

"Alright, Carmen," she said, flipping open the yellow folder. "You'll be joining our junior class. And you're turning seventeen next month?"

"Yes, on the seventeenth," I answered.

"Oh! Your golden birthday, how fun! I'm a seventeenth baby, too, but in March," she laughed.

She scanned my records. "Looks like you were taking Algebra II, English III, American History, Government, and Biology. Is that still accurate?"

"Yep, and I was also taking French."

"Perfect," she said, fingers tapping swiftly across the keyboard. "We have space in all those classes. You've got one open slot, though; would you prefer an elective or a study hall?"

"Study hall, please," I answered without hesitation.

She nodded and clicked through a few final screens. "Done. I'll print your schedule now."

Just as the printer finished spitting out the page, a loud bell rang through the building.

"That's the end of homeroom," she explained as she handed me my schedule. "Don't worry. There are five-minute breaks between classes, so you'll have plenty of time to find your way around."

Miss Meijer stood up and opened a nearby file cabinet. She flipped through a large binder labeled *LOCKERS*, scribbled something down on two sticky notes, and handed one to each of us.

"These are your locker numbers and combinations. Don't lose them, though, if you do, we can always get you another copy."

We stood, clutching our schedules and sticky notes, and I felt the butterflies in my stomach flutter a little faster now.

"Alright, you're both all set," she said brightly. "Have a great first day, and don't hesitate to come find me if you need anything."

We thanked her and walked out of the office together, glancing down at our schedules before heading in opposite directions. The day had just begun.

Chapter Eleven

Karina

The bell rang, cutting through the classroom chatter and signaling the end of the second period. I exhaled and packed my things, slinging my backpack over my shoulder. So far, the day had been... okay. I had math first, then science, and next was P.E., followed by lunch. After that, it was world history, study hall, and finally English. It was a full day, but manageable.

Instead of heading straight to the gym, I used the break to find my locker. I dug out the sticky note from my pocket and read the number: *346*. Walking down the hallway, I read the numbers aloud under my breath like a chant. *"333... 334... 335..."* I finally found it between a dented locker covered in stickers and one with a broken handle. I double-checked the combo: *36-24-04*. I turned the dial slowly, holding my breath. Click. It opened on the first try, a *small victory*. I placed the two textbooks I'd been lugging onto the top shelf, savoring the weight lifted from my shoulders, literally and figuratively. But that moment of peace shattered like glass.

"Well, look who it is."

The voice behind me was unmistakable. I didn't even have to turn around to know who it was. *No, not today. Please not today.* I turned slowly. It was the girl from the mall, her platinum blonde hair practically glowing under the fluorescent lights, who stood just a few feet away, arms folded, lips curled into a smug smile. Leah was beside her again, whispering something under her breath and giggling. A new addition, a tall boy with short, dark, curly hair and a letterman jacket, stood with them.

"Hi," I said, stiffening and straightening my back to look more confident than I felt.

She smirked. "So this is where you ended up."

"I'm Steven," the boy said casually, ignoring the tension. He motioned toward the queen of mean. "And this is Amber." *Amber,* I thought. *So that's her name.* Steven tilted his head. "So today's your first day? Why'd you transfer schools?"

I opened my mouth. "My family just moved here, and I—"

"Don't talk to the trash, Steven," Amber snapped, cutting me off. "It's better just to throw it out." She tossed her hair with a practiced flick, then grabbed his hand. "Come on, we'll be late for math." And just like that, they walked away.

My shoulders sagged.

I closed my locker slowly, the metallic clunk echoing louder than it should have. It was only my first day, and I already had a target on my back. *Perfect.*

I found my way to the gym and checked in with the teacher. Since it was my first day, I didn't have gym clothes yet, so I was excused from participating. I sat off to the side while everyone else played volleyball, using the time to scribble through some science notes and mentally try to shake off Amber's words.

When the bell rang, relief flooded me. *Lunchtime.* I wasn't particularly hungry, but I grabbed some cheesy fries, a fruit cup, and a can of pop, comfort food in a strange place. I paid for my lunch and stepped into the cafeteria. It was buzzing with noise and motion. Every table was crowded with clusters of friends laughing, trading snacks, and chatting. I paused for a moment, overwhelmed. Then I saw he, Carmen, sitting alone at a table near the far-right corner. She was picking at her food with her headphones in, as usual. Without hesitation, I walked over and took the seat beside her. She looked up briefly, gave me a slight nod, then returned to her meal. And just like that, I felt grounded again. Even in a sea of strangers, at least I wasn't alone.

"How's it going?" I asked after a minute of silence had passed. She looked up from her fries.

"Not bad. You?"

"Same," I replied, though the knot in my stomach begged to differ. I was about to tell her about my locker run-in with Amber, but I didn't get the chance because she turned up beside us. *Speak of the devil.*

"I was hoping to find you here," Amber's sugary-sweet voice sliced through the cafeteria noise like a blade. She strolled up to our table like she owned the place, Leah and Steven flanking her like backup dancers. In her hand was a neat stack of hot pink flyers. She pulled a small folded paper from her pocket and slapped it onto my tray. It was a receipt. *Total: $18.00.*

"What's this?" I asked, already knowing I wouldn't like the answer.

Amber folded her arms. "That's how much it cost to dry-clean the outfit *you* ruined."

"It was an accident. I didn't *ruin* anything," I said, steadying my voice. "I said I was sorry you spilled your drink, but it wasn't my fault."

She raised a perfectly plucked brow. "Correction: *you* slammed into me and spilled my drink all over *me*. So yeah, your fault." She barely finished the sentence before turning to a girl with glossy black hair who was passing by. "Chloe!" Amber shouted.

Chloe paused. Amber handed her one of the pink flyers. "It's my sweet sixteen next Friday. Theme's vintage glam."

"Oh my God, thank you, Amber! I can't wait." Chloe beamed and walked off, already telling someone.

Amber turned back to me with a smug grin. "Don't expect one yourself. I don't invite charity cases."

The words hit harder than I expected, sharp and personal. Before I could respond, Carmen shot so fast that she nearly knocked her chair over.

"What is your *problem*?!" she snapped, her voice ringing across the cafeteria. Heads turned.

I reached out and grabbed her arm, trying to tug her down. "Carmen, it's fine. Let it go."

Amber's smile grew cold. "You've got your sister fighting your battles now?"

"Leave her alone," Carmen said, eyes narrowed, fists clenched at her sides.

"Seriously, sit down, don't make a scene," I pleaded, heart thudding.

Amber laughed, flipping her hair with theatrical flair. "Relax. You two are used to being invisible, don't start acting like you matter now."

That was it for Carmen. "Get out of here," she snapped. Her voice was low, dangerous.

Amber's smug expression faltered for just a second before she turned with a dramatic scoff. "Come on, guys," she said, and Leah and Steven followed her as she walked away from us.

When they were finally gone, Carmen sat back down, her face still burning red. "You okay?" she asked me, her tone gentler now.

"Yeah," I said quietly. "Thanks... for standing up for me."

We finished our lunch in silence. The food barely tasted like anything anymore. When the bell rang, we tossed our trays and headed out, the cafeteria noise roaring back to life behind us.

Chapter Twelve

Liv

My shift was a whirlwind of learning: how to make everything from lattes to frappés, how long to heat the breakfast sandwiches without burning them, and how to distinguish between a cappuccino and a latte. One thing became crystal clear: I'm terrified of the steam wand. Every time that hiss screamed to life, I jumped like it was coming for me.

We'd just gotten through a mid-morning rush, and for once, I realized I hadn't spilled anything in two hours. Small victories. I glanced at the wall clock; my shift had technically ended six minutes ago, time to clock out. I walked over to the office and knocked on the door.

"Come on in," Anna called from inside. I pushed the door open and stepped in.

"Hey, I just noticed I'm a few minutes over my shift. Is there anything else you'd like me to do before I head out?"

Anna looked up from a stack of papers and smiled. "Nope, you're good. You did a great job today, Liv. Especially for your first day."

"Thanks," I said, feeling a tiny bubble of pride.

I headed to the break room, grabbed my bag, clocked out, and said a quick goodbye to Zara and Trent, who gave me a high-five on my way out.

Out in the parking lot, I climbed into my car and finally checked my phone. *Nina: Two missed calls.* I dialed her back as I settled in with the open door, the air warm and buzzing around me.

She picked up after the first ring. "Hello?"

"Hey, I'm sorry I missed your call. I just got off work."

"That's right, today was your first day. I forgot," she said. "How'd it go?"

"It was good! A little overwhelming, but honestly, kind of fun. The people are nice, and once I get the hang of the drink menu, I think I'll be fine."

"I'm so glad," Nina said.

"Actually... I have something to tell you."

"Okay?"

"I'm transferring schools." That caught me off guard. Nina had been studying business and photography at the college near our old town, the school she'd dreamed of for years.

"What? Why? You *love* that school."

"I did," she said. "But something's missing. *You're* missing."

My breath hitched. "Nina..."

"I miss you, Liv. I've been thinking about it a lot and want to be where you are."

"I miss you too," I whispered, already half-smiling, half-nervous.

"I'm moving to New York," she said, her voice soft but steady.

I sat up straighter. "Are you serious? Nina, you can't just uproot your whole life for me."

"I'm not doing it *just* for you. I'm doing it for *us*. You're my home, Liv. I don't want to keep loving you from a distance."

God, I love her. Every piece of me wanted to say yes, scream yes.

"I love you, too," I said instead, the words sticking in my throat. "So... when are you coming?"

"I'm going to finish the semester here, then start my senior year in New York this fall. But there's one thing I wanted to ask before I commit."

"Anything."

"Do you think... Could I stay with you this summer? Before I move into the dorms?"

I smiled so wide it hurt. "That would be awesome. Seriously. I'll talk to my mom tonight; I don't *think* she'll say no."

"Thank you," she breathed. "And hey, if she does, it's okay. I'll still visit and move in closer to fall."

"I'll do everything I can," I said. "I can't wait to see you."

"I have to run to class in ten. But I love you, Liv."

"I love you, too."

We hung up, and for a long second, I just sat there, staring at my reflection in the rearview mirror. My heart was whole and racing at the same time. I turned the key in the ignition, the engine rumbling to life. This summer might just change everything, *if* Mom says yes.

And I hope she says yes.

Chapter Thirteen

Karina

Like this morning, Carmen and I sat together on the bus ride home. As we neared our stop, we moved to the front of the bus. The brakes gave a soft squeal as the bus pulled over, and the driver opened the door with a familiar hiss.

"Have a good night," she said as we stepped onto the gravel shoulder of the road. Behind us, two more students got off, a boy and a girl. I recognized them from this morning; they'd been in the car we passed on the way to the bus stop.

I turned toward them. "Hi, I'm Karina, and this is my sister, Carmen. We just moved in last week."

"Hey," the girl said with a warm smile. "I'm Sarah, and this is my brother, Brett."

Brett nodded but kept walking, hands shoved in his hoodie pocket.

"You work at Joey's Pizza, right?" I asked him.

"Yep," he said without breaking stride.

We started walking up the road together, the late afternoon sun casting long shadows behind us. When we reached their driveway, Brett paused, facing the house, while Sarah stopped beside me. Carmen continued up the road toward our place, headphones on her head.

"So, how was your first day?" Sarah asked. She was petite, with light brown wavy hair that grazed her shoulders and striking hazel-blue eyes. Her frame was thin, her collarbones gently outlined beneath her T-shirt. She had a natural, delicate kind of beauty, someone who seemed shy at first glance but wasn't afraid to speak her mind.

"It was alright," I said. "My teachers are all nice, and the school's easy to navigate."

"Yeah, it's not very big," she laughed. "So, you just moved in; how are you liking it so far?"

"I love it. Our house is gorgeous, and I appreciate the quiet atmosphere here. It's a big change from our old place; we lived in a suburb before, lots of noise, neighbors practically on top of each other."

"Same. I grew up in a tiny apartment before Brett and I moved in with our aunt and uncle."

"Sarah," Brett called sharply from a few feet away.

She rolled her eyes. "What? It's not a secret, Brett." He muttered something under his breath and turned back toward the house.

"I saw you two in the car this morning. Was that your aunt?"

"Yeah, that was Aunt Rhea. She drops us off on her way to work, but we take the bus home. I'm sure she could give you and your sister a ride in the mornings."

"Seriously? That would be amazing, thank you."

"No problem," Sarah said with a smile. "It's nice to have new people around. We should hang out sometime. Are you free after school tomorrow?"

I nodded. "Yeah, I am."

"Cool!" She swung her backpack off her shoulder and pulled out a pen and a scrap of paper.

"Write your number. I'll call you later."

I wrote down our home phone number and handed it back.

"Awesome. Talk soon," she said, then jogged up her driveway. I turned and continued home, a little bounce in my step. I'd made a friend, a *real* one.

When I walked through the front door, Carmen was already curled up on the couch, still wearing her headphones, swaying slightly to her music. I spotted Liv in the kitchen, talking to Mom. Her face was practically glowing. Something was up. "What's going on?" I asked.

"Nina's coming to live with us!" Liv said, beaming.

"Just for the summer," Mom clarified, holding her hands like she needed to slow the excitement. "She's transferring to Riverbend in the fall."

"That's awesome, Liv. I'm so happy for you." I dropped my backpack on the floor and sank into a chair.

"But," Mom added, giving Liv a pointed look, "this comes with rules." Liv sat up straighter, hands clasped before her like she was about to accept an award.

"Number one: no closed doors. Number two: She helps with housework and pitches in for groceries. Number three: She needs to get a job. I'm not having her lounging around here all summer."

"Done, done, and *done!*" Liv squealed, practically bouncing on her toes. "Thank you, thank you, thank you!" She rushed out of the room and bolted up the stairs, already dialing.

Mom shook her head, half-smiling. "Let's hope they don't drive each other, or the rest of us, crazy." I laughed and leaned back in my seat, feeling the warmth of something missing lately: things falling into place.

Chapter Fourteen

Carmen

I sat at my desk in my room, buried in math homework. Ugh, I hated math. None of it made sense to me. I had the radio on, the soft hum of music filling the room as I listened to a new song I'd heard recently, *Bitter Sweet Symphony*. The melancholy tune played in the background, but my focus kept drifting. Halfway through the song, I heard a voice, a little girl's.

"...can you help me... I'm scared..."

I froze. My heart skipped. I quickly turned off the radio and closed my book, trying to steady my breathing.

"I can help you," I whispered, unsure if I was even speaking aloud.

I slowly turned my chair around, scanning the room. There was nothing at first. Then, the closet door creaked open, almost like it had a life of its own. My breath caught in my throat as she appeared again, the little girl. She crawled out of the closet and stood in the doorway, her movements stiff and unnerving. She wore a green dress, her long, dark blonde hair pinned back at the sides, her face a mixture of fear and uncertainty.

"Why are you in the closet?" I asked, my voice trembling slightly.

...I have to hide... she whispered, her voice distant, like an echo.

"Hide from what?" I asked, my curiosity rising, though a knot of unease tightened in my stomach. She didn't look quite right; there was something off about her. She appeared almost translucent, her edges blurry, like she wasn't entirely real. Suddenly, the closet door slammed shut behind her, making me jump.

...I have to go, or I'll get in trouble... she murmured, her voice growing fainter.

Before I could say anything more, she turned around and vanished into thin air. I blinked, hoping for a second that my imagination was running wild. But it wasn't. I stood frozen in place, trying to understand what had just happened. I had never seen things like this before, not like this. Shadows, yes, but not people. And this little girl... she wasn't just a shadow. *Was* I hallucinating?

Just then, there was a knock on my door.

"Are you okay, sweetheart?" Mom's voice called from the other side. "I heard a door slam." Mom heard it, too. I wasn't imagining things.

"I'm fine," I said, quickly composing myself. "It was an accident. I'm sorry." I didn't want to tell her until I realized what was happening.

"Alright, well, dinner's in twenty minutes. Are you finished with your homework?" she asked, her voice soft.

"Almost," I said, forcing a smile.

"Good. I'll call you down when it's ready." She left, closing the door behind her.

I let out a shaky breath. Okay, Mom heard the door slam, which meant I wasn't losing my mind. But she didn't hear the girl speak. Only I did. Was there something else going on here? Karina mentioned the kitchen cabinets being wide open the other day, but no one admitted to opening them. Was it possible there was something... more? Something I couldn't quite understand?

~~~~~~~~~~

Dinner that night was quiet, though the warmth of Mom's homemade chicken pot pie filled the house with a familiar sense of comfort. It was one of her specialties, made only a few times a year, as the pie crust took forever to make from scratch.
~~~~~~~~~~

"So, how was your first day of school?" Mom asked as we dug into our plates.

"It was good," Karina replied, her tone nonchalant. I noticed she was avoiding eye contact with me. She must've been keeping whatever happened with Amber to herself. I wasn't going to bring it up, either, not yet.

"Did you make any new friends?" Mom asked, looking between the two of us.

I shook my head, and Karina answered, "One, but not at school. Sarah, from the end of the street. We met when we got off the bus today. We're going to hang out tomorrow after school."

"That's wonderful, honey. Do you have her number? I'd like to speak to her mom first," Mom said, a little too eagerly.

"Please don't embarrass me, Mom," Karina groaned. "And yes, I have her number. But she lives with her aunt and uncle."

"Oh, don't worry, I won't embarrass you. I just want to introduce myself," Mom insisted. "I mean, it's not like we have many neighbors."

"Okay, okay," Karina sighed.

I smiled, glad to see Karina had made a friend. She never had any at our old school, though Mom didn't know that. Karina had always spent hours at the library after school, claiming she was hanging out with friends, but I never saw anyone with her.

"Oh, Carmen, don't forget," Mom said, turning to me as she wiped her mouth with a napkin. "You have a doctor's appointment after school on Thursday. Liv's going to take you."

"Do I have to go?" I asked, already dreading it.

"Yes, you do," she said firmly. "We need to get your medications sorted out. You've been struggling, and you don't tell me everything."

"I haven't been struggling," I muttered, mostly to myself. But the words felt hollow. Sure, I was seeing more, hearing more than I ever had before. But it wasn't hard. It wasn't *difficult*. It felt strange; everything around me had shifted, and the air in this house was thicker. I couldn't shake the feeling that something wasn't right. It felt like I was being watched... all the time.

I knew if I mentioned that to Mom, she'd dismiss it as "just the air outside," or something equally logical. But I knew what was happening. I *felt* it. Whatever was going on here, I had to keep it to myself, for now.

Chapter Fifteen

Karina

April 21ˢᵗ, 1998

It's the following day, and I was at my locker during break before the last class of the day.

Amber strutted with her usual crowd, her blonde hair pulled up in a perfect butterfly clip. She stopped and looked me up and down like I was some stain on the tile floor. "Did your mom dress you in the dark again?" she sneered, loud enough for everyone nearby to hear. Her friend Leah burst out laughing, and I felt my face burn as I stared down at my faded jeans and oversized flannel. I wanted to disappear but could only slam my locker shut and walk away, pretending her words didn't follow me down the hall.

After school, I found myself sitting with Carmen on the bus again. I would have sat with Sarah, but her brother,

Brett, claimed the seat next to her before I had the chance. He was a senior, and I couldn't help but notice how protective he seemed of her. As the bus pulled up to our stop, we all got off, and I followed Sarah and Brett down the street toward their house while Carmen headed in the opposite direction, walking toward our place.

We walked up a gravel driveway that led to a stunning, dark green Victorian-style house. It was strikingly similar to ours, but while ours was maroon and had seen better days, lacking landscaping, Sarah's home was pristine. The front garden was lush and well-maintained, a testament to the care her aunt and uncle must have put into it. Intrigued by their family, I asked, "So, what do your aunt and uncle do?"

"Uncle Matt's a real estate agent, and Aunt Rhea used to teach two classes at Riverbend College a few years ago, but now she owns a shop right off campus," Sarah explained.

"That sounds cool. What kind of shop?" I asked, curious.

Sarah pushed open the front door, and we stepped inside. The moment I crossed the threshold, I was struck by the eclectic charm. It wasn't cluttered, but knick-knacks were everywhere, crystals, unique statues, and captivating photographs. Each surface seemed to hold a carefully chosen decor piece, giving the space a cozy, welcoming feel. It was immaculate, with a warmth that made it feel both lived-in and loved.

"A curiosity shop," Sarah said, and that explanation made perfect sense. We headed to the kitchen first, where Sarah pulled a fresh veggie platter from the fridge. "Let's go to the basement," she added, motioning for me to follow.

I trailed behind her as we walked down the hallway, and she opened the door to the basement. At first, I was puzzled. Why would we eat in a basement? The cellar at our old house was unfinished, cold, and uninviting, a place we only ever went to for laundry. However, that was nothing compared to the basement of our new home. It was dark, musty, and damp, a far cry from the warmth and charm of Sarah's house.

Not all basements are like that. As I descended the stairs, I was surprised to find clean, smooth walls and sleek, modern flooring. Two couches faced each other in front of a stylish wet bar on one side, while two oversized bean bag chairs were arranged in front of an entertainment center. In between, a tall card table with four stools created a casual, inviting space. The basement starkly contrasted with the rest of the house, which retained its classic Victorian charm.

We sat on one of the couches, and Sarah set the veggie platter on the coffee table between us. I grabbed a cucumber slice and popped it into my mouth, savoring the crispness.

"So, I'll be honest," Sarah started, breaking the silence. "I saw you in my science class yesterday, and I wanted to introduce myself, but you left right after the bell rang before I could get to you."

"Oh, I'm sorry about that," I said, feeling a little guilty for not noticing her.

"No, no, it's fine," Sarah reassured me with a smile. "I was just excited to learn you were our new neighbor. The thing is, I don't really have any close friends. I have a lot of people I talk to at school, but they're not my friends."

"Same here," I admitted. "Back at my old school, I had people to talk to during class, but none were friends."

"That's awesome!" Sarah exclaimed, then paused, realizing the awkwardness of her words. "I mean, not awesome, but... You know what I mean? It's nice that we have that in common."

I chuckled. "Yeah, I get it. It's not great that neither of us has real friends, but it's nice that we can be friends now."

"Exactly!" Sarah grinned, grabbed a bell pepper from the platter, and took a bite. "So, what do you like to do outside of school?"

"I love to read," I said, feeling too enthusiastic. "I try to read two to three books a week."

"Wow," Sarah said with wide eyes. "I like to read, but not *that* much. I usually manage to finish about two books a month."

I laughed, waving her off. "Hey, it's not a competition. Everyone reads at their own pace."

"I have a lot of hobbies, so I usually just read before bed," she continued, reaching for another veggie.

"Like what?" I asked, grabbing another slice of cucumber.

"I knit, I paint, though I'm not very good at either. I make scrapbooks, I'm in the French club, I ride my bike, take tumbling classes, and sometimes I help Aunt Rhea in the garden."

"Wow, you keep yourself busy," I said, genuinely impressed.

"I also have tons of homework," Sarah added. "I'm taking two electives this semester and no study hall."

"Which electives?" I asked, intrigued.

"French and psychology," she replied.

"Psychology?" I raised an eyebrow. "Do you know anything about schizophrenia?"

"Not much," she said, flipping open her backpack and pulling out her psychology textbook. She scanned the index until she found what she was looking for and opened the book. "I know people with schizophrenia often hear or see things that aren't there, and they can have mood and behavioral issues."

"Why do you ask?" she added, glancing up from the book.

"My sister Carmen," I said quietly. "She was diagnosed with schizophrenia when she was eleven."

"Oh, I'm sorry," Sarah said, her voice softening with sympathy.

"It's okay," I replied, though I didn't feel entirely okay about it. "But what kind of mood and behavior issues can there be?"

Sarah flipped through the book, her finger scanning the text. "Let's see... Behavioral symptoms can include agitation, repetitive movements, aggression, hostility, or even self-harm. Moods can swing from anger and anxiety to elevated moods or inappropriate emotional responses."

I shook my head. "Yeah, that doesn't sound like Carmen."

"Well," Sarah hesitated, "is she on medication?"

"Yes, but she still hears things all the time. The medication hasn't helped. She told me about it two years ago."

"Hmm..." Sarah's brow furrowed as she thought. "I'm not a doctor, and I've only been taking this class for a few months. But maybe you should just trust her if she says she's okay. Sometimes the meds take time, but everyone's different."

"Yeah, you're probably right." I felt a sense of relief, but that nagging uncertainty was still in my chest.

We switched topics, talking about the latest movies and the characters from the books I'd been reading. The hour passed quickly, and before I knew it, I realized I needed to head home to start my homework.

"Well, I should probably get going," I said, standing up. "I've got homework to do."

"Yeah, me too," Sarah said with a sigh. "But we should hang out again tomorrow after school." She smiled. "I'm happy we're friends."

"Me too," I agreed, smiling. We planned to meet up the following day, and I left her house and walked home feeling like I'd found someone I could connect with.

I pushed open the door and stepped into the house. Liv was sprawled on the couch, eyes glued to the TV, while Mom was still at work. I sighed, relieved to have a moment of quiet. I went upstairs to my room, my footsteps soft against the carpeted stairs. As I reached the top of the stairs, I heard Carmen's voice drift through the slightly ajar door of her room.

"Why do you have to hide?" she said, her tone sharp but quiet, as if she were conversing with someone. Curious, I took a few silent steps toward her door, trying to stay calm so she wouldn't hear me...

"What's your name?" she asked, her voice filled with curiosity and uncertainty. My heart rate quickened. Something about this didn't feel right. I gently pushed the door open, not wanting to startle her. Carmen was facing the door, but she jolted when she saw me, her eyes wide with surprise.

"Knock much?" she snapped, her usual edge to her voice returning.

I hesitated, standing in the doorway. "Sorry, I just... who were you talking to?" I asked, my voice low to keep the concern from creeping in.

Carmen rolled her eyes and sighed... her shoulders stiff. "No one. I was reading out loud." I studied her carefully, narrowing my eyes. "Seriously, Carmen?" I crossed the room, closing the distance between us. "There's no one here. So why were you talking like that?"

Her gaze flickered momentarily, unsure of what to say, before she straightened her posture, her tone defensive. "Seriously, Karina. I was reading out loud. Now, please get out of my room." I stopped, a pang of frustration rising in me. I wanted to press further, but she wouldn't open up.

I turned to leave, my hand on the door handle. But before I could pull it shut, I glanced back at her. "You know you can tell me anything," I said quietly, almost hesitantly. "I won't tell anyone, not even Mom." The words hung in the air, but she didn't respond. I could feel her eyes on me, though, even as I closed the door behind me, the sound of it clicking softly in the silence. I stood there momentarily, leaning against the door, feeling the weight of the unspoken tension between us. But when no answer came, I walked away, unsure what to make of the conversation or the silence.

~~~~~~~~~~

April 22nd, 1998

The following day after school, I walked home with Sarah and Brett, while Carmen headed in the opposite direction toward our house. When we got to Sarah's place, she grabbed the veggie platter from the fridge and set it on the kitchen table. We decided to get a head start on our homework while we snacked. I pulled my assignments from my backpack, and we began with science since we shared that class.

We barely progressed when Sarah's aunt walked in through the back door.

"Hey, Aunt Rhea," Sarah greeted her.

Rhea smiled warmly. "Hey, honey. Is this Karina?" she asked, her gaze shifting toward me.

"Yeah. Nice to meet you," I said, with a slight wave.

"Nice to meet you, too." Rhea gave a friendly nod. "Well, I don't mean to interrupt your study time. I'm just grabbing a drink, and then I'll be back outside." She walked over to the fridge, pulled out a pitcher of iced tea, and set it on the counter. After grabbing a glass from the cupboard, she
~~~~~~~~~~

poured herself some tea, her movements casual and effortless. "Would you girls like some?"

"Yes, please," Sarah answered.

"Yes, thank you," I added, smiling politely.

Rhea filled two more glasses and, as she walked them over to the table, something strange caught my attention. Across the room, a door began to creak open by itself. My body froze. The door swung wider, inch by inch. I stared at it, a sense of unease creeping up my spine.

Rhea didn't seem phased at all. "Oh, don't mind that," she said, chuckling lightly. "It's just the ghost."

I blinked, unsure if I had heard that correctly. "Ghost?" I repeated, my voice quieter than I intended.

"Oh, she's just kidding," Sarah quickly reassured me, smiling at me. "Aunt Rhea always jokes about that. The door hinge is loose, and it always does that. She likes to say it's because we've got a ghost."

I let out a nervous laugh, relieved but still curious. "It must be the old houses," I said. "We have some cabinets that do the same thing at my place."

"Must be," Rhea agreed, smiling as she set the glasses before us.

The moment passed, but I couldn't help feeling like there was something strange in the air, something I couldn't quite put my finger on. It was probably just the way they'd said it, like it was all so casual, but there was a lingering chill I couldn't shake.

Later that evening, when I returned home, I sat at the dinner table with Liv and Carmen. Mom was working another night shift, just the three of us. We ate quietly, the hum of the TV in the background as usual. But as I chewed, my thoughts drifted back to Sarah's house. The door. The ghost joke. It wasn't a big deal, but something about it felt... off.

Chapter Sixteen

Carmen

"So, how was it with your new friend, Sarah?" Liv asked Karina as she took a sip of her drink.

"It was good. We worked on some homework," Karina replied with a shrug.

"Nice," Liv said, then turned to me. "Carmen, your appointment's at four tomorrow, so we'll need to leave right after you get off the bus. I'll be waiting at the end of the street. Karina, do you want to come with us, or are you good?"

"I'll be fine," Karina said. "I might head over to Sarah's again."

"Okay," Liv nodded.

The cabinet door behind her began to creak open with a long groan. We all froze, eyes locked on it.

"It's just an old hinge," Liv said, brushing it off with a smile.

"Sarah's aunt Rhea blames it on a ghost," Karina added casually.

Liv laughed. I forced a laugh, too, but something inside me twisted. Rhea said it was a ghost. And this wasn't the first time the cabinets had opened independently. Ever since we moved into this house, strange things have been happening. Too many to ignore.

After dinner, while Liv and Karina cleaned up, I slipped into the small library where Mom had set up the computer. I sat down, opened the browser, and typed the word *"ghosts."*

I clicked through articles, reading everything I could. Spirits could move objects for different reasons. The more I read, the more I thought about the little girl I kept seeing. Maybe she wasn't a hallucination after all. Perhaps she was a ghost.

She didn't seem dangerous, at least not yet.

One article mentioned poltergeists, while another discussed earthbound spirits, souls that couldn't move on and remained tied to the physical world. Could that be what she was?

I kept reading, absorbing as much as I could. Finally, I cleared the search history, in case Mom checked.

Something was happening in this house. And I needed to know what.

~~~~~~~~~~

I was jolted awake that night by my closet door creaking open again.

Heart racing, I pushed myself up on my elbows and fumbled for the switch on my bedside lamp. The soft glow filled the room... and there she was.

The little girl stood just a few feet from my bed, half-shadowed by the light. I'd tried asking her name the day before, but Karina had interrupted before she could answer.

"What's your name?" I asked quietly.

...my name is Shiloh...

Her voice echoed in my mind, soft and distant, like a memory I never had.

I wanted to know more... to be sure my ghost theory wasn't just in my head.

"When did you die?"

...when I was thirteen...

Suddenly, the closet door slammed shut with a violent *bang*. Shiloh flinched. Her eyes went wide with fear.

"What's wrong?" I asked, sitting up straighter.

...I have to hide or he'll get mad...

"Who? Who's mad at you?"

...my father... she whispered, and then she vanished.
~~~~~~~~~~

I leaned back against the headboard, my chest tight with unease. She'd died at thirteen and was still afraid of her father. Why?

Driven by instinct, I threw off my blanket, tiptoed downstairs, and powered on the computer. In the search bar, I typed: *thirteen-year-old girl, dead*, followed by our address.

Nothing.

I didn't know what year she'd died… only how old she'd been. It wasn't enough.

I erased the search and tried something else: *Can people talk to ghosts?*

Many results appeared, most stating the same things: stories, theories, and warnings.

Then something caught my eye: a website for a local shop that offered psychic readings.

Rhea's Curiosities.

My stomach flipped. Wasn't that Sarah's aunt's name?

I scribbled down the shop's address and phone number on a notepad, then carefully deleted the search history. The last thing I needed was my mom or sisters asking questions.

I crept back upstairs, heart still pounding, and slid beneath the covers.

Something wasn't right. And I was going to find out what.

~~~~~~~~~~

April 23rd, 1998

The next day, after school, Liv was already waiting at the end of the road, parked there. I stepped off with Karina, Brett, and Sarah as the bus pulled up with a loud hiss. Without a word, Karina peeled off with the other two, heading toward Sarah's house. I climbed into the passenger seat of Liv's car.

She gave me a tight smile. "Ready?"

I didn't answer. We both knew I wasn't.

The drive to the doctor's office took about thirty minutes. We didn't talk much, just the soft hum of the tires on the road and the occasional click of her turn signal. Outside, the city blurred past. Inside, I tried not to think about what was coming.

Liv filled out the new patient paperwork at the office, and her handwriting was quick and precise. I sat beside her, picking at a thread on my sleeve. The receptionist called my name just five minutes later.

A woman with short brown hair, round glasses, and a bright purple scarf greeted me. She looked like someone who knitted her sweaters and drank herbal tea with honey.

"Carmen? Come on back," she said warmly.

I followed her down a quiet hallway into a small, softly lit room. The walls were painted a deep, soothing blue. A
~~~~~~~~~~

plush loveseat sat across from an armchair angled in the corner, a box of tissues on the table between them. Everything about the room screamed *comfort*, which only made me more anxious.

"Go ahead and take a seat, and we'll get started," she said.

I sat on the loveseat, my fingers clenched around the edge of a cushion.

"I'm Dr. Wilson," she began, settling into her chair with a notebook on her lap. "Your mom emailed me yesterday, explained a bit of what's been going on. She said your sister would bring you."

"Yeah," I muttered.

I didn't want to be here. I never did. Doctors always say the same thing: *Your mind plays tricks on you. Be patient. The meds will help.* But they never did.

"So, you were first diagnosed with schizophrenia at eleven. Is that right?"

"Yes," I said, staring past her at the bookshelf behind her shoulder.

"And when you got that diagnosis, how did it feel? Did it help things make sense?"

I hesitated. "It upset my parents. But it gave a reason, I guess... for why I hear things other people can't."

Dr. Wilson nodded, scribbling something down. "You said 'hear.' In the present tense. Do you still hear things now, even while on your medication?"

I considered lying, saying no, and claiming that everything was fine. But I knew she probably already knew about the hospital visit last week. There's no point in getting caught in a lie.

"I do," I admitted. "Sometimes."

"That must be frightening," she said gently.

"It's not," I replied, more sharply than I meant to.

She gave a small, understanding smile. She asked the same questions slightly differently for the rest of the session, trying to coax me into opening up. I gave her the answers she wanted to hear, or at least enough to get through the hour.

Finally, she clicked her pen closed and pulled out her prescription pad.

"I'm going to adjust your medication," she said. "This should help stabilize the episodes a little more. We'll check in again next month, okay?"

I nodded and took the slip of paper. Liv was waiting in the lobby, reading a magazine.

We drove home in silence, again. The car felt heavier this time.

We stopped at the pharmacy on the way back. Liv handed over the prescription while I sat in the passenger seat, watching the sky darken through the windshield.

The pills would be new. But the feeling? That was always the same.

~~~~~~~~~~

That night, after dinner, I was supposed to start my new medication.

I stood in the bathroom, the soft buzz of the overhead light filling the silence. The mirror reflected a tired version of myself, with eyes shadowed and lips pressed into a flat line. I opened the cabinet and took out the orange prescription bottle, the label still crisp and unread by anyone but me.

I twisted off the cap and shook one pill into my palm. It sat there, small and chalky, like it didn't matter, but it did. My thumb brushed over it, hesitantly. Its weight felt heavier than it should.

If what I'm seeing and hearing is real... if she's real... maybe I don't have schizophrenia.

Maybe I'm not broken. Perhaps I've been right this whole time, and no one ever believed me.

I stared at the pill for a few more seconds before quietly grabbing a piece of toilet paper. I wrapped the pill in it, folded it over carefully, and dropped it into the bathroom trash can. Then I repeated the process with the other two I was supposed to take tonight—slowly, methodically, like a ritual.

The pills were gone. But not taken.
~~~~~~~~~~

I stared into the mirror one last time before switching off the light and returning to my room.

The hallway was dim, the walls casting long shadows in the glow of the nightlight. The house was too quiet, as if it were holding its breath. Karina was probably still working on homework, and Liv had gone to bed early. I had the house and the silence to myself.

I closed the door behind me in my room and turned on the small lamp by my bed. Its warm glow filled the space with a soft, golden haze. I moved to the closet and slowly opened the door, revealing only my clothes and a few storage boxes, as it always looked during the day.

But things never happened during the day.

I sat on the edge of my bed, staring at the dark space inside the closet, waiting.

The minutes passed. I didn't check the clock. I just waited, listening to the quiet, the hum of the house, the creaks in the walls that might've been footsteps. I didn't feel afraid, not exactly. More... expectant. Like something was supposed to happen. Like something *would*.

"Shiloh," I whispered, barely loud enough to hear. "Are you there?"

No answer.

But still, I waited. Because if Shiloh came back, if I saw her again, then everything the doctors said could be wrong.

And maybe I wasn't sick. Perhaps I'd been haunted this whole time.

And that was somehow... better.

I lay back against the pillows but kept my eyes fixed on the open closet door, my heart beating in slow, deliberate thumps. The light stayed on, and my mind stayed awake.

And I kept waiting.

~~~~~~~~~~

April 24th, 1998

The next morning, Karina and I walked to Sarah's house. Rhea had offered to drive us all to school. The air was cool, the sky still wearing that pale early-morning gray.

We climbed into Rhea's car, Karina and I in the backseat with Sarah, while Brett called shotgun up front.

"Last day of your first week," Rhea chirped as she backed out of the driveway. "How are you two liking it here so far?"

"It's nice," Karina said, trying to sound casual, though I could tell she was still a little tense from yesterday.

"Thank you for driving us," I added.

"Oh, no trouble at all. It's on my way to work," Rhea said with a smile in the rearview mirror.

I leaned forward slightly. "Where do you work?"

"I own a shop on campus," she said.

My heart skipped. "What kind of shop?"
~~~~~~~~~~

"A curiosity shop," she replied. "We carry antiques, old books, artifacts, crystals, things that make you wonder, you know?"

That was it. *Rhea's Curiosities.* The place on the website.

"Does your shop offer services, too? You know, besides selling items?" I asked, trying to sound casual.

"We do," she said, glancing at me with a knowing grin. "A friend of mine is a psychic. She gives readings, mostly to tourists, but locals stop by too."

"That sounds amazing. I'd love to visit sometime."

"I'd love to have you," she said. "You've got an inquisitive energy about you."

I tried not to overthink that. *Inquisitive energy.* What did that even mean?

We arrived at school about twenty minutes early. Karina and I headed to the cafeteria to kill time before homeroom. The place was half-lit, half-empty, with the sleepy clatter of trays and murmurs from early arrivals. Breakfast was the usual disappointment: wrapped sandwiches, slightly soggy French toast sticks, and lukewarm juice.

Karina bought an orange juice and we sat at one of the side tables. I kept glancing around, my mind still spinning with thoughts of Rhea's shop and Shiloh.

A few minutes passed before trouble arrived.

Amber.

She sauntered with her usual entourage: Steven and Leah, who laughed too quickly and echoed everything she said. Her eyes locked on Karina.

"Hey, Karina," she said in a singsong voice, fake sweetness dripping from every syllable.

I tensed instantly.

"How was your first week?" Amber asked, then laughed like she'd made the funniest joke in the world.

Karina stared at her, confused and uncomfortable.

"Just leave her alone," I said, trying to keep my voice calm, but sharp enough to warn her off.

Amber smiled, and in one swift, deliberate motion, she reached across the table and tipped Karina's juice onto her lap.

Karina gasped and jumped to her feet as the liquid soaked into her pants.

"Why would you do that?" she cried.

Amber shrugged, already turning away. "Had to make it even, didn't I?"

She laughed again, her friends joining in, and the three of them walked off like nothing had happened.

I stood up, walked calmly to the napkin dispenser, and returned with a thick stack. Karina was still standing there, frozen in shock and humiliation.

"Here," I said quietly, handing her the napkins and helping dab at her clothes. The front of her jeans was soaked, and orange juice clung to the hem of her hoodie.

"I hate her," Karina muttered under her breath.

"Yeah," I said. "Me too."

We did our best to clean her up before the bell rang, but she still looked miserable. As we walked toward homeroom, I glanced over my shoulder at Amber.

I wasn't going to forget what she did.

And next time... I wouldn't just sit there.

~~~~~~~~~~

Later that day, during study hall, I was scribbling through a math worksheet when someone slid into the seat beside me. I glanced up, expecting a random classmate needing a pencil.

It was Brett.

"Hey," he said, flashing a crooked smile.

"Hi," I replied, a little caught off guard.

"Why are you sitting by yourself?"

I shrugged, eyes back on my paper. "I like being by myself."

"Oh." He paused. "Is it okay if I sit with you anyway?"

I looked at him for a second, trying to read his expression. He didn't seem like he was teasing or trying to
~~~~~~~~~~

be annoying. It wasn't *that* weird; after all, we did ride to school together, and he was my neighbor.

"Sure," I said, and went back to my homework.

A few quiet minutes passed. I thought maybe he'd gotten bored and would move on, but instead, he leaned slightly toward me and asked, "So... why did you move here?" I looked up again, taken aback. His voice wasn't nosy, it was careful. Curious, but not pushy. I hesitated. "It's okay if you don't want to talk about it," he added quickly.

"No, it's fine," I said, shifting in my seat. "My parents got divorced. Then my mom got a job promotion here... we packed up and left. It happened kind of fast."

"That sucks," he said. "My mom left when I was little. And my dad... well, he's not around. That's why Sarah and I live with our aunt and uncle."

I blinked, not expecting him to say something that real. "I'm sorry. That must've been hard."

He shrugged, offering a soft smile. "It was. But it's the past now." There was a pause. He leaned in just a bit closer, not enough to make me uncomfortable, just enough that I could smell his shampoo, something citrusy and clean. "So," he said, eyes flicking to mine, "would you wanna hang out after school?"

Wait—*what?*

"Hang out?" I repeated, probably sounding like an alien.

"Yeah, I don't know. We could... watch a movie? Talk?" He rubbed the back of his neck. "Only if you want to."

Okay. He *was* asking me out.

I'd never had a boyfriend before. I'd never really wanted one. Or a friend, for that matter. Keeping to myself was easier and safer. No one asked questions when you were quiet. No one expected explanations. But now, Brett didn't feel like someone to whom I had to explain myself. He just felt... normal. And kind of nice.

"Umm... sure," I said, a little too quietly.

His smile widened. "Cool. Want to come over right after school?"

"Okay," I said again, this time more confidently.

We didn't say much after that. Just sat there, side by side, pretending to focus on homework. But there was this quiet, comfortable feeling between us.

And I didn't mind not being alone for the first time.

~~~~~~~~~~

After we got off the bus, the four of us, Karina, Sarah, Brett, and I, walked up the familiar path to their house. The late afternoon sun cast long shadows across the yard, and everything felt comfortably ordinary... until Karina turned to me.

"You heading home?" she asked, clearly expecting I'd split off toward our place.
~~~~~~~~~~

"She's hanging out with me," Brett cut in casually, slinging his backpack higher on his shoulder.

Karina blinked, surprised. "Oh," she said, glancing at Sarah. They exchanged a look, a grin that made my stomach nervously twist.

"Is that okay?" I asked Sarah, just to be sure.

"Totally," she said with a laugh. "Have fun."

We all filed into the house through the kitchen. Sarah grabbed a veggie tray and two water bottles from the fridge while Karina sat at the table. Brett rummaged in the pantry for popcorn and pulled out two cans of pop, placing them next to the microwave. The air smelled faintly of butter and cinnamon, a comforting blend of snack food and something warm baking in the oven earlier.

Once the popcorn had finished popping, Brett dumped it into a bowl and motioned me downstairs. I did, heart-thumping, a little more complicated than I wanted to admit.

The basement was cozy, with dim lighting, thick carpet, and a low table situated between two oversized beanbag chairs. Brett set down the popcorn and cans and then turned toward a shelf crammed with DVDs.

"Got a preference?" he asked, glancing over his shoulder.

"Nothing scary," I said immediately.

He laughed softly. "Noted." His fingers grazed over the spines until he pulled two movies. He turned around, holding them up like a game show host presenting the final prize.

"You pick."

One was called *Titanic*. A classic romance. The other, *Men in Black*, appeared to be a goofy sci-fi comedy. My brain immediately began decoding the more profound meaning. Was this a test? A way to figure out if I saw this as a date? Would he think I wanted to be friends if I picked the comedy? If I chose the romance... what would *that* mean?

I wasn't sure if I wanted anything beyond friendship. I didn't *have* close relationships. I had enough going on; with my diagnosis, with Shiloh, with everything, I didn't even understand yet. But there was something comforting about Brett. He didn't press. He didn't judge. He just... showed up.

After a long moment of internal debate, I pointed to one of them.

"This one," I said.

He smiled like he hadn't been expecting that, but liked the choice anyway. "Good pick."

He put the disc into the player, grabbed the remote, and settled into the bean bag chair beside mine. The movie started, the screen filling with underwater footage of a sunken ship.

I stole a glance at him. Brett was tall and lean, with that naturally athletic build that looked effortless. His tousled brown hair fell slightly into his blue eyes; eyes that always seemed to be paying attention, even when he wasn't trying.

I popped a few pieces of popcorn into my mouth, trying to focus on the movie and *not* on the fact that I might be on my first... date.

About an hour and a half in, just after the iceberg hit, Brett paused the movie.

"It's over three hours long," he said, stretching his arms. "We can finish it another time. It's getting late."

"Okay," I said, standing up with him.

As we climbed the stairs, the sounds of Karina and Sarah saying goodbye floated through the hallway. I started to grab my bag, but then I hesitated.

"Hey, can I use the bathroom real quick?" I asked.

"Yeah, down the hall, first door on the right," Brett said.

I followed the dark wood hallway, noticing all the family photos along the walls. Some were recent: smiling kids, summer vacations, messy birthdays. Others were older, sepia-toned portraits in delicate frames.

I used the bathroom, then lingered as I walked back, drawn to one photo in particular.

I froze.

Two young girls, maybe around ten or eleven, stood side by side in the picture, one with dark curls and a sweet, almost shy smile. The other... was Shiloh.

My stomach dropped.

It was her. The little girl I'd been seeing. The one everyone said *wasn't real*. But this was proof: a photograph in *this* house. And I'd never been here before. I'd never seen this photo. She wasn't in my imagination. Shiloh was real.

I must've been staring too long, because Brett came beside me.

"You okay?" he asked, concern in his voice.

I pointed to the photo. "Who's this?"

He leaned in. "That's Aunt Rhea when she was little."

"And the other girl?"

"I think... her best friend. She died not long after that picture was taken."

My throat tightened. "Do you know her name?"

He shook his head. "Can't remember."

"Do you know how she died?" I asked, trying to sound casual.

"Some accident, I think. You'd have to ask Rhea."

I nodded slowly. Next time I visit, I could find a way to talk to her. Alone.

"Carmen! Let's go!" Karina's voice called from the front door.

I jumped a little, snapped out of the moment. I gave Brett a quick goodbye, grabbed my bag, and followed Karina out the door, heart still pounding.

Shiloh wasn't a dream. She wasn't a hallucination. She was a memory. Some people had forgotten. But I hadn't. And now... I had proof.

Chapter Seventeen

Karina

May 21st, 1998

It's almost the end of the school year, and I couldn't be more relieved. Not excited, not hopeful. Just relieved. Amber hasn't let up; if anything, she's gotten worse. Relentless. Sharper. Crueler.

I used to love school. I was the kid who raised her hand first, *liked* homework, and looked forward to walking into class every day. Learning used to feel like something I was good at, something I could count on when everything else was uncertain.

But since we moved, and I started at this new school, that love has been quietly dismantled, piece by piece, word by word.

Now, I wake up every morning with a knot in my stomach, heavy and tight. Amber makes sure of that. She's turned the halls into something cold and hostile with her perfectly polished hair and venom-laced smile. She doesn't need to shout. Her whispers are worse. Cutting. Precise. She laughs when I pass by, twists her words like knives, and convinces everyone else to follow her lead without ever lifting a finger. Amber had been careful never to bother me when Carmen was around. Deep down, she was afraid that Carmen might do something. And honestly, I was a little thankful for that. The few times Carmen had stepped in, it shut Amber up fast. But even then, I wasn't sure how far my sister would go to defend me. Would she hit her? Or just throw back some sharp words and threats like she always seemed to have ready? I didn't know. And part of me wasn't sure I wanted to find out.

Some mornings, I lie there, staring up at the ceiling, trying to summon the courage to get up. I wonder how something I once loved so much could become something I'm now afraid of.

And most days, the fear wins. Not in a big, dramatic way. Just in the quiet, invisible way that makes hope feel out of reach.

Right now, it feels like I'm holding my breath, waiting for the year to end, and wishing it had never begun.

I signed up for a few at-home summer courses, hoping to get a head start on my sophomore year. Any chance I had at graduating early felt worth it; anything to put distance between me and Amber. She was making my life miserable, and every day at school felt like walking into a storm without an umbrella.

There are only eight school days left. Eight long, dragging days. And then... summer.

Twelve weeks of freedom. Twelve weeks without whispered insults, fake smiles, and the weight of her shadow following me down every hallway.

I just had to make it a little longer.

I sat on the bus ride home next to Sarah, watching the world blur by outside. Carmen, meanwhile, was sitting with Brett, as usual. They'd been spending a lot of time together lately, but I hadn't seen them do anything beyond talking or watching movies. It didn't seem like they were in a relationship, but still... I couldn't help but wonder. Sarah had the same suspicion, and we'd shared a few unspoken glances about it.

The bus jolted to a halt at our stop, and we all filed off. Sarah had a dentist appointment after school, so I figured I'd go home for once. This would be the first time since we started hanging out last month that I wasn't heading to her house after school.

Before walking home, I stepped off the bus and waved goodbye to Bethany, our bus driver. But as I walked, I noticed Carmen was following me. She wasn't going to Brett's like she usually did.

"You're not going over to Brett's today?" I asked, turning to face her.

"Not today," she replied. "His uncle needs help working in the shed."

"You two have been spending a lot of time together," I said, a little surprised.

"So have you and Sarah," Carmen shot back, her tone flat.

"Yeah, but we're friends. Friends hang out," I said with a shrug, trying to keep the conversation light.

"Exactly. *Friends'* hangouts." She emphasized *friends*, her voice hinting at something I couldn't quite place.

I could tell she didn't want to talk anymore, so she quickly walked ahead of me. But I jogged a few steps to catch up with her.

"Do you like him?" I asked, my voice a little quieter now.

"He's nice," she answered simply.

"Yeah, he is. But do you like him... like that?"

She hesitated, her steps faltering just a moment before she said, "I don't know. Maybe."

"Have you asked him how he feels?"

"No," Carmen replied shortly.

"Are you going to?"

Carmen suddenly shouted, "Karina!" Her voice was louder than I expected, catching me off guard. I stopped in my tracks, taken aback by the sharpness.

"I'm sorry," I said quickly, feeling bad. "I just... I'm excited for you. You've never really had any friends before, and neither have I. I'm happy for you, Carmen. You seem happy, and I just—"

"It's fine. I'm sorry I shouted." She sounded more tired than angry, and I could feel the tension in her voice melt away. "The truth is... I do like him. And that scares me. I've never felt this way about anyone before, and I don't want to ruin it."

"Are you scared of telling him how you feel?"

"No," she said, her voice small. "I'm scared of him finding out about... You know, my issues."

I frowned. "That's ridiculous."

"It's not." She stopped walking momentarily, her hands stuffed deep into her pockets. "It's not normal, Karina. It's... weird. And when he finds out, he might look at or treat me differently." Her words dropped into the space between us like stones. "Just like how you treat me differently."

"Me? I don't treat you any differently," I said, a little too quickly.

She looked at me, her eyes softer than I expected. "Not anymore. But when I was first diagnosed? You, Mom, and Liv started treating me like I was made of glass. Like, if you said the wrong thing, I was going to break. Mom still treats me that way. You and Liv have eased up, but... You still treat me like I'm broken."

Her words hit me harder than I expected. I let out a slow breath, the weight of her truth sinking in. I'd never realized how much my actions and words had affected her. When Carmen was diagnosed, I was barely ten years old. Mom had sat me down and explained that Carmen was sick and that we had to be careful around her from then on. But I didn't understand it. To me, Carmen had always been Carmen; no different than before.

I stopped walking, suddenly feeling overwhelmed. "I'm sorry I made you feel that way," I said, quietly but sincerely. "I never thought of you as broken or damaged. To me, you've always just been my sister. And I love you. I would never want to change you."

Carmen reached out, her arms pulling me into a hug before I could say anything else. I wrapped my arms around her, holding her tight. We stood there momentarily, holding each other, before pulling apart and walking home together.

I didn't know what the future held, but in that moment, I knew one thing for sure: I wouldn't let anything come between us again.

~~~~~~~~~~

We stepped inside, and Carmen went straight to her room without saying a word. I dropped my backpack in the foyer and headed into the kitchen. Mom was at the table, both
~~~~~~~~~~

hands wrapped around a mug of coffee, her gaze fixed on something far beyond it.

"Everything okay?" I asked, making my way to the fridge. I pulled out the orange juice, opened a cabinet, and grabbed a glass.

She didn't look up. "Your father called."

I froze, the jug halfway to the glass. Slowly, I turned to face her. "What?"

We hadn't seen or heard from Dad since the divorce was finalized. When they sold the house, everything went through the lawyers. He never even came to say goodbye; he just hid at his brother's place while we packed up and moved on. Now he was calling?

"What did he want?" I asked, my voice tight.

Mom's eyes stayed on her cup. "He wants to see you."

I blinked. "Just me? Not Carmen? Not Liv?" I already knew the answer before she nodded.

"No," I said firmly. "No. If he wants to see *me*, he sees *all* of us. He doesn't get to pick which kid he wants to love today."

"Karina," Mom said gently, "your father has made some mistakes, but he's still your father. You shouldn't shut him out forever. If he's trying to be part of your life, maybe—"

"No," I cut in. "He doesn't get a gold star for showing up late. He *left*. He didn't call. He didn't write. He didn't even say goodbye. And now what, he just gets to come back like nothing happened?"

Mom sighed. "At least he's trying. Some fathers don't try at all." Her voice grew quieter. "Mine didn't. He walked out when I was eight, and I've seen him three times since. That's it."

I stared at her, my anger twisting into something more complicated. I could see the hurt in her eyes, buried under the years. And maybe that's what made me soften, just a little.

"I'll see him," I said finally. "One time. That's it. I'll listen to what he has to say. But I'm not making any promises."

"Okay," she said, her voice barely above a whisper.

I turned back to the counter, screwed the cap on the orange juice, and put it back in the fridge. The glass in my hand suddenly felt useless, so I slid it back into the cabinet.

After that conversation, I didn't feel like drinking anything.

Or eating.

Or talking.

I just walked upstairs, a hollow weight sitting in my chest.

Chapter Eighteen

Carmen

May 22nd, 1998

I stood in the bathroom, finishing up my morning routine. After brushing my teeth, I returned the toothbrush to the holder and opened the cabinet above the sink. My pill bottle sat in its usual spot, almost empty. I twisted off the cap and tapped the remaining pill into my palm. Then, like I had done every day for nearly a month, I wrapped it in a tissue and dropped it into the trash.

I hadn't taken my medication in weeks.

And honestly? I felt better. Clearer. My head wasn't foggy anymore. I could think, focus, and *feel*. The weight that used to sit on my chest like a stone had lightened. I still heard the voices, and I still saw the little girl, Shiloh, but if my theory was correct, the meds were never meant to help with that anyway.

I finished getting ready and headed downstairs for breakfast. Mom and Liv were already at work, so it was just Karina and me. She spread cream cheese onto a bagel while I popped a Pop tart into the toaster. We ate in comfortable silence, a state that only exists when both people understand each other without needing to say much.

Once we were done, we grabbed our backpacks and headed out. The walk to Brett's house took about twelve minutes, and we arrived just as he and Sarah stepped outside. Perfect timing. We all climbed into Rhea's car, and she drove us to school.

It had been almost a month since Shiloh first told me her name, and I still hadn't found a way to bring her up to anyone. I'd only seen her a few times since, each time fleeting, like she was just passing through. She never stayed long, never said another word. But the way she looked at me... it was like she *wanted* to speak. Like something was keeping her from it.

I didn't know what she needed yet. But I was starting to think that whatever it was, I was the only one who could help her.

<div align="center">~~~~~~~~~~</div>

At lunch, Brett, Karina, Sarah, and I sat at our usual table in the corner of the cafeteria.

We'd started sitting together a few weeks ago, and it still felt a little surreal, being part of a group, like I belonged. It was new. It was... nice.

After my walk with Karina yesterday, her words played on a loop in my head. *Do you like him? Are you going to tell him?* The truth was, I didn't know how. Brett and I had been hanging out more, usually once or twice a week after school, depending on his part-time job.

We watched movies or played games with Karina and Sarah most days. Our conversations were easy but light. Surface-level. He hadn't tried to kiss me or make a move. Part of me appreciated that. The other part? It made me wonder what he was waiting for... or if he was waiting at all.

"Carmen, what do you think?"

I blinked, suddenly aware that everyone was looking at me. I'd zoned out completely.

"What?" I asked, straightening in my seat.

Brett chuckled and said, "Bowling. Saturday. The four of us. You in?"

"Oh, yeah. Sounds fun," I said, maybe too quickly.

He leaned a little closer, just enough that his shoulder brushed mine. "You coming over later?"

I nodded, and he smiled before turning back to his lunch. That smile stirred something in my chest, something hopeful, yet also heavy.

I knew I wanted to take the next step. I wanted to be honest with him. But the question that kept circling in my mind was one I couldn't escape.

What is the truth?

Do I hear voices?

That I see a ghost no one else can?

That I've been off my meds for a month because I think she's *real*?

How do you even begin a relationship with that?

~~~~~~~~~~

May 23rd, 1998

Karina and I walked over to Rhea's house after lunch. As we reached the driveway, we spotted Rhea handing Brett the keys, though not without a mini lecture.

"Watch your speed. Don't run any red lights. And please, *please* fill up the tank this time," Rhea said, tossing him the keys like she'd done it a hundred times before.

"Don't worry, Aunt Rhea. I got this," Brett replied with a confident grin as he slid into the driver's seat.
~~~~~~~~~~

I climbed into the front passenger seat, and Karina took the back with Sarah. Brett started the ignition, and we backed out of the driveway.

The drive to the bowling alley took about seventeen minutes. Brett kept his eyes on the road, and we didn't talk much. Karina and Sarah filled the silence from the back seat, chatting animatedly about the Backstreet Boys and some upcoming concert being aired on the Disney Channel. I listened, half-smiling, enjoying how normal everything felt for once.

We paid for our games and picked up our shoes upon arrival. Karina and Sarah went to order drinks while Brett and I found our lane. I laced up my rental shoes and stood to grab a ball.

I ran my fingers along the rack until I found a nine-pounder that didn't feel too awkward in my hands.

Brett was up first. He grabbed his ball, took a few straightforward strides, and successfully launched it down the lane. The pins exploded.

"Strike!" Sarah called from behind us.

Brett turned around smugly, walking back like he was on a runway. Okay, that was impressive. I don't think I've ever bowled a strike in my life.

Sarah was up next. She knocked down six pins on her first try and two more on her second. Not bad.

Then it was my turn.

I walked up the lane, took a deep breath, and rolled the ball. It veered slightly to the right and clipped two pins. It wasn't terrible... but my spare was a total bust; a clean gutter ball.

"Nice try," Brett said, grinning as I returned to our seats.

I sipped my pop and shrugged. "I haven't done this in years."

Brett gave my knee a light pat, and his touch was reassuring. "It's okay. No judgment. Honestly, that strike? Total fluke. I've only done that like three times in my life."

I smiled, grateful he wasn't trying to impress me too hard.

Karina took her turn, knocking down five pins and three more. She raised her arms like a champ anyway, and we all laughed.

The game continued in this manner: easy, fun, filled with playful teasing and occasional high-fives. And things felt light for the first time in a while, like I could let my guard down. Like I wasn't the girl with secrets or shadows. Just a regular teenager, bowling with her friends.

This could be what normal felt like.

~~~~~~~~~

After playing two games, Karina and Sarah wandered off to the arcade, leaving Brett and me alone in the food court. We slid into a booth near the window, the glow of neon
~~~~~~~~~

lights from the claw machines flickering in the background. I sipped my pop, still catching my breath from laughing at Karina's ridiculous victory dance.

The conversation started off light; jokes about who had the worst bowling form (me), favorite childhood cartoons, and the terrible concession stand pizza. But then Brett shifted in his seat and got quiet for a moment.

"Carmen, I... I've wanted to tell you something." I glanced up from my drink. His tone was different, serious. I nodded, giving him room to speak. He took a breath and exhaled slowly. "I like you." His words hung there between us. He looked nervous, like he was waiting for the ground to open up beneath him. I had suspected, but he'd never done anything that crossed the line from friendly to... this. "I think you're amazing," he went on. "You're smart, funny, and beautiful, and I really like being around you."

My heart picked up speed. I searched his eyes, trying to find the right words. "I like you too," I said, a small smile tugging at the corners of my lips.

His face lit up with a mix of relief and joy. "Really? I've wanted to say something for about two weeks, but it never felt like the right time."

"I know what you mean," I said. "That first day you asked me to hang out, I wasn't sure if it was a date. I didn't even know if I was ready for something like this. But then we kept spending time together, and I started feeling it, too."

He reached out and gently placed his hand over mine on the table. My pulse jumped a little, but I didn't pull away.

"Would you like to go out on an actual date?" he asked, hopeful.

I nodded. "I'd love to." A pause. Then I added, more hesitantly, "But... can I ask you for one thing?"

"Anything," he said instantly.

"Can we keep it just between us? At least for now?"

His expression softened with understanding. "Yeah. Of course. Whatever makes you comfortable."

We sat there longer, the quiet between us no longer awkward, but warm and easy. We made plans for the following Saturday; something simple, just the two of us. And for the first time in a long while, maybe things were finally starting to fall into place.

~~~~~~~~~~

May 30th, 1998

The following Saturday, I was upstairs preparing for my first official date with Brett. After breakfast, I took a shower and let my hair air-dry, the soft waves falling naturally over my shoulders. I wasn't big on makeup, but I swiped on some mascara and tinted lip balm; just enough to feel a little extra polished. I pulled on my favorite pair of jeans and a flowy top, then checked the mirror one last time.
~~~~~~~~~~

Liv and Karina were curled up on the couch, watching TV downstairs.

"Where are you going?" Karina asked as I passed by the living room.

"Over to Brett's for the afternoon. I won't be home for dinner," I said, trying to sound casual, even though my stomach was full of nerves.

Outside, I followed the familiar gravel path to Brett's house. We'd hung out plenty of times before, but this felt different, more charged, more real. Now that it was officially a *date*, I couldn't help but feel like I had to impress him.

I stepped up to the door and knocked. A few seconds later, Brett opened it, smiling.

"Hey. You look nice," he said, giving me a quick once-over that warmed my cheeks.

"Thanks," I smiled.

"You ready?"

"Yeah."

He quickly said goodbye to Rhea, then walked with me to the car. Ever the gentleman, he opened the passenger door for me. I slid in, my heart thudding a little harder than usual. Once in the driver's seat, he started the car and backed out of the driveway.

We didn't talk much during the drive, but it wasn't awkward at all. The radio played softly between us, and I wondered where he was taking me. Brett had kept our plans a surprise, and the longer we drove, the more curious I became.

After almost an hour, he turned off the highway and said, "We're here."

I looked out the window and gasped. A sprawling open field lined with rows of parked cars stood on one side of the road. Across the street, a large sign glowing in bright lights read: *County Fair*.

I couldn't help the excited squeal that escaped me. "You remembered!"

Brett grinned as he pulled into the grassy lot. "Of course. You told me it was one of your favorite memories."

It *was* one of the last good ones before everything changed. I hadn't told him the whole story, but the fact that he remembered that detail meant more than I could say.

We exited the car and joined the crowds walking up the gravel path to the fairgrounds. At the ticket booth, I reached for my wallet.

"Let me pay half," I said.

"No way," he said, pulling out a ten-dollar bill. "My treat."

After we got our hands stamped, we walked through the gates and into a colorful world of flashing lights, swirling rides, and mouthwatering smells. Music floated through the air, and kids ran past us holding cotton candy and giant stuffed animals.

"Where to first?" Brett asked.

I scanned the grounds and spotted a ring toss booth with a tall man in a cowboy hat calling out to passersby. "How about that game?"

"Let's do it."

We walked over, and the man greeted us with a smile. "Five rings for a dollar. Land one, win a prize!"

Brett handed him a dollar, took the rings, and gave me three. I completely missed my first two throws.

"Your turn," I said, laughing.

Brett aimed and hit the target on the first try. Then again on his second.

"Show-off," I teased.

"Third time's a charm," he said, eyeing the last ring in my hand.

I took a deep breath and threw; this time, the ring clinked perfectly onto the bottle. The booth owner cheered, grabbed a stuffed panda from the top shelf, and handed it to Brett. He turned and gave it to me.

"For the record, you softened it up for me," he said with a wink.

The next few hours flew by. We went on five rides, played more games, and grabbed food; cheesy fries for me, a corn dog for him. It was hot, so we ended our loop around the fairgrounds with cold lemonades and found a bench in the shade.

"I'm having such a great time," I said, sipping my drink. "Thank you."

"I am, too," Brett said. "This was a good idea."

We sat quietly for a moment, enjoying the fair buzz around us. After a while, he leaned toward me. "We should probably head out soon. Anything else you want to do before we go?"

I glanced around, then saw it: the Ferris wheel. "That," I said, pointing.

He smiled. "Perfect ending."

We walked over, handed the ride operator our last tickets, and were led into a gondola. Brett stepped in first and offered me his hand as I climbed in. We sat side by side as the wheel began its slow climb. The view grew wider with each turn; the fairgrounds sparkling below us, the fading sun painting the sky in soft gold and pink.

At the very top, the wheel stopped. We sat suspended above the world.

Brett shifted closer, gently draping his arm around my shoulders.

"Thank you for this," I said quietly.

"I'm glad you're having fun."

I turned to him, and for a moment, neither of us said anything. He looked at me, his eyes flicking to my lips. I leaned in the rest of the way.

Our lips met; soft, warm, and perfect. He pulled back, his face glowing with a smile, and I smiled back, my heart pounding.

We kissed again, just as the wheel started moving.

He reached for my hand again when we climbed out of the gondola. This time, he didn't let go. We walked back to the car, fingers intertwined, and the world buzzed with the magic of first love.

Chapter Nineteen

Karina

June 2nd, 1998

It was officially the last day of school. Rhea had just dropped us off, and we walked through the front doors together before heading in different directions.

As I made my way toward homeroom, a familiar voice cut through the noise of the hallway.

"Karina!" Amber called out, striding toward me with that fake smile she always wore when she was about to say something nasty. "Glad I caught you."

I sighed. "What do you want, Amber?"

"I saw your name on the list in the guidance office; you signed up for summer school." Her grin widened.

"Not that I'm surprised," Leah said, appearing at her side.

Amber laughed. "I already knew you weren't the brightest, but summer school? You must be even dumber than I thought."

I rolled my eyes and turned to walk away.

"I hope you flunk," she shouted after me, her laughter echoing down the hallway.

I clenched my jaw and kept walking. Just one more day, I reminded myself. One more day, then I'll be free for twelve weeks.

When I got to homeroom, I slipped into my usual seat by the window, pulled out a book, and buried myself in it. Reading always helped pass the time and tune out the rest of the world.

After a few minutes, I sensed someone standing in front of me. I looked up. It was Steven.

"Hey, Karina. Can I talk to you for a second?"

I stared at him, unamused. Why would *he* want to talk to me? He was Amber's friend, which meant anything he had to say was probably not worth hearing. I dropped my gaze and went back to reading.

"I'm sorry," he said quietly.

That made me pause. I glanced up. "Sorry for what?"

He hesitated, then leaned in slightly. "I'm sorry for the way Amber treats you. And for never saying anything. I should've stood up for you."

I watched him, confused. Steven had always been silent in the background while Amber did her thing. Leah occasionally jumped in, but Amber was the ringleader.

"She'd kill me if she knew I told you this, so please don't say anything," he added, lowering his voice. I gave a slight nod for him to continue. "Amber... she doesn't have it easy. Her mom's a drunk, and her mom's boyfriend.... he's not a good guy. Amber crashes at my place most nights and stays with Leah on weekends. She acts tough at school, so no one knows how bad things are at home. When she's not around people, she's... different. Nicer. I'm not saying it excuses how she treats you, but I thought maybe you should know."

I sat there, unsure of what to say. No, it didn't excuse her behavior, but it did explain some things.

"I won't say anything," I finally said, then returned to my book.

Steven nodded slightly and walked away, just as the bell rang for homeroom.

~~~~~~~~~~

The rest of the day passed uneventfully. I cleaned my locker, returned my textbooks, and picked up the new ones for my summer classes: geometry, American History, English II, and Biology. If I complete everything over the summer, I'll get to skip tenth grade and move straight into
~~~~~~~~~~

eleventh grade in the fall. The thought both excited and terrified me.

After the final bell rang, I gathered my things and headed outside to catch the bus. Carmen sat with Sarah and me again, since the seniors were already done for the year, and Brett was off until college started. Carmen had mentioned he'd be attending the local college, Riverbend, to study social work.

I still hadn't decided what to do, but I was leaning toward something in literature; maybe publishing or editing. It felt right, even if I didn't have it all figured out yet.

Sarah couldn't hang out today; her family had dinner plans to celebrate the end of the school year, so Carmen and I walked home together. I dropped my backpack and headed to the kitchen for a snack when I got through the door.

Mom was sitting at the table with a woman I didn't recognize. She had reddish hair, wore scrubs, and laughed with Mom like they were old friends. I figured she must be a coworker. Still, it was nice to see Mom smiling. She tried to maintain the appearance of being okay, but since the divorce, that spark in her had dimmed. I couldn't blame her. Even though he wasn't the most incredible dad or person, he was still her husband. I imagined a part of her probably still loved him, in some buried, complicated way.

When they noticed me standing there, Mom turned with a warm smile.

"Karina, honey, this is my friend Julie. We work together."

"Nice to meet you," I said politely.

"You too," Julie replied. "You're the youngest, right?"

"Yeah. I'm fifteen."

Julie turned back to Mom. "And you've got one still in high school and one in college?"

"Carmen's still in high school; she just turned seventeen last month, on the seventeenth. Her golden birthday," Mom said with a smile. "And Liv's nineteen. She's taking a gap year... or two. Still figuring things out."

"Oh, that's great," Julie said. "I took a gap year after high school. It was honestly the best thing I've ever done. I traveled to three countries. Sounds cliché, I know, but I found myself." She tilted slightly and added, "That's when I realized I wanted to go into nursing. I wanted to help people."

I turned to Mom. "What made you want to be a nurse?"

"I didn't, actually," she said, glancing at Julie, then back at me. "I was in medical school. I wanted to become a doctor."

"Really?" Julie said, clearly surprised. "What happened?"

Mom looked down for a moment, then at me. "Your father," she said softly. "He convinced me it wasn't a career for a woman. Being a doctor was a man's job, and nursing made more sense for me." She shook her head, her smile fading a little. "It's my biggest regret: not going after what I wanted."

"He *said* that?" I asked, stunned; another reason to resent him. I didn't understand why she still encouraged me to visit him.

Mom gave a slight shrug. "He thought he was doing what was best for me."

No, he didn't, I wanted to say. He just wanted to keep her small. I bet he dressed up his words and made them sound concerned that she wouldn't be wise or strong enough. Nursing was often considered the "safer" option.

I looked at her. "Would you ever consider going back? To school, I mean. To become a doctor."

She laughed lightly. "Oh, honey, I don't know. It's been almost twenty years. We just moved, and it's not the right time for something that big."

"But would you *think* about it?" I asked gently. I wanted her to have something just for her. Something that made her proud and happy. After everything she'd been through, maybe this could be her chance.

She looked at me for a long moment, then smiled. "I'll think about it," she said.

~~~~~~~~~~
~~~~~~~~~~

Mom and Julie had already left for their night shift at the hospital, so Liv made dinner, and I helped her clean up afterwards. We stood side by side at the sink; she washed, I dried. The clinking of dishes and the sound of running water filled the quiet kitchen.

"There's a book fair in town next week," I said. Setting down a dry plate. "Want to go?"

She handed me a bowl, still dripping. "What day?"

"Monday, I think."

She shook her head. "I can't. Nina's moving in this weekend, and I told her I'd help her job hunt Monday."

"Oh. Okay." I tried to keep my voice neutral, but I could feel a small knot forming in my chest.

Last summer, Liv and I had been inseparable. We spent most of those long, hot days going to book fairs and yard sales, even just hanging out on the porch, talking about everything and nothing. It was like having my best friend home for the first eight weeks. But during the final stretch of summer, she started disappearing, making excuses, saying she had other plans, sometimes not saying anything at all. That must've been when she met Nina.

Now, with Nina moving in, I knew things would change again. Maybe permanently.

I dried the last dish silently, trying not to let the disappointment show. "I'm gonna read for a bit before bed," I said quietly.

Liv nodded without looking up. "Alright. Goodnight, kiddo."

"Night," I said, heading upstairs, feeling more alone than I had just a few minutes before.

Chapter Twenty

Liv

June 6th, 1998

I was just about to clock out at the end of my shift when my manager called me.

"Hey, Liv!" She glanced over at me, eyes tired but focused. "Can you grab the trash and take it out before you head out? I know your shift ended five minutes ago, but we're shorthanded. I need to finish payroll, and we can't leave the counters empty."

I felt a flash of frustration. Nina was supposed to be at my house by three o'clock, and it was already thirty minutes past two. I needed to get home before she arrived, but I didn't want to make a fuss.

"Sure thing," I said, keeping my tone even.

I set my bag down, sighing quietly as I moved to the trash bins. In under three minutes, I had emptied all six cans, replaced the bags, and rushed the trash outside. That had to be a record.

Once home, I ran straight upstairs. There was no time to waste. I stripped off my work clothes, pulling on jeans and a loose, blue tank top that fluttered as I moved. My hands shook a little as I brushed my hair and teeth, nerves bubbling inside me.

This would be the first time seeing Nina in almost seven weeks. I missed her more than I cared to admit. We kept in touch, two phone calls a week, but it wasn't the same as being with her in person. Nina was the kind of person who lit up a room just by walking into it, always positive, always spreading joy. And I loved her more than I could say.

When I finished getting ready, I rushed downstairs and sat on the front steps, staring down the street. I didn't want to look too eager, but my heart beat twice. Four minutes later, I saw her; Nina's car turning the corner, headlights cutting through the late afternoon light. She parked quickly, jumped out, and before she even grabbed her bags, she was running toward me.

When she was close enough, I opened my arms, and we collided. It was like a breath I didn't know I'd been holding was finally released. We clung to each other, holding on as if we could somehow make up for all the time apart.

A few inches separated our faces before she pulled back, smiling with that familiar gleam in her eyes. She leaned in, and I met her halfway. Our kiss was slow and soft, yet it felt like everything at once. When we finally pulled away, we just smiled at each other, the kind of smile that said everything words couldn't.

After what felt like an eternity, we began bringing in her belongings: three suitcases stuffed with clothes and two plastic totes of dorm essentials. We carried her bins of dorm supplies to the basement, planning to store them all until she needed them in the fall.

Since my bed was only a twin, Nina had to sleep in the office, where we had a pull-out couch. We rearranged the space, moving the desk against the wall to clear room for the bed. I grabbed a spare set of sheets from the linen closet and made the bed for her, feeling oddly domestic.

Once her sleeping area was set up, we moved her bags upstairs to my room. I'd cleared out space in my closet and dressers so she'd have somewhere to store her clothes. We unpacked, chatting between bags, catching up on everything and nothing at all.

When we finally stopped for a break, we flopped onto my bed, squeezing together on the small mattress. Our legs tangled, elbows bumping as we tried to make ourselves comfortable. We laughed at how ridiculous it was; two people on a twin bed meant for one, but I didn't care.

There, lying together, face to face, we talked about silly and profound things, memories we'd missed sharing, and thoughts we hadn't yet voiced. I never wanted that moment to end. With Nina beside me, everything else faded away.

Four Years Ago

It was the summer after my freshman year, and my friends and I had decided to check out a local outdoor market in town. The place was buzzing with activity; booths lined the street, offering everything from quirky trinkets to fresh food, and social clubs and events promoted their causes. I was having fun, but my attention drifted when I saw something that piqued my interest.

My friends had stopped at a makeup booth, absorbed in testing shades and swatching products. I took the opportunity to wander away, heading toward a booth I'd noticed earlier but had been hesitant to approach. It was an LGBT Pride booth. Something about it made me curious, but also nervous. I wasn't sure why, but the thought of standing there with my friends felt too exposed. I wanted to do this alone, without their eyes on me.

As I approached the booth, I saw a girl sitting behind it with dark hair and a warm smile. She looked up from a reading pamphlet, as if she'd been waiting for someone like me to come over.

"Hi," she greeted, her voice soft yet confident.

I hesitated for a moment before speaking. "I have a question."

"Sure. Ask me anything."

I took a deep breath, then let it out slowly, unsure how to phrase what I'd been thinking. "How do you... Come out?"

She didn't seem surprised by the question, but her expression softened, as if she understood the weight behind it. "Well, it's different for everyone," she said, her voice reassuring. "And everyone does it at their own pace. There's no right or wrong time to come out. It can be scary, though. You never really know how the person you're telling will react."

She reached over to the table, picking up a brochure with a calming design. She handed it to me with a gentle smile. "Here. Read this. It has examples of how to say it and steps to consider. I found it helpful when I was figuring things out."

I took the brochure, my fingers brushing against hers for a split second. I glanced at the title: Scared to Come Out? My heart beat a little faster. I folded it up quickly and shoved it into my pocket. "Thank you," I said, my voice barely above a whisper.

"What's your name?" she asked, her smile still warm, her eyes kind.

"Liv," I replied, feeling a little braver now that the moment had passed.

"Well, good luck, Liv," she said, offering me one last smile. "I'm Nina."

I smiled back, a small but genuine smile, feeling something stir inside me, like a door quietly creaking open. "Thank you, Nina," I said before leaving the booth.

As I walked back toward my friends, I couldn't help but think about the conversation. I didn't know where this journey was going, or what would come of it, but for the first time, I felt like maybe I wasn't alone in it.

Eleven Months Ago

It was the summer after I graduated from high school, and Karina and I had decided to spend the day at a book fair on a local college campus. After a while, I left Karina to browse the books alone, stepping away to use the bathroom. When returning to find her, I turned the corner and accidentally bumped into someone.

"Sorry," I quickly said, stepping back.

"Oh, it's no problem," the girl responded, and I looked up to find myself face to face with Nina. I recognized her instantly. The last time I'd seen her was at the Pride booth a few years ago. She gave me a warm, familiar smile. "Hey, you look familiar," she said, a playful glint in her eyes.

"Yeah," I said, a smile tugging at my lips. "We met a couple of years ago at a market sale."

"That's right!" she said, her eyes lighting up. "You were the one asking about how to come out. Liv, right?"

Her remembering my name made my heart skip a beat. "Yeah, that's me," I said, slightly nervous.

"So did that brochure help you at all?" Nina asked, her tone gentle and kind.

I hesitated for a second before answering. "Yes, but I still haven't come out. I don't know... I'm just not ready yet."

"And that's okay," she said softly. To my surprise, she reached out and gently touched my wrist, her fingers warm against my skin. "There's no pressure to do it before you're ready. You do it at your own pace."

I felt my cheeks heat up, and I quickly bit my bottom lip to hide the smile that wanted to escape. Her touch lingered for a second, and I couldn't help the flutter in my stomach.

"So, are you here with anyone?" Nina asked, her voice light as she changed the subject.

"My sister," I answered, trying to calm my emotions. "Are you here with anyone?"

She shrugged casually. "Just a couple of girlfriends."

"Girlfriends?" I echoed, suddenly unsure if I had heard her right.

She laughed softly, shaking her head. "Oh no, not like that. Just friends who are girls. I don't have a girlfriend." She paused, her gaze meeting mine with something unreadable in her eyes.

"Oh," I said, feeling a wave of butterflies flit through my stomach, the kind I hadn't felt in a long time.

"Do you have a girlfriend?" Nina asked, her voice light but with a hint of curiosity.

I laughed nervously, shaking my head. "Me? No... I don't."

Nina's smile turned a little more mischievous, and before I could react, she reached out and gently stroked my arm with her fingers, sending a shiver down my spine. "Do you want a girlfriend?"

I felt my heart race, and I couldn't stop the smile that spread across my face, despite my best efforts. "Um... no," I stammered. She looked at me, confused for a split second. "I mean, yes. Yes, I do want a girlfriend." My voice softened, and I glanced away. "I'm just... afraid of my family finding out."

She nodded slowly, understanding in her eyes. "They don't have to find out, Liv," she said, her voice comforting.

I looked down at my shoes, my heart pounding as I gathered the courage to ask what I'd been thinking since the moment we'd run into each other.

"Hey, I'm sorry, am I making you uncomfortable?" she asked, her voice unsure.

"No, no," I reassured her, my smile gentle.

She leaned in a little, her eyes soft. "I just... want to make sure you're okay."

I took a breath, feeling like my chest would explode from the nerves. "Umm, Nina?" I looked up at her, my heart beating louder than ever. "Would you... Would you like to go out with me?"

Her eyes softened, and the world seemed to slow down momentarily. She smiled, and I felt like I could breathe again. "Yes," she said, her voice like a melody. "I would love to."

~~~~~~~~~~
~~~~~~~~~~

June 8ᵗʰ, 1998

That Monday, after breakfast, Nina and I headed into town so I could help her look for a job. We stopped by three fast-food places and two clothing stores, each time watching her walk out with a new application tucked under her arm. After hours of driving around in the late spring heat, we checked the local campus for any openings.

There, Nina grabbed applications from a cozy little diner, a tucked-away bookstore, and the campus gym. We were hot, tired, and sticky from the sun, but her energy never dipped. She was determined and adorable while doing it.

Before we headed home, Nina turned to me in the car and said, "Hey, I want to see where you work."

So, we made one last stop at the coffee shop. I spotted Zara behind the register and Trent working the espresso machine inside.

Zara looked up and grinned the second we walked through the door. "Coming in on your day off? You must miss us."

Trent glanced over. "Who's your friend?"

"Hey, guys," I said as we approached the counter. "This is Nina, my girlfriend."

They both responded in unison, smiling. "Hi, Nina!"

We ordered some drinks and found a quiet corner table by the window. A few minutes later, Zara came over, still in her apron, with her drink in hand. "I'm on break. Mind if I join?"

"Not at all," I said, scooting to make room.

"So," Zara said, leaning in with a curious smile, "how did you two meet?"

I smiled, glancing at Nina. "We met about four years ago at a market sale."

"I was working at a Pride booth," Nina chimed in. "Liv came up to ask for some advice."

Zara raised an eyebrow. "Advice?"

"On coming out," I said softly, feeling a little blush creep up my neck.

"We didn't talk again for a long time," Nina added. "But then, last summer, we ran into each other again..."

"And I asked her out on a date," I said with a grin.

"And now," Zara said, eyes wide with amusement, "you're living together?"

Nina laughed. "Only for the summer. I will move into my dorm this fall. But... who knows? Maybe after I graduate, we'll get a place together."

She looked at me as she said it, and I could feel my heart do a tiny backflip. I smiled back, unable to hide how happy I was. Hearing her say it, *maybe we'll get a place together*, made it feel a little more real.

Chapter Twenty–One

Carmen

Mom was on the night shift, so Liv made dinner as usual. Nina helped, though it was pretty clear she wasn't at home in the kitchen. Still, she followed Liv's directions carefully, smiling the whole time. Once everything was ready, we sat around the table with Swedish meatballs, one of Karina's favorite dishes. I had a feeling Liv made them on purpose. Perhaps she felt guilty for spending the whole day with Nina while Karina was with Sarah instead.

Not long after we sat down, Karina broke the silence. "So, have you had any luck finding a job?" she asked Nina, poking at her meatballs with her fork.

"I picked up a bunch of applications," Nina replied, reaching over to gently rest her hand on Liv's. "But I'm thinking of applying to the bookstore on campus. It's close to where Liv works, so maybe we'll see each other more. Depends on our shifts."

Liv smiled and gave her hand a little squeeze. "That would be nice."

Then Nina turned to Karina and me. "So... do you guys have any fun summer plans?"

"Well, I've got summer school," Karina said with a shrug. "And I'll hang out with Sarah when she's free."

"Summer school?" Nina raised an eyebrow. "I thought Liv said you're a straight-A student."

"I am," Karina said quickly. "It's to get ahead."

"Why the rush?" Nina asked, tilting her head.

Karina straightened in her chair. "If I finish the core classes over the summer and take extra classes instead of a study hall next year, I might be able to skip a year and graduate early."

"Why do you want to graduate early?" Liv asked, her brow furrowed. "College isn't going anywhere."

"I just... I want to get started. You know, get to college, get a better job..." Karina trailed off.

But I noticed something Liv and Nina didn't. Karina looked away when she said that; it was a classic sign she was lying. I've known that about her since we were kids. Liv has a higher voice, and Mom used to fidget with her wedding ring; at least, until she stopped wearing it after the divorce.

I knew the truth. Karina wanted to escape high school because of Amber, the girl who had been tormenting her since the start of the school year. It wasn't about getting ahead. It was about getting *away*.

After dinner, Liv and Nina stayed behind to clean up, and Karina disappeared into the library to read. I flopped onto the couch in the living room to watch TV. From where I sat, I could partially see into the kitchen through the archway. The house's layout was open in the front but more maze-like toward the back; the library was located down the hall, the office was across from it, a half-bath was situated under the stairs, and the bedrooms were all upstairs.

As Liv and Nina finished drying the last dishes, they headed toward the living room to join me. But before they made it to the couch, we all heard it: a low creaking sound. Not the usual settling of an old house. It was... different.

They froze.

"That's creepy," Nina said, turning back toward the kitchen.

I stood up and followed them in. Four cabinet doors stood wide open.

Liv sighed and walked over to close them. "It's the house," she said, sounding casual. "The hinges are loose. It happens."

Nina raised an eyebrow. "Right. And here I was thinking you had a ghost."

She wasn't wrong. I didn't say anything, but I felt I knew who, or what, had opened the cabinets. Shiloh. I hadn't seen her in a while, but every time I did, she looked scared. Maybe this was her way of trying to tell me something.

Something I still didn't understand.

We spent the next couple of hours watching TV, but the eerie moment lingered in the back of my mind. Around eleven, I called it a night. Karina had gone to bed an hour earlier,

~~~~~~~~~~

June 9th, 1998

The creaking of my closet door pulled me out of sleep. My eyes snapped open, and I glanced at the clock. It was just after four in the morning. I groaned softly and reached for the lamp on my nightstand, the soft glow filling the room.

Just like all the other times, Shiloh emerged, crawling slowly out of the shadows of my closet. She stood in the doorway, her translucent form flickering faintly in the light. But tonight, something was different.

Her eyes looked hollow. Her cheeks glistened like she'd been crying.
~~~~~~~~~~

"Shiloh," I whispered, sitting up straighter. "What's wrong?"

...he's mad at me... I need your help... her voice echoed in my mind, small and broken.

"I can help," I said quickly, trying to keep my voice steady. "Just tell me what to do."

...you need to tell her... she doesn't know...

"Tell who?" I asked.

...Rhea... she doesn't know...

I felt a chill run through me. "What do you want me to tell her, Shiloh?"

But before she could answer, her form shimmered and vanished.

I didn't sleep the rest of the night.

I lay in bed, staring at the ceiling, her voice haunting me, repeating repeatedly in my head. *Tell Rhea... she doesn't know...* But what didn't she know? And why was Shiloh so afraid?

By morning, I had a plan. I'd go to Rhea's house and ask to visit her shop. Maybe being in that space would help me understand more.

That afternoon, I walked over to Rhea's. Brett wasn't home; I knew his schedule by heart. Rhea's car was in the driveway, which was a good sign.

I knocked on the front door, and a moment later, Matt opened it.

"Carmen, how are you?" he asked, wiping his hands on a towel like he'd just finished something outside.

"I'm good. How are you?"

"Doing well. I just finished mowing the lawn. It's been a productive day. Brett's at work, if you're looking for him."

"I know," I said with a small smile. "I'm here to see Rhea."

"She's in her office. Come on, I'll walk you up."

He stepped aside to let me in and led me up the stairs, down a quiet hallway lined with framed pictures and faintly scented candles. He knocked gently and opened the office door.

"Honey, Carmen's here to see you."

Rhea looked up from her desk. "Carmen, sweetheart! Come in."

Matt gave me a friendly nod and left us alone.

I stepped into the office, quietly taking in the space. One entire wall behind Rhea's desk was covered in books. Titles on *parapsychology, philosophy,* and *occult studies* filled the shelves; heavy, academic-looking volumes. I remembered she used to be a professor, so it made sense... but still, something about those books sent a strange shiver down my spine.

"I was wondering," I said, clearing my throat, "would it be okay if I came with you to your shop sometime?"

Rhea smiled warmly. "Of course. You're welcome anytime. I'm heading in tomorrow morning, just for a couple of hours. I can take you if you'd like."

"That would be great," I said, trying to hide my nerves. "Thank you."

"Come by around nine," she said. "I'll be heading out shortly after."

"Okay. I'll see you then."

I gave her a grateful nod and turned to leave. As I went downstairs, Matt finished a cup of coffee in the kitchen. I said goodbye, and he waved with a smile.

As I walked home, my thoughts spun in circles. Shiloh was trying to tell me something important, something she wanted Rhea to know. I had to figure out *how* to say it... and *what* it meant.

~~~~~~~~~~

June 10th, 1998

Rhea and I drove the thirty-some minutes out to her shop, nestled just off the Riverbend campus where Liv worked, and now Nina too, ever since she got the call back from the bookstore yesterday.

We parked in front of a quaint brick building with ivy curling around its windowsills. A chime above the door rang softly as we stepped inside.
~~~~~~~~~~

The air was thick with the scent of incense and aged paper, rich and musky, like stepping into a dream. Every surface was carefully curated; leather-bound books stacked beside shimmering crystals, jars labeled in looping, delicate script, filled with dried herbs and unfamiliar substances. Faux candles flickered from wall sconces, casting shifting shadows over shelves lined with tarot decks, talismans, and bundles of sage. The entire place felt enchanted, as if it existed halfway between this world and another.

I wandered toward the metaphysical section, running my fingers along spines titled with words like *Spirits*, *Witchcraft*, *Shadow Work*, and *Ghost Lore*. A few months ago, I might've dismissed all of this. But now... now I knew ghosts were real. So who was I to say what else might be true?

"Your store is amazing," I told Rhea, still wide-eyed.

"Thank you," she said, her voice warm. "It's been one of the greatest joys of my life. A leap I'm so glad I took."

Just then, the front door chimed again. A young man and woman entered, both with an aura of calm confidence.

"Oh! Carmen, this is Viola and Luca," Rhea said. "They help out around the shop. Viola does intuitive readings. Luca helps with customers and logistics. Viola, Luca, this is Carmen, my neighbor."

"Hi, Carmen," they said in perfect unison, smiling. Then they slipped into the back room while Rhea opened the register.

I picked up a slim book titled *Echoes of the Other Side* and leafed through it. The words resonated with something I couldn't quite name.

About half an hour later, the shop was officially open. Rhea had retreated to her office, and Luca manned the front. I walked over to him.

"Where's Viola?" I asked.

"In the back," he said. "She has a reading in twenty minutes. Getting the room ready."

"Mind if I go see?"

He smiled and gestured. "Be my guest."

The back room was dimly lit, cozy, and strange. A low table sat in the center, surrounded by plush floor cushions. Tapestries blanketed the ceiling and walls, and candles glowed gently in every corner. Viola was just lighting the last of them when I stepped in.

"Carmen," she said, surprised but not unkind. "Hi."

"Can I ask you something?"

"Anything."

I hesitated, then: "Is all of this... real? I mean, are *you* really psychic? Or is it just for show?"

She smiled gently. "Some people believe. Some don't. But belief plays a role. If you don't believe in the energy around you, it's harder to feel it. Harder to connect."

"What can you *do*?"

"I do readings. Tarot and other things. I can sense energy," she said. "Sometimes the air in a room feels different; denser, colder, heavier. Sometimes it drops suddenly. You just know something's there."

"That happens in my house," I said, my voice barely above a whisper. "As soon as I walk through the door, the air changes. It's harder to breathe."

Viola studied me for a moment. "It can be instant, yes. That sounds like more than a coincidence. Is something going on?"

I nodded slowly. "There's more. I hear voices sometimes. Not out loud, more like... in my head. Since I was eleven, my parents have taken me to doctors. They said it was schizophrenia, but the medication has never worked. And lately... I've been seeing someone."

"Who?" she asked softly.

"A little girl. I've never seen her before. But she's in our house. She's scared. She talks to me and says she's hiding from *him* and needs help. Last night, she told me I had to tell someone something."

"Who?"

"Rhea."

Viola's eyes widened.

"She told me her name is Shiloh."

Viola stepped back slightly, stunned. "Carmen, I think you need to talk to Rhea."

~~~~~~~~~~

After Viola finished her reading, thirty minutes later, we gathered in the back room.

"What's going on?" Rhea asked, taking a seat on one of the cushions. I looked at Viola, silently asking her to start.

"I think Carmen has a gift," Viola said. "She might be a medium."

Rhea looked at me, surprised but not doubtful. "Really? Carmen, why didn't you tell me?"

"I didn't know what it was. I thought I was sick. Everyone told me I was."

"What changed?"

"Moving into that house," I said. "Something always feels off. The moment I step through the door, it's like walking through fog; cold, heavy. And I keep seeing this little girl. She told me her name is Shiloh. Then I saw her picture in your house. But I saw *her* first."

Rhea's face went pale. She sat back, her voice quiet. "I thought... I thought she might still be around."

"You've seen her?" I asked.
~~~~~~~~~~

"Once. I was eighteen. She was standing in the hallway. Just for a second. After I bought the house from my mom, more things started happening; cabinet doors opening, lights flickering, the sense of someone there when I was alone."

"What happened to her?"

"She died just before her fourteenth birthday. She was hit by the train that runs behind my house in the woods."

"Was it an accident?"

"We don't know. Shiloh was deaf. She wore a hearing aid, but without it... she couldn't hear a thing. We played together all the time. I used to go over after school, to your house, and we'd go into the woods. Her parents didn't let her go alone. But that day..."

She didn't finish.

"I think she's stuck," I said. "She said someone's mad at her. She said I had to tell you something. And there's something else. There's another presence. A man, I think. But his voice is... warped. Like a growl."

Rhea and Viola exchanged a look.

"What?" I asked.

Viola leaned forward. "That voice, you said it feels different?"

"Terrifying. Like it doesn't belong in this world."

"I believe you," Viola said. "And I think Shiloh is scared of whatever this is."

Rhea reached out gently. "Carmen, would you be okay if we came to your house? Discreetly. I have the necessary equipment and a team that can conduct the investigation. We might be able to help."

"I don't want my mom or sisters to know. Not yet."

"That's fine. When you have the house to yourself, call me. We'll come quietly."

~~~~~~~~~~

On the way home, Rhea shared more about Shiloh with me.

"She was a year and a half older than I. We were the only kids on the block around the same age. I was five when we met. My mom brought me to their house and introduced us. Her mother explained to me that Shiloh was deaf. She had a hearing aid, but sometimes you needed to repeat things twice."

I looked out the window as we turned down our street.

"How am I supposed to find out what she wants to tell you if I can't even control when I see her?"

"It'll take time," Rhea said. "Some people believe ghosts show you a replay; just memories trapped in a loop. Others say they reveal themselves for a reason: to reach someone. Or to protect something."

"But Shiloh talks to me. She's not a memory."
~~~~~~~~~~

"No," Rhea agreed softly. "She's still here. And she's trying to trust you."

I swallowed hard. "Then I have to help her."

"You will," Rhea said. "Just take it one step at a time. We'll figure this out, together."

Chapter Twenty–Two

Karina

June 24ᵗʰ, 1998

It's already been three weeks since school ended, and I'm nearly halfway through my summer school work. The days have blurred together; quiet, slow, predictable. I've hung out with Sarah a few times, but she's been busy lately, focusing on her hobbies and tumbling classes. I don't blame her, but I still feel the space where our time used to be.

Being out of school has made things easier. I haven't had to see Amber. I haven't had to hear her whispers behind my back or dodge how she stares at me like I'm something less human. Without her, the noise quiets. But even in the silence, there's still this heavy feeling in my chest, a kind of sadness that lingers, even when everything is calm.

Liv has been wrapped up in Nina; she's always with her, always laughing, or off at work.

Mom's been working long shifts, coming home late and tired. Carmen disappears most of the time, either with Brett or locked in her room. Lately, the house feels too big and too quiet at the same time.

And it's Wednesday. The day I finally agreed to see Dad.

I've been putting it off since school let out, letting his calls go to voicemail. But he kept pressing, and eventually, I ran out of excuses. I don't want to go; not really. But part of me just wants to get it over with, to finally say the things I've been holding in.

I know exactly what I want to say.

If he wants a relationship with me, it has to include Liv and Carmen. He can't keep pretending they don't exist. They're his daughters, too. Just like me. And they didn't do anything to deserve the way he's pushed them away.

I hate him for that.

He hates Liv for being gay, something she didn't choose, something she can't change. And he hates Carmen because of her diagnosis, because he doesn't believe her, thinks she's making it up for attention or sympathy. But I *know* that's not true. I remember how she looked when they found out, how scared she was of being seen differently and broken in their eyes.

She never wanted this.

None of us did.

And I don't know what will come of today. Maybe nothing will change. Perhaps he won't listen. But at least I'll know I tried.

At least I'll have said it out loud.

~~~~~~~~~~

Liv dropped me off at the diner on her way to work. Neither of us said much during the drive; just the low hum of the radio and the occasional click of the turn signal. When she pulled up to the curb, she glanced at me, like she wanted to say something but wasn't sure what.

"You'll be okay," she finally said.

I nodded, but I didn't feel okay. Not even close.

When I entered the diner, the smell of syrup and old coffee hit me. The place was quiet, just a few scattered customers and the faint clatter of dishes from the kitchen. I kept my head down as I walked to a booth near the window, hoping no one noticed the anxiety practically radiating off me.

I slid into the booth, my palms damp and my heart tapping a nervous rhythm in my chest.

A waitress approached, cheerful and warm, like the person who remembered birthdays and regular orders.
~~~~~~~~~~

"Hi, honey. My name is Tracy, and I'll be taking care of you today," she said with a bright smile. "Can I get you started with something to drink?"

"Um... a Sprite, please." I tried to smile back. "I'm meeting someone; he should be here soon."

"No worries. I'll get that for you and give you both a minute when he arrives." She gave a quick nod and walked off toward the drink fountain.

When she brought it, I sat there, my fingers wrapped tightly around the glass. The ice clinked softly as I took a small sip. My eyes drifted to the door and the clock, then back to the door again.

Every minute felt like five.

I hadn't seen Dad in months. Not since the day when everything cracked open and started falling apart. He'd been calling more lately, trying to sound casual and pretending he hadn't just decided to cut himself off from two-thirds of his family. But I knew why he was reaching out.

Because I was the easy one. Because I wasn't a disappointment like Liv and Carmen in his eyes.

Ten minutes passed.

Then the door chimed, and I looked up.

There he was; same old collared shirt, sleeves rolled to the elbows like always. He scanned the room, spotted me instantly, and smiled like nothing had ever gone wrong between us. I didn't smile back. He walked over to the booth, arms already open, expecting... what? A hug? Some kind of reunion moment? As if months of silence and hurt could be brushed away with a single embrace? I didn't move. Just sat there, frozen, watching the disappointment slowly settle in his face as he dropped his arms and sat across from me.

"I was hoping for a hug," he said, trying to laugh it off, but it sounded more like a sigh.

I shrugged, unwilling to give him anything, not a smile, comfort, or forgiveness. Not yet.

"Hi, Dad," I said instead. My voice was flat. Distant.

He leaned forward, elbows on the table, trying to close the space between us. "You look older," he said softly. "More grown-up."

I didn't answer.

He looked down at the table, suddenly feeling how thick the air had gotten and how heavy this moment was.

"You've been putting this off," he said quietly.

"Yeah," I replied. There was no point in pretending otherwise.

"Because you're angry."

"I'm not just angry." I looked at him then. "I'm disappointed. And I'm hurt." He nodded slowly, but didn't interrupt. For once, he just let me talk. "I don't understand how you can just pretend nothing's wrong. Like, Liv doesn't exist because she's gay. Or Carmen, just because she has something you don't believe in. They're your daughters, too. They didn't stop being your kids when life got inconvenient for you."

"I didn't stop loving them," he said, his voice quiet.

"Then where were you?" I snapped, the words tumbling out faster now. "When Liv needed you, when Carmen was scared and confused, she needed someone to believe her."

He didn't answer.

The silence between us stretched, filled only by the hum of the overhead lights and the murmur of distant conversations. I could feel the tears building behind my eyes, but I refused to let them fall, not here, not for him.

"I don't know if we can have a relationship," I said. "Not unless you're willing to try with them, too. I won't pretend everything's fine just because it's easier for you to only deal with me."

He looked at me for a long time, and for a moment, I thought maybe he finally understood.

"I'm trying," he said. "I don't know how to fix everything. But I'm here. And I want to be better."

I didn't know what to say to that. Not yet.

So instead, I took another sip of my Sprite and stared out the window, letting the silence speak for me.

The waitress returned after a few minutes of heavy silence. "Hi there, sir. Can I get you something to drink?" she asked politely, pen poised.

"Coffee, please," Dad replied with that same practiced smile he always wore with strangers. Friendly. Harmless. Polished. Classic Dad, warm to the world, cold to the people who needed him most.

Tracy returned a moment later with a steaming cup and set it gently in front of him. "Here you go," she said, pulling out her notepad. "Are we ready to order, or do you need a few more minutes?"

I hadn't even looked at the menu, too busy counting the seconds until I could leave. But I didn't want to make her wait. "I'll just have the special," I said quickly.

Dad skimmed the menu like he suddenly cared, then closed it and handed it back. "Chicken salad sandwich, please. With onion rings. Thank you." Tracy smiled and jotted it down, then disappeared toward the kitchen, leaving us alone again in the awkward quiet.

I dropped my gaze to the table, picking at the skin around my fingernails. I could feel him watching me, waiting for an opening.

"So, I was thinking…" he began, too casually. "I saw online that the county fair is coming up in a few weeks. Maybe you let me take you? Like old times. You used to love going."

I didn't look up. "Are Liv and Carmen invited too?" There was a pause, long enough to know I'd struck a nerve.

"I was thinking it would just be us," he said, his voice cooler now. *Of course.*

I looked up then and met his eyes. "Then no. You either get all of us, or none of us."

His expression soured. "Karina, come on," he said sharply, frustration cutting through the thin mask of patience. The sound of it made me flinch, like a door slamming somewhere inside me. "You're my daughter. If I want to take my daughter out, I should be able to."

"You have three daughters," I said evenly.

He leaned back in the booth, jaw tense. "I can't just pretend everything's fine," he muttered. "Your sisters have disappointed me in ways you don't understand. You're not a parent. You don't get it. Fathers want their daughters to grow up right, go to college, find good jobs, fall in love with a good man, and get married. Walk them down the aisle."

My stomach turned.

"Successful lives?" I asked, my voice thick with disbelief. "That's your definition? A 'good job' and a walk down the aisle?"

He nodded. "A good job, a nice house. Stability. That's not too much to hope for."

I blinked at him, then shook my head slowly. "Is that why you convinced Mom not to go to med school? Because you thought being a nurse was more 'appropriate' for a woman?"

He didn't answer at first. Just clenched his jaw and dragged his tongue slowly across the inside of his lip, something he always did when he was mad and couldn't say what he wanted to say.

"She told you about that, huh?" he said finally.

"Yeah," I said. I stood up. There was nothing left to talk about. Everything I'd hoped he'd hear, everything I wanted him to realize, he was never going to. He was too deeply entrenched in his beliefs, too blinded by the idea that love should only manifest in a certain way, that daughters should only turn out the way *he* had imagined.

"Goodbye, Dad," I said softly. He didn't move. Didn't speak. I walked away from the table, from him, from the bitter silence he'd built between all of us. I pushed open the diner door and stepped out into the street, the sunlight blinding for a second. But I kept walking. And this time, I didn't look back.

I rounded the diner's corner and leaned against the cold brick wall, letting the weight of everything finally hit me. The tears I had fought to hold back during that entire conversation spilled down my face like a flood breaking through a dam. My breath came in short, sharp bursts, and I covered my face with both hands, sliding down the wall until I was curled into myself at the base of it.

For a long time, I just cried. I let it all go; the hope I had clung to, the disappointment that had hollowed me out, and the hurt I never wanted to admit was still there.

I must have sat there for over thirty minutes, until the tears slowed and my chest stopped heaving. My face felt raw, and my limbs heavy as I finally pushed myself to my feet.

I didn't take the direct route to Liv's work. I went the long way, around the back of the building, down a side street, then along a row of shops, just in case Dad lingered nearby. I didn't want to see him again. Not now. Maybe not ever.

The walk was about twenty minutes, but I welcomed it. Every step gave me space to breathe, settle, and piece myself back together.

When I arrived at the coffee shop, Liv's job, the scent of espresso and baked goods wrapped around me like a blanket. She was behind the counter, focused on the espresso machine, a girl with long, dark hair working beside her, chatting with a customer. I slipped quietly into a corner booth near the back and sat down, wrapping my arms around myself. My head still ached from crying.

A few minutes later, Liv spotted me. Her face shifted instantly, softening from a barista's mode to a big sister's mode. She brought me a warm cappuccino and sat across from me without saying anything at first, just being there.

Her voice was gentle when she finally spoke. "Didn't go well?"

I shook my head, barely able to meet her eyes. "No. There's no changing him. I'm done."

She didn't look surprised, but she still looked sad. "I'm sorry, Karina. I know you used to look up to Dad."

I swallowed hard, my fingers curling around the warm cup. "I just... I hoped I was wrong. Maybe he'd realized how wrong he was—about you, Carmen, everything. That he'd want his family back."

Liv's expression softened even more. She reached across the table and placed her hand gently over mine. "... if you still wanted to have him in your life, I wouldn't be mad. I know he doesn't want to see Carmen or me, but that doesn't mean you should cut him out if you still want him around."

"You sound like Mom," I said, my voice low.

She gave a small smile. "She's wiser than we give her credit for."

"Yeah, she is. But no," I added after a beat. "I don't want anything to do with him. Not anymore."

Liv squeezed my hand once, then let go. "Okay. That's your choice to make. And for what it's worth... I'm proud of you."

I smiled faintly, grateful but exhausted. I sipped the cappuccino, warm, a little sweet, and strong enough to ground me.

Liv glanced at her watch and sighed. "I've got to get back to the counter. Do you want to stay here until my shift ends, or should I call you a cab?"

"I'll wait," I said. "It's only a couple of hours. I brought a book."

She nodded, standing up. "Alright. I'll check on you when I can."

As she walked away, I opened my bag and pulled out my book. I wasn't sure I'd be able to focus on the words, but it felt good to hold something steady in my hands, something that made sense when the rest of the day hadn't.

And for the first time since leaving that diner, I didn't feel alone.

Chapter Twenty–Three

Carmen

June 25th, 1998

Mom and I were in the car, heading to another doctor's appointment. The silence between us settled thickly, only the hum of the engine and the occasional click of the turn signal filling the quiet.

Mom finally spoke after a few minutes, just past the turn off our road. "Has the new medication been helping?"

I hesitated, watching the trees blur past the window. I hadn't taken the pills in weeks, not since I realized they weren't doing anything. Not for what I was dealing with. But I didn't want to have that conversation. Not yet.

"Yeah," I said, trying to sound casual. "They've been helping."

Mom smiled, relief softening the lines around her mouth. "That's great. Maybe these are the ones that finally work for you."

She flipped on the turn signal, slowing for the next intersection. "Have you… heard anything since starting them? Any voices?"

I thought about lying again, but something in her voice stopped me. If I said no, she'd know it wasn't true. She could always tell. So I gave her something in the middle.

"Some," I said quietly. "But not as much. It's been better."

She nodded, eyes on the road, but her smile grew. "I'm happy to hear that."

I looked away, back out the window, the guilt heavy in my chest. I wanted to tell her the truth. That the voices weren't symptoms, that the little girl I'd been seeing was real. Her name was Shiloh, and she was a ghost trapped in our house. There was something dark there too, something worse.

But now wasn't the time.

Not yet.

I still didn't know precisely what Shiloh needed from me or how I could help her. Until I was sure, I had to keep it to myself. Keep her safe. Keep us all safe.

So, I stayed quiet, tracing the path of the power lines out the window as the car carried us forward again in silence.

~~~~~~~~~~

After my doctor's appointment, Mom dropped me off at Brett's house before heading home. I stepped out of the car, the sun warm on my face, and made my way to the front door. My nerves buzzed quietly under my skin. I hadn't told Brett much yet, but I wanted to.

I knocked, and a moment later, I heard footsteps inside. The door opened to Brett's familiar grin.

"Hey," he said, stepping aside to let me in. "I thought you had a doctor's appointment today?"

"I did," I said, brushing a strand of hair behind my ear. "We just got back."

He closed the door behind me. "Wanna hang out upstairs for a change?"

I hesitated. We'd been seeing each other for almost a month, movies, late-night phone calls, long talks in the basement, but I had never been in his room. I wasn't sure what that meant, and I wasn't sure what *I* wanted it to mean.

Still, I nodded. "Sure."

He led me up the stairs, giving me space to enter his room first. It was larger than I expected, with soft blue walls, covered in posters and framed sketches. A double bed sat in the center of the room, flanked by two small lamps glowing with a soft amber light. It felt warm, personal, and lived-in.
~~~~~~~~~~

I sat on the edge of the bed, resting my hands in my lap. Brett shut the door quietly and joined me, sitting just close enough for our shoulders to brush. He looked at me momentarily, gently tucked a lock of hair behind my ear, and leaned in to kiss me. I kissed him back, slow and thoughtful. We stayed like that for a moment, calm, connected, before he pulled away. There was something profound in his eyes now.

"Carmen," he said carefully, "can I ask you something? It's kind of personal, but... I've just been thinking about it."

My chest tightened a little. "What is it?"

He hesitated, his eyes searching mine. "This is the third doctor's appointment you've had since we started hanging out. I swear I'm not trying to push, but... are you okay?"

I held his gaze. For a second, I considered brushing it off. But something in his voice, his concern, his patience, made me want to tell him the truth.

I took a deep breath. "When I was eleven, I was diagnosed with schizophrenia." His eyebrows lifted slightly, but he didn't interrupt. "I've been going to check-ins, mostly about the meds," I continued. "That's what the appointments are."

He nodded slowly. "Is... is the medication helping?"

This was the moment. I couldn't keep dancing around it. Not if I wanted him to know the real me.

I shook my head. "I don't think I have schizophrenia. I used to believe I did, because that's what everyone said. But no matter what medications I tried, the voices never stopped. The things I saw never went away." I drew in another breath, steeling myself. "Lately, I've started to figure it out. The voices. The visions. They're real. I'm not sick, I have a gift."

He blinked. "A gift?"

"I can see spirits. Communicate with them. Ghosts." I watched his face for a reaction, ready for disbelief or pity. "I haven't told anyone else in my family. Not yet. However, I visited Rhea's shop a few weeks ago, and she introduced me to her friend Viola. She's like me. Viola said I might be a medium." Brett was quiet for a long moment. Then he nodded, slowly.

"Like... like Viola. I've seen her at the shop a couple of times. She always exuded a calm energy. Like she *knew* things."

"She does," I said. "She helped me make sense of everything."

Brett sat back slightly, his expression unreadable. "And you believe it? That it's not just in your head?"

"I *know* it's not," I said firmly. "There's a little girl, her name is Shiloh, who's in our house. And something else, something darker. I don't know what it is yet. But it's real. I can feel it."

Brett looked at me for a long time. And then he did something I wasn't expecting. He reached out, took my hand in his, and gently squeezed it.

"Thank you," he said. "For telling me."

"You don't think I'm crazy?"

He gave a soft laugh. "No. I think you're the bravest person I've ever met."

Relief washed over me, warm and dizzying. For the first time in a long time, I felt safe telling someone the truth and being believed.

"I don't know what's going to happen," I admitted. "But I need to help her. I need to figure this out."

"Then we will," he said. "You're not alone in this, Carmen. I've got you."

He leaned in and wrapped his arms around me, pulling me into a warm embrace. I closed my eyes, breathing him in, the scent of his cologne and his heart's steady beat. When he pulled back just enough to look at me, his eyes searched mine for something unspoken. Then he kissed me.

I kissed him back, deeper this time, letting myself fall into the feeling. He believed me. *He believed me.* And in that moment, something inside me loosened, like a weight I didn't know I was carrying had finally been lifted.

I felt safe.

I trusted him.

And more than anything, I wanted him.

We sank back onto the bed, our lips still connected. He gently brushed the hair from my face, his fingers soft against my skin, then hovered over me, his gaze locked with mine. His expression was full of something tender and open, something that made my breath catch.

"I love you, Carmen," he whispered.

A rush of warmth spread through me. I smiled, my heart fluttering. "I love you, too," I said.

He kissed me again, slow and meaningful. I pulled him closer, wrapping my arms around him, feeling the strength and safety in his presence. His hand cupped my cheek, then slowly, cautiously, moved to trace the curve of my waist. My body responded instinctively, arching toward him, craving more of this closeness; this moment that felt entirely ours.

"Do you want to?" I whispered.

He paused, his forehead gently resting against mine. "Are you sure?" he asked softly. "We don't have to. Not unless you want to."

I looked into his eyes; those kind, steady eyes that had only ever made me feel seen. "I want to," I said, and kissed him again, pulling him closer as everything else in the world faded away.

~~~~~~~~~~
~~~~~~~~~~

We lay there in silence, bodies entwined beneath the covers, the warmth between us lingering. My head rested on Brett's chest, rising and falling with each steady breath. His fingers drifted up and down my arm in gentle strokes, a quiet rhythm that made me feel safe and anchored.

"That was... amazing," I whispered, still caught in the softness of the moment.

He smiled, his voice hushed and sincere. "*You* were amazing."

He pressed a kiss into my hair. "I love you, Carmen."

I tilted my face toward him, heart full, and smiled. "I love you, too."

I wanted to stay like that forever, suspended in the stillness, wrapped in him. But the real world waited outside the walls of his room. It was almost seven, and I knew I had to get home before dinner.

Reluctantly, I slipped from his embrace and sat up, drawing the blanket over my chest as I reached for my clothes. The cool air kissed my skin as the moment's spell began to fade. I sat on the edge of the bed with my back to him, quietly pulling on my bra and T-shirt. Then my jeans, one leg at a time.

Behind me, I heard Brett shifting, getting dressed too. No words passed between us, just the soft rustle of fabric and the hum of something unspoken hanging in the air.

Once we were clothed again, he came around the bed and stood before me. He wrapped his arms around my waist and pulled me close, resting his chin gently on my shoulder. I melted into him, resting my head against his neck.

"I'll walk you down," he said quietly.

We moved softly through the house, each step careful, almost reverent. Rhea was in the kitchen, humming as she stirred something on the stove. She didn't hear us slip past.

At the front door, Brett followed me outside and down the driveway. The air was calm now, the sun just sinking below the horizon. He pulled me into one final hug, holding on like he didn't want to let go.

Neither did I.

Then I turned, heart full and aching all at once, and walked the short path home, the memory of his touch still warm on my skin.

Chapter Twenty–Four

Karina

I was curled up in our library in my comfy chair, lost in a book. After a few solid hours of schoolwork, relaxing with a good story felt like a reward well-earned. The grandfather clock in the corner chimed seven, deep and resonant, like something out of a movie. I'd just finished a chapter and figured it was a good time for a break.

As I stepped out of the library, Carmen came in through the front door, her cheeks a little pink and her hair slightly windblown.

"Hey," I said.

"Hey," she replied, smiling, but it was the kind of smile you try to hide.

"Brett's?" I asked, already knowing the answer.

"Yep," she said quickly, walking toward the living room, flopping onto the couch like nothing was up. But something was. She was glowing in a way that screamed *something had happened.*

I headed into the kitchen, where Liv was making dinner and Nina was perched at the breakfast table, watching as if she were trying to learn through observation. The smell of garlic and butter filled the room.

Mom had left about half an hour ago for her night shift. Twelve hours on her feet again. She'd been working a lot lately, nights, weekends, anything she could pick up. I missed having her around, but I was proud of her. She was doing what she loved, and it showed.

I sat down next to Nina.

"How much longer till dinner?" I asked.

"Just a few more minutes," Liv said, stirring something on the stove. "Can you get some plates down?"

I got up, grabbed four plates from the cabinet, and then pulled out silverware, setting it on the counter. Liv plated the food with practiced ease, rinsed the pan, and handed me two plates to carry to the dining table. Nina and Liv followed with the rest.

"Carmen! Dinner!" Liv called out. Moments later, Carmen shuffled in from the living room and took her seat. We dug in.

Dinner was simple: garlic butter chicken, rice, and steamed broccoli. I started with the broccoli, because if you eat your greens first, it counts as being healthy, right?

"So, Carmen," Liv said, shooting her a knowing look, "you've been spending a lot of time with Brett. Is there something going on?"

Carmen immediately looked down, hiding her face behind her fork. "Yeah... there is," she admitted with a soft smile.

"I knew it!" I grinned.

"It's still new," she said, a little bashfully. "I like him, he likes me... but can we talk about something else now?"

Respecting her privacy, Nina picked up the conversational baton. "Something hilarious happened at work today," she said, setting down her water glass. "This guy came in asking for *that new book about the internet,* but all he could remember was that it had a blue cover and maybe a floppy disk."

Liv chuckled. "No way."

"I handed him a copy of *The Internet for Dummies*," Nina said, grinning. "He asked if you could catch viruses by typing too fast. Then he paid in cash, winked at me, and warned me to 'be careful because it's almost Y2K.' Emily and I just lost it after he left."

We all burst out laughing.

It wasn't a big moment, but it was the kind that made me grateful for quiet nights, shared meals, and the weird, wonderful stories that come with them.

~~~~~~~~~~

June 26th, 1998

After knocking out a few hours of schoolwork the next morning, I walked over to Sarah's house. Rhea answered the door and let me in with a warm smile.

"She's in the kitchen," she said quietly, and I could tell something was off even before I stepped inside.

Sarah was at the table, a half-eaten plate of food in front of her. Her eyes were red and puffy, and she looked like she'd been crying.

"Hey," I said gently, walking over. "What's wrong?"

Sarah didn't answer me right away. Instead, she glanced at Rhea, her voice small. "Can I be done for now? I promise I'll finish it later."

Rhea nodded softly and took the plate from the table. "You did great, honey. Go hang out with your friend."

Sarah stood without a word and gave me a subtle nod, motioning for me to follow. We stepped onto the back deck and sat on the old swinging bench. The air was quiet, the kind that felt heavy with something unspoken.

I hesitated, then asked, "What was that about?"

She took a deep breath before answering, her voice low. "I have anorexia."

I froze. The words hit me harder than I expected. Sarah had always been thin, but I'd never noticed her struggling
~~~~~~~~~~

to eat. She always seemed so disciplined, so in control. I thought she was just health-conscious. I didn't know there was more underneath it.

"It started when I was younger," she said, looking straight ahead. "Like eight or nine. I'd hide food. Skip meals. At first, no one noticed. But after a year, I started dropping weight fast, and Aunt Rhea took me to the doctor."

I stayed quiet, listening.

"I saw a nutritionist and got better for a while, but... It's something that comes back. I've had ups and downs. Lately, it's been worse again. Aunt Rhea noticed last month and took me back in. Now I'm on a meal plan, in therapy again, and I'm not allowed to go to my tumbling classes."

I nodded slowly, letting it all sink in. "Why didn't you tell me before?"

"Because I was ashamed," she said, barely above a whisper. "Only Aunt Rhea, Uncle Matt, and my brother know. I didn't want anyone else to see me in a different light. But I've been struggling, and I wanted you to know because... you're my friend. I love you. I just didn't know how to say it."

Tears welled up in her eyes again.

I reached over and squeezed her hand. "Thank you for telling me. I'm so sorry you've had to carry this. I don't judge you at all. I'm here for you, whatever you need, always."

She wiped at her cheeks, a small, grateful smile flickering across her face. "Thanks. Just being here helps. That's enough."

I leaned over and wrapped my arms around her. She melted into the hug, letting the tears fall freely. The bench swayed slowly beneath us as the sun warmed our backs, and for a long moment, neither of us said anything. We didn't need to.

"I think Carmen and your brother are dating," I said, breaking the silence on the swing after a few quiet minutes.

Sarah raised an eyebrow and tucked a strand of hair behind her ear. "I had a feeling something was going on. He's been... suspiciously cheerful lately."

I chuckled. "Same with Carmen. Yesterday, she came home trying to hide this ridiculous smile, like she didn't want me to know how happy she was. I swear she was blushing."

Sarah laughed softly. "Brett's never had a real girlfriend before. He asked a girl out last year, but she turned him down. He took it hard for a bit, but... I think this is the first time I've seen him genuinely happy in a long time."

Her expression softened, and she turned to face me more directly. "Our mom left when I was two. Dad wasn't around much either. Brett was only five, but he stepped in. He basically raised me."

My chest tightened. "That must've been so hard. For both of you."

Sarah nodded. "It was. We didn't even know how bad it was until later. When I was seven and Brett was ten, our uncle, Uncle Matt, found out Dad had been leaving us alone for days. Sometimes longer. He got a lawyer and fought for custody. We've lived here with him ever since."

I hesitated, then asked, "What happened to your dad?"

She looked down at her hands. "He went to jail for a few years for child neglect. He's out now, but... we don't talk to him."

"And your mom?"

"She showed up again a few years ago," Sarah said, her voice quieter now. "She said she wanted to reconnect but wasn't in a place to be a parent. She left again, but we keep in touch sometimes. Emails, mostly."

Initially, I didn't know what to say, so I just murmured, "I'm sorry."

Sarah offered a faint, understanding smile. "It's okay. It sucked, yeah. But Uncle Matt and Aunt Rhea gave us a real home. And Brett? He's always been there. He deserves someone who makes him smile like Carmen does."

~~~~~~~~~~

After leaving Sarah's house, I made my way back home, the conversation we'd just had still echoing in my mind. The
~~~~~~~~~~

walk felt longer than usual, each step weighed down by the heaviness of everything we'd shared. When I finally reached the front door, I pushed it open and stepped inside, greeted by the quiet hum of the house.

I climbed the stairs slowly, my legs moving on autopilot. From down the hallway, I could hear Liv and Nina laughing behind a closed door, soft, familiar sounds of comfort and friendship. I paused momentarily, considering knocking, maybe even joining them, but something in me hesitated. I didn't want to interrupt their joy with the storm brewing inside me.

Instead, I quietly slipped into my room and shut the door behind me. The room felt still, like it had been waiting for me. I dropped my bag to the floor and collapsed onto my bed, staring blankly at the ceiling. The weight of the afternoon pressed down on my chest, thick and inescapable.

Everything Sarah and I had talked about, the pain, the memories, the vulnerability, had cracked something open inside me. I tried to hold it together, but the emotions came rushing in like a flood I couldn't stop. My vision blurred, and without meaning to, I started to cry. Not just a few tears, but the kind of crying that comes from deep within, from a place you don't always let people see. And in that moment, alone in the quiet of my room, I let myself feel all of it.

Chapter Twenty–Five

Liv

Nina and I lay tangled together on my too-small twin bed, the kind of closeness that made everything else feel far away. We were reminiscing about one of our last dates before the move, just a few days after I came out, and not long after Dad walked out. She knew the guilt I carried, how I kept wondering if my truth had broken something in my family. But I saw it more clearly over time: I wasn't the one who left. He was.

Six Months Ago

It was just after lunch when Nina picked me up from my house. We headed to the mall, music playing and windows down. We wandered through the shops, trying on ridiculous sunglasses and laughing until our sides hurt. At the photo booth, we snapped a strip of silly pictures, grinning, making faces, and stealing a few kisses. Before we left, we shared a strawberry milkshake in the food court, sipping from the same straw and smiling like idiots.

We drove to a nearby park and wandered through the cool afternoon air, surrounded by the quiet hum of nature. After a while, we found an empty bench and sat down, talking about everything and nothing as time passed. Later, we headed back to the car and pulled into a quiet corner of the parking lot, where we curled up in the back seat, sharing a few unhurried, breathless kisses.

The kisses deepened, growing slower and more intimate, and with each passing moment, I felt myself falling even closer to her. I had never felt more connected, as though time had stopped just for us, leaving nothing but the warmth of her touch and the softness of her lips. It was as if every kiss brought us closer, weaving our hearts together in a way words could never capture

~~~~~~~~~~

I had just gotten up to use the bathroom when I heard soft, muffled sounds coming from Karina's room. It was hard to miss; her door was slightly ajar, and the quiet sobs echoed in the house's silence. I paused, my heart sinking. I never liked hearing her upset, especially when I wasn't sure how to help.

I knocked gently on her door, then cracked it open just enough to peer inside. "Karina? Are you okay?" I asked, my voice soft but filled with concern.
~~~~~~~~~~

She was sitting on her bed, her face hidden in her hands as she wiped her eyes. When she saw me, she quickly composed herself, blinking away the remnants of tears. "I'm fine," she said, her voice shaky, almost too quickly.

I didn't believe her. I walked over and sat on the edge of her bed, my legs hanging off the side. The space between us felt heavy. "You're not fine," I said gently, watching her closely. "What's going on?"

She let out a long sigh, her shoulders slumping as she wrapped her arms around herself. "I just feel... alone," she admitted, her voice barely above a whisper. "I don't know. Everything feels off. It's like nothing is right anymore."

The words hit me harder than I expected, the weight of her sadness settling over me. "Is it because I haven't been around as much? Since Nina moved in, I know I've been distracted. I'm sorry, I should've been there more." We used to spend hours together, just the two of us, but lately, I'd been so caught up with Nina that I hadn't noticed how much I'd distanced myself from Karina. The guilt tightened in my chest.

"No," she said quickly, her eyes avoiding mine. "It's not that." I could tell she was lying; she wouldn't even look at me. Her gaze flickered to the window, then to the floor. "I'm happy for you. Really. It's just... everything else. The divorce, moving, and the stress of school. It's a lot to handle."

Her voice faltered again, and I could see the strain in her face. The walls she'd built up over the years seemed to crack just a little bit, and I wanted so badly to help, to pull her out of whatever storm she was in. But all I could do was listen.

She took a deep breath, as if trying to steady herself, and shook her head, offering a small, forced smile. "I'm fine. Seriously. It's just that time of the month, and I'm extra moody. I'm sure it's nothing."

I didn't believe that either. I knew there was more she wasn't saying, but I could tell she wasn't ready to talk about it. I reached over and gave her shoulder a soft, comforting squeeze. "Okay," I said, my voice quiet but reassuring. "But you know you can talk to me about anything, right?"

She nodded, though it seemed half-hearted, her eyes still far off. I stood up slowly, giving her space, and smiled gently. "I'll leave you alone now. But I'm here if you need me."

I could tell she appreciated it, even if she wasn't ready to open up. As I closed the door behind me, I couldn't shake the feeling that there was so much more going on with her than she was letting on. But I'd wait. I'd give her the time she needed, whenever she was ready to let me in again.

Chapter Twenty–Six

Karina

July 4th, 1998

I woke up with that same familiar weight pressing down on my chest, the heaviness that made even breathing feel like a chore. Another day of schoolwork, quiet reading, and aching loneliness that never seemed to disappear. I sighed and sat up slowly, rubbing my eyes like that would somehow clear the fog inside my head. There was a cloud over me, dark, heavy, unmoving. I'd never felt this kind of sadness before, not like this.

Lately, the first thing I had to do every morning was cry, just a little. Not sobbing. Just a quiet ache that leaked out through my eyes. My emotions felt like they were running in all directions at once, and no matter how hard I tried, I couldn't seem to pull myself together.

I dragged myself to my desk and stared blankly at the calendar pinned to the corkboard above it. Grabbing a marker, I scratched out yesterday's date. When I glanced at today's box, something unexpected caught my eye.

July 4th.

A holiday.

I blinked, surprised. I'd almost forgotten. I remembered now, Mom had mentioned she was taking the day off so we could all go into town to watch the fireworks at the park. A small spark flickered inside me. Not joy exactly, but close. A warm little reminder that today didn't have to be heavy.

Today could be different.

I went to the bathroom, went through the motions; used the toilet, brushed my teeth, dragged a brush through my hair, and tied it back into a low ponytail. In front of the mirror, I paused for a moment. My reflection looked pale and tired. But I was trying.

Back in my room, I opened the closet and pulled out a pair of blue jean shorts and a red T-shirt, smiling faintly at the accidental holiday spirit. I grabbed my white sneakers from the floor and slipped them on. For once, I decided schoolwork could wait. It was a holiday. I owed myself one day of peace.

As I headed downstairs, the comforting smell of eggs and bacon wrapped around me like a blanket. I followed it into the kitchen, where Mom plated five breakfasts with her usual quiet focus. Liv and Nina were already seated at the table, chatting about something that made Nina laugh. I took the empty seat next to Liv.

"Morning, sweetheart," Mom said, glancing up at me with a smile.

"Morning," I replied, my voice still groggy but steady.

A moment later, Carmen came down the stairs and slid into the chair beside me. Mom brought over the plates, placing one in front of each of us, then finally sat down at the head of the table.

"So, I was thinking," Mom said, sipping her orange juice. "Since we all have the day off, let's go out and do something fun before the fireworks tonight."

"Like what?" Liv asked, already halfway through a forkful of eggs.

"Well," Mom began, setting her glass down, "I thought we could pack up the car, make a picnic, and head out to the lake for a few hours. About thirty minutes from here, I looked it up last night."

"It's probably going to be packed," Carmen said flatly.

"Yeah, probably," Mom agreed, "but we haven't done anything together since the move. I thought spending the day outside, just us, might be nice."

Carmen shrugged. "I suppose."

Mom looked around the table. "What about the rest of you? Everyone okay with that idea?"

We all nodded.

"Great," she said, smiling. "After breakfast, pack up whatever you need, we'll leave around eleven."

For the first time, I felt something shift, just a little. The weight was still there, but it was lighter, not gone, but manageable. And maybe, just maybe, today could be a small step back toward feeling like myself again.

After breakfast, I returned upstairs to pack for the lake, the familiar heaviness still hanging around me like a weighted blanket I couldn't shrug off. I grabbed my backpack from my room and quietly moved through the routine, swimsuit, sunglasses, sunscreen, a book I haven't started yet, a towel, and flip-flops. Each item felt like it required more effort than it should have, but I pushed through it. Packing for a day at the lake should've felt exciting, something to look forward to, but my mind drifted to darker places, as if some part of me didn't want to feel light again.

Once everything was packed, I sat on the edge of my bed for a while, letting the silence wrap around me. My eyes traced the seams in the floorboards, the slow swirl of dust in the air, the way the light from the window didn't quite reach the room's corners. I didn't cry, I just sat there, feeling like a shadow of myself.

Eventually, I stood up and forced myself downstairs. The smell of fresh fruit and bread greeted me in the kitchen, and I found Mom at the counter assembling sandwiches and threading strawberries, melon, and grapes onto wooden skewers.

"Need any help?" I asked, my voice softer than I intended.

She looked up and gave me a gentle smile that always made something ache a little in my chest. "Yes. Could you grab the cooler from the basement?"

I nodded and turned on my heel, heading down the hall. I opened the basement door and flicked on the light, though the old bulb overhead sputtered before settling into a dull, flickering glow. As I descended the wooden stairs, each step creaked beneath my feet. The basement smelled like dust and cement, and the air was damp and cool against my skin.

Our storage corner sat in the shadows, cluttered with plastic bins, unused holiday decorations, and mismatched furniture from the old house. I spotted the cooler wedged between a stack of folding chairs and an old fan. I grabbed it with both hands, trying not to look too long at the dark corners where spiderwebs draped like abandoned curtains. The unfinished concrete floor gave off a chill, and something about the place always made my skin crawl, as if the silence down there was heavier than the silence upstairs.

With the cooler in hand, I hustled back up the stairs, heart beating a little too fast for comfort. I pushed the door open with my shoulder and brought the cooler into the kitchen, setting it down on the floor near the counter with a soft thud.

"Thanks, honey," Mom said warmly, patting my arm before returning to her sandwich assembly line.

She packed everything into the cooler: wrapped sandwiches, fruit kabobs, bags of chips, a few cans of pop, and bottled water, then closed the lid and slid it over by the front door when she finished.

About twenty minutes later, we were ready to go. The house buzzed with movement; doors opening and closing, sandals slapping against hardwood, sunscreen tossed into tote bags. We piled everything into the car, and our backpacks and towels were shoved into the trunk. Then, we finally climbed inside.

Carmen called shotgun, which was no surprise, so I ended up in the backseat with Liv and Nina. Nina immediately began humming along to some made-up tune while Liv flipped through the CDs in her case, flipping through scratched discs in bright plastic sleeves. Mom started the engine, and we backed down the driveway, gravel crunching under the tires.

As we pulled onto the main road, chatter filled the car, mostly Liv and Nina, laughing and swapping stories. I leaned my head against the window and stared outside. Trees passed in blurs of green, and telephone lines drew invisible lines across the sky. I stayed quiet, half-listening but not really absorbing a word.

The weight hadn't disappeared. It never really did. But today, it felt just a little lighter. Just enough to notice the warmth of the sun on my arm, the sound of laughter, and the soft hum of the road beneath us.

And for now, that was enough.

~~~~~~~~~~

We pulled into a packed gravel lot, the tires crunching as Mom carefully eased the car into one of the last open spots. The moment we stepped out, the sounds of summer wrapped around us; laughter, splashing water, the distant hum of music from a nearby portable radio, and the high-pitched jingle of the ice cream cart's bell.

We followed a narrow dirt path toward the lake, our arms full of folded chairs, towels, bags, and the cooler Mom had packed earlier. The trail curved slightly, fully revealing the lake: sparkling under the midday sun, its surface dotted with floaties, paddleboards, and kids diving off the edge of a wooden dock. Families were scattered across the grassy shore, some grilling, others playing catch, a few just lying on their backs with their eyes closed, soaking in the heat of the July afternoon.
~~~~~~~~~~

After some searching, we found an open patch of grass near the edge of the lake, under a large tree that cast a generous patch of shade. We spread two beach blankets and unfolded our chairs in a loose semicircle. Mom popped open a striped umbrella and angled it to shade the cooler, then sank into her chair with a tired but contented sigh.

Liv and Nina didn't waste a second; they dove into their bags, grabbed their swimsuits, and headed off to change in the nearby restrooms. Within minutes, they sprinted back barefoot across the grass, laughing and daring each other to be the first in the water. Liv jumped in without hesitation, while Nina squealed at the cold before slowly lowering herself in.

Mom leaned back in her chair, sunglasses on, letting the sun soak into her skin. She looked peaceful, her hands resting in her lap, her eyes closed. Carmen sat cross-legged on the blanket, her Discman in her lap and oversized headphones covering her ears. She tapped her fingers to the beat of whatever moody '90s song she was listening to, probably something by The Cranberries or Alanis Morissette.

I stayed in my chair, pulling my book from my bag: *The Golden Compass.* I'd picked it up at a school book fair last year, drawn in by the cover with its mysterious armored bear and the sense of adventure it promised. I opened to where I'd left off and began reading, letting the world of daemons and parallel universes carry me away from my thoughts.

After a few chapters, the heat from the sun began to sink deep into my skin, and sweat prickled along the back of my neck. The pages stuck to my fingers. I looked up at the lake and saw Liv and Nina splashing each other, their laughter carrying across the water. The temptation was too much.

I slipped my shirt over my head, revealing my dark green one-piece swimsuit, and kicked off my flip-flops. The grass was warm beneath my bare feet as I strolled toward the lake, the sounds of the world around me softening under the steady hum of summer.

The first step into the water was shocking, cold, and sharp against my hot skin, but in the best possible way. I waded in carefully, letting the water climb higher with each step until it reached my waist. A breeze rippled across the surface, and goosebumps rose along my arms. I didn't want to get my hair wet, so I stayed in that sweet middle ground, lowering myself just enough so the water lapped at my shoulders.

It felt good, calming, and grounding. I floated in place for a few minutes, letting the water carry away some of my heaviness.

Eventually, I made my way back to our spot on the grass. My skin tingled as it dried in the sun, and I wrapped myself in a towel before sitting back in my chair. Mom had started unpacking the cooler and handing out foil sandwiches. Carmen was already munching on a fruit kabob, chewing slowly with her eyes still half-closed behind her headphones. Liv and Nina rushed over, dripping wet and laughing, snatching their sandwiches like they hadn't eaten in days.

Mom handed one to me: turkey and cheese, my favorite, and I took it with a small smile. I sat back, unwrapped it slowly, and took a bite.

The sandwich was simple, nothing fancy, but in that moment, it tasted like everything good about summer: warm sun, cold water, family, and the comfort of a meal made by someone who loves you.

For the first time in a while, I felt like maybe... just maybe, I could let myself enjoy it.

~~~~~~~~~~

After a few hours at the lake, our energy finally wore thin. The sun had begun to dip lower in the sky, casting golden light over the water, and the laughter that once filled the air had mellowed into the soft chatter of tired families packing up their blankets and bags. We were sun-drenched, waterlogged, and ready to go home.

We gathered our things in a quiet rhythm: folding chairs, damp towels, empty pop cans, and the leftover fruit
~~~~~~~~~~

kabobs that had started to wilt in the cooler. Mom tossed the trash into a nearby bin while Carmen unplugged her Discman and carefully rewound the CD. Liv and Nina still had wet hair, clinging to the backs of their necks as they trudged up the path in their flip-flops, each step sounding like a quiet slap against the packed dirt.

The drive home was peaceful. The car was filled with silence that followed a full day, the kind that didn't feel awkward, just comfortably still. The windows were cracked, letting in the warm evening air and the scent of sunscreen and lake water that still clung to our skin. I rested my head against the window, watching the trees blur past in the fading light; my thoughts drifted, but they were quiet.

Once home, I made a beeline for the shower, desperate to wash the day's stickiness from my skin. The scent of sunscreen, sweat, and lake water swirled down the drain as I stood under the hot stream, letting it rinse the last of the afternoon. When I stepped out, I wrapped myself in a towel, pulled on an oversized T-shirt and a pair of soft cotton shorts, and towel-dried my hair until it stopped dripping.

Feeling fresh but pleasantly tired, I padded back to my room, the floorboards cool under my feet. I climbed onto my bed and lay on my stomach, the familiar comfort of my mattress sinking beneath me. I pulled *The Golden Compass* from where I'd left it earlier, opened it to my bookmarked page, and let myself fall back into the world I had temporarily left behind.

With everything I'd been feeling lately, the heaviness in my chest, the thoughts that crept in when the world grew too quiet, the constant sense that something inside me was unraveling. It was a relief to disappear into another world for a while. The sadness didn't go away exactly, but it softened, like a dimmer switch turning the volume down on my pain. For those moments, I wasn't just a girl fighting her way through the fog; I was somewhere else, somewhere safer.

Reading has always been that for me. A quiet place. A hidden door to a world where I didn't have to be *me* for a little while. Where everything made more sense than it did in my own life.

Outside my window, the sky was turning shades of purple and orange. Soon, it would be time to head out again, for fireworks, laughter, and the joy I'd almost forgotten how to feel. But for now, I stayed where I was, curled up with a book, letting my heart rest in a world that asked nothing of me but to turn the page.

~~~~~~~~~~
~~~~~~~~~~

A knock at my bedroom door jolted me back to reality, yanking me out of the world of armored bears and parallel universes.

"Come on, we're leaving now," Liv called from the hallway.

"Okay, be right there," I replied, sliding my bookmark between the pages and setting the book down on my nightstand. My heart lingered in the pages momentarily, reluctant to let go of that world. But I stood up, dressed quickly in jeans and a zip-up hoodie, and padded barefoot down the stairs. The air in the house was cooler now, carrying the smell of fresh laundry and the faint echo of laughter from earlier in the day.

We loaded into the car, Mom in the driver's seat, Carmen beside her, and the rest of us tucked in the back, still carrying the warmth of the lake day in our hair and on our sun-kissed skin. It was only a fifteen-minute drive to the park, just far enough for the hum of the road and the rhythm of the tires to lull us into a comfortable silence. I cradled two thick picnic blankets, their familiar weight grounding me. Mom, Liv, and Nina carried fold-out chairs, their metal legs clinking as we crossed the crowded park lawn.

We found an empty patch of grass just wide enough for all of us, far enough from the noise but close enough to see the sky. The last hints of sunlight were fading from the horizon, leaving streaks of peach and lavender melting into navy blue. Crickets chirped in the grass, and the air held that specific warmth of a summer night just before it cools.

We set up our chairs and spread the blankets over the grass, anchoring the corners with water bottles and flip-flops. Liv and Nina unfolded their chairs side by side, and Carmen settled on the blanket in front of Mom and me. I chose the chair beside Mom, leaning back and pulling my knees to my chest.

The crowd around us buzzed with anticipation; kids chasing each other with glow sticks, families unwrapping snacks from crinkling bags, and teenagers lighting sparklers that hissed and sizzled in the dark.

"The sky's just about ready," Mom said, settling into her seat and sipping from a water bottle. "This has been such a nice day. Did you girls have fun?" she asked, her voice soft, content.

"The *best* day," Nina said immediately, glowing in that way only someone freshly in love could. She had settled behind Liv and now wrapped her arms around her, chin resting on Liv's shoulder.

"I had a great time," Liv echoed, leaning back into Nina's arms, their fingers interlocked casually, comfortably, like it was second nature.

"It was nice," Carmen added, sitting cross-legged on the blanket, earbuds out now, her gaze on the sky.

"I'm glad we were able to spend time together," I said quietly, meaning it more than I could express. I looked at each of them for a moment; Mom's eyes were soft with peace, Carmen was unusually relaxed, and Liv and Nina looked like they belonged entirely to another world.

I turned away when I caught Nina sneak a kiss against Liv's cheek, small and private, the kind of thing they thought no one would notice. My heart twinged, not out of bitterness, but something quieter. I missed having that closeness with Liv, the kind we used to share before things shifted. Before her world made space for someone new, it didn't have the same room for me.

But I didn't say anything. I wouldn't make her choose. I didn't want to be a weight she had to carry or a guilt she didn't deserve. She deserved to be happy. And even if it stung sometimes, I knew love wasn't something you should ever make someone feel bad for choosing.

So I smiled softly, leaned back in my chair, and let my head tip toward the stars beginning to flicker above.

The voices around us faded into background noise, children laughing, someone strumming a guitar far off, the occasional crack of a pop can being opened. It all blurred into a gentle hum that calmed the part of me that still felt like it was holding its breath.

I closed my eyes momentarily and waited for the first firework to light up the sky.

After waiting a few minutes in the dark, the sky suddenly cracked open with a loud bang. I flinched slightly at the sound, even though I had been expecting it. A brilliant flash followed, painting the clouds in shades of violet and crimson. Sparks bloomed like fiery petals, spreading across the night in slow, graceful arcs before fading into ash. Another explosion chased the first, this time in electric blue, then emerald green, each burst chasing away the shadows for a heartbeat before the darkness returned.

Watching fireworks feels like standing inside a living sky, like the stars are being shaken loose. Every explosion thunders through me, echoing in my ribs and settling somewhere deep in my chest, where all the quiet sadness usually lives. For just a little while, the noise in my head goes silent. The heaviness I've been carrying, the sadness, the loneliness, the invisible weight that's followed me for weeks, seems to scatter with the sparks, like maybe it was never as permanent as I feared.

Each burst of color seems to hold something more than light, memories, hope, and reminders that the world is still capable of beauty even when everything feels broken. People around me cheer and gasp, but I stay quiet, soaking it in like I don't want to miss a second. I tilt my head back and let my eyes blur, allowing the colors to melt into a kaleidoscope of emotions.

In those moments, I feel small, but in the best possible way. I'm not invisible, but connected. I feel like I'm part of something bigger than myself, bigger than the sadness and the past. I'm just a single person under a vast, exploding sky, grateful for a moment of peace that feels like magic.

~~~~~~~~~~

After the fireworks ended, the sky still shimmered faintly with smoke trails and fading sparks, like echoes of the magic we'd just witnessed. Mom, Liv, and Nina started packing up our chairs and folding the blankets, chatting softly about which fireworks had been their favorite. Carmen and I went to find the bathroom before the drive home, and Mom nodded, too distracted with loading the cooler into the trunk to notice how quickly we slipped away.

We weaved through a slow-moving tide of people, families, couples, kids on their parents' shoulders, all heading toward the exits with sleepy eyes and empty snack bags. The air was loud with chatter and the shuffle of feet, but it still felt warm and pleasant, humming with leftover energy from the show.

We finally found the restrooms near the park's pavilion, where a long line had already formed outside the women's side. Carmen and I took our place in the back, quietly
~~~~~~~~~~

waiting. We were only a few people from the front when I heard it; sharp, fake-sweet, and unmistakable.

"That you again? You're *everywhere*, aren't you?"

I turned slowly. Amber.

She stood behind us, arms crossed tightly over her chest, flanked by Leah and Steven like they were her entourage. Her blonde hair was pulled back into a slick ponytail, her lips curled into that smug smirk I'd learned too well. Her voice was louder than necessary, like she wanted everyone around us to hear.

I breathed and straightened my back, trying not to let my nerves show. I was so tired of this, of the passive-aggressive jabs, the whispers, the looks that lingered just long enough to hurt. I didn't want to fight. Not again. Not tonight.

"Amber," I said calmly, "can you just drop whatever this is? I've apologized for everything. What happened at the mall wasn't intentional. I paid for your dry cleaning. I've done everything I can to make it right. What more do you want from me?"

She laughed, that cold, hollow sound that never quite reached her eyes. "I want you to disappear," she spat. "You're like a roach stuck to the bottom of my shoe."

"Just leave her alone," Carmen snapped before I could say anything else. Her voice was sharp, unshaking.

Amber stepped closer. "I've told you before, your sister doesn't scare me."

Carmen's fists were clenched at her sides, jaw tight like she dared one of us to respond. Before I could open my mouth again, Carmen stepped forward.

And then, out of nowhere, *crack*.

Carmen's fist flew through the air and connected with Amber's jaw in one clean, brutal punch. The sound was unmistakable, flesh against flesh, and Amber stumbled back, eyes wide, almost losing her balance.

"You *bitch!*" she screeched, holding her face. She looked more shocked than hurt.

"I told you to leave her alone!" Carmen shouted, her voice full of fire and something more profound, something protective. "You don't get to treat her like she's nothing. Not anymore. Now get out of here."

Amber stared at us for a long moment, breathing hard, her face flushing with fury and embarrassment. Then she flipped us off with a trembling hand, turned on her heel, and stormed back into the crowd with Leah and Steven trailing behind her like stunned shadows.

A few people nearby had stopped to stare, their conversations paused mid-sentence, their expressions a mix of curiosity and disbelief. I felt heat rise in my cheeks, but I didn't care. Not really.

Carmen turned to me, still breathing heavily, her hand curled protectively against her chest. "Are you okay?"

"I'm fine," I said, and I meant it. For once, I felt... okay. Maybe even strong. I looked down at her hand, already red and swelling slightly at the knuckles. "But is *your* hand okay?" I gently took it in mine, brushing my thumb over the bruising skin.

"I'm fine," she repeated with a small, satisfied smile. "Don't tell Mom."

I smiled too. "I won't," I said. "But remind me never to make you mad."

She laughed softly, and for the first time all night, the tension between us melted into something familiar: sisterhood. Fierce and complicated and honest.

And honestly, if anyone deserved a punch in the face... It was Amber.

Chapter Twenty–Seven

Carmen

Karina and I walked back to the car, the cool night air brushing against my skin, a sharp contrast to the fire still burning in my knuckles. My hand throbbed with every heartbeat, a dull, aching reminder of what I'd done. I still couldn't fully process it; my fist connecting with Amber's smug face, the way she'd stumbled back in shock. I had never hit anyone before. I wasn't even sure I'd meant to. But something in me had snapped.

Since before school started, Amber had been tormenting Karina for months, and I'd just... had enough. I couldn't let her keep breaking down my sister. I wouldn't.

We reached the car, and I shoved my aching hand deep into my hoodie pocket, hiding it before Mom could see. I knew the bruises would darken by morning, but right now, the adrenaline was still too loud in my veins to care.

"Took you long enough," Liv said from the backseat as we climbed in.

"The line was long," Karina replied casually, sparing me from having to say anything. I kept quiet, staring out the window as we pulled away from the park. The crowd's chatter faded behind us, replaced by the hum of the tires against the road.

The ride home was silent, not uncomfortable, but quiet in the way nighttime sometimes demands. Everyone was tired. Fireworks had come and gone, and the magic of the evening had settled into a hush.

Once home, we all crept, unloading the car, folding blankets, and kicking off our shoes. It was already past eleven, and no one had the energy for anything more. The lights turned off one by one, and the doors clicked shut.

I climbed the stairs to my room, peeled off my clothes, and slipped into soft pajamas. The bathroom light flickered when I brushed my teeth, one of those small things I usually ignored but suddenly felt eerie in the house's silence. When I returned to my room, I crawled under the covers, hoping for sleep, hoping maybe tonight would be different.

But peace never lasted long.

I had only been lying there for a few minutes when I heard it; my name, carried on a breath that wasn't mine.

...Carmen...

I sat up, heart already picking up speed. I reached for the lamp on my nightstand and flicked it off, letting the room fall into shadows.

"Shiloh?" I whispered into the dark.

Like all other times, the closet door creaked open slowly and deliberately. The blackness inside seemed deeper than the rest of the room, like it led somewhere else entirely. And from that darkness, Shiloh stepped forward, pale and translucent, her eyes full of worry.

...Carmen... I need help...

I sat up straighter, the weight of the covers falling from my lap. "What can I do, Shiloh?"

...He's here... she said, her voice barely above the wind. *He's mad...*

I leaned in, a knot forming in my stomach. "Who's here? Who's mad at you?"

Before she could answer, the closet door slammed shut behind her with a violent bang that shook the walls. I flinched hard, my heart leaping into my throat. I stood, stepping toward her, desperate.

"Shiloh, I want to help. Just tell me what to do."

...I can't... she said, her voice breaking. *He's mad at you, too...*

"Mad at *me*?" I asked, my voice barely a whisper. "Why?"

...He doesn't want you to help...

And then it happened.

The air changed, turned thick and heavy, charged with something cold and angry. Instantly, it was as if invisible claws had ripped through the space between us. I didn't even see it coming. I just *felt* it.

A burning, icy sting tore across my back. I gasped and stumbled backwards, hands clutching at my sides. The pain was sharp and sudden, like something had slashed me open with freezing blades.

There was nothing, no attacker, no shape, no shadow. just the raw and unmistakably real sensation. My breath came in ragged gasps, and a tremor spread down my spine. I turned toward the mirror, my hands shaking, and lifted the hem of my shirt.

Three long, red scratches marred my skin. Blood trickled slowly down the curve of my back. The sight of it made my stomach twist.

Something had *attacked* me.

And I couldn't see it.

I spun back around to face Shiloh, but she was gone and vanished, like she had never been there at all. The closet door was shut again, sealed in silence.

Fear flooded me. I wasn't just dealing with a ghost anymore. This was something else, something darker. Something dangerous.

Still shaking, I left my room and walked down the hall to the bathroom, flicking on the light with trembling fingers.

I grabbed a washcloth, ran it under cold water, and gently dabbed at the scratches, flinching with every touch.

My reflection stared back at me, wide-eyed, pale, and rattled. I had known the dead could reach out... but never imagined they could *hurt* the living.

I needed help. I couldn't handle this on my own. Not anymore.

In the morning, I was going to find Rhea and Viola. I had to tell them what happened.

And I had to figure out what this spirit wanted, before it decided to do more than scratch.

~~~~~~~~~~

July 5th, 1998

Before anyone in my house was awake the next morning, I left. I slipped out quietly, the cool air brushing against my skin as I stepped into the sleepy morning light. The sun had just crested the rooftops, casting long shadows over the sidewalk. Birds chirped in the distance, filling the quiet with a calm rhythm that almost made me feel normal again. But the weight on my shoulders hadn't lifted, not even with the promise of a new day.

I walked briskly, my sneakers thudding softly on the pavement, my mind replaying the night before repeatedly,
~~~~~~~~~~

Shiloh's trembling voice. The closet slamming shut. The sharp pain across my back. The blood. I hadn't slept at all.

It only took about ten minutes to get to Rhea's house, though my thoughts made it feel longer. When I reached the porch, I hesitated momentarily, then knocked.

Brett opened the door almost instantly, as if he'd been expecting me. He greeted me with a smile, but it faded when he saw my face.

"Carmen?" he asked, stepping aside so I could come in. "Is everything okay?"

"I need to talk to your aunt," I said, quiet but firm.

His brows pinched together. "Is it about…?" He didn't say it, but we both knew what he meant.

I nodded.

"She's in the kitchen."

I followed him through the warm foyer, where the scent of breakfast wafted through the house: eggs, sausage, and maybe something sweet, like cinnamon. It should've been comforting, but all I felt was the hollow ache in my stomach.

When we walked in, Rhea was plating food in the kitchen. Matt and Sarah were already seated at the table, joking quietly with each other, unaware of the storm brewing behind me.

When Rhea turned around and saw me, her expression lifted.

"Carmen," she said, surprised. "What a nice—"

"Can I talk to you?" I interrupted gently, stepping closer to the counter.

She paused for a beat, reading the tension in my voice. Then she nodded, set down the plates, and motioned for me to follow. "Let's go to my office."

Brett came with us, staying close. Rhea didn't notice until we reached the top of the stairs and stepped into the cozy office filled with books, crystals, and herbs. She stopped short and turned to him.

"Brett, why don't you go have some breakfast? I think Carmen wants to speak privately."

"I know what's going on," he said softly.

Rhea looked between us; her eyes suddenly sharper. Protective. "You told him?"

"I did," I admitted.

She hesitated, clearly torn between shielding her nephew and letting him stay. Finally, she sighed and waved her hand. "Alright. Just stay quiet and listen."

We stepped into the room, and Brett closed the door behind us. I moved to the center of the room while Rhea sat behind her desk. Brett stood beside me and gently took my hand. His warm fingers grounded me.

"What's going on?" Rhea asked, her voice low and serious now.

I took a slow breath. "I saw Shiloh again last night. She came to me. She was terrified... she said *he* was mad."

"Who?' Brett asked, concern lining his voice.

"She didn't say, just 'he.' But then... something happened." I hesitated. My throat tightened. "I don't know how to explain it."

Rhea leaned forward, her eyes fixed on mine. "Just tell us."

Without speaking, I turned around and lifted the back of my shirt, exposing the three long, angry scratches down my back. The air in the room changed.

Rhea inhaled sharply. Brett froze beside me.

"Oh my god..." he whispered, and gently reached out, tracing the edge of one with his fingers. I winced.

Rhea stood quickly and came around the desk, her eyes wide. She didn't touch me, just looked.

"Something *did* this to you?" she asked, her voice tight.

I nodded. "I didn't see anything. I just felt it, like claws, cold and sharp. It hurt. And then when I looked in the mirror..." I trailed off, letting the wounds speak for themselves.

Rhea's expression darkened. "This isn't just a restless spirit. This isn't a ghost. What you're dealing with now... is something darker. *Malevolent.*"

"I need to help Shiloh, " I said, returning to face them. "Whatever else is in that house, she is scared of it. She keeps coming to me for a reason."

"I understand that," Rhea said gently. "But Carmen, you need to watch out for *yourself*, too. Spirits like Shiloh are drawn to you because you're open, which means other things can find you. Things that don't want help, they want control. Or destruction."

I swallowed hard. "So, what do I do?"

"We'll figure it out, " Rhea said. "You're not alone in this. But we need to be careful. Whatever this is, it knows you now. And it won't stop just because you're trying to help."

Brett squeezed my hand. "I've got your back. Whatever it is, we'll face it together.

I nodded, my fear still present but not as loud as it had been. For the first time in a while, I felt like I had people who believed me, people who would fight with me, not against me.

And that made all the difference.

Chapter Twenty–Eight

Karina

Mom had just finished setting breakfast on the table; bowls of warm, creamy oatmeal that still let off curls of steam. She'd arranged toppings like she always did on mornings when she had the energy: plump blueberries, tart raspberries, juicy strawberries, and a little container of brown sugar, which was *my* favorite.

Most people would say oatmeal was a healthy breakfast, but not how I ate it. Mom added fresh fruit, and Liv always made hers into a picture-worthy masterpiece, arranging berries in neat little rows, as if she were prepping it for a magazine cover. Carmen liked hers simple, with just a drizzle of maple syrup.

But me? I went full sugar-fiend. I piled on four, sometimes five, tablespoons of brown sugar and let it sit there, melting slowly into a thick, sticky syrup. I waited for it to sink into the oatmeal before stirring it all together, turning it into a rich, gooey mess of sweet comfort. It was the best part of my morning, hands down.

By the time I started eating, Liv was halfway through her bowl. She had her headphones slung around her neck, bobbing her head to a beat only she could hear as she ate. Just as I took my first spoonful, the front door opened.

"Carmen?" Mom called from the kitchen, a hint of confusion in her voice.

Carmen stepped inside a few seconds later, still in her hoodie and sneakers, cheeks pink from the cool morning air.

"I thought you were still in bed. Where did you go so early?" Mom asked, turning in her seat.

"I had to talk to Brett about something," Carmen replied casually, brushing a strand of hair from her face. "Sorry for not telling you."

"That's okay," Mom said, her voice light but firm. "Just give me a heads-up next time, alright?"

Carmen nodded and sat down at the table, pulling her bowl closer. She grabbed the bottle of maple syrup and poured a thin stream over her oatmeal, stirring it slowly.

We ate silently for a moment, the soft clinking of spoons the only sound.

Then I glanced at Carmen and asked, "Why'd you have to go to Brett's so early? Couldn't you have just called him after breakfast?"

She didn't answer right away. Her eyes stayed on her bowl as she took a bite, chewed slowly, and finally said, "He has work this morning. He had to leave by nine."

"Okay," I said, nodding, "but you *could* have just called him. We have a phone. That's all I meant."

Carmen's spoon clinked sharply against her bowl as she set it down.

"What's the big deal?" she snapped, her voice suddenly tense. "It was private. I didn't want anyone to hear."

I blinked, taken aback by the edge in her tone.

"I wasn't trying to pry," I said quietly. "I'm sorry."

She didn't respond immediately; instead, she returned to eating, as if the conversation had never happened.

Mom glanced between us, clearly picking up on the shift in energy but choosing not to comment. Liv pulled one headphone back on, pretending to zone out, but I knew she was still listening.

Carmen had been distant lately. It wasn't just this morning; it had been building for weeks. Like she was carrying something heavy around, but didn't want anyone to see it. And now, seeing how tightly she guarded that early morning visit to Brett, I was more sure than ever: she was hiding something.

And I was going to find out what it was, not to be nosy or to get her in trouble, but because she was my sister, and she was scared, whether she admitted it or not.

~~~~~~~~~~

Later in the day, after spending a few hours hunched over my summer schoolwork, I felt a mix of exhaustion and relief. I was almost done, maybe another week or two, and I'd finally finish all my assignments, a small victory, but a victory nonetheless.

I pushed my books aside, stretched my arms over my head, and decided I needed a break. I headed downstairs, planning to curl up in the quiet library with a book. The house was still and warm, filled with the faint ticking of the clock and the low hum of summer outside the windows. Liv and Nina had already left for work, and Mom had gone to her shift at the hospital a little earlier. That left only Carmen and me at home.

Walking into the living room, I saw her curled up on the couch, absently watching TV. When I entered, she barely glanced at me, her eyes fixed on the screen, her expression distant.

Because it was just the two of us, no distractions, no one else around, I figured it might be my only chance to talk to her. Really talk.
~~~~~~~~~~

I walked over and sank into the opposite end of the couch, tucking my legs under me and leaning back against the armrest, facing her. She said nothing, but I saw her thumb pause on the remote before she muted the sound. The room settled into silence except for the soft rustling of the trees outside.

I waited a few moments, trying to choose the right words.

"You've been distant lately," I finally said, my voice soft. "Like... something's going on. Like you're hiding something."

Carmen didn't respond right away. She didn't even look at me, just stared at the muted screen, her body tense.

"You've been spending a lot of time with Brett," I added, watching her reaction.

"Yeah, so?" she said at last, her voice quiet, guarded.

I hesitated, unsure if I should even ask, but the question had been gnawing at me for days.

"Are you... You're not pregnant, are you?"

That got her attention. Her eyes widened in shock, and she let out a short laugh, shaking her head.

"What?" she said, almost amused. "No. Oh my God, Karina."

"I mean... you've been sneaking out, going over there all the time, and acting weird. I don't know what else to think."

I took a deep breath, trying to calm the growing nerves in my chest. "So... you're not?"

"No, Karina," she said more firmly, "I'm not pregnant."

Relief flooded through me, loosening something tight inside my chest. "Okay. Good. I just... I had to ask."

"Jesus," she muttered, running a hand through her hair. She looked tired, more tired than she'd admit. "You think I'd keep something like that from everyone?"

"I don't know," I said honestly. "Lately, I don't know anything about what's going on with you. You don't talk to me. You barely even look at me."

"I'm just dealing with stuff, okay?" she snapped, sharper than before. "Not everything is about you."

"I never said it was," I replied, stung. "But I'm your sister. You used to talk to me. I miss that."

She stood up abruptly, the tension in her body spilling over. "Believe what you want, Karina. I'm fine."

And just like that, she turned and walked out of the room, her footsteps heavy on the stairs as she disappeared down the hall.

I sat there in the silence she left behind, staring at the muted TV screen, feeling a familiar hollowness settle into my chest.

Carmen and I had never been super close, not like Liv and me, but we *used* to talk. We laughed and even confided in each other when things got hard. Now she acted like I was a stranger, which hurt more than I wanted to admit.

A knot formed in my throat, and I blinked hard, trying to keep the tears at bay. I didn't want to cry, not again.

Lately, even on the good days, I still felt like I was outside of everything. Life was happening around me, but I wasn't part of it. I was just floating there, invisible, waiting for something to change. Something to make me feel less... worthless.

Nothing was the same anymore. Not our family, not this house, not even my sisters. And I was starting to wonder if it ever would be again.

I sat on the couch, the dim light of the living room casting soft shadows across the walls. My body felt heavy, like gravity had doubled just for me, pressing me into the cushions as if the weight of my thoughts had manifested into something tangible. I let the tears fall, warm and silent, sliding down my cheeks in a slow, steady stream. I didn't bother to wipe them away. There was something strangely comforting in letting them fall, not having to pretend, at least for a little while.

I cried quietly, swallowing the sobs in my throat so Carmen wouldn't hear me from upstairs. She'd already brushed me off, shut down, and walked away. The last thing I wanted was her pity, or worse, her irritation. So, I kept my grief hidden, like always, tucked inside where no one could see just how dark things had gotten.

I tried to fight it; the thoughts that haunted me. I wanted to push them aside, bury them, distract myself with anything that didn't hurt. But they always found their way back in, curling around the edges of my mind like smoke under a door. They whispered to me in the silence, louder than any shout.

Maybe no one would miss me if I were gone.

Everything could be easier without me.

Maybe I'm just... too much.

These weren't fleeting thoughts; they were constant. Heavy. Relentless. The kind that kept me awake at night, staring at the ceiling with tears slipping silently onto my pillow. The kind that made my chest feel like it was caving in. The type that scared me because sometimes... they started to make sense.

And then came the darker thoughts. The ones I never said out loud. The ones I couldn't take back if I were to act on them.

What if I just stopped trying?

What if I made it all stop?

What if the pain could just... end?

They terrified me, not just because I had them, but because sometimes they didn't feel like a warning, they felt like a promise. A way out.

I hugged my knees to my chest, pressing my forehead against them, trying to breathe through the storm. I didn't want to feel like this. I didn't want to be this version of myself; this fragile, broken girl who felt invisible even in a room full of people. I wanted to be stronger. I wanted someone to notice without me having to scream. I wanted someone to *care*.

But in that moment, it was just me and the quiet. Just me and the tears. Just me and the fight to keep going.

And I wasn't sure if I was winning.

Chapter Twenty–Nine

Liv

July 7th, 1998

I had just clocked out from my shift at the coffee shop, wiping the last traces of espresso grounds from my apron before hanging it up. My feet ached, and I smelled like steamed milk and cinnamon syrup, but there was still something satisfying about finishing a long shift. I waved goodbye to Zara and Trent, who were still on the clock for another few hours.

"Hang in there," I called as I pushed through the door. Zara gave me a mock salute, and Trent flashed a tired smile. Just two more hours for them.

I made my way to the car, tossing my bag into the passenger seat and debating what to do next. It was only a little after two, and Nina didn't get off work at the bookstore until three. A quick visit wouldn't hurt, and honestly, I just wanted to see her.

The drive over was short, only five minutes, but the change in atmosphere was instant. The cozy little shop sat nestled between a florist and a vinyl record store, its windows cluttered with displays of bestsellers, staff picks, and a few dusty classics. As soon as I walked inside, the comforting smell of old paper and patchouli incense wrapped around me like a warm blanket. It was quiet and peaceful, one of those places where time seemed to stand still.

Nina stood behind the counter, ringing up an elderly woman with short white hair and a worn tan leather purse that had been loved for decades. She noticed me the second I walked in and gave me a soft smile, her eyes lighting up in that way that still gave me butterflies.

I waited by the door, not wanting to interrupt. The older woman handed over a crisp ten-dollar bill and chatted pleasantly with Nina while she counted change.

"Have a great day," Nina said, handing the woman her purchase in a paper bag.

"Thank you, dear," the woman replied, giving me a brief nod as she made her way toward the exit.

When the door chimed shut behind her, I made my way up to the counter.

"Hey, you," Nina said, leaning on her elbows and kissing me across the counter.

"Hey," I replied, smiling. My shoulders relaxed without me even realizing it.

"Are you shopping, or just stopping by to say 'hi'?" she teased, her tone playful.

"Both," I said, letting the smile linger. "I want to get Karina a book. Something like a peace offering for being kind of... absent lately."

Nina raised an eyebrow in that thoughtful way she always did when trying to solve a problem. "Hmm. What does she like again? Fantasy? Adventure?"

"Yeah, both. Anything with a cool world, magic, or quests. She needs a distraction that'll sweep her away for a while."

"I've got just the thing." Nina stepped out from behind the counter, motioning for me to follow her. We walked down one of the side aisles, the wood floor creaking under our feet.

She skimmed her fingers along the spines of the books, murmuring to herself, until she paused and pulled one free. "This one just came in last week. It's the second Harry Potter series, *The Chamber of Secrets*. People are loving it."

I took the book from her hands and turned it over in mine, reading the summary on the back. "You know, this is perfect. She read the first one not too long ago. I think she'll love it."

"Good," Nina said with a grin. "Let's get you checked out."

She scanned the book at the counter and punched a few buttons on the register.

"You get the friends-and-family discount, of course," she said, flashing a cheeky smile.

"Perks of dating the cashier," I said, nudging her playfully.

She told me the total. "That's $14.36."

I handed over a twenty, and she made change, gently placing the receipt and bills in my hand.

"Thank you," I said with a smile, tucking the book into my bag. I leaned in for another quick kiss, then gave her a half-hug over the counter. It was awkward, but sweet.

"See you at home," she said as I backed toward the door.

I walked out into the late afternoon sun, feeling lighter than I had in days. Maybe it was the book. Maybe it was Nina. Perhaps it was just that rare, perfect in-between moment when the world didn't feel so heavy.

~~~~~~~~~~

When I got home, the house was quiet except for the soft hum of the air conditioner and the faint rustle of pages turning. I headed toward the library, and sure enough,
~~~~~~~~~~

Karina was curled up in her favorite armchair by the window, legs tucked underneath her, nose buried deep in a book. She looked peaceful, almost like she belonged there more than anywhere else, safe in her little world.

I knocked gently on the doorframe, not wanting to startle her too much. She jumped a little anyway, her eyes blinking quickly as she looked up. She must not have heard me come in, completely lost in her book, like always.

"Hey," I said, stepping into the room.

"Hey," she replied, her voice soft, her expression warming when she saw me.

I walked over slowly, feeling a little nervous and unsure. "I, um... I have something for you." I slipped my bag off my shoulder and unzipped the front pocket. Carefully, I pulled out the book and handed it to her. "It's just a little something... my way of saying 'sorry' for being so distracted lately. I know you've been feeling kind of down, and I've noticed. I should've said something sooner."

She looked at the cover and instantly lit up. Her eyes widened, and a smile bloomed like a sunrise. "*Harry Potter and the Chamber of Secrets?*" she asked, delighted. "Thank you, Liv!"

She stood up and set her book on the end table without hesitation. She threw her arms around me in a tight hug, surprising me a little. I wrapped my arms around her and held her close. It wasn't a quick, polite hug. It was the kind of hug where you can feel how much the other person needed it. Her head rested against my shoulder, and I didn't let go.

We stayed like that for a while, just holding each other. No words. Just quiet understanding. I didn't need to ask what was wrong; I could feel it in the way she clung to me. I could tell she'd been carrying something heavy lately, and if this one small gesture could lift even a bit of that weight, it was worth it.

After nearly a minute, she finally pulled away, her eyes glassy but still smiling. She plopped back into her chair with the new book in her lap like it was a treasure she'd been waiting for.

"I'm going to start it right now," she said eagerly. She slipped a bookmark into the book she had been reading, then carefully placed it aside. Her fingers traced the new book's spine before she opened it to the first page and began to read.

I stood there for a moment, watching her. Something about how she looked in that moment, peaceful, content, maybe even hopeful: it made my heart ache in the best way.

I turned to leave but glanced back just before walking out the door. She was already completely absorbed, a soft smile on her lips. And for the first time in a while, she looked happy.

And seeing her like that... made me feel a little lighter, too.

Chapter Thirty

Carmen

July 16ᵗʰ, 1998

It had been nearly two weeks since something attacked me in my bedroom, leaving three jagged scratches down my back. The wounds had stopped stinging a few days ago, but the fear, that lingering, crawling feeling of being watched, hadn't faded so easily. I kept waiting for something else to happen, but all I got was silence: silence, and Brett.

He'd barely left my side since that night, only stepping away when work called. He was watchful, patient, and comforting whenever I was with him. And today, after lunch, I was going to see him again. I needed to.

The walk to his house took just under fifteen minutes, a familiar path down the gravel road. The sun was high overhead, and the air was warm, filled with the scents of dust and pine. As I came up the long driveway, I spotted him outside, sitting on the front steps, elbows resting on his knees like he'd been waiting a while. He stood the second he saw me and walked toward me with open arms.

Without hesitating, I closed the distance between us, wrapping my arms around his waist and resting my head against his chest. His heartbeat thudded steadily under my cheek, grounding me.

"How are you feeling?" he asked softly, brushing his hand down my back before pulling slightly away to look at me.

"I'm okay," I said. "It doesn't hurt anymore."

He leaned down and kissed the top of my head, gently and reassuringly. Then he looped an arm around my shoulders, and we walked inside. The house was quiet. His Uncle Matt was at work, and Sarah was hanging out with Karina at my house. Rhea was in the backyard, digging in her garden as she often did when she needed to clear her mind.

Brett closed the door behind us. "What do you want to do?"

I paused for a moment. It had been three weeks since that night, the first time we'd been that close. Since then, a great deal has happened. Between the scratches, the nightmares, the secrets, and the growing weight I felt pressing down on my chest, I just wanted to feel safe again. To feel close to someone who made the noise go quiet.

Without answering, I reached for his hand and gave it a small tug.

He looked at me, questioning but trusting, and followed me up the stairs and into his room. When he shut the door behind us, I turned to face him.

Without speaking, I stepped into his arms and kissed him. Not shy, not hesitant, just full of all the emotions I didn't know how to say aloud. He kissed me back, just as eager, his hands wrapping around my waist and pulling me closer. Still holding on, I walked backward until the backs of my knees hit the edge of the bed. I pulled him down with me, our bodies falling in sync.

For a few minutes, it was just us: lips, breath, the sound of rustling sheets. The tension and ache in my chest slowly began to unravel. When he pulled back and looked into my eyes, his breathing was heavy, his face flushed.

"We don't have to go further if you don't want to," he said, his voice low and full of care. "Not unless you're sure."

I held his gaze and nodded. "I want to."

I reached up and cupped his face, drawing him back down to me. We kissed again, deeper this time, slower. He carefully peeled my shirt over my head, like I might break. I did the same with his, and for a moment, we just looked at each other, skin to skin, breath to breath. Then we fell together onto the bed, and the rest of the world faded away.

Every movement was soft. Every kiss meant something. And in that quiet space, I let go of everything else; the darkness, the fear, the invisible thing that had marked me. For a while, there was only Brett and the safety of his arms.

And I didn't feel alone for the first time in a long time.

~~~~~~~~~~

After the quiet storm of our time together, Brett and I lay tangled under the soft weight of his bedsheets, the afternoon sun casting lazy streaks of gold across the floor. My head rested gently on his chest, his heartbeat slowing beneath my ear like a song meant only for me. His fingers traced idle circles on my arm, feather-light, as if even now he couldn't stop touching me.

"That was... even better the second time," I whispered, my voice barely audible, my cheeks warming with shy vulnerability.

"I've heard it gets better the more you do it," Brett replied, his tone playful but soft, his fingers brushing back a strand of hair that had fallen in my face.

I hesitated a moment, biting the inside of my cheek. Then, quietly, I asked, "Have you... done it a lot before?"
~~~~~~~~~~

He didn't answer right away. I felt his chest rise with a steady, honest breath. "No," he said finally, turning slightly to look at me. "You were my first."

My heart did a small flip. "You were mine too," I admitted, a little nervous and relieved.

Brett leaned down and kissed my head gently, his lips lingering just a second longer than necessary. Then he wrapped his arms around me tighter, like he never wanted to let go.

We lay like that for a while longer, wrapped in the comfort of silence and each other, the kind of silence that doesn't feel empty but full of all the things we didn't need to say aloud. But eventually, we got dressed, sharing quiet smiles and light touches as we pulled our clothes back on, grounded again by the real world waiting just beyond Brett's bedroom door.

Rhea stood at the kitchen counter downstairs, snacking on pistachios and thoughtfully watching birds outside the window. Her sleeves were rolled up, and her hands were busy but relaxed. Brett and I sat down at the kitchen table, and the faint creak of the chairs gave away our arrival.

Without turning around, Rhea said, "Don't think I don't know what you two have been up to."

I blinked, stunned, and glanced over at Brett, whose eyebrows raised with a silent laugh. I could feel the heat rise in my face.

"We didn't—" I started, but Rhea turned around and gave us both a look that said, don't even try.

"I'm not going to give you a lecture," she said, cracking another pistachio between her fingers. "I was young once. I get it. Just promise me you're being safe. Emotionally and physically."

Brett leaned back slightly in his chair, nodding calmly. "We are," he said, his voice casual but sincere.

Rhea studied us both for a moment, her gaze not judgmental, but maternal, almost protective. Then she popped another pistachio in her mouth and said, "Good."

I laughed, tension melting away. The moment felt strangely perfect, warm, grounded, and safe. The world hadn't stopped turning. The dark shadows that haunted me at night were still out there somewhere. But in that kitchen, in the company of two people who mattered so much, everything felt okay, if only for now. And sometimes, 'okay' was more than enough.

Rhea pulled out a chair and joined us at the table, her expression shifting from casual to serious as she leaned forward, hands folded. The energy in the room changed instantly. There was no more light teasing, no more warmth from stolen moments. It was time to talk about what really mattered, what was happening in that house, and how to stop it before it hurt someone else.

"We need a plan," she said firmly. "Whatever attacked you, Carmen, isn't going to stop. And the longer we wait, the stronger it may become."

I nodded slowly, the weight of her words pressing down on me. "Mom's working the night shift tomorrow night. She leaves a little after six and won't be home until seven in the morning."

"What about your sisters?" Brett asked, his voice low but urgent.

"Liv and Nina are going out of town for the night. They got tickets for some concert a couple of hours away."

"That helps," Rhea said, already shifting into strategy mode. "That just leaves Karina."

Brett leaned forward. "I'll ask Sarah if she can have Karina over for a sleepover. She's been wanting to hang out with her anyway."

"That would be perfect," Rhea nodded. "With her out of the house, we can focus on the spirit without worrying about her safety. I'll talk to Viola and Luca; we'll meet at your place around eight. We need to go in prepared, and we need to do this right."

The room felt heavier as she spoke, like the air thickened with something unseen. This was real. It was not a nightmare, not a passing haunting. Something had attached itself to my home, and we planned to face it.

I swallowed hard, unease creeping up my spine like a cold draft. "It's all starting to feel too real. I can't shake this feeling that something will go wrong."

Brett reached for my hand across the table, his thumb brushing my knuckles. "I'll be with you, Carmen. You're not doing this alone."

"No," Rhea and I said at the same time.

He looked stunned. "What? Why not?"

Rhea turned to him, her voice gentle but unyielding. "It's too dangerous, Brett."

He frowned. "I'm not a kid. I can handle myself. I won't let Carmen walk into that house alone while something's in there."

I looked at him, my heart twisting with both love and fear. "Please, Brett. I love you, but if something were to happen to you... If I had to watch you get hurt too..." My voice caught, and I looked away, blinking back tears. "I couldn't live with that."

Brett leaned back, frustrated, but said nothing at first. The silence between us was thick with emotion.

"We're not trying to push you away," Rhea added, more gently this time. "But if this thing is as strong as we suspect, we need a clear head and trained hands in that house tonight. Viola and Luca have done this before. Let them lead."

Brett exhaled sharply, rubbing the back of his neck. "Fine," he said reluctantly. "But I'm coming over right after. I want to know you're okay."

I gave him a small smile. "Okay. I'll call you when it's over."

He nodded, though his jaw was still tight. "I'll be waiting."

As the plan settled between us, a strange quiet fell over the room. This wasn't just about ghosts anymore. This was war. And tomorrow, we'd finally confront whatever lurked in the shadows; whatever had left marks on my skin, haunted Shiloh's ghost, and poisoned the house we tried to make a home.

Whatever happened, it would all come to a head tomorrow night...

~~~~~~~~~~

July 17th, 1998

The day I had been both dreading and waiting for was finally here.

Everything had fallen into place just as planned. Mom had just pulled out of the driveway for her night shift at the hospital, completely unaware of what was about to unfold in her house. Liv and Nina had left hours earlier, road-tripping to the concert they'd been talking about for weeks. And Karina, sweet, curious Karina, was safe. She'd been
~~~~~~~~~~

with Sarah since early afternoon, tucked away in the comfort of a sleepover, blissfully unaware of the danger that still clung to the shadows of our home.

Now, I was alone. Alone in the house that had never felt comfortable, not yet...

The silence pressed in on me from every direction, heavy and unnatural. It wasn't the peaceful quiet that comes when a house settles. No, this was the kind of silence that listens, watches, and waits.

Even though nothing had happened in days, no whispers, slamming doors, or Shiloh, I knew it wasn't over. It wasn't gone. And deep down, I had the chilling sense that it knew what we were planning... and was just waiting to strike back.

I'd just hung up the phone after a call with Brett. Hearing his voice helped calm my racing heart. We hadn't said anything particularly profound, but something about his steadiness, the way he said "You'll be okay," made me believe it, if only for a moment.

"I'll be waiting for your call," he had said. "I love you."

"I love you, too," I whispered back before hanging up, reluctant to sever the connection.

Now the house felt colder. Emptier.

I stood in the middle of the living room, arms wrapped tightly around myself, listening to the creaks of the old wood floor, the faint hum of the refrigerator, and the wind whispering through the trees outside. Every little sound felt amplified, ominous. Every shadow stretched just a little too far.

I stood at the top of the stairs, my eyes wandering to the hallway, the one that led to the bedrooms and the closet where Shiloh always appeared. I felt like something was lurking, waiting just beyond my vision, like it had sunk deeper into the house's bones, watching with unseen eyes, biding its time.

I tried to shake the feeling, but it clung like a second skin.

The worst part wasn't the fear. It was the waiting.

Waiting for the others to arrive. Waiting for the spirits to show their faces again. Waiting for the storm that had been building for weeks to finally break.

I took a deep breath, turned on every light in the house, and sat on the edge of the couch. Rhea had said they'd be here by eight. That gave me less than an hour to sit with my thoughts. Less than an hour to prepare myself to walk straight into the unknown.

To face whatever it was that had hurt me.

To find the truth about Shiloh.

To reclaim my home, or burn whatever haunted it to the ground.

And in the middle of all that fear, a tiny flicker of resolve sparked inside me.

Tonight, something was going to come to an end. One way or another.

~~~~~~~~~~

Eight o'clock finally rolled around, and as if on cue, I heard the sound of car doors shutting just outside. My heart skipped a beat. I stood from the couch, wiped my palms against my jeans, and walked to the front door. The air felt heavier now, like the house itself was holding its breath.

Outside, the last hints of daylight clung to the horizon in dusky streaks of pink and blue. Viola's car had just parked at the curb, and I saw Rhea stepping out from the back seat. In the front, Viola and Luca were already out of the car, stretching and looking around. Then I noticed another vehicle parked behind them, one I didn't recognize.

Who's that? I wondered, narrowing my eyes.

I walked down the porch steps just as Rhea approached me. She gave me a soft, reassuring smile and gently squeezed my shoulder.

"You ready for this?" she asked, her voice low and steady, like an anchor.

I nodded, though my stomach was fluttering with nerves. "As ready as I'll ever be."

I glanced over at Viola and Luca, who were helping a young man I hadn't seen before unload a ridiculous number of bags from the trunk of the second car. He had
~~~~~~~~~~

shaggy brown hair that curled slightly around his ears, and a shadow of stubble along his jaw. He looked older than me, but not by much, maybe in his early twenties. He moved quickly, slinging one heavy bag over his shoulder while reaching for another.

"What is all that?" I asked, taking a step closer.

"Equipment," Viola said simply as she adjusted the strap on her shoulder.

"What kind of equipment?" I asked again, still trying to wrap my head around the number of duffel bags they hauled up my driveway.

"Cameras. EMF detectors. Audio recorders. Anything we might need to document or identify a presence," said the young man, walking toward me with the final two bags in hand.

"Carmen, this is Micah," Viola said, gesturing between us. "Micah, meet Carmen." Micah smiled politely, almost sheepishly. "Nice to meet you, Carmen. I hope we can help you."

"I hope so too," I said quietly, still feeling the buzz of anxiety under my skin.

Rhea must've sensed it because she stepped beside me again and rubbed my shoulders gently. "Let's go inside. We'll set everything up and walk you through how it works, okay?"

I nodded again, more slowly this time, and led the group up the porch steps and into the house. The second Viola crossed the threshold, she paused and staggered slightly, catching herself on the doorframe.

"I see what you mean," she murmured. "The energy shifts the moment you walk in... like an invisible curtain of static just hanging in the doorway."

Relief flickered in my chest. So, I wasn't crazy. Someone else could feel it, too.

I led them into the kitchen, where they immediately began working. They unzipped bags and laid out gadgets on the counter: compact cameras, handheld audio recorders, and something that looked like a high-tech walkie-talkie with a row of tiny bulbs on top.

"What's that?" I asked, pointing.

"EMF detector," Micah said, holding it up for me to see. "It measures electromagnetic fields, magnetic, radio, or otherwise. Spirits tend to give off energy spikes, and this helps us track them."

He turned a dial, and the little lights flickered to life in a soft hum, casting a faint glow across the counter's surface. The buzzing sound it emitted was subtle, but it made the hairs on the back of my neck stand up.

And just like that, it hit me.

The fear. The tension. The weight of everything we were about to face.

The room spun slightly. My chest tightened. Tears welled in my eyes before I could stop them, and my breathing quickened.

"Carmen?" Viola noticed immediately and crossed the room. She didn't hesitate. She just opened her arms and wrapped them around me like a blanket.

"It's okay," she whispered against my temple. "We've got you. You're not alone anymore."

I held on tightly, letting her words sink in, allowing the comfort of her presence to steady me. Because tonight, we were going to face the darkness. But at least I wouldn't be doing it alone.

~~~~~~~~~~

After nearly thirty minutes of setting up gear and testing each piece to ensure it worked properly, we were finally ready to begin. The atmosphere was heavy and tense, and every slight noise seemed amplified. Once everything was in place, we turned off every light in the house, plunging ourselves into near-total darkness. We decided to start upstairs, in my bedroom, where most of the strange occurrences had occurred.

Micah held the night vision camera, its green glow casting eerie shadows across the walls. Luca had the regular digital video camera set to record in low light. Rhea carried an audio recorder and a flashlight in one hand. At the same
~~~~~~~~~~

time, Viola took the lead with her notebook and a list of pre-written questions, carefully crafted to provoke a response from any entity that might be present.

We entered my bedroom slowly, like we were stepping onto sacred ground.

"Is anyone here with us?" Viola asked, her voice deliberately steady, almost robotic.

Silence.

"Can you tell us your name?" she asked again, scanning the room with her eyes, still nothing; no creak of floorboards, no whisper in the air.

The room felt dead. Or too alive in all the wrong ways.

Luca quietly moved around the space, recording every corner, every shadow. Rhea held the recorder out like a divining rod, hoping it would catch something our ears couldn't. I stood by the doorway, watching, waiting... hoping that nothing would happen, but knowing, deep down, that something always did.

Then, just as the minutes dragged into a tense lull, I felt a sudden chill, like icy fingers crawling down my spine. My breath caught in my throat. That's when I heard it: a voice.

Familiar.

Shiloh.

...you can't be here...

It was a whisper, but it felt inside my head. Echoing. Warning.

"Shiloh just spoke to me," I said, my voice shaking.

Rhea turned to me, eyes wide. "What did she say?"

"She said we can't be here."

Viola didn't miss a beat. "We're not here to hurt you," she said clearly, addressing the room. "We just want to talk."

That's when the nausea hit, fast and hard. My stomach turned. My legs buckled, and I stumbled backward, barely catching myself against the wall.

"Are you okay?" Rhea said, rushing to my side, one hand out to steady me.

"I... I don't feel so good," I managed to say, my vision blurred.

Then it came again, this time louder, more guttural.

...get out...

The voice was not like before. This was something darker, more profound. Something that didn't want us there, and wasn't afraid to show it.

Suddenly, a searing pain tore across my back, sharp and sudden like claws dragging through my skin. I cried out, collapsing forward onto the floor.

"Carmen!" Viola shouted, running to me. "What happened?!"

I could barely speak. "My back..." was all I could manage through the pain.

Viola gently lifted the back of my shirt and gasped. "Oh my God…"

Rhea moved to look and let out a horrified breath. Three long, jagged scratches ran diagonally across my back, already oozing blood.

"He said 'get out,'" I said, through gritted teeth. "The voice, it wasn't human. It sounded like a growl."

Viola's face turned pale. Her hands trembled as she lowered my shirt. "I don't think we're dealing with a spirit," she said, her voice barely above a whisper. "This is something darker. Let's wrap this up and get downstairs. We need to clean you up."

None of us argued. We gathered our equipment and returned to the kitchen as quickly as possible. The brightness of the overhead light was jarring after so much time in the dark. I sat backwards on a kitchen chair, gripping the edges tightly as Rhea disinfected the wounds with peroxide. The sting was sharp, and I winced as it bubbled against the open scratches.

Meanwhile, Micah and Luca set up at the kitchen table with the cameras and audio recorder, reviewing the footage and sound.

A few minutes later, Micah suddenly removed his headphones, his face ashen. "Guys," he said urgently. "You need to hear this."

He pressed play. At first, it was just our voices and the creaks of the floor. Then, beneath all of it, low, gravelly, unmistakable, came the voice.

...leave now... You do not belong here...

The room fell utterly silent. No one breathed. No one moved.

"I think you may be right," Luca finally said, his voice barely audible. "This... this isn't a ghost."

I looked at Viola. "Then what is it?"

Her expression was grave. She stared at me for a long moment before speaking. "It's something that's never been human. Never walked the earth like we do. We're dealing with something much older, much darker."

She took a slow breath before saying the word that would change everything.

"A demon."

It hit me like a punch, a *demon*. The word echoed in my mind, sinking in like ice water. I looked around the room. Everyone's face mirrored the same realization: this was beyond us. This was dangerous.

For three long minutes, no one spoke.

"We're not prepared for something like this," Viola said finally. "We need help. From someone who knows how to deal with this kind of entity. A professional."

Rhea nodded. "Let's wrap this up for tonight and return another day with better protection. Carmen, I don't want you sleeping here alone. You can stay in Brett's room tonight."

I didn't hesitate. "Thank you," I said, the fear finally breaking through my voice. I felt hollow and shaken. But above all, I was grateful not to be alone.

Even if I couldn't shake the feeling that whatever was upstairs... wasn't done with us yet.

~~~~~~~~~~

I lay on my stomach across Brett's bed, the cool sheets pressing gently against my burning skin. Every movement sent a dull ache radiating from the scratches on my back, sharp reminders of what had just happened. The pain was deep, not just physical but emotional, spiritual. I felt hollowed out.

Brett had stayed downstairs with Rhea and the others. She was filling him in, explaining everything that had happened, what they had seen, what they had heard, and what had marked me. I was glad he wasn't up here. I couldn't face another person right now. Not while I was barely holding myself together.

The room around me was dimly lit, just enough moonlight seeping through the curtains to give everything a silver sheen. Outside, I could hear the soft chorus of crickets and the faint rustle of leaves swaying in the night breeze. It was peaceful, deceptively so. The kind of calm
~~~~~~~~~~

that sits on top of something much darker. A calm that feels like it's watching you, waiting.

My thoughts spiraled, tumbling over one another like a storm inside my head. I couldn't stop hearing Viola's voice in my mind, over and over again:

"A demon."

Just two words. But they echoed with the weight of everything I didn't understand. Everything I *feared* to understand.

A demon.

The word tasted like metal in my mouth. Bitter. Cold.

What were we even dealing with? How do you fight something like *that*? Something you can't see, something you can't touch, something that doesn't bleed, doesn't sleep, doesn't *die*? I was already overwhelmed when I thought it was just a ghost. Even that was easier to accept. I could make sense of it. But this... this was different.

I pressed my face into the pillow, trying to focus on the steady sound of my breathing. But it wasn't constant. My chest tightened, and a wave of panic bloomed inside me, hot and crushing. My thoughts were spinning out of control:

How do we get rid of it? What if it doesn't leave? What if it comes for my family next?

My Mom. My sisters.

How do I protect them from something like this?

The helplessness hit me like a brick wall. I wanted to scream. I wanted to tear something apart. But instead, the pressure inside me cracked open, and tears spilled down my cheeks. I tried to keep quiet, to keep my sobs hidden in the fabric of the pillow, but I couldn't hold them in. I cried until my shoulders shook, until I couldn't breathe right.

I didn't want this, any of it.

I just wanted my life to return to the way it was before I discovered the truth. Before I realized that the strange things I saw and heard weren't in my head. Before I found out I had some kind of *gift*, if you could even call it that. Back when I thought maybe I was just imagining things, hallucinating, losing my mind.

At least then, I had control over the fear. I could convince myself it wasn't real. That I could stop it if I just tried hard enough.

But now? Now I know better. And the truth was so much worse than the lie.

Because the voices I used to hear in the quiet moments, the whispers in the dark, were scary. But they were nothing compared to *this*. Nothing compared to what had left marks on my skin. Nothing compared to what had spoken with that voice, that *growl*, that rage.

This wasn't just a haunting. It was a warning. And I didn't know how to listen to it without falling apart.

I curled tighter into myself, every muscle aching with the weight of everything I couldn't fix. I felt small, like a child in a nightmare with no one coming to wake me up. And the worst part was knowing this wasn't a dream. This was real. And it was only just beginning.

The silence around me deepened. The crickets outside quieted momentarily, like they were holding their breath.

I pressed a hand over my mouth, trying to stop the sobs from rising again. I didn't want anyone to hear. I didn't want to be the weak one. But the truth was, I was scared.

More scared than I'd ever been in my life.

And beneath all the tears and all the fear, one thought pulsed through me like a heartbeat I couldn't silence:

What if it's not done with me yet?

~~~~~~~~~~

I don't know how long I was alone in Brett's room. It could have been twenty minutes or two hours; the seconds had blurred into each other, stretching out like a dull ache in my chest. Time didn't move as it should when you were drowning in fear, when the silence pressed down on you like a weight you couldn't lift.

The pillow beneath my cheek was damp, soaked with the tears I couldn't stop. My body felt heavy, like my grief and fear had become a part of my bones. I didn't move. I didn't
~~~~~~~~~~

speak. I just *existed*; silent and still, hoping that if I stayed quiet long enough, maybe the pain would pass.

Then the door opened with a quiet creak.

I didn't lift my head. I didn't have the strength. I kept my face buried in the pillow, my body motionless, as if I could pretend I was already asleep and maybe he wouldn't say anything. The footsteps that followed were soft, hesitant. Brett. I knew his walk as well as I knew my own heartbeat.

He didn't speak at first. He must've thought I was sleeping. I listened as he moved gently through the room. The faint rustle of fabric told me he was changing. Slipping out of his clothes and into pajamas. Then the mattress dipped beside me as he climbed in and settled beside me, close but not crowding me. Respectful. Gentle.

There was a pause. A beat of silence that felt like it lasted a lifetime.

"You're awake," he said quietly. I felt his gaze on me, warm and steady. "You've been crying."

It wasn't a question. He already knew. My eyes were swollen and raw, and I was sure the moonlight catching through the window had lit up the streaks on my face like silver rivers. My chest hitched, and more tears welled up without warning. I still didn't say anything. I didn't know how. The words were buried somewhere beneath the weight of everything I was feeling.

I started to cry again. Slowly at first, then harder, as a storm builds from a drizzle into something heavier. That's when I felt Brett shift closer, his arm wrapping gently around my shoulders. He pulled me into him, his body warm and grounding. I didn't resist. I couldn't. I needed that comfort like I needed air.

He held me firmly but not too tightly, like he knew exactly how much I could take before it would hurt my back. His presence felt like a dam against the chaos in my head; strong, constant, unshakable.

"I'm so sorry," he whispered into my hair, his voice thick with emotion. "I've got you."

That was all he said. But it was enough.

The words broke something open inside me, not in a bad way, but in a way that finally allowed me to let go. To surrender to the pain I had been trying to hold inside. My fingers curled into the fabric of his shirt as I wept harder than I had all night. The fear, the guilt, the helplessness, it all came pouring out of me, raw and unstoppable.

Brett didn't try to hush me. He didn't offer empty words or pretend he had the answers. He just held me. He let me cry. He let me feel everything I needed to feel, and he didn't let go.

His hand moved slowly up and down my back in soothing circles, careful not to touch the wounds. His breathing was calm and steady, something I could anchor myself to. I closed my eyes, letting his presence wrap around me like a blanket of safety in the middle of the storm.

Eventually, the sobs softened. My breathing slowed. The tension in my muscles started to fade, little by little, as the exhaustion took over.

Wrapped in his arms, I let his warmth calm the trembling in my soul. The fear lingered like a shadow at the edge of my mind, but I didn't feel alone for the first time since everything happened.

And in that small, quiet moment, curled against him, my face pressed to his chest, I cried myself to sleep.

Not because the fear was gone.

But because I finally felt safe enough to close my eyes.

Chapter Thirty–One

Karina

Sarah clicked the remote just as the movie credits began to roll, the soft hum of orchestral music fading into the room's quietness. The TV screen dimmed to black, leaving us in the soft glow of the string lights draped across her basement ceiling.

We had spent the entire day together, talking, laughing, and playing games until our cheeks ached. After dinner, we curled up with bowls of popcorn and watched two movies back-to-back. It was the kind of night I'd always imagined when I thought about what a real sleepover would be like.

I didn't want to admit it out loud, not even to myself, but this was my first sleepover. Sure, I'd stayed at my grandparents' house and sometimes at my aunt's, but this was different. This was *special*. This was me spending the night at a friend's house, with no grown-ups orchestrating our every move. It felt like a small milestone I hadn't known I was waiting for.

It was nearing midnight, and the fatigue was starting to settle in. I stretched and yawned from my spot in the soft beanbag chair.

"I'll be right back," I mumbled, standing up and brushing popcorn crumbs off my pajama pants. "I need to use the bathroom."

"Can you grab me a water on your way back?" Sarah asked, already halfway through rearranging some pillows on the couch.

"Sure," I said, heading quietly up the stairs.

The hallway was dimly lit, illuminated only by the soft nightlight near the bathroom.

After washing my hands, I padded into the kitchen, trying not to make too much noise. But as I turned the corner, a low murmur of voices reached my ears.

"I know someone in Connecticut who might be able to help," a woman said, her tone hushed but urgent.

I froze for a moment, then peeked around the corner. Rhea, Sarah's aunt, was seated at the kitchen table with three other adults. Papers and a file folder were spread before them, and the atmosphere felt tense. Serious, focused, like they were planning something important.

When I entered the room, all four looked up, startled by my sudden appearance.

"Oh, I'm sorry," I said quickly. "I was just grabbing some water for Sarah."

Rhea's expression softened into a smile. "Oh, no worries. Help yourself, Karina."

I walked to the fridge, feeling awkward under their collective gaze. Something about the energy in the room made me hesitate. Their eyes were calm, but the calmness masked something more profound. I didn't want to pry, but the words slipped out before I could stop them.

"Is... everything okay?"

There was a brief pause.

"Everything's fine," Rhea said smoothly. "Karina, these are my colleagues: Viola and Luca. And this is Micah, a friend of ours." She gestured to each of them, then added, "This is Karina, Sarah's friend. She's staying the night."

"Nice to meet you," I said, sounding casual.

"You too," Viola replied, giving me a polite nod. Luca offered a small wave, and Micah returned it with a friendly smile.

I could feel that strange tension under the surface again, like I had walked in on something secret. Something important. I didn't press. Instead, I grabbed a bottle of water from the fridge and quietly returned downstairs.

When I returned, Sarah was fluffing the couch cushions and laying out blankets. She looked up as I handed her the water.

"Thanks," she said. "Took you a while. Everything okay?"

"I didn't realize your aunt had people over," I said, sitting down and pulling the blanket over my legs.

"She does?" Sarah blinked in surprise.

"Yeah, Viola, Luca, and Micah, I think. They were talking in the kitchen."

"Oh, I know Viola and Luca. They've been around before. Micah's new, though. Must've been a last-minute thing."

I hesitated. "They all stopped talking when I came in. Like... completely silent. It felt kind of weird."

Sarah frowned slightly. "Maybe it was personal. Rhea sometimes has work meetings at night. She doesn't always tell me what they're about."

"Yeah. That makes sense, I guess," I said, though the uneasy feeling still lingered.

We let it go after that, not wanting to overthink it. The couch cushions were surprisingly comfortable, and soon we were settled under our blankets, the room filled with the soft rustle of fabric and the occasional creak of the house settling for the night.

As my eyes started to drift closed, I couldn't help but wonder, what kind of work meeting happens at midnight?

~~~~~~~~~~
~~~~~~~~~~

July 18ᵗʰ, 1998

The following morning, Sarah and I woke up around the same time, both of us blinking sleep from our eyes as golden sunlight spilled through the basement windows. The air was cool and still, filled only with the soft rustling of blankets as we slowly sat up and shook off our grogginess.

Neither of us said much; we were still wrapped in the warmth of sleep and that peaceful morning quiet that seems to hang in the air after a long, memorable night. After tidying up the makeshift beds, we padded up the stairs, drawn by the smell of something cooking.

When we entered the kitchen, I froze for a second.

At the table, Carmen sat whispering with Brett. Rhea was standing near the counter, leaning against it with a mug in her hand, clearly having been mid-conversation with the two of them. Like the night before, the room went strangely still when we walked in.

"Morning, girls," Rhea said brightly, smoothing over the awkward silence with practiced ease. "Did you sleep well?"

We both nodded and slid into the empty chairs at the table. Sarah yawned and rested her elbows on the table, while I stole another glance at Carmen. Her hair was damp, like she'd showered here, and she wore the same sweatshirt from yesterday. She looked too comfortable, like someone who hadn't just arrived for breakfast.

"What are you doing here?" I asked her, narrowing my eyes.

Carmen smiled, a little too quickly. "Came over for breakfast," she said casually.

I didn't say anything immediately, but I knew she wasn't telling the truth. She'd spent the night here. And I had a feeling Brett was the reason why.

Rhea stood and walked over to the stove. "How do eggs and bacon sound?"

"Just egg whites for me," Sarah said automatically.

There was a pause, short but heavy with unspoken meaning. Rhea and Sarah exchanged a look, the kind that says more than words ever could. It wasn't just about breakfast. It was about care. It was about history.

"Okay," Rhea said gently, "but you're having five of them. And juice."

Sarah let out a soft sigh and leaned back in her chair. "Fine," she muttered, not meeting anyone's eyes.

I remembered what she'd told me last night while we were curled up on the couch. She'd been struggling lately, some tough days that felt heavier than others. She spoke softly, like she was afraid the words might break her if she said them too loudly. I listened as best I could, offering no solutions, but simply being present. She didn't want advice. She just didn't want to be alone with it.

While Rhea cooked, the kitchen filled with the sound of sizzling bacon and the clinking of utensils. The smell of eggs and melted cheese made my stomach rumble. Twenty minutes later, she brought plates to the table; eggs light and fluffy, with cheese melting perfectly into the folds, the bacon crisp, and tall glasses of juice that looked freshly squeezed.

It was one of those rare meals where everyone was quiet, not because there was nothing to say, but because the food and the moment felt sacred in a small, simple way.

After breakfast, I gathered my things from the basement: my overnight bag, pillow, and the hoodie I almost left behind. I came upstairs and lingered near the front door, slipping on my shoes. Carmen was still saying goodbye to Brett near the kitchen. I could hear the low murmur of their voices, then caught sight of them as she leaned in close.

He whispered something to her, something too quiet for me to catch, and she gave him a quick, familiar kiss. The kind that didn't seem new. The kind that said this had been going on for a while.

"I'll call you," she said softly, then turned and walked out the front door with me.

We made our way down the driveway in silence, the gravel crunching under our shoes. The late morning sun was warm against our faces, and neither of us said anything for a while.

Then, after a few minutes, I broke the silence.

"I won't tell Mom," I said quietly.

Carmen didn't look at me. "Tell Mom what?"

"That you spent the night with your boyfriend."

She kept her eyes straight ahead. "I told you, I just came over for breakfast."

I gave a half-laugh, not even trying to hide my disbelief. "Uh-huh. Sure."

Carmen didn't answer. She just kept walking, arms crossed, her expression unreadable. Maybe she thought I didn't understand, that I couldn't possibly know what it meant to keep something secret just to protect your peace. But I did, more than she realized.

We walked the rest of the way home in silence. But I knew, without needing her to say it, that she appreciated me not pushing harder.

~~~~~~~~~~

It was just after three in the afternoon, and the house was tranquil, the stillness that made it feel like time had slowed down. I was curled up in the library, nestled in the deep leather armchair by the bay window, with a book on my
~~~~~~~~~~

knees and a half-empty mug of tea cooling on the side table. The sunlight slanted through the glass, warm against the wood-paneled walls, casting long, golden shadows across the floor.

I had just started rereading the same paragraph for the third time when the sharp opening of the front door broke the silence. Voices followed, muffled at first but quickly rising in intensity.

"It wasn't that big of a deal!" Nina's voice rang out, edged with exasperation.

"*Not* a big deal?" Liv shot back, louder.

I set my book down and rose from the chair, cautiously moving toward the hallway. Their voices echoed from the foyer, sharp, tense, and unmistakably in the middle of a fight. From the archway near the staircase, I watched them face off, with bags slung over their shoulders.

"Correct, Liv," Nina said, arms folded. "I didn't do anything! You're acting like I was the one flirting with her. *She* was the one coming on to *me*!"

Liv's mouth twisted in frustration. "But you didn't *stop* her from flirting with you."

"What was I supposed to do?" Nina threw her hands in the air. "Start a scene in the middle of the crowd? I didn't want to be rude!"

"I'm not saying you had to be rude," Liv snapped, "but a simple, 'I have a girlfriend,' would have sufficed."

They were both flushed, Liv with anger, Nina with defensiveness. It was rare to see them in this state. Usually, they moved in sync, a unit, always laughing or finishing each other's sentences. But now, there was a crack between them, and I had no idea what to do.

I stepped forward hesitantly. "What's going on?"

Liv's eyes flicked to me. For a split second, I thought she might soften. But then her expression hardened, and she snapped, "It's none of your business, Karina."

She turned sharply and disappeared up the stairs without another word.

I stood there, stunned, her words still ringing in my ears. I hadn't expected her to lash out. Not like that. My face flushed with heat, a mix of embarrassment and hurt. I hadn't meant to intrude. I just wanted to know if everything was okay.

Nina lingered in the foyer, her shoulders slumped slightly now that Liv was gone. She turned toward me, her face softening with an apologetic smile.

"She didn't mean it," she said gently, stepping closer. "She's just mad at me. Not you."

I nodded, even though I didn't feel reassured. Nina gave my shoulder a gentle squeeze, comforting but brief, then picked up her bag and started up the stairs.

I stood alone in the foyer for a long moment, replaying the exchange repeatedly in my head. I knew Liv hadn't meant to snap at me, at least, I hoped she hadn't, but her words still stung. I felt like I had walked into something I wasn't supposed to see. Like I'd been caught in the blast radius of someone else's pain.

I debated following them upstairs. I could say something. Offer to talk. Try to smooth things over. But I didn't move. Something inside me, some small, anxious voice, told me to leave it alone. To not make it worse.

So I turned and strolled back to the library.

I sank into the chair, curled my legs beneath me, and pulled the book back into my lap. But the words on the page swam before my eyes, meaningless and distant. I didn't even try to focus this time.

Instead, I let the tears come quietly, steadily.

I didn't sob. I didn't make a sound. I just sat in the golden light, warm and aching, tears tracing slowly, silently down my cheeks. I wasn't even sure if I was crying because Liv had yelled at me, or because I'd felt so helpless, so small, in the middle of something I couldn't fix.

Maybe both.

The library felt a little colder than it had before. A little quieter. And for the first time since arriving in that house, I felt like I didn't quite belong.

Chapter Thirty–Two

Liv

I was lying flat on my back, staring at the ceiling, my hands cradling my head like I was trying to keep everything from spilling out. My chest felt tight, like all the thoughts circling in my mind were pressing down on me, refusing to let me breathe. I was trying, really trying, not to let it get to me. But it was.

Nina and I never fought. That was one of the things I loved about us, how easy it always was, how we just *got* each other. The only real fight I could even remember was way back, before I came out, and even then, that had more to do with me and the fear I carried than with her. I hadn't seen her in over a week, and she'd begged me to sneak out to see her. I didn't, and it hurt her. We argued, sure, but it hadn't left a scar.

This one felt different. Heavier. It wasn't just a bump in the road; it had settled in my chest like a stone.

I was genuinely angry, not just hurt or confused. I was mad at Nina.

That stupid lunch. That waitress. When it happened, I'd been sitting across the table, and she started flirting, smiling, and laughing like I wasn't even there. Nina didn't flirt back, not in a technical sense. But she didn't shut it down, either. She just let it happen. And that was what got to me. Not what the waitress did, but what Nina didn't do.

A soft knock pulled me out of the spiral.

I blinked and sat up, pushing a breath through my teeth. "Come in," I called, my voice quieter than intended.

The door creaked open, and there she was.

Nina stepped into my room hesitantly, her expression unreadable at first. She closed the door behind her and crossed the room slowly. Then she knelt before me, her eyes wide with something raw, maybe regret, or fear.

"Liv..." Her voice was barely above a whisper. "I'm so sorry."

Her eyes met mine, and I could see the weight she was carrying. "I should've said something to her. I should've told her to back off right away. But I froze. You know how bad I am with confrontation; I've always struggled with it, but that doesn't excuse it. You were sitting right there, and I just let it happen. That was wrong, and I'm sorry."

I looked at her, feeling the weight in my chest shift, still heavy, but different now. I exhaled slowly.

"I'm not mad at you," I said, and my voice cracked slightly. "I'm mad at myself."

Her brows drew together, confused.

"I hate how I felt in that moment. Jealous. Insecure. Like maybe I wasn't enough. I know it wasn't your fault. That waitress was completely out of line. But it still got under my skin. And I think..." I trailed off for a second, trying to find the right words. "I think it scared me. Because just the thought of someone else thinking they had a shot with you made me feel like maybe you'd realize you could do better than me."

Nina's face crumpled, and she reached for my hands, wrapping hers around them gently.

"Liv," she said firmly, "you are *not* replaceable. Not now, not ever. You are my girl. I love you so much. You are the only one for me. No one could ever take your place. Not even close."

A lump formed in my throat, and I felt tears prick at the corners of my eyes.

"I love you, too," I whispered.

She stood, pulling me up, then wrapped her arms around me. I melted into her embrace, arms locking around her like I'd fall apart if I let go. And maybe I would.

Because I did love her so much, it scared me. The thought of losing her, of her walking away, of not having her in my life, was unbearable. I couldn't even let myself imagine it. I wouldn't survive it.

So, I just held on, and she did too, and in that moment, it was enough.

Chapter Thirty-Three

Carmen

July 20th, 1998

Three days.

It had been three long, sleepless, aching days since that night, the night everything unraveled again. The night I was attacked for the second time. And since then, every breath I took felt like it was on borrowed time. My body still bore the signs, long scratches along my back stung every time I moved too quickly or leaned too far, reminders etched into my skin of something I still didn't fully understand.

I hadn't slept properly since. Not really. I closed my eyes, sure. Drifted into shallow, restless dreams. But every creak, every shift in the air, sent a jolt of adrenaline through my body. I was jumpy, constantly on edge. The nights were the worst, silent, suffocating, full of the stillness that feels like it's holding its breath.

Mom had the night shift again, and the thought of being alone in that house, *our* house, which no longer felt like home, was too much. So, just after midnight, I packed a small bag and came over to Brett's. He hadn't asked questions, just welcomed me in and offered his bed like it was the most natural thing in the world. And I clung to that, the quiet comfort of someone who made me feel safe, who didn't ask me to explain the unexplainable.

Now, in the faint morning light slipping through the slats in his blinds, I felt him shift beside me.

Brett was trying to be quiet, easing out of bed in that half-careful, half-clumsy way people do when they don't want to wake someone. But I was already awake. I had been staring at the ceiling for hours, counting my breaths, listening to the clock ticking like it was trying to hold me together.

I rolled over slowly, wincing as the healing cuts on my back pulled beneath my shirt. Brett caught the movement and turned.

"Hey," he said softly, sitting on the edge of the bed. "You awake?"

I nodded and pushed myself up with more effort than I let on. "Yeah."

He studied my face for a beat, like he could see the fatigue I was trying to hide. "How are you feeling?"

"I'm okay," I replied automatically.

He didn't look convinced. "Are you sure?"

"I mean… it doesn't hurt *that* bad," I added, forcing a weak smile. It was a lie. The pain was a dull, persistent throb, especially in the mornings when everything was stiff and raw. But pain, I could handle. It was everything else I wasn't so sure about.

He reached out and placed a gentle hand on my shoulder. The contact grounded me, just for a moment.

"I have to be at work by nine," he said, his voice tinged with regret. He leaned in and kissed my forehead, and I tilted my head slightly, just enough to take in his scent, clean soap, faint coffee, and something that was just *him*. I glanced at the clock on his nightstand. 8:07. I wanted to ask him to stay. Beg him, even. But I didn't. I couldn't.

Instead, I slid out of bed and wrapped my arms around him. He was still shirtless, warm and solid beneath my touch. I pressed my face into his chest and closed my eyes, breathing him in like a lifeline.

He pulled me into him entirely, arms strong around me, chin resting lightly on my head. "I'll be home right after five," he murmured. "Will you be okay until then?"

I nodded into his chest, then gave him a playful push, a silent way of telling him to go. To live his life. To not worry too much about the mess I had dragged into it.

He smiled, just a little, then disappeared into the hallway to get ready.

I stayed behind in his room, sitting on the edge of his bed, staring at the same clock approaching eight-thirty. The silence stretched around me, no longer comforting. My mind picked up right where it had left off, spiraling.

How did my life get here?

Just a few days ago, everything felt complicated, but manageable. I was sleeping at someone else's house because mine might be haunted. Or worse, *cursed*. Violated by something unseen, unknowable. *Violent.*

After the attack, Rhea pulled me aside. She and the others stayed late, not just for comfort but for answers. Viola had mentioned someone in Connecticut who *might* be able to help, not a guarantee, just a possibility. And they were still waiting for him to call back.

That was three days ago.

Three days of waiting, wondering, feeling like the walls of my home were closing in. Like something was watching. Waiting.

I didn't know how long I could handle this limbo, being trapped between fear and hope. Between wanting to pretend nothing was wrong and knowing that something was.

And then there was Shiloh.

She had been terrified of the thing in the house. I saw it in her eyes; she kept glancing over her shoulder, flinching at nothing. Whatever had attacked me... she knew it, or sensed it. And somehow, it terrified her.

But *Shiloh* didn't scare me. She *never* had. Even in the beginning, when I didn't understand what she was, there had always been a softness to her. Sadness, maybe. Loneliness. Not violence.

And now, more than ever, I knew I needed to help her. Not just to figure out what was happening, but to save her. She didn't deserve to be caught up in this, trapped with something that haunted and hunted her.

None of us did.

I pressed my palms against my eyes, trying to hold back tears. I didn't have the energy to cry. My body was sore, my nerves frayed, my heart pounding with unanswered questions.

I just wanted it to stop.

I just wanted to feel *safe* again.

~~~~~~~~~~

I lingered in Brett's room long after he'd gone. The space felt heavier without him in it, like the air itself was weighed
~~~~~~~~~~

down by everything we weren't saying. I sat there, silent, for what felt like hours, letting the stillness wrap around me. The shadows from the curtains crawled slowly across the carpet as the sun shifted in the sky. Eventually, I forced myself to move. I gathered my things with stiff hands, my mind still buzzing, and made my way downstairs, each step heavier than the last.

Rhea was at the kitchen table, a mug of coffee in her hand, flipping through the pages of a worn book. Something dense, too many footnotes, probably about symbols, spirits, or things normal people didn't even believe existed. She looked up as I entered, but didn't say anything immediately. I slid into the seat across from her, the chair creaking beneath me, and rested my arms on the table.

We sat like that for a few quiet minutes, the only sounds coming from the ticking clock and the occasional rustle of paper. It was strangely comforting.

Then she spoke. "How are you holding up, Carmen?" Her voice was soft but steady.

I stared at the tabletop for a second before answering. "I don't know what to do," I admitted, and my voice cracked slightly. "Four months ago, when I heard voices in my head... I wasn't even scared. Not really. I just assumed it was hallucinations, like everyone told me it was. But I didn't think it was *real*."

I looked up at her, eyes wide with a mixture of fear and exhaustion.

"But now..." I continued. "Now, everything I hear, everything I *see*, I know it *is* real. And I don't know how to handle it. I don't even know *what* I'm dealing with half the time. Demons. Spirits. Things we don't even know how to fight. I feel like I'm being thrown into a war I didn't enlist for."

Rhea closed the book and pushed it aside. Her expression softened. "This is a lot for anyone to handle," she said gently. "Let alone someone your age. You're only seventeen, Carmen. You should be worried about what outfit to wear, who's going to prom with whom, or which college will send you a letter first. Not... 'how do I banish a demon from my house?'"

"It's not fair," I said, almost whispering.

"No," she agreed. "It's not."

I swallowed hard. "I didn't ask for any of this. I didn't go looking for it. And now I can't turn it off. It's always there, the voices, the energy, the feeling like something is watching me. And the worst part? I can't even tell my mom. I mean, what am I supposed to say? 'Hey, Mom, by the way, the house is haunted, and I can see things that shouldn't exist.'? She'll think I've lost my mind. She'll call a doctor. She'll try to *fix* me."

Rhea didn't interrupt. She let the words come, let me say what I needed to say.

"What if she doesn't believe me?" I went on. "What if she *does* and still can't handle it? I just... I don't want to be taken away or medicated into silence. I'm scared of what will happen if I tell her. But I'm also scared of what happens if I don't."

Rhea leaned forward slightly, her tone calm but serious. "There's every chance she'll be skeptical at first. That's natural. People are scared of what they don't understand. But when you decide to tell her, whenever that is, you won't be alone. I'll stand with you, Carmen. And your mom, she might not believe it coming from someone else, but hearing it from *you*, seeing how real this is for you... It'll be harder for her to dismiss. Especially when she sees you're not making this up, that you're grounded, sane, and still her daughter."

She reached across the table and placed her hand over mine. "You're not alone in this. You never have been. And you never will be."

Her words settled something in me, not enough to make the fear disappear, but enough to remind me that I wasn't facing this entirely in the dark. There were people, *real* people, who were on my side. They believed me.

But that comfort came tangled with something else: the knowledge that this couldn't stay hidden forever. Sooner or later, the truth would have to come out. And when it did, things would change. Whether for better or worse, I didn't know.

But I knew one thing.

The secret wasn't going to stay a secret much longer.

~~~~~~~~~~

After talking with Rhea for a while, I finally went home. The sun hung low in the sky, casting an orange glow across the gravel road that led to our house. The summer air was thick and unmoving, pressing against my skin like a weighted blanket. My feet dragged with every step, my thoughts running faster than my legs ever could.

I wasn't sure why I was strolling; maybe I was avoiding going home, or I didn't want the quiet moment to end. Either way, I wasn't prepared for what was waiting when I stepped through the front door.

"Carmen?" Mom's voice called out from the kitchen.

I froze mid-step. That wasn't right. She wasn't supposed to be home. She was supposed to be working a double shift, covering for Julie, her friend from the hospital. My stomach dropped a little, as if my body instinctively sensed I'd just walked into something I wasn't ready for.

I peeled off my shoes by the door and cautiously entered the kitchen. My mom stood at the counter, stirring something in a saucepan. She was still in her scrubs, but her
~~~~~~~~~~

hair pulled back in a loose bun, like she'd been home for a while.

"Hi, Mom," I said, trying to sound casual.

She turned and gave me a small smile, though there was something measured in her eyes. "Sit down, honey."

I did as she asked, sinking into one of the chairs at the table, arms folded loosely across my chest. I could feel the tension building before she even said a word.

She turned off the stove, wiped her hands on a dish towel, and joined me at the table. Her eyes searched mine for a second, and I could see she wasn't trying to pick a fight. She looked more... unsure than anything. This conversation was just as uncomfortable for her as it was about to be for me.

"First of all," she began slowly, "I'm glad you've found someone you care about. I think it's great that you're seeing someone. That's part of growing up."

I nodded slightly, unsure of where this was going but feeling it wouldn't be great.

"But..." she continued, pausing as if testing the ground beneath her words, "I'm not okay with you sleeping over at a boy's house. You're still young, Carmen. I know you probably think you're ready for everything, but there are things I want you to wait for. And this is one of them."

I swallowed hard. My face flushed immediately, and I looked down at my hands in my lap.

"I'm not saying you need to stop seeing him," she added gently. "But no more sleepovers. Okay? That's not negotiable."

"I'm sorry, Mom," I said quietly, my voice barely above a whisper.

She softened. "I'm not angry with you. I just... I want you to be older before you make those kinds of choices. Intimacy isn't just physical. It comes with weight and consequences, including emotional ones. I just want you to be ready."

I nodded again, cheeks burning. My mind raced. *Does she know? Can she tell?* The possibility made my heart thud against my ribs.

"I understand, Mom. I won't stay over again. I'm sorry."

She didn't answer right away. The room fell into a brief silence, filled only by the faint hum of the refrigerator and the soft clinking of her spoon against the coffee mug she hadn't touched.

Then, after a long pause, she tilted her head slightly and asked, "Do you love him?"

The question caught me off guard. It wasn't judgmental. Just curious, maybe even a little wistful. Like she remembered what it was like to be my age and feel something big and terrifying for the first time.

This was new to me, and I wasn't exactly the type to open up about my feelings, especially not to my mom. But the way she asked it made me want to meet her halfway.

"I do," I said softly. "He understands me. When I'm with him... I feel safe."

Her face relaxed a little at that. She reached across the table, her hand covering mine for a moment. "Well, I'd love to meet him officially. Can he come to dinner sometime? I have a few days off next week. Maybe we can make an evening out of it, something low-key, just us."

A part of me tensed at Brett sitting across from my mom in this kitchen, with all its quiet expectations. But another part of me warmed at her effort. She was trying, and that mattered more than I realized.

"I can ask him," I said, a small smile tugging at the corners of my mouth.

She smiled back. "Good."

And for a moment, the air between us felt a little lighter. Maybe things weren't perfect. Perhaps I was still keeping too many secrets. But at least for tonight, we were talking. And that was a start.

~~~~~~~~~~

Later that evening, after I figured Brett would be home from work and settled in, I picked up the phone, and dialed the number to his house. My heart beat faster as it rang. I
~~~~~~~~~~

knew he'd expect me to come back over, maybe to talk or distract ourselves from everything we didn't know how to handle. But I couldn't. Not tonight.

Rhea answered the phone, her voice warm as always. "Hello?"

"Hi, it's me. Can I talk to Brett?" I asked.

"Of course, sweetie. Hold on just a second," she said.

I heard the faint sound of movement, soft footsteps, and the rustle of the phone changing hands. Then a moment later, Brett's voice came through the line.

"Hello?"

"Hey," I said softly.

"Hey, beautiful," he replied, his voice instantly lighter. "I thought you were coming back over. Everything okay?"

I sighed, leaning back on my bed, staring at the ceiling as the words formed. "My mom caught me coming home today."

He paused for a second. "Oh."

"I can't sleep over anymore."

There was silence on his end, just the sound of him breathing. I knew he understood. We both knew this day was coming. Still, hearing it out loud made it real in a way it hadn't been before.

"She wants to have you over for dinner," I added after a moment, trying to steady my voice. "To talk to us. I don't know what about. Maybe it's just one of those 'get to know the boyfriend' dinners or her way of trying to keep a tighter leash. I'm not sure."

"I'd love to come to dinner," he said quickly, without hesitation.

That surprised me. "Really?"

"Of course. If it makes her feel better and gives me a chance to prove I'm not some sketchy guy trying to steal her daughter away in the middle of the night, I'll wear my nicest hoodie," he joked.

I laughed a little, but the smile soon faded. "I'm just scared."

His voice softened again. "Of what?"

"What if something happens to you?" I said quietly.

I wasn't just talking about awkward family conversations or overprotective parenting. I meant the *other* things that crept into my room at night, whispered in my head, that I still couldn't understand. The kind of things Rhea and Brett were only beginning to wrap their heads around.

"Nothing is going to happen," he said. But I could hear the hesitation under his words. He didn't fully believe it either. He just wanted *me* to believe it. And I loved him for trying.

"You don't *know* that," I said, my voice suddenly trembling. "I don't know that. I can't predict what's going to happen anymore, Brett. I don't know the rules. I don't know what's coming. And I'm scared that you'll be caught in the middle if something happens, if things worsen. And you'll get hurt."

He was quiet for a long time before he spoke again. "It'll be okay," he said softly. "And if something *does* happen, something we can't explain, I'll be there. With you. When the truth comes out, whatever it is, we'll face it together."

My heart ached at how easily he said it. I didn't know if that made him brave or just reckless. Maybe both. But I clung to it anyway.

"Mom said next Tuesday works best for dinner," I said. "You work until three that day, right?"

I heard him rustling papers, probably checking his schedule on the desk. "Yeah... hang on... yeah, I'm off at three. I can be there."

"Okay. I'll let her know." I paused, letting the silence fill between us before adding, "I'll call you tomorrow. I love you."

"I love you, too. Goodnight, Carmen."

"Goodnight," I whispered, and ended the call.

I sat there momentarily, the quiet in my room pressing around me. I stared at the phone, wishing I could crawl through it and into a world where things were simpler, where my biggest problem was a curfew or a pop quiz, not an invisible threat lurking behind every normal moment.

But then, for the first time in what felt like weeks, I had an idea, something small, something bright.

I walked over to my desk and pulled open the bottom drawer where my old sketchbook lay buried beneath loose notebooks and tangled headphones. I hadn't opened it in months, not since before everything changed. Before the voices. Before the visions. Before the fear.

I sat in my desk chair, cracked the cover open, and stared at the first blank page. My hand hovered over it, unsure where to begin. But then I started sketching.

At first, it was simple lines. Shapes. Half-formed thoughts. But soon, they began to take on form, eyes, shadows, light, and emotion. I didn't try to control what came out. I just let it pour onto the page.

And slowly, as the pencil moved, I felt the heaviness lift. My thoughts drifted not into the terrifying unknown but into something quieter, something peaceful.

This was my escape. My way of making sense of a world that had stopped making sense. I could disappear into drawing just like Karina disappeared into her books. I could find light in the middle of the dark, even if only for a little while.

I sketched until my hand ached and the sky outside turned black, and for once, I wasn't afraid of the dark.

Chapter Thirty–Four

Karina

July 26th, 1998

After nearly eight long weeks of pushing myself harder than I ever thought I could, I finally finished all my summer school work. The last assignment had been completed that morning, and closing my book felt like slamming the door shut on a chapter I hadn't been sure I could survive. I stared at the book for a few seconds afterward, almost waiting for something to go wrong; to realize I'd missed a test, or forgotten an entire section. But nothing happened. I was *done*.

In three weeks, I'd go back to school, not to start tenth grade like I was supposed to, but to take the placement exams that would determine if I could officially skip to eleventh grade. The idea still made me nervous, but it also made me kind of proud. I had done this. *Me*. I hadn't cheated or cut corners. I'd stayed up late, worked through weekends, and kept going even when my brain screamed at me to give up.

And I was proud of that. Not because anyone told me to be, but because it felt like it was *earned*.

Of course, the downside was that skipping a grade meant I'd be in the same year as Amber. That part stung. Being in her orbit again meant dodging her sharp words, her fake smile, and that constant sense that she was watching and waiting to cut me down the second I let my guard down. But even so... it was one *less* year of dealing with her overall. And that was worth something.

I needed a break, a real one. So, when Liv offered to take me to work, I jumped at the chance. She only had a four-hour shift at the coffee shop near the town square, and I hadn't left the house in days. I hadn't *wanted* to, if I was honest. But today felt different. I needed air. I needed color. I needed to remember that life wasn't just stress, assignments, and survival.

A small book fair was happening in the square while she worked, and I'd been looking forward to it all week. I hadn't seen Sarah since our sleepover a while ago; she'd been busy with her own life, and even though I understood, it still left a weird emptiness I tried not to dwell on. But books... books never left.

So I wandered through the rows of tents and stalls along the sidewalk, the smell of kettle corn and warm pavement lingering in the air. The fair wasn't huge, but it was cozy in the best way. Each table held stacks of paperbacks, their covers faded by sun and time, or brand-new indie titles with crisp spines and handwritten price tags. A few local authors were signing copies under colorful umbrellas, and everywhere I looked, people were smiling, flipping through pages, and carrying little treasures beneath their arms.

I took my time.

I had just enough allowance money to get a few books, maybe three, if I budgeted right. Still, that didn't stop me from filling my basket with twelve "maybe" choices. I wandered from table to table, picking one up, putting another down, flipping through first chapters, and reading the blurbs like they held the answers to something bigger than just plot. There was something comforting about the whole process, as if I were piecing myself back together with every page.

Eventually, I found a shaded bench and sat down, my basket beside me. The narrowing-down process took almost another hour, and it was hard. It felt like saying goodbye to people I hadn't even met yet. But when I finally settled on four books, I felt good about it. Like I was walking away with the right ones. Like they were waiting for me.

I returned to the coffee shop with my bag and my heart a little heavier.

Inside, the scent of espresso and vanilla hit me instantly. The place was busy; people lined up at the counter, talking over the soft hum of music and the occasional hiss of the steamer. Liv was working the register, helping a customer with a polite smile and quick hands. Her hair was tied up in a messy bun, a smudge of something, maybe coffee, on her apron.

She caught my eye and gave me a little wave, her expression warm despite the rush of activity. I found an empty booth in the corner, far from the noise, and slid in. I opened the first book from my haul and started to read. It didn't take long for the words to pull me in.

After the crowd thinned out, I felt someone approach. I looked up to see Liv setting a cup down in front of me, my favorite, a vanilla cappuccino, still steaming, with a tiny heart drawn in the foam.

"You earned it," she said, slipping into the seat beside me. "How was the fair?"

I smiled, cupping the warm mug in both hands. "It was perfect," I said, taking a slow sip. "I narrowed it down to four books. Took me almost an hour."

She laughed. "That sounds like you."

I leaned against the booth cushion, relaxing for the first time all day.

"I've got about two hours left," Liv said after a moment. "But what do you say, after I'm off, we go see a movie? Your choice. Total decompression night."

I looked up at her, surprised and touched. "Really?"

"Really. And yes," she grinned, "we can get a large popcorn. Extra butter. I won't judge."

I nodded, smiling for real now. "That would be amazing."

She hugged me quickly before standing and heading back behind the counter. "Don't fall too deep into your book. Save a little of your brain for the movie."

I watched her go, my heart feeling full in a way I hadn't felt in a long time. I had survived the summer. I had pushed through the loneliness, the pressure, the self-doubt. And in this quiet little moment, with a book in my lap, coffee in my hand, and someone who cared about me just a few feet away, it all felt like it had been worth it.

~~~~~~~~~~

Liv and I stood in line outside the box office, the warm evening air buzzing with people's chatter and the smell of buttery popcorn drifting from the open theater doors. A neon sign overhead flickered slightly, casting a soft glow over everyone waiting.
~~~~~~~~~~

I was caught between two movie options: *Saving Private Ryan*, a heavy, action-packed war film with Tom Hanks that I knew would be intense, and *Dr. Dolittle*, a comedy with Eddie Murphy that promised to be light and funny. My brain felt fried from all the summer work I'd just finished, and honestly, I didn't want to think too hard. I just wanted to laugh, to escape.

"I think we should go with the comedy," I said finally.

"Dr. Dolittle, it is," Liv said with a smile, and she bought our tickets. Her voice had that easy, comforting calm that always made me feel safe.

We walked into the lobby, heading toward the concessions line. The colorful candy displays and giant pop machines gave the place a familiar, almost magical feeling, like, for a few hours, nothing else in the world existed outside this building.

But then I heard a sharp, familiar laugh that twisted my stomach.

Amber.

I froze for a second but didn't turn around. I stared straight ahead at the menu board above the counter, pretending I hadn't heard her. Maybe she wouldn't see me if I acted like I didn't see her.

We got our popcorn and drinks, Liv paid without a second thought, even tossing in some chocolate to share, and we entered the darkened theater. As we walked up the aisle to find seats, I kept looking over my shoulder, but there was no sign of Amber yet. We slipped into two seats near the back, close enough to see the screen clearly but far from most of the crowd. I sank into my chair and let out a breath.

Just as the previews started, I saw them enter: Amber, Leah, and Steven. Of *course,* they picked the same movie. Just my luck. As they walked past our row, Amber's eyes locked onto mine. She tilted her head slightly and gave me a look that wasn't quite a smile, more like a smirk wrapped in malice. A flash of something cruel passed across her face, like she already had a plan.

I looked away quickly, pretending to be fascinated by the Coke commercial on the screen.

The movie started, the lights dimmed, and I tried to focus on the talking animals and the jokes for a while. People around us were laughing. Liv nudged me a few times when something funny happened, and I smiled back, even if it didn't quite reach my eyes.

About halfway through, I whispered, "Be right back," and stood up. I needed to use the bathroom, not just for the obvious reason, but to breathe, to reset. The theater felt tight, as if it were closing in.

When I entered, the bathroom was empty. The quiet echoed off the tiled walls, the fluorescent lights buzzing faintly above. I went into a stall, did what I needed to, and lingered momentarily, taking a breath.

Then the door opened.

I knew who it was before I saw her.

When I stepped out, there she was; Amber was leaning against the sink like she'd been waiting.

I avoided eye contact and washed my hands slowly at the sink. My pulse was thudding in my ears. She said nothing at first, but I could feel her eyes on me, like hot coals burning holes into my back.

When I turned to leave, she moved, stepping directly in front of the door.

"Let me out," I said, keeping my voice calm.

Her arms crossed over her chest, and she smirked. "You know," she said, her voice smooth and sharp, "I could've pressed charges. Your sister *assaulted* me, remember? I still might."

I didn't respond. I knew better than to engage. Amber thrived on attention, especially the kind that gave her a sense of power.

She stepped closer. "I told you before to stay away from me. And here you are. Again. Just ruining my day with your existence."

"How was I supposed to know you were going to the movies?" I asked, trying to keep the tremble out of my voice.

She ignored me. "You, Karina, are exactly what I always thought: pathetic, a stupid, inconsiderate loser. You walk around like people want you here. Like you matter." Her voice dropped, venomous. "You *don't*. I hate you. You're a waste of space. You'd be better off dead."

She turned and walked out, the echo of her words ringing in the quiet.

I stood frozen for a second, breath caught in my throat. My hands were shaking. I waited a few minutes before gathering myself enough to walk out. I just wanted to return to Liv, sit down, and pretend this didn't happen.

But she wasn't done.

The moment I stepped out into the hallway, I felt her hands shove me hard. I stumbled and fell, knees hitting the sticky, soda-covered floor of the corridor.

"Bitch," she spat, towering over me for a second before sauntering away, laughing.

I stayed there, stunned. The hallway felt blurry and too loud at the same time. My knees ached, and my chest hurt worse. I pushed myself up slowly, cheeks burning, and rushed back into the bathroom. I locked myself in a stall and let the tears fall.

What had I done to deserve this? Why was she so determined to hurt me?

I didn't have answers, only the burning in my throat and the weight of every cruel word she'd thrown at me.

Minutes passed. I don't know how many.

Then I heard the door creak open.

"Karina?" Liv's voice was gentle but laced with concern. "Are you in here?"

I swallowed hard and tried to make my voice sound as normal as possible. "Yeah... I'm fine. My stomach doesn't feel good. Just give me a minute. You should go back to the movie."

There was a pause. Then she said, firmly, "I don't care about the movie. Let's just go home, okay?"

"I'm sorry," I said, voice cracking.

"Don't be sorry. None of this is your fault." She paused again. "I'll go get our stuff."

And just like that, she left; not out of frustration, not because she was giving up, but to take care of me.

I sat in the stall for a few more seconds, listening to the sound of the hand dryer going off in the distance and the hum of the air vents above me. I wiped my face, breathing slowly.

I didn't know how much longer I could handle this.

Two more years. Two more endless, dragging years trapped in the same school halls, the same suffocating classrooms, the same cafeteria filled with whispers, stares, and laughter that wasn't meant to be kind. And worst of all, two more years of her.

Amber.

The thought of it made my stomach twist. It felt like standing at the base of a mountain I didn't have the strength to climb. Every time I tried to breathe, the weight of her words pressed down on my chest. Maybe it would get easier, or I'd grow numb to it, stronger, or wiser. But the truth was, whenever I saw her, she would corner me, throw a look across the room, or whisper something cruel just loud enough for me to hear; it felt like a fresh wound. And I was running out of bandages.

How was I going to make it?

It wasn't just the bullying; it was the isolation as well. The way people saw what was happening and looked away. The way teachers acted like they couldn't do anything because Amber was charming when she wanted to be. Polished. Untouchable. Everyone saw the surface version of her: the perfect student, the friendly smile, the girl who could win over a room with a joke and a toss of her hair. But they didn't see what she did behind closed doors, quiet corners, girls' bathrooms, and empty hallways where no one was watching.

I did.

And I was tired. So tired of pretending it didn't matter. Tired of acting like I was okay.

Because I wasn't.

The truth was, I was surviving, not living. I was walking through my days like I was holding my breath underwater, counting the seconds until I could come up for air; except there was no air, and I didn't know if I'd ever reach the surface again.

Two more years. How was I supposed to keep my head up for that long? How was I supposed to pretend it didn't hurt, like I wasn't slowly disappearing?

I didn't have the answers. I just knew I couldn't keep going like this.

Something had to change.

Or I was going to break.

Chapter Thirty–Five

Carmen

July 28th, 1998

I walked over to Brett's house a little after three. The afternoon sun started to dip lower in the sky, casting golden light across the area, making everything look softer and quieter. Brett was scheduled to finish work around this time, so I figured he'd pull into the driveway soon. But, truthfully, he wasn't why I was heading over today.

Not entirely, anyway.

It had been a few days since I'd been to the house. Brett and I spoke on the phone every morning and every night; we always made time for that, even when we were exhausted or overwhelmed. But phone calls weren't the same. His voice helped, but it wasn't like being with him. I felt safer when I was around him. More grounded. Maybe I didn't have to carry all of this alone.

But it wasn't just Brett who gave me that feeling. Rhea did too.

Being in that house, with its creaky floors and lived-in warmth, felt like stepping out of a storm. My house still felt tense and fragile, like one wrong word could cause everything to shatter. So, walking the familiar gravel path toward Brett's porch, feeling the sun on my back and the weight of the drawing in my bag, I felt nervous but also calm, as if I was doing something that mattered.

I knocked lightly on the door.

Rhea answered almost immediately, her expression brightening when she saw me.

"Carmen," she said, smiling warmly, "come on in."

I stepped inside, greeted by the subtle scent of cinnamon and something baking. Rhea always had something going on in the kitchen, even if it was just tea. The house felt like a place where nothing bad could touch you.

I followed her to the kitchen and took a seat at the table. Without asking, she poured two glasses of iced tea, added a lemon wedge, and carried them over. She placed mine gently before me and sat across from me, folding her hands around her glass like always.

"Brett should be home soon," she said.

"I know," I replied softly, then paused. "I came to see you."

She raised her eyebrows slightly, curious but not surprised. I reached into my bag and carefully pulled out the piece of paper I'd been carrying around for the past two days, tucked between the pages of a book to keep it from bending. My hands felt a little shaky as I handed it over to her.

She took it gently and slowly unrolled it. Her smile faded, but not in a bad way. Her expression changed, softened, and became unreadable. I watched her closely, trying to decipher what she was feeling. Sadness, maybe. Or was it something like joy? Maybe both. Her eyes didn't leave the paper.

It was the drawing I had started the night I felt like I couldn't breathe from everything happening. I had worked on it for hours, shading and redrawing until the image matched what I saw so clearly in my mind.

Shiloh.

"Is this how she appears to you?" Rhea asked, her voice quiet but steady, like it took effort to speak.

I nodded. "Yeah," I said. "This is how I see her."

She stared at the drawing for a long time. "She was wearing this dress," she murmured. "That exact one. When they found her body."

The words made my chest ache. I hadn't even known that part. I just drew what I saw.

"I was at school when it happened," Rhea continued, her eyes still fixed on the paper. "It was February, but it was warm that day. Unusually warm. I remember walking home without a coat, thinking how strange it felt for the middle of winter."

Her voice began to crack around the edges.

"My mom was waiting for me on the front steps. That was rare. She never waited outside. Her face looked strange, sad, almost blank. I didn't even have to ask her. I just *knew* something was wrong." She breathed slowly and deeply, like she was trying to steady herself. "She told me they found Shiloh in the woods, just past the train tracks. She didn't give me the details. Said I didn't need to know. But I've imagined them ever since, anyway. I think part of me needed to."

The room was quiet for a moment, and the only sound was the soft clinking of ice shifting in our glasses.

Rhea's eyes moved over every inch of the drawing. The gentle lines in Shiloh's face. The way her dress flowed slightly, as if caught by a breeze. Her eyes, half-hopeful, half-haunted. I had tried to capture the sadness I saw in her, the longing that clung to her spirit.

"This is very detailed," Rhea said eventually, her voice thick with emotion. "You're very talented, Carmen. I don't think you even realize how much."

"Thank you," I said quietly. "I just... I thought you should have something of her. Something real. Not just a memory."

Rhea reached across the table and touched my hand. Her fingers were warm and steady. "This means more than you know. I've never had anything like this before. It's like... she's still here. In some way. Thank you, Carmen. Truly."

I didn't know what else to say. So I just nodded, and for the first time in a long while, I felt like maybe I had done something right. Something good. Maybe I'd given someone a little light in all this darkness.

~~~~~~~~~~

Later that evening, after Brett had gotten home and we spent some time curled up on the couch in his living room, it was starting to edge toward dinner time. The sun was beginning its slow descent, casting long golden shadows over the neighborhood. We decided to walk back to my house, our fingers laced tightly together as we stepped into the warm hush of early evening. The air smelled of cut grass and honeysuckle, and a gentle breeze carried the sounds of birds chirping and leaves rustling in the woods..
~~~~~~~~~~

Everything felt still, peaceful, almost like the calm before a storm.

We didn't talk much on the walk back, but we didn't need to. Sometimes, silence said everything. Brett would lean over to press a soft kiss to my temple or my cheek, and each time he did, the weight I always carried in my chest felt a little bit lighter. I squeezed his hand a little tighter every time.

But the moment we stepped through my front door, I felt that heavy, familiar shift in the atmosphere. It was like walking into a house with no windows, like the light couldn't quite reach inside. The air grew thicker, colder somehow, and that sickly twist in my stomach returned almost instantly. It was subtle, but it was real. And Brett knew I felt it. He didn't say anything, but the way his thumb started to rub slow circles against the back of my hand told me he sensed my discomfort.

We walked toward the kitchen, where the bright overhead light flickered faintly before steadying. Mom stood at the counter with her back to us, plating dinner. The comforting aroma of lemon chicken, garlic, and herbs enveloped me like a warm blanket, momentarily dulling the strange sensation that always accompanied being home.

She turned when she heard us enter, brushing a strand of hair from her face with the back of her hand.

"Hey," she said, giving us a tired smile. "Dinner's almost ready. Just waiting on the garlic bread, it needs a few more minutes."

"It smells amazing," Brett said, offering her a friendly smile.

"Thank you," Mom replied, clearly appreciating the compliment. Her tone softened just a little. "Do you two want to help get the table set?"

"Of course," I said.

She handed me a large bowl of pasta glistening with olive oil and herbs and then passed Brett a plate of golden, lemon-roasted chicken. We carried the dishes into the dining room, where the evening light filtered through the curtains in hazy amber streaks. I motioned for Brett to sit and returned to the kitchen to grab three glasses and a water pitcher. The soft clink of glass against the table felt grounding, somehow normal.

When the garlic bread was finally out of the oven, Mom brought it into the dining room, setting it on the table with a practiced ease. She finally joined us, her eyes flicking between Brett and me as we sat.

"Help yourselves," she said, gesturing to the spread before us.

Brett reached for the pasta first, scooping a generous portion onto his plate before adding a piece of the chicken. I followed suit, grabbing a slice of garlic bread before piling food onto my plate. Mom did the same, and for a few minutes, we all ate in silence, the only sound the soft clatter of silverware and the occasional contented sigh.

"This is delicious, Mrs. Woodlen," Brett said after a few bites, glancing up with sincere appreciation.

"Thank you, Brett," Mom replied, her expression warming slightly. She sipped her water and asked, "So, you live with your aunt and uncle, right?"

"Yes, ma'am," he said, nodding. "We moved in with them about eight years ago."

"If you don't mind me asking," she continued carefully, "how come you live with them and not your parents?"

Brett hesitated momentarily, not out of discomfort, but out of care. His voice was quiet, but steady when he finally spoke.

"My mom left when I was little, and my dad... he wasn't around much. When I was ten, my uncle Matt found out what was happening and fought for custody. My dad was eventually arrested for child neglect."

There was a long silence. I remembered the first time Brett had told me that, not long after we started spending time together. I remembered how vulnerable he had been and how much it meant that he trusted me with that part of his story. Hearing him repeat it in front of my mom felt like something sacred.

"I'm so sorry," Mom said, her voice soft, the judgment gone. "That must have been incredibly difficult."

"It was," Brett admitted. "But... It's all in the past now. I'm grateful for the life I have. For the people in it." He looked at me when he said that, and I felt something shift in my chest, a quiet ache, a sweet one.

After another quiet moment, Mom dabbed the corner of her mouth with her napkin and asked, "Are you planning to go to college in the fall?"

"Yes," Brett said, sitting up a little straighter. "I'm going to stay local; go to school here so I can still live at home."

"What are you studying?" she asked.

"Social work," he replied.

"Family services," I added with a small smile, beating him to it.

Brett laughed gently. "What she said."

"That's a noble path," Mom said with genuine approval. "You're going to do great in that field."

"That's the plan," Brett replied, glancing at me again. "I've seen what happens when families fall apart. I want to be someone who helps keep them together. Or... help people feel less alone."

For the first time in what felt like days, I saw a flicker of something gentle cross my mother's face. Something close to pride, or maybe hope. She didn't say anything right away, but I saw it. She saw Brett. Really saw him.

And maybe, for the first time in a long while, she saw *me* too.

~~~~~~~~~~

After dinner, Brett and I helped Mom clean up the kitchen. We rinsed dishes, stacked leftovers into containers, and wiped down counters in comfortable silence. The plates' clinking and the dishwasher's soft hum were oddly soothing. There was something almost domestic about it, like a glimpse into a version of life that felt normal, a version I didn't get to see very often anymore.

Once the kitchen was clean, we moved into the living room. Mom grabbed a carton of ice cream from the freezer and scooped generous helpings into mismatched bowls. We sat together; Mom in her favorite armchair, Brett and I on the couch, our knees brushing as we ate. The incredible sweetness of the ice cream was a comforting contrast to the weight of the day.

After a few minutes of laughter and easy conversation, the topic returned to college.

"I never asked," Mom said, looking at me thoughtfully. "Have you given any thought to what you want to study?"

I paused, my spoon halfway to my mouth. It wasn't something we had ever really talked about before. I always assumed I'd attend college, but what about the specifics? Those were harder to grasp.
~~~~~~~~~~

"Maybe art," I said slowly. "I love drawing, but I'm not sure I'm good enough to do something with it, professionally."

"Your drawings are amazing," Brett said immediately, his tone firm, no hesitation. "At least the few I've seen are incredible. You've got real talent, Carmen."

I smiled, warmed by the compliment. "Thanks."

"If not art," I continued, "I think I'd want to do something that helps people. I don't know what exactly. I just... I want to make a difference."

"You could be a nurse," Mom offered with a teasing smile, the kind that said she was half-joking, half-serious.

I laughed, but there was a hint of nervousness in it. "I don't think I'm smart enough for medicine."

"You can do anything," Brett said softly, touching my shoulder gently. His touch was grounding.

The moment should have felt warm and full of possibilities. But then it changed.

The air in the room shifted.

It wasn't dramatic, unlike in horror movies, where doors slam and gusts of wind blow. It was subtle, like a whisper brushing against the back of my neck. A cold sensation crawled down my spine. I shivered, even though the room wasn't cold. And then I heard it.

The voice.

Deep. Raspy. Possessive.

She's mine... you're mine...

It repeated over and over, like a chant. It didn't sound like a threat. It sounded like a promise. My breath caught in my throat. I could feel my body tense, like my muscles were reacting before my brain could catch up. Every hair on my arms stood on end.

Brett noticed immediately. He turned to me, eyebrows knitting together in concern.

I looked at him and shook my head slightly, barely perceptible, but he understood. He always did.

While Mom was distracted with her dessert, I leaned toward him, my voice barely a whisper.

"I can hear it," I said. "It's talking to me again."

Brett didn't hesitate. He placed his bowl on the coffee table and stood up, forcing a casual tone into his voice. "Thank you so much for dinner, Mrs. Woodlen, but it's getting late. I should probably head home."

I followed his lead. "I'll walk you," I said, sounding casual. "Is that okay, Mom?"

She looked up, surprised but not suspicious. "Of course, sweetheart. Just be home by ten."

We cleaned our dishes quickly, placing them in the sink before leaving. Night had fallen while we were inside; now the sky was dusted with stars. The temperature had dropped just enough to be noticeable, and the cool air felt like a refreshing breeze after the suffocating heat in the house.

We didn't talk as we walked. We moved quickly, almost like we were being chased.

Neither of us wanted to be on the street longer than necessary. By the time we reached his house, my hands were trembling slightly.

Rhea was in the kitchen, humming as she flipped through mail.

"Aunt Rhea," Brett said, his voice serious.

She turned, immediately picking up on the tension in the air. "How was dinner?" she asked, her voice light but cautious.

"It was good," Brett said, "but something happened."

She looked at me, her face suddenly drawn tight with concern. "What is it?"

I took a breath and told her everything. "I heard it again. The voice. It said... *she's mine, you're mine'*... over and over. I think it was talking about Shiloh. I felt it. The same energy as before. He's not gone. And I don't think he ever left."

Rhea's face paled. "Are you okay? Did he touch you again?"

"No. But... it felt close, as if it could have. Like it was just waiting." I took a deep breath. "We have to do something," I said. "We can't just wait around for him to attack again. He can't hurt her, Shiloh, can he?"

Rhea didn't answer right away. She looked down, thinking, processing. "I don't know. But you're right. We can't afford to wait. I'll call Viola and see what she can do. Maybe she can find something to help until Donald—"

"—The guy in Connecticut?" Brett asked.

Rhea nodded. "Yes. If he can come, if not, we need a plan."

She excused herself and went upstairs to her office to make the call. Brett and I headed to his room to wait, our minds spinning. We sat on the edge of his bed, neither of us saying much, both listening for any sign that something had followed us.

Twenty tense minutes passed before Rhea called us into her office.

Her face was serious but hopeful. "Viola got in touch with Donald. He won't be able to come here, at least not soon. But he sent a list of instructions for a house cleansing ritual that might help contain the entity or weaken it until more permanent help arrives."

She handed me a printed email, and I scanned its contents: candles, salt, incantations, symbols, and timing.

"Carmen," Rhea said gently, "when will your house be empty again?"

I frowned. "I'm not sure. Mom works nights, but Karina, Liv, and Nina are usually home in the evenings. They don't work past six."

Rhea nodded slowly. "Then we'll do it during the day. The sooner, the better."

I looked up at her and then at Brett. "Okay," I said. "Let's end this."

~~~~~~~~~~

August 3rd, 1998

A few days later, everything was in place. The plan had been carefully crafted, and every detail was checked and double-checked. Timing was crucial. By early afternoon, the house would be empty, at least as empty as it could be. Mom was working at the hospital. Liv and Nina were at work until five, and Karina had made plans to spend the day at Sarah's, and I made sure she left before anyone else arrived.

Brett had stayed home. As much as it hurt not to have him by my side, I couldn't risk him getting hurt. He didn't like it, he wanted to be with and protect me, but he understood why I asked him to stay away. This was dangerous. The energy in the house was unpredictable, and every moment it seemed to grow stronger.

Just after two o'clock, Rhea pulled into the driveway with Viola, Luca, and Micah in tow. I opened the door before they could even knock.
~~~~~~~~~~

"Come in," I said, stepping back. My voice felt small in the house's space, like the walls themselves were listening.

Everyone filed in, each carrying bags or boxes of supplies; candles, herbs, oils, items I couldn't name but somehow felt were important. They moved with urgency, wasting no time. The air felt heavy already, like the house knew what we were planning.

Viola took charge, as she always did. "The first thing we have to do is a sage cleanse," she explained, calm but firm. "I'll light the sage and walk it through every room. The goal is to disrupt any dark or lingering energy."

Rhea looked over at her. "What exactly does that do?"

"Sage has been used for centuries for purification," Viola said. "It doesn't banish spirits, but it can weaken them, strip them of their hold in the space. After that, we'll anoint the top of every doorway with blessed oil to create a boundary against reentry. And finally, we'll say a protection prayer together. Strength in unity."

I nodded. "Okay. Let's do it."

Viola struck a match and lit the bundle of sage. A thin stream of smoke curled into the air, its scent sharp but strangely comforting. She moved with intention, her footsteps slow and deliberate as she passed through each room, whispering something under her breath. The smoke trailed behind her like a ribbon, clinging to the corners of the walls and ceiling.

I stayed close to Rhea as we followed. The others split up, checking rooms and placing candles at key points. Despite the steady movements and hushed concentration, a tension hung over us all, as if something were waiting.

We had just finished upstairs. Viola snuffed out the sage and pulled a small bottle from her bag, its contents amber in the light.

"Time for the oil," she said. "We need to be quick."

She stepped toward the first doorframe, lifting her hand. And then it happened.

Every door in the house slammed shut at once.

The sound thundered through the walls, sharp, violent, and final. I jumped so hard I nearly dropped the candle I was holding. The energy in the house changed instantly. It wasn't just heavy now, it was *hostile*.

And then, I heard it.

...you're wasting your time... this is my house...

The voice, *that* voice, was like gravel and smoke, thick with malice. It echoed inside my head, vibrating through my bones. It wasn't loud, but it felt *close*.

"I just heard *it*," I whispered, heart pounding.

Viola's eyes narrowed. "It knows what we're doing. It's angry. We need to move, *now*."

Without hesitation, she began anointing the doorframes upstairs, her fingers swift but steady. Rhea followed close behind, reciting a prayer under her breath. We moved like a unit, room by room, each of us focused and alert.

Then we moved downstairs.

Luca took the lead, walking toward the staircase with a determined stride. But as he reached the top step, my breath caught in my throat.

There, just behind him, *a shadow.*

It wasn't a trick of the light. It was real. Humanoid, dark as night, but not *solid.* It shimmered like smoke, radiating a cold chill.

"Luca!" I screamed, just as the shadow lunged.

But I was too late.

Luca's body jerked forward, and he tumbled down the stairs. The sound of his body hitting each step was sickening. He landed hard at the bottom, groaning in pain.

"Luca!" Viola cried, bolting after him. We all ran to his side.

He rolled onto his back, wincing. "I'm okay," he muttered through clenched teeth. "Just... bruised."

"Babe, you just got pushed down a flight of stairs," Viola said, panic flickering behind her eyes. "You're *not* okay."

"I'm *fine*, Vi. Really. Nothing's broken." He sat up with Rhea and Micah's help, his face pale but determined. "Let's finish this before one of us *really* gets hurt."

I helped Viola to her feet, and for a second, our eyes met. Her face was taut, but there was a fire in her gaze.

"It's trying to scare us," she said. "But we don't scare easily."

I nodded, even though my hands were shaking. "Let's end this."

Viola finished applying the last of the blessed oil to the downstairs doorframes, her movements deliberate and steady, despite the lingering tension in the air. The house was quiet, *too* quiet, and every creak of the floorboards beneath our feet felt louder than it should have. When she turned back to us, she pulled out a small stack of papers and handed one to each of us.

"Our final step," she said softly, her voice low but firm. "We'll stand together and recite the prayer aloud, as one. Our unity is our strength."

We formed a circle in the center of the living room, just before the fireplace. I could feel the residual heaviness in the room pressing on my shoulders like a weight, but I took a deep breath and unfolded the paper in my hands. Viola gave a small nod, signaling it was time.

All at once, we began reading in unison:

"Almighty God, Father, Son, and Holy Spirit, we humbly pray for your protection from all evil spirits..."

The words left my mouth clearly, but I felt an almost immediate pressure, like something pushing back. The air grew denser, thick, and suffocating. My stomach churned, and a wave of nausea hit me out of nowhere. I wasn't the only one feeling it. I glanced at Viola, and I could see the tension in her brow, the way she clutched her paper just a little tighter. But we kept going.

"...We ask you to fill every space with your presence and power, driving away any demonic influence..."

The temperature dropped suddenly. A chill seeped into the room, creeping along the walls like a shadow with intent. I clenched my jaw and pushed forward, my voice shaking but steady.

"...Lord, we ask you to break any chains that the devil has on us and pour upon us the precious blood of your Son, Jesus..."

I felt it then, a presence, like something angry circling us, pacing the edge of our circle.

The candle flames flickered wildly. Still, we didn't stop.

"...In the name of Jesus, we command all demons to leave us forever. Amen."

As the final *"Amen"* left our lips, something *shifted*.

It was as if someone had pulled back a heavy curtain. The dense, oppressive energy that had filled the house for months suddenly lifted. The air felt lighter and breathable again, as if we had opened all the windows and let in fresh air. A warm breeze seemed to pass through the room, brushing against my skin like a comforting touch.

I blinked and looked around.

"...It feels lighter in here," I said, my voice barely above a whisper. "Did it work?"

Viola took a slow, steady breath, her eyes scanning the room. "The energy is definitely different. I think... I think it did."

A deep, unfamiliar sensation welled up in my chest: relief. Real, honest relief. For the first time in what felt like forever, I didn't feel the weight of something watching me. There was no whisper in the back of my mind, no growl echoing from the shadows. It was *quiet*. It was *peaceful*.

A soft smile broke across my face, and I realized how long it had been since I'd felt anything close to joy. Hope flickered to life again, warm and tentative.

We began to clean up, snuffing out candles, carefully packing away the ritual items, and folding the prayer papers. Everyone worked quietly, the silence now calm instead of eerie. There was no urgency, just a shared understanding that something had changed.

When everything was packed and ready to go, I looked at each of them: Viola, Rhea, Luca, and Micah, and felt a wave of gratitude I couldn't put into words.

"Thank you," I said softly, my voice thick with emotion. "Thank you all so much."

One by one, they pulled me into their warm, strong, and reassuring hugs. I held on tight, not wanting to let go, not just of them, but of this moment.

Because for the first time in a long time… it felt like maybe we had a chance.

<div align="center">~~~~~~~~~~</div>

September 25th, 1998

It had been two months since the demon was banished from our home; two months since the constant weight on my chest had finally lifted. For the first time in what felt like forever, I could breathe without fear, sleep without waking in a panic, and walk through my house without looking over my shoulder. The silence, once eerie, was now comforting. Peaceful. Still.

The sickening feeling that once haunted my house was gone. No more cabinet doors left hanging open, no more violent attacks, no more cold drafts cutting through warm rooms. Every trace of a demonic presence had disappeared from my life. And finally, Shiloh was gone too.

That last part lingered in my heart more than I wanted to admit. A part of me missed her; I missed seeing her quiet, solemn presence in the corner of my room or hearing her soft footsteps in the hallway at night. Initially, she had been a source of fear, but over time, she'd become something else entirely. Familiar. A reminder that I wasn't crazy. That I wasn't alone. I had to believe that she'd found peace, that wherever she was now, it was somewhere better, somewhere safe.

Life had slowly, gently begun to piece itself back together. School had picked up again, and for once, I didn't dread the routine. I was doing well, actually, better than I ever had. Maybe it was because the darkness had cleared, or I finally believed in myself again. Either way, it felt good.

I still heard voices from time to time, faint whispers that echoed in the back of my mind when I was away from home. They no longer screamed or demanded, no longer clawed at my sanity like they once did. Now, they were barely more than a murmur, like fragments of a fading dream. It was nothing compared to the relentless torment I used to endure. Just the occasional flicker, a reminder of what once was, but even those were growing quieter with each passing day.

Brett and I had grown even closer. We still talked every night before bed, and most afternoons we found time to meet up at his place, or the park, even just walking home from school. He made me laugh. He made me feel seen. And most importantly, he made me feel safe. Sometimes we'd sit quietly together, and that was enough. Other times, he'd talk about his time in college, and I'd imagine a future that didn't feel so impossible anymore.

I still visited Rhea often. Her home had become a sanctuary for me; a place where I could unwind, talk openly, and feel at ease. And now and then, I'd drop in to see Viola, Luca, and Micah. It was strange how close I'd grown to them in such a short time. They weren't just people who had helped me survive something terrifying; they were people who had stayed. People who still cared.

At home, things had returned to normal. Liv was still working at the coffee shop most days, always coming home with the scent of roasted beans and vanilla. She seemed happier, more herself, and I was glad. Nina had officially moved into her dorm a few weeks back. The campus wasn't far, just thirty minutes away, but the deal Mom had made with her about staying with us only lasted through the summer. The house felt a little emptier without her laughter echoing down the hallways. I missed her, but I was proud of her. She was building a life for herself, just like we all were.

And Mom was still working long shifts at the hospital, doing her best to keep everything running smoothly at home while juggling the chaos of her job. I hadn't told her what had really happened, not yet. A part of me wanted to. I knew I'd have to eventually. But every time I thought about sitting her down and explaining it all, the voices, the haunting, the ritual, I froze. How could I make her believe something that, not long ago, I could barely believe myself?

For now, I let her believe the version of the story that made sense to her: that the medication was finally working.

That I was feeling better because of the pills, not because a demon had been forced out of our home. I was still pretending to take them, still going through the motions because I didn't want to give her any more reason to worry. She looked so relieved lately, like a weight had also been lifted off her shoulders. I couldn't take that peace away from her. Not yet.

But the guilt lingered, quiet and constant. And I knew the truth wouldn't stay hidden forever.

Things were quieter now. Calmer.

But not empty. Not sad.

Just... better.

And that made it okay.

~~~~~~~~~~

It was finally Friday, and I was genuinely excited about the weekend for the first time in weeks. The day seemed to move slowly, each ticking minute pulling me closer to something I'd been quietly looking forward to all week: two full days with Brett. He had somehow managed to get Saturday and Sunday off, which felt like a minor miracle.

Ever since he started college last month, things had shifted. Not in a bad way, just... different. Between his classes, study time, and part-time job, our time together had become limited to a few stolen hours here and there, quick meetups after school, late-night phone calls, or
~~~~~~~~~~

walking me home when he had the energy. I missed him. Missed the way he made everything feel lighter. Calmer. Safe.

So, knowing we had the whole weekend ahead of us, no work, no school, no rushing off, made something warm settle in my chest. We hadn't even decided what to do yet, and honestly, it didn't matter. We could just hang out in his room watching old movies, go for a long drive without a destination, or sit in the park sharing ice cream and stories. As long as we were together, it would be enough.

This weekend wasn't just a break from the week; it felt like a much-needed reset, a chance to breathe again and *be* without pressure. And I couldn't wait.

The bell rang, signaling the end of lunch, its sharp buzz echoing across the cafeteria. Karina, Sarah, and I were still seated at our usual table, lingering for a few extra moments before heading to class. The late-September sun peeked out from behind the clouds, casting soft light through the windows onto the tables. Karina and Sarah were doing most of the talking, chatting animatedly about Karina's birthday in a week.

Karina wasn't having a big party; she never wanted that kind of attention. However, Mom had planned something more intimate - just a small family dinner at home. Mom had requested the day off to spend the afternoon cooking Karina's favorite meal. Sarah was coming over. Liv and

Nina would be there, and Brett had promised to stop by after work. The thought of everyone being together under one roof again, without any tension or lingering shadows, felt comforting.

I didn't say much during the conversation. I was happy listening, soaking in the normalcy. My birthday back in May had been quiet. I hadn't wanted a party. Everything had still felt too raw, too unstable. But we'd had cake, ice cream, and a few small presents. It was simple, peaceful. And at the time, that had been more than enough.

As the lunch crowd started packing up, I tossed my wrapper in the trash and followed the stream of students toward the hallway. When I got to class, my teacher met me at the door, holding a yellow slip of paper.

"Carmen? The guidance counselor wants to see you."

I took the note, a flicker of worry sparking in my chest. "Okay," I said, glancing down at the slip as if it would offer more clues. It didn't; just my name, the time, and the room number.

As the bell rang, students filtered into classrooms around me. The noise dulled as I walked through the hall alone, my footsteps echoing off the linoleum. Everything felt quieter, heavier, like the building was holding its breath.

When I reached the guidance office, I hesitated briefly before knocking gently.

"Come in," Miss Meijer called.

I pushed open the door and stepped inside. The office was neat and cozy, and the soft scent of a cinnamon candle burning on her bookshelf filled the air.

She smiled warmly at me and gestured to the chair before her desk.

"Hi, Carmen. Don't worry, you're not in trouble," she said quickly, as if reading the flicker of anxiety on my face. "I just wanted to check in and see how you're doing."

Relief swept through me, but I remained cautious. "Okay," I said slowly, sitting down.

She reached for a file on her desk and opened it. I noticed my name on the tab.

"I know we didn't talk about this last year when you started here," she began, her tone careful, "but we have your medical history on file. It's standard for all new students who transfer in."

I stiffened a little, bracing myself. *So that's what this is about.*

She continued, "It says you were diagnosed with schizophrenia when you were eleven?"

"Yeah," I replied, keeping my tone neutral.

She glanced up from the folder. "How did that feel at the time, getting that diagnosis?"

I shrugged, trying not to overthink my answer. "It explained what I was experiencing back then, so I guess it helped make sense of things."

"And now?" she asked gently. "Do you still experience hallucinations?"

I took a breath and gave the same answer I'd rehearsed so many times before, the answer my mom believed, the one that made everything easier. "No. The medication's working."

She nodded slowly, jotting something down in the folder. "I see. That makes sense. And it would explain the dramatic improvement in your grades this year. We're only two months in, and already you have nearly all As and one B. That's a huge jump from last year."

I could feel her studying me, but her tone wasn't accusatory, just curious.

"Well, like I said, the meds are helping. I can concentrate better. I'm not cheating, if that's what you're thinking," I added, a bit more defensively than I meant to.

"Oh, no, no," she said quickly, holding a hand. "I didn't mean to suggest that at all. I just wanted to hear it from you. Your perspective. Not just what's written down in your file."

She smiled again and stood, smoothing down her blouse. "Thank you for coming in, Carmen. You can head back to class now."

I nodded, stood, and walked out the door, my mind replaying the conversation. It had gone fine, better than expected, but something still left me uneasy. Perhaps it was because I was becoming too adept at concealing the truth.

Too good at lying.

Chapter Thirty–Six

Karina

I sat at my desk in American Literature, the afternoon sunlight slanting through the blinds, casting long golden lines across the floor. The air was quiet except for the soft scratching of pencils and the faint hum of the overhead lights. Mrs. Hooper stood at the whiteboard, writing our vocabulary list for the upcoming week in her graceful, looping handwriting. She always wrote carefully, as if each word mattered, not just in spelling but in meaning.

We had just finished our vocabulary quiz for this week, and I felt confident. I'd studied every night, and I was sure I aced it. The words had come easily to me, like pieces clicking into place.

My notebook was open on my desk, the edge of the pages slightly curled from wear. I carefully copied the new list of words as they appeared one by one on the board:

acrimonious, affable, edict, disseminate, imbue, precipitate, bequeath, forbear, hiatus, and *doggedly.* Each week, we got ten new words, and by Friday, we were expected to know how to pronounce them, spell them, define them, list their synonyms and antonyms, and use each one in a sentence. It was a challenge, but it was the kind I liked, the kind that made me feel like I was growing sharper, more capable.

English had always been my favorite subject, but it felt even more personal this year. It was because I now understood words better, how they could be tools, weapons, or lifelines. And maybe it was because of Mrs. Hooper.

She was, without a doubt, my favorite teacher I'd ever had. She had a way of making literature feel alive, like the words on the page were breathing. Today, her long black curls were pulled to the side in a thick braid that hung over one shoulder. Her skin was a warm, deep brown that glowed under the classroom lights, and she wore a colorful, handmade-looking knit sweater, paired with sleek black pants and ankle boots. Subtle gold eyeshadow shimmered on her lids, and her reading glasses rested on her head like a crown. A pen was tucked behind one ear, ready to be used at a moment's notice.

She always carried herself with a quiet confidence. She spoke to us as if we were adults, as if our thoughts and opinions mattered. She didn't just teach; she listened, which made a difference.

Another reason I loved this class was that it was one of the few places I could breathe easily, because Amber wasn't in it. Since I'd completed my sophomore year over the summer and jumped ahead to eleventh grade, I now shared most of my classes with her. She was in three others with me, and I could feel her eyes on me in each one. Watching. Waiting. She always found some small, cruel way to twist my day.

But not here.

This classroom felt like a haven for learning, thinking, and being. And even though Amber was still a dark cloud that followed me through the hallways and hovered over lunch tables, she couldn't get to me in this room, not with Mrs. Hooper's calm voice guiding us through poetry and prose, nor with the words themselves standing guard around me.

I glanced back down at my notebook, underlining the word *doggedly*. It reminded me of myself lately; persistent, determined, clinging to hope like it was the only thing keeping me afloat. Maybe that's why I liked vocabulary so much. Sometimes, it felt like the words knew me better than people did.

And in this moment, surrounded by quiet concentration, the soft tap of Mrs. Hooper's marker against the board, and the rustle of notebook pages turning, I felt something I didn't always feel at school.

Safe.

Class ended shortly after, and the bell rang, its sharp tone echoing through the quiet classroom. I quickly packed up my things, slipping my notebook into my bag and slinging it over my shoulder as I joined the flow of students heading into the hall. My next class was P.E., not my favorite, but not my least favorite. It was somewhere in the middle. I liked being active, but I didn't like being around so many people, especially not people like Amber.

The hallway was crowded as usual, a blur of conversations, laughter, and the occasional shove from someone trying to beat the bell. I kept my head down and moved quickly, eventually pushing the girls' locker room door open. The familiar scent of body spray, detergent, and rubber gym mats hit me immediately. The room was already noisy and bustling with students finding their lockers, laughing with friends, and complaining about the upcoming class.

I went to the extended bench near my locker, dropped my backpack, and spun the lock. After retrieving my gym clothes, a black T-shirt, and stretchy gray shorts, I scanned the room for an available changing stall. Thankfully, one was open. I slipped inside, changed quickly, and stuffed my school clothes into my locker.

Once I was ready, I walked out into the gymnasium. The tall ceiling lights lit the ample space, gleaming beneath the polished wooden floor. A few students were already stretching or chatting in small groups while we waited for Mr. Marceli.

Mr. Marceli stood near the center of the gym, clipboard in hand. He was tall, broad-shouldered, and muscular; he looked like someone who lived at the gym. But his appearance didn't match his personality. He was one of the kindest teachers in the building, known for turning even the most dreaded P.E. days into something at least mildly enjoyable. His booming laugh made class feel more like a game than a chore.

Still, not every day was fun and games. Some days were filled with fitness assessments and laps around the gym, leaving everyone sore and grumbling. Today, though, felt different. There was a kind of energy in the air, the good kind that promised something fun was coming.

As the last students filed out of the locker room, the sharp blast of Mr. Marceli's whistle rang through the gym. That was our cue to get into formation: five rows of six. I hurried to the front row, positioning myself close to the teacher. It wasn't just about being eager to participate. I did it on purpose because Amber was in this class too, and the closer I stayed to the teacher, the less likely she was to bother me. It didn't always work, but sometimes the distance helped.

Once we were lined up, Mr. Marceli led us through our usual warm-up routine: twenty-five jumping jacks to pump blood, followed by toe touches to stretch out our hamstrings, and finally a sixty-second plank. The plank was always the worst. Sixty seconds felt like six hundred, and by the end of it, my arms were shaking and my core felt like it was on fire.

After we finished, Mr. Marceli clapped his hands to get our attention. "Alright, listen up!" he shouted over the chatter. "Today, we're playing Scooter Capture the Flag. There will be two teams. Each team will have four guards, and the rest of you will work to steal the opposing team's flag and get it back to your side. Helmets on, no crashing into each other intentionally, and have fun. Let's go!"

Excited murmurs rippled through the group as we headed to the equipment room to grab scooters and helmets. The scooters were those little square ones with wheels, which you had to sit on and push with your feet. They looked simple, but moving quickly on them took real coordination and leg strength without flipping over.

Once everyone had their gear, we split into teams and rolled out onto opposite sides of the gym. Our flags were placed at the far ends, and the game began with another blast of the whistle.

What followed was thirty minutes of chaos and laughter. Students scooted wildly around the gym, trying to dodge opponents and sneak past the guards. A few crashes happened, nothing serious, just the usual clumsy falls and exaggerated groans of defeat. I didn't manage to capture the flag, but I did block someone from stealing ours, which felt like a small victory.

By the time Mr. Marceli blew the final whistle, no team had secured a win. It was a draw; we were all red-faced, sweaty, and breathless. Still, the energy was high, and the mood was good.

We put the scooters back in the storage room and returned to the locker room to change out of our gym clothes. I moved quickly, eager to get back into my regular clothes and head to the next class.

As I slung my backpack over my shoulder and stepped back into the hallway, I felt lighter. It could be the exercise. Maybe it was the laughter. Or it was the satisfaction of getting through another class without a single word or glare from Amber.

Whatever it was, I'd take it.

Chapter Thirty–Seven

Liv

The soft hum of the espresso machine and the murmur of conversation filled the cozy coffee shop. The scent of fresh coffee beans and baked goods lingered in the air like a warm blanket. I stood behind the counter, straightening a stack of napkins, when the front door opened and a woman in a long tan coat stepped inside. She looked in her early forties, her hair neatly pulled back, and her expression relaxed as she approached the register.

I straightened up and smiled warmly. "Hi, welcome in! What can I get started for you today?"

She smiled back, scanning the menu briefly before saying, "Can I please have a medium latte with hazelnut?"

"Of course," I replied, tapping the option on the computer. "Would you like that hot or iced?"

"Hot, please. And I'll also take a cheese danish."

"Absolutely," I added the pastry to her order and gave her a friendly nod. "Okay, your total comes to $3.36. Will that be cash or card today?"

The woman pulled a five-dollar bill from her wallet and handed it over with a polite smile. "Here you go."

"Thank you." I accepted the bill and slid open the register drawer with a soft *ding*.

I counted out her change, one dollar and sixty-four cents, and handed it to her.

"Here's your change. Your order will be ready in just a couple of minutes. Feel free to take a seat, and I'll bring it out to you if you'd like."

"Thanks," she said, stepping to the side.

I turned to the espresso machine and got to work. I filled the portafilter with freshly ground espresso beans and tamped it down before locking it into place. The rich aroma filled the air as the hot shot of espresso poured into the cup. I steamed the milk until it was velvety smooth, added a splash of hazelnut syrup, and then combined everything to create the perfect latte. A little foam on top, a soft swirl of the spoon, and it was done.

Next, I walked over to the pastry case. Using a pair of silver tongs, I carefully picked a golden-brown cheese danish from the display and slipped it into a crisp white paper bag. Before returning to the counter, I folded the top and wrote a small "Thank you" with a marker.

"Here you go," I said, smiling as I handed the woman her hot hazelnut latte and the bagged pastry. "One hot hazelnut latte and a cheese Danish. Enjoy, and have a wonderful day."

She returned the smile, her hands wrapping around the warm cup. "Thank you so much."

"You're very welcome."

She sat by the window, and I returned to my station behind the counter, already spotting the next customer making their way inside. I glanced at the clock, *one more hour.*

~~~~~~~~~~

When my shift ended, I wiped my hands on a towel, grabbed my bag from the break room, and headed to the front to clock out. The familiar *beep* of the time clock marked the official end of my day, and I let out a quiet sigh of relief as I pushed open the glass door and stepped outside. The late-afternoon sun cast a soft, golden hue across the parking lot, and a gentle breeze rustled the trees lining the street.

I went to my car, unlocked the door, and slid into the driver's seat. The scent of coffee still clung to my clothes, warm and comforting. I started the engine, backed out of my space, and turned onto the road, going through town toward Nina's dorm. The streets were calm, a slow lull
~~~~~~~~~~

between the weekday rush and the weekend buzz. It felt peaceful.

When I reached her building, I parked along the curb, turning off the engine with a quiet click. I grabbed my bag, locked the doors behind me, and climbed the front steps.

Inside, the air was cooler, smelling faintly of laundry detergent and whatever someone had just microwaved down the hall. I took the stairs two at a time, familiar with the creaky spots on the second-floor landing. When I got to Nina's room, I knocked lightly.

A few seconds later, her roommate opened the door. Cassie was wearing a hoodie and holding a half-eaten granola bar.

"Hey, Liv," she said with a friendly smile.

"Hey, Cassie. Is Nina here?"

She shook her head. "Not yet. She left class around three, but she hasn't come back. Probably stopped somewhere."

That was odd. Her class had ended at least fifteen minutes ago. Nina wasn't usually late without texting, but I shrugged it off.

"Mind if I hang out and wait?"

"Not at all," Cassie said, stepping aside and motioning me in. "Make yourself at home."

I walked in, dropped my bag gently on the floor, and sat cross-legged on Nina's neatly made bed. The room was familiar now; photos of family and friends pinned to the corkboard, a string of fairy lights lining the ceiling, and the faint scent of vanilla from a wax warmer on Cassie's desk. Occasionally glancing at the door, I flipped through a magazine to pass the time.

About ten minutes later, I heard footsteps in the hallway. Nina's key turned in the lock, and the door swung open. She walked in carrying a small brown paper bag, her cheeks flushed from the cool air outside.

"Hey!" she said brightly when she saw me. "Sorry, I'm late. I had to stop and pick something up."

"No worries," I said, standing up to greet her. "I haven't been waiting long."

She crossed the room and sat down beside me on the bed. "Actually," she said, her voice shifting into something more playful, "I picked something up for you."

I blinked in surprise. "For me? Why?"

Nina grinned. "Because I love you. And... I saw this and thought of you."

She reached down, picked up the bag from where she'd set it on her desk, and handed it to me.

"What is it?" I asked, curiosity piqued.

"Open it and find out," she said, eyes bright with anticipation.

I laughed softly and unfolded the top of the bag. Inside, nestled carefully in tissue paper, was a vinyl record. My heart jumped slightly when I pulled it out and read the label.

"Separate Ways by Journey?" I said, almost in disbelief.

"It's the single," she said proudly. "I had to hunt it down online and order it. It took a few weeks to arrive, but I knew it'd be worth it. I remembered you saying it was your favorite song."

I looked down at the record, running my fingers over the cover. "I love it," I said, smiling at her. "Seriously. I'm excited to play it. You're amazing."

Nina gave a slight shrug and a bashful smile. "I just wanted to do something nice. You've had such a hard year. You deserve little moments of joy."

I leaned over and hugged her tightly. "Thank you," I whispered. "This means a lot."

She hugged me back just as tightly, and for a moment, the chaos of the world outside seemed to melt away. We were just two lovers, sitting on a bed, surrounded by warmth, music, and love.

~~~~~~~~~~

I spent about an hour with Nina before heading home. Her roommate, Cassie, had left to study at the library, giving Nina and me some much-needed time to catch up. Ever since she started school, we hadn't had much time to really *be* together, not in the way we used to. So it felt good to be
~~~~~~~~~~

close again, like real girlfriends, sharing space, laughter, and something that felt like home.

When I finally said goodbye and slipped into my car, the sun was already beginning its descent, casting soft amber light across the tops of the trees. When I pulled into the driveway, it was nearly five o'clock, and I knew I had to get dinner started. Mom was working the night shift at the hospital again, and it was my turn to handle the evening meal.

I carried my bag inside, dropped it in my room, and tied my hair in a loose bun before heading into the kitchen. The house was quiet except for the faint hum of the refrigerator and the muffled voices from upstairs; Karina and Carmen, no doubt, buried in homework, the kind of background noise that felt normal.

I opened the fridge and leaned in, scanning the shelves for inspiration. A few chicken breasts were on the bottom shelf, along with a carton of eggs, a nearly full jar of marinara sauce, leftover spaghetti in a Tupperware container, and two heads of broccoli tucked into the crisper drawer. My mind clicked into gear. I knew exactly what I could pull together.

Chicken parmesan: simple, comforting, and always a hit.

I took the chicken out to thaw quickly in the microwave while I grabbed the eggs from the fridge and some breadcrumbs from the pantry. I mixed garlic powder, parsley, and a little paprika from the spice cabinet into the breadcrumbs. I whisked the eggs in a shallow bowl, poured the breadcrumbs onto a plate, and prepped a dish with flour for dredging.

I coated each piece of chicken one by one; first, the flour, then the egg wash, and finally the breadcrumb mix. The scent of seasoned breading was warm and savory, even before the chicken hit the pan. I heated a skillet on the stove, added a few tablespoons of olive oil, and set the first piece of chicken in. It sizzled on contact, the sound crisp and satisfying.

While the chicken cooked, I microwaved the leftover spaghetti and set a pot of marinara on the back burner to warm. Once the chicken was golden and cooked, I laid a slice of provolone over each piece, covered the skillet with a lid, and let the cheese melt into a gooey blanket.

I steamed the broccoli in the microwave with butter, salt, and pepper until tender but still bright green.

By the time everything was ready, plates stacked, steam rising from the food like the promise of comfort, the house smelled amazing. The air was filled with the rich aroma of garlic, cheese, and tomato, mingled with the buttery sweetness of broccoli.

I wiped my hands on a dish towel and walked to the bottom of the stairs.

"Karina! Carmen! Dinner's ready!" I called.

A moment later, I heard the sound of chairs scraping against the floor above and the thud of footsteps on the stairs. Carmen was the first to appear, her hair in a messy bun, still holding a pencil. Karina followed, nose still buried in a paperback book, which she only lowered once she caught a whiff of what was waiting at the table.

"Oh wow, it smells amazing," Karina said as she sat.

"Chicken parm?" Carmen guessed, grinning.

"Yup," I said, placing a plate before her. "And leftover spaghetti, so double points for being resourceful."

We all sat at the table, the three of us, plates full, the evening light casting a warm glow through the kitchen windows. We didn't say much at first, just the clinking of silverware and the occasional hum of approval as someone took their first bite. There was something comforting about the quiet that spoke of healing and normalcy.

"This is really good, Liv. You always do such a great job," Karina said between bites. She grinned and added in a mock whisper, "Sometimes even better than Mom. But don't tell her I said that."

I laughed, shaking my head. "Your secret's safe with me."

After dinner, Karina stayed to help me clean up, like she always did. We moved around the kitchen in sync, chatting as we rinsed plates and stacked them in the dishwasher. It was one of those quiet, comforting routines that made everything feel normal.

Once we finished, we headed into the living room, where Carmen was already curled on the couch. I let Karina pick the movie, and she wandered over to the DVD shelf in the corner before holding up a familiar case.

"Hook?" she asked.

"Classic choice," I said, settling onto the couch as she popped it into the player. About halfway through the movie, just as the Lost Boys were about to confront Captain Hook, Carmen suddenly stood up, her expression unreadable.

"I'll be right back," she mumbled quickly, and without waiting for a response, darted out the front door.

Karina sat up straighter, watching the door swing closed behind her. "What do you suppose *that* was about?"

I frowned, trying to think. "Maybe she remembered she was supposed to meet up with Brett? I'm not sure..."

We glanced at each other, both a little puzzled. The movie was forgotten momentarily as the atmosphere shifted ever so slightly.

Chapter Thirty-Eight

Carmen

I ran as fast as my legs would carry me toward Brett's house, my lungs burning with each breath. The last sliver of sunlight had disappeared behind the horizon, leaving the street cloaked in a dim, eerie twilight. The shadows stretched long across the pavement, and everything around me felt too still, too quiet. My heart pounded not just from the sprint, but from the voice echoing in my head.

It had happened again.

After everything, cleansing, prayers, oil, and sage, I thought it was over. I *believed* it was over. We all did. The energy had shifted, the weight in the air had lifted, and for the first time in what felt like forever, I'd been able to sleep without fear. But now? Now I wasn't so sure. Had we been wrong? Had we missed something?

I reached the front porch and banged on the door, frantic and breathless. The force of the bang stung my knuckles. After a few seconds, the door creaked open, revealing Sarah.

"Carmen?" she said, eyes wide. "Are you okay?"

I nodded quickly, though I didn't look like it. "I'm fine, just... I need to see your aunt. Right now. Is she home?"

"She's out back," Sarah said, stepping aside to let me in. She looked worried, like she wanted to ask more but didn't.

"Thanks," I murmured, already moving past her. I darted through the familiar hallway, pushing open the sliding door that led to the back patio.

Rhea was sitting on the porch swing, a blanket over her lap and a book in her hand. She looked up when she first heard the door, smiling, until she saw my face.

"Carmen?" she said, her smile fading. "What's happened?"

I stepped onto the patio, struggling to catch my breath. "I heard her," I said.

Her eyes sharpened with understanding. "Shiloh?"

I nodded, my throat dry. "She said my name. Three times. 'Carmen, I need your help.' I didn't see her, but I *heard* her. Clear as day."

Rhea immediately set her book aside. "Come here," she said gently, patting the seat beside her. "Sit with me. Breathe."

I took a deep breath, then another, and sank into the swing beside her. The creaking of the chains was the only sound for a moment.

"I thought she was gone," I said. "I thought she had moved on, but now... now I don't know what to think."

Rhea looked out into the darkened yard, her expression thoughtful. "It's possible she never left. Maybe something is still anchoring her here; something unfinished."

"She said she needed my help. That's not the first time, remember? Back when everything first started, I *felt* that urgency in her. Like she had something she wanted me to know."

Rhea nodded. "Exactly. She might be trying to reach out because that message, whatever it is, still needs to be delivered. The demon might have been suppressing her presence all along."

I bit my lip, my mind racing. "So, what should I do? Wait? Try to contact her somehow?"

"I think... we wait," Rhea said gently. "Right now, the best thing we can do is be open to whatever she needs. The cleansing ritual may have finally given her enough space to come through. It might take time before she's strong enough to reach you again."

I exhaled, trying to calm the buzzing in my chest.

"I'll talk to Viola in the morning," Rhea continued. "She'll know if there's something more we can do. Something safe."

"Can I come with you?" I asked quickly.

Rhea gave me a small smile. "Don't you have plans with Brett tomorrow?" "I do," I said, "but this is more important. He'll understand."

Rhea nodded, touched by the seriousness in my voice. "Alright. I'm heading over around nine. Just be here a little before, and we'll go together."

"Thank you," I said quietly. "I don't want to mess this up. If Shiloh's still here, I want to help her. I *have* to help her."

Rhea reached over and squeezed my hand. "We'll figure this out, Carmen. You're not alone."

And for the first time since I heard Shiloh's voice, I believed that.

~~~~~~~~~~

September 26th, 1998

The following morning, I woke up just before eight. The soft light of early morning filtered through my curtains, casting pale stripes across the floor. For a moment, I just lay there, staring at the ceiling, my thoughts already on what the day might bring. I still couldn't shake the sound of Shiloh's voice from my head; it had echoed through my
~~~~~~~~~~

dreams like a whisper, lingering long after I opened my eyes.

But there was no time to sit and dwell on it. I had to be ready. I kicked off the covers and swung my legs over the edge of the bed, my feet hitting the cool hardwood.

With a quiet yawn, I stood up and padded down the hall to the bathroom.

The house was still. I could hear the gentle hum of the refrigerator downstairs and the faint chirping of birds outside. No one else was up yet.

I stepped into the shower, letting the hot water wash over me, warming and waking me up at the same time. The steam quickly filled the small bathroom, fogging the mirror and creating a soothing cocoon of warmth. I closed my eyes briefly and tried to quiet my racing mind, but Shiloh's voice still echoed faintly: *"Carmen, I need your help."*

After I stepped out of the shower, I towel-dried my hair until it was damp rather than dripping, then wrapped the towel around myself and headed back to my bedroom. I moved quickly, grabbing a pair of light blue jeans and a soft, fitted T-shirt from my dresser. It was a chillier day, a crisp fall morning, when you could see your breath if you exhaled outside. I slipped on a blue zip-up jacket and zipped it halfway, letting the collar rest comfortably against my collarbone. I sat on the edge of my bed to lace up my favorite blue Converse, scuffed and worn, but still my go-to.

Once I was dressed, I headed downstairs to grab a quick breakfast. The kitchen was quiet, the air smelling faintly of the cinnamon candle Liv had lit the night before. I grabbed a clean bowl from the cupboard, pulled a cereal box from the pantry, and poured a generous serving, followed by milk from the fridge.

I ate quickly, the ticking clock in the corner reminding me that I only had about ten minutes before I needed to leave. I barely tasted the cereal as I shoveled it down, my mind still buzzing with nerves and anticipation.

Today could start something important: answers, maybe even closure. I was going to meet Rhea, and from there, we'd go to her shop to see Viola. If there was any way to reach Shiloh, I had to be ready to understand what she needed from me. I wanted to help her; I *needed* to.

I rinsed my bowl in the sink and placed it in the dishwasher. One last glance at the clock told me it was time to go. I grabbed my bag and slung it over my shoulder. Then, I reached for the front door handle, pausing just long enough to take a deep breath.

I stepped outside and began the walk toward Rhea's house, the morning chill brushing against my skin like a quiet reminder; something was waiting.

And I was finally ready to face it.

I arrived at Rhea's just as she stepped off the porch and headed toward her car, keys jingling in her hand. She spotted me and smiled softly.

"Ready?" she asked, already opening the driver's side door.

"I'm ready," I said, giving her a nod as I walked around to the passenger side.

I slid into the car, buckled up, and we pulled out of the driveway. The drive to the shop was quiet, but not uncomfortably so. The sun was climbing slowly in the sky, casting golden light through the trees that lined the road, their leaves just beginning to turn with the arrival of autumn. I stared out the window, my thoughts heavy, swirling with Shiloh's voice and the unease it left in my chest.

We reached the shop in just under thirty minutes. Rhea parked in her usual spot out front, and we headed inside. As always, the familiar scent of dried herbs, aged wood, and faint incense filled the air the moment we stepped in. It was oddly comforting.

Rhea went behind the counter and immediately began her usual opening tasks: checking the till, turning on the lights in the back, and flipping the sign on the door to "OPEN." I wandered the shop floor, idly browsing the shelves even though I'd seen everything before. Rows of crystals, bundles of sage, tarot decks, and worn books with cracked spines all felt like a second home now.

Not long after, the bell above the door chimed softly, and Viola walked in with Luca right behind her. They were carrying coffee cups and chatting casually, their energy calm and warm.

"Carmen!" Viola said brightly when she spotted me. Her face lit up with genuine joy, and she hugged me quickly but affectionately. "It's so good to see you."

"Hey, Carmen," Luca said with a smile, giving me a little wave.

I smiled back, but it didn't quite reach my eyes. They didn't think anything of me being there. Over the past two months, I'd stopped by a handful of times just to talk, visit, and feel grounded. But as I opened my mouth, the tone of my voice gave everything away.

"I need to tell you something," I said seriously.

Viola's smile faded slightly, and she glanced at Rhea, who was now behind the counter, watching us closely.

"She's hearing Shiloh again," Rhea said, stepping forward.

Viola's eyes snapped back to mine, her expression shifting instantly to concern.

"I thought she had moved on after the house cleansing," Viola said slowly. "You're sure it was her?"

"I didn't see her," I said, my voice steady but low. "But I heard her. She said my name. She said, *'Carmen, I need your help,'* and she repeated it. Three times."

"That's strange," Viola murmured, her brow furrowing. "We were so certain the cleansing had allowed her spirit to move on. There must be something anchoring her here."

"That's what Rhea said," I replied. "That maybe there's unfinished business; something she still needs me to do. Maybe something she never got to tell me."

Luca, who had been listening quietly, crossed his arms. "Spirits don't always move on because the negative energy is gone. Sometimes their purpose and reason for staying are deeper than we can see."

"What can we do?" I asked, my voice barely above a whisper.

Viola took a breath, her expression thoughtful. "Well, there are a few options. We can try to reach out to her. There are ways to communicate openly and safely. But... we can also wait. Let her come to you when she's strong enough. Whatever's happening, it sounds like she's trying. The choice is yours, Carmen. What do you want to do?"

I hesitated, staring down at my shoes. The weight of the decision felt heavier than I expected. "I'm not sure yet," I admitted. "I need some time to think. I don't want to rush it... or make it worse."

Viola gave me a soft smile and placed a comforting hand on my shoulder. "That's okay. Take your time. Go ahead and walk around, clear your head. Don't worry about us; we're always here for you. This shop, this space, it's yours too now."

She pulled me in for another hug, this one longer, more grounding. I let myself breathe it in; the warmth of people who cared, the safety of being somewhere I was believed.

"I'll get things ready to open," she said gently. "And when you're ready, we'll face this together. One step at a time."

I nodded, swallowing hard against the knot in my throat. "Thank you," I said quietly. "For everything."

~~~~~~~~~~

After spending a few quiet hours drifting around the shop, watching customers come and go, and feeling the low energy in the space, I finally made a decision. I'd browsed every shelf, read the spines of old books, fingered the edges of hand-labeled jars, and let the soft flicker of candlelight and scent of dried herbs settle my thoughts. My nerves had slowly smoothed out into calm determination.

I walked to the back room, where Viola was setting up for a psychic reading she had scheduled for later in the afternoon. The room was dim, cozy, and quiet, lit by soft lamps and warm-toned candles. The faint scent of sandalwood hung in the air.
~~~~~~~~~~

"Carmen, hey," Viola said brightly when she saw me enter. She stood near a small round table draped in a deep purple cloth embroidered with golden thread. "Come help me choose something. I just bought these new candles, and I can't decide which one to light for the reading and which to take home."

She held up two candles, one in each hand. I stepped closer and leaned in to smell them. The first had an earthy, musky scent, like damp soil, cedarwood, and something ancient. The other was sweeter, almost like vanilla or spiced honey. They were total opposites, but each had an intense, distinct energy.

I inhaled deeply from each again, letting the scents wash over me. "I like this one for here," I said, pointing to the earthy candle. "It smells like the shop; mystical, grounded... like something's hidden in the air, waiting to be discovered."

Viola nodded in agreement. "Good choice. I like it too; it has a depth to it. Perfect for this space."

She placed it on the table in a simple brass holder, carefully arranging crystals and a deck of tarot cards beside it. Then she glanced over at me, her hands pausing. "So... have you had time to think about what you want to do? About Shiloh?"

I shifted slightly, my fingers grazing the back of a wooden chair. "Yeah," I said quietly. "I think I want to wait, just for a little while. I don't want to force anything, and I don't want to risk pushing her away if she's trying to come through in her own way. I want to give her the space to reach me first, if she can."

Viola studied me for a moment, her expression calm and understanding. "I think that's wise, Carmen. Spirits have their own timing. If she's calling to you now after all this time, there's a reason, and she'll come again when she's ready. You'll know when the moment is right."

I smiled softly at her, grateful for her reassurance and presence. "Thanks, Viola."

"Of course," she said, returning the smile with warmth in her eyes. "You're stronger than you realize, you know. Trust your instincts, they're rarely wrong."

I gave her a small, grateful wave as I turned to leave the room. She nodded and returned to her preparations, carefully arranging a cloth over the table as the candle flickered to life behind her.

As I stepped back into the central part of the shop, I felt a strange mixture of anticipation and calm. I didn't know when Shiloh would reach out again, or what she needed from me, but I was ready now, or at least more prepared than before.

And for now, that was enough.

Chapter Thirty–Nine

Karina

I've been lying in bed for what feels like forever, hours slipping by since I first opened my eyes this morning. I haven't moved much, just staring blankly at the ceiling, silently pleading to get up, do something, to *be* someone. The sunlight is already creeping through the blinds, signaling it's well past noon, but I still can't summon the energy to rise. My limbs feel like they're weighed down by something invisible, something heavy and suffocating. It's like a thick, dark cloud is hovering over me, pressing in, stealing my breath, blurring my mind. I want to shake it off, but I can't. I don't know how.

Nothing feels right anymore. Nothing feels like *me*, not since before the move.

When we first moved, I told myself it was just a phase, that things would settle eventually, that I'd adjust. I gave it time. I tried to be patient. But instead of getting better, it's only gotten worse. I feel like a stranger in my skin. I used to feel joy. I used to laugh without forcing it. I used to look forward to the day ahead, especially school. I loved school once. Now, just the thought of going makes my stomach turn. The place I used to feel alive in now fills me with dread. I avoid people. I avoid myself.

There's something inside me that feels broken. I don't know how to describe it exactly, but this emptiness has taken root within me, growing slowly and quietly every day. I find myself having thoughts I never used to have; dark thoughts, scary ones. I try to push them away, but they keep creeping back in, stronger each time. I don't want to do anything. The things I used to enjoy feel meaningless. Food doesn't taste right. Music sounds dull. Even my reflection feels unfamiliar.

I wish I could explain it to someone, make them understand, but I'm afraid. I'm worried they won't get it. Or worse, they will and look at me differently forever. I just want to feel okay again. I want to wake up one day and not feel this crushing weight on my chest. I want to return to the version of myself that felt excited about life. I miss that person so much. I don't know where they went.

And I'm scared I'll never find them again.

Eventually, I finally managed to pull myself out of bed. It doesn't feel like a victory, more like surrender. My body moves slowly, almost reluctantly, as if gravity is stronger today. I don't bother changing out of my pajamas or brushing my hair. What would be the point? I'm not going anywhere. No one will see me. There's no performance to put on today; just the quiet obligation of schoolwork waiting on my desk like a shadow I can't ignore.

I shuffle over to my desk and sit down, slumping into the chair as I unzip my backpack. The sound of the zipper is loud in the stillness of the room. I start pulling things out: one textbook, then another, then a third, stacking them in an uneven pile next to my lamp. Then come the folders, five of them, each a different color. Five matching notebooks follow, one for each subject. There's something comforting about the color coordination, like a small corner of order in a day that otherwise feels shapeless.

The blue folder is for math, the green folder is for science, the yellow folder is for social studies, the red folder is for English, and the purple folder is for Spanish. It's a system I've stuck with for years. It just makes sense to me. Blue feels cold and distant, like numbers. Green reminds me of nature and the earth, which is obviously related to science. Yellow is bright and historical, somehow evoking the feel of old parchment and sunshine. Red is bold and passionate, perfectly fitting English and all its emotions. And purple? Purple feels like language; rich, layered, sometimes confusing. That's Spanish.

Sarah disagrees with my system. Her color choices are entirely different, and she refuses to accept that science should be green. We once had a whole conversation about it, half-serious, half-silly. I told her that when I think of science, I think of trees, plants, ecosystems, and the natural world. That's green. She laughed and said she thought of beakers and chemicals; blue or gray, definitely not green. We never agreed. I still think I'm right.

I decided to start with math because I hate it the most, and I always do my homework in order from least favorite to favorite. It's my little strategy for getting through the day: suffer first, reward later. I flip open the math textbook to page forty-seven. The assignment is to take notes on Chapter Six and complete fifteen practice problems. My heart sinks a little when I see the topic: fractions and algebra, a combination I dread. I stare at the first problem long before picking up my pencil.

It takes nearly an hour. Every answer feels like a guess. By the end, my hand aches, and my brain feels foggy, but I'm relieved to be done. One subject down.

Next is science. I open the green folder, take out the worksheet, and stare at the heading: "Introduction to Chemistry." Just the word *chemistry* makes me tense up. This year's science class feels like it was written in another language. I don't understand half the terminology, and nothing sticks, no matter how many times I reread the textbook. Each question on the worksheet feels like a riddle, and I wasn't given the clues, either. I try my best, flipping through the chapters and taking an occasional guess. After forty-five exhausting minutes, I finish, barely confident in my answers.

I give myself a break with Spanish. Today, it's a simple worksheet on verb conjugations and vocabulary review. I finished it in less than fifteen minutes. It's one of the only subjects that feels manageable lately, like I can breathe when I'm doing it.

Then comes social studies. The assignment is to write a five-paragraph essay on a chosen historical topic. I pick one quickly, something we discussed in class last week, and start writing. It takes almost an hour, but the words come easier than they did with math or science. History has a narrative to it, a story I can follow.

Finally, I save the best for last: English.

Our homework is to study vocabulary and read a few chapters of *The Great Gatsby*. I start with the vocab. I grab a stack of index cards and begin making flashcards. On one side, I write the word in black ink. On the other hand, I carefully jot down the definition, a few synonyms, a couple of antonyms, and a sentence that helps lock the meaning in my mind. It's time-consuming, but oddly soothing. I like how structured it is; how each word starts to make more sense when I break it down.

When I finish the flashcards, I pull out my copy of *The Great Gatsby*. We were only assigned a few chapters for the weekend, but I already read the book the day after we started it in class. Still, I like going back. Rereading allows me to see what I missed the first time: little details, lines of dialogue that hold more meaning now, and subtle moments I rushed through before. I get lost in the story again, the world of Gatsby and Daisy and all their beautiful, tragic mess.

I read for about an hour before I finally put the book down. My eyes are starting to blur, and the day is winding down, even though I barely left my room. I pack everything back into my backpack, organizing it just how I like; folders stacked by color, books zipped neatly into place.

There's something a little satisfying in that, just a small piece of control in a world that feels mostly out of it.

I crawled back into bed once I finished my homework. That was all I had the energy for; eating, showering, and reading felt too much. I didn't care to do anything more. I didn't *want* to. All my motivation was used up just getting through those assignments. The rest felt hollow and drained, as if I were running on fumes. So I lay there, staring at the ceiling, not thinking. Just existing. And somehow, even that felt exhausting.

No matter how hard I tried to push the dark thoughts away, Amber's voice kept echoing. Her words, *"Kill yourself"*, looped endlessly, like a cruel whisper I couldn't block out. It didn't matter how much I tried to drown it out with distractions or logic, it was always there, waiting in the silence. I couldn't turn it off. I couldn't escape it. Her voice had embedded itself into my thoughts, and I could only sit with its weight, trying not to fall apart.

I kept making lists in my head, trying to count all the reasons *not* to do it. I'd go over them repeatedly, clinging to anything that might anchor me. But no matter how many reasons I found, the one reason *to* do it always felt louder, heavier, like it outweighed everything else. It was a constant, suffocating loop, hope trying to rise, only to be crushed beneath the weight of something darker. And in that cycle, I began to believe the lie that nothing would ever improve.

Chapter Forty

Carmen

After spending the morning and most of the early afternoon with Rhea, Viola, and Luca, talking and letting the day drift by, I found myself back at Rhea's house, waiting. The sun had already begun to tilt westward in the sky, casting a soft golden glow through the windows. Everyone else had left their respective homes, but I stayed behind. Brett would be home in about thirty minutes, so I couldn't bring myself to go.

Rhea didn't seem to mind. She handed me a bottle of water, said something about needing to finish some paperwork, and disappeared down the hallway. I wandered into Brett's room, which felt familiar and untouched, like stepping into a memory that hadn't aged.

I sat cross-legged at the edge of his bed, the mattress giving slightly beneath me. It was firm but not uncomfortable, the kind of bed that doesn't ask questions, just lets you sit. I looked around, quiet and still, letting the silence wrap around me.

The room was tidy, almost startlingly so. Not a single item seemed out of place. His bed was neatly made, the corners tucked in like someone had taken time to do it right. A dark gray comforter lay perfectly smoothed, with no wrinkles or bunches. His desk was clean, with a couple of pens and a notebook arranged side by side. The shelves above it were lined with a few books, some fantasy novels, a couple of textbooks, and one or two with spines so worn I wondered how many times he'd read them.

No clothes were strewn across the floor. No cluttered piles in corners. No empty pop cans, greasy pizza boxes, or snack wrappers lying forgotten. It wasn't the chaos you'd expect from a teenage boy balancing school, work, and whatever life threw at him. It was the opposite. It was curated. Controlled.

Even the air smelled clean, like linen and cedarwood, a subtle cologne or maybe just the scent of fabric softener clinging to everything. That smell lingered in his room, even the first time I'd been here. It wasn't artificial or overpowering. Just... pleasant. Like something intentional.

As I sat there, I studied the room more closely, almost like it reflected Brett himself. It made me wonder: Was this who he was? Neat, organized, deliberate? Or was it a version of himself he maintained for others, for company? For me?

There's a strange intimacy in being alone in someone else's room, especially when they're not there. It feels like reading a diary without permission, not because you're rifling through drawers or snooping, but because even *being* there lets you see parts of them they don't talk about out loud. The arrangement of things, the books he chose to keep within reach, and the lack of mess felt like clues. Clues to a version of Brett I didn't entirely know yet. Or maybe one he didn't want to be known too deeply.

I wondered if he rushed to clean up whenever he knew someone was coming over, if he smoothed out his comforter and cleared off his desk so his room wouldn't betray him. Or maybe, just maybe, this was how he lived all the time. Maybe this careful order was how he made sense of the world. Perhaps it helped him feel in control.

I shifted slightly, glancing around again, feeling strangely like I didn't belong and didn't want to leave. Something was soothing about the room's stillness, the way everything waited in its place, untouched.

And then I heard the faint click of the front door opening. A low and familiar voice floated through the hallway.

Brett was home.

I heard him before I saw him; the familiar creak of the second step on the stairs, the soft thud of his sneakers hitting the hallway floor, the subtle brush of his fingertips as they curled around the doorknob. There was a brief pause, like he hesitated just a moment, maybe knowing, or hoping I was already there. Then the door opened, and there he was.

The second his eyes landed on me, his entire face lit up. That effortless smile spread across his lips, warm and familiar, and for a moment, all the nerves slowly building in my chest faded away. I couldn't help it, my smile mirrored his, like we were wired to do so the moment we saw each other.

"Hey, you," he said, his voice soft and affectionate, carrying the warmth that made me forget the rest of the world. He stepped into the room, leaned down, and kissed me, slow, sweet, and grounding.

I closed my eyes and melted into it for a second. When he pulled away, I gently brushed a strand of hair behind my ear and asked, "Oh, I almost forgot. How was your test yesterday?"

"It was good," he said as he kicked off his shoes and approached the bed. "Some kid in my psychology class walked out during our test."

"Seriously?" I raised an eyebrow, surprised. "Must've been brutal."

He chuckled, flopping down on the bed behind me. "I thought it was easy, but who knows. Maybe I bombed it, and I'm just living in denial."

He grinned as he reached for me, wrapping his arms around my waist and gently pulling me back to rest against his chest. I let my body relax into his, feeling the steady rhythm of his breathing behind me, the way his heartbeat slowed after a long day. The silence between us wasn't heavy or awkward; it was peaceful, familiar, and safe.

After a few minutes, his voice came quietly, brushing against the back of my neck. "So... what did you do all day?"

I stiffened slightly, not enough for him to notice, I hoped, but enough to feel the tension pull tight inside my chest. I had been waiting for this question, playing out the conversation in my mind repeatedly, but now that it was here, the words caught in my throat.

I didn't want to lie to him. I never did. But I also didn't want to worry him, not again.

Still, I couldn't hide it. Not this.

"I went with your aunt to her shop today," I said carefully.

"Oh yeah? How was it?"

"It was... good. Nice. It felt good to see everyone again."

I hesitated, biting my bottom lip, trying to find the courage to keep going. He felt so solid and trusting behind me, and the idea of shattering that trust made my stomach twist.

"And I needed to talk to Viola because..." I drew in a breath. "I heard Shiloh again."

The air shifted. Brett's body tensed behind me, and I felt him pull back just slightly to look at me more fully. His eyes locked onto mine, sharp with sudden intensity.

"What?" His voice was low but urgent. "I thought that was over. I thought you weren't hearing things anymore."

"Not exactly," I said, lowering my eyes. "It's been quiet at home. I haven't heard or felt anything there in two months. But... sometimes, in other places, I still hear voices. Not all the time. Just... sometimes."

He didn't speak. I could feel him processing, trying to stay calm and not panicking, even though I could practically hear his thoughts racing.

"Yesterday," I continued, my voice softer now, "... I heard Shiloh. She called out to me."

Brett ran a hand through his hair and sat up straighter, his expression unreadable. "If Shiloh can come back... does that mean the demon can, too?"

I swallowed hard. The question was one I had already asked myself a dozen times. "I don't know," I admitted. "Viola doesn't think Shiloh ever fully left. She thinks something might be tethering her here, keeping her spirit grounded. The house cleansing weakened her connection, but it didn't erase it. It just... took time for her to regain the strength to speak to me again."

"I don't want you getting hurt," Brett said quietly. His voice was soft but firm, threaded with concern. He reached for my hand, his thumb brushing over mine in slow circles.

"Shiloh's not dangerous," I said quickly, holding his gaze.

"You don't know that," he replied, and though his tone wasn't accusing, there was a weight behind his words.

"Yes, I do," I said, but my voice faltered slightly. "I mean... I *think* I do. I've never felt afraid of her. Not once. I don't feel fear when she's around. I feel... sadness, as if she's scared. Like she's lost, and she needs someone."

He watched me for a long moment, his expression softening with something like helplessness.

"I just don't want anything happening to you," he said. "Not again. Not because of all of this."

"I know," I whispered. "But I don't think she wants to hurt anyone. She's not like that. She just... needs to be heard. And maybe I'm the only one who can help her."

He didn't argue. He pulled me closer again, wrapping his arms around me like a shield, like he could protect me from ghosts, memories, and things that don't belong in this world. I sank into him, grateful for how he held me; fiercely, gently, like he didn't want to let go.

And for now, that was enough.

We didn't talk for the next hour. We didn't need to. We just lay there together in the quiet, the hum of the world fading around us like background noise. My head rested on his chest, rising and falling in rhythm with his breath, while his arm was draped around me, holding me close in that gentle, effortless way of his. There was a quiet comfort in it, no words, no expectations. Just closeness. Just warmth. Just *us*.

It felt safe, like nothing outside this room could reach me. It was as if time had paused and left us behind, tucked away in our own little world.

Eventually, I shifted slightly, lifting my head just enough to look at him. His eyes were closed, but his breathing hadn't slowed as it does when someone is asleep. I studied the calm lines of his face for a moment, then quietly asked, "Can I ask you something?"

He opened his eyes slowly, a small smile tugging at the corner of his mouth. "Ask me anything," he said, his voice low and inviting.

I hesitated, suddenly unsure why the question had been on my mind for so long, but I couldn't let it go now that it was there.

"Do you normally keep your space this clean?" I began carefully, "or... do you just do it because I come over?"

For a moment, he didn't answer. Instead, he took a slow, deep breath, his eyes drifting from mine to some faraway place in his memory. And just like that, I regretted asking. I hadn't meant to dig too deep or press on something sensitive, but maybe I had without realizing it.

When he finally spoke, his voice was quieter than before, more thoughtful. "Growing up... before we moved in with our aunt and uncle, our place was a mess."

He paused, his fingers lightly tracing slow, absent-minded patterns on the blanket between us.

"Dad was never around after Mom left. I was too young to understand how to take care of things. The dishes would pile up for days, sometimes weeks. Our bedding didn't get washed. We'd wear the same clothes for days before we finally did laundry, if we did it at all."

He swallowed hard, and I could feel the heaviness behind each word like he was reliving it.

"I used to think that was normal," he continued, his eyes still not quite meeting mine. "Living in clutter. The smell of old food. Dirty clothes are in every corner. I didn't realize there was another way to live. Those things didn't have to feel so... forgotten."

He took another breath, steadier this time. "Then we moved here. And everything was different. From the first day, the counters were spotless, and the house smelled like lemon and fresh laundry. We had clean clothes in our drawers every week, and clean sheets without having to ask. It was the first time in my life that I realized how much space could affect how you *feel*, that a clean room can quiet your mind. That a made bed can make you feel like you've got some kind of control."

He finally looked back at me, and there was something raw in his gaze, something vulnerable that made my chest ache.

"I keep it clean because I *need* it to be clean," he said. "Because it reminds me that I'm not there anymore. That I got out of that place. That I'm not that kid anymore. And yeah," he added with a slight smile, "maybe part of it is because you come over, and I want you to feel comfortable here. But mostly... It's for me. It's how I breathe."

My heart swelled at the honesty in his voice, the courage it must've taken to say all of that out loud. I cupped his cheek, brushing my thumb lightly across his skin.

"Thank you for telling me," I whispered. "And... I'm happy you're here now, that you have this space. That you made it your own."

He nodded, and I leaned in to kiss him, soft, slow, and grateful.

We didn't say anything for a while. We didn't need to.

Some truths remain in the air long after being spoken, shaping the silence into something deeper, something sacred.

As I rested my head back on his chest, listening to his heartbeat, I realized something: sometimes, love is found not in grand gestures or perfect words but in the quiet spaces we create for one another, the ones where we feel seen, safe, and strong enough to share the hardest parts of who we are.

Chapter Forty–One

Karina

A knock at my door jolted me out of the daze I'd been sinking into, dark thoughts looping endlessly, swallowing everything else. I flinched at the sound, as if it had physically shaken something loose in me. My heart raced as I sat up slowly, trying to mask the storm I was drowning in.

"Yeah?" I called out, my voice hoarse and unsteady, though I tried to make it sound normal.

The door creaked open a few inches, and Liv poked her head through the gap, her expression curious but cautious.

"Dinner's ready," she said, then tilted her head. "Are you okay?"

I hesitated for just a second too long. "Yeah. I'm fine," I replied quickly, forcing a smile that didn't quite reach my eyes. "I just don't feel well."

Another lie.

She stepped into the room more, concern flickering behind her eyes. "Are you sick?"

I turned away so she wouldn't see my face as I opened my drawer. "No. Just tired. I didn't sleep well."

Lie after lie. They slipped out too easily, like they'd been rehearsed. I pulled out a pair of sweatpants and slipped them on, replacing the pajama shorts I'd worn all day, as if putting on real clothes might help me feel like a real person. It didn't.

When I turned back to her, I gave her a quick nod, silently asking her to leave it alone. She seemed to get the message. Without another word, she turned and walked back out, leaving the door open.

A few moments later, I followed her down the stairs, walking like my body belonged to someone else, like I was only borrowing it for now. The familiar sounds and smells of dinner filled the air: the faint clatter of cutlery, the comforting aroma of herbs and spices, and the murmur of voices. It should've made me feel grounded and safe, but it didn't.

Mom and Carmen were already at the table, chatting softly about something I didn't catch. I slipped into my usual seat beside Liv and across from Carmen, trying to match the rhythm of a typical evening.

"Dinner smells great, Mom," I said, because I was supposed to say something.

"Thanks," she replied with a smile. "It's your grandmother's recipe. She used to make it all the time when I was your age."

I nodded, not tasting her words. I pushed food around on my plate, chewing without paying attention, as I pretended to be part of the conversation. But my mind wasn't there. It was miles away, locked onto the plan I had made.

The decision I had come to.

It sat heavy in the center of my thoughts, impossible to ignore. While everyone else talked about their day, school, and whatever show Carmen was obsessed with this week, I was counting down silently. I told myself this was the right choice, for the best.

That *everyone* would be better off.

I glanced around the table, watching the people I loved most laugh and share stories. And somehow, that only made the ache worse. The guilt dug in deeper, the sadness heavier. They looked happy, and I didn't want to ruin that. I didn't want to be the weight they had to carry, not anymore.

So, I smiled when they smiled. I nodded in the right places. I kept playing the part.

But inside, I was breaking.

And no one knew.

After dinner, Mom, Carmen, Liv, and I drifted into the living room, as we always did on nights when no one had plans and everything felt normal. We cleared the dishes together, laughing at Carmen's comment that Liv stacked the plates like a game of Jenga, and then made our way to the couch with bowls of popcorn and fuzzy blankets.

We browsed through DVD options for a few minutes, half-heartedly debating before settling on a family favorite, *Dumb and Dumber*. We didn't even have to argue about it. We'd all seen it at least a dozen times, maybe more, but somehow, it never stopped being funny. Harry and Lloyd, with their over-the-top stupidity and completely ridiculous adventures, made it impossible not to laugh. Their nonsense felt like the kind of humor that stitched us together, even for a little while.

The four of us squeezed onto the couch, shoulders brushing, blankets overlapping. Mom curled up on one end with her tea, Liv leaned against the armrest with a pillow in her lap, and Carmen sat cross-legged beside me, already quoting the opening lines before they were fully spoken. I took the last spot, nestled in between them, feeling their warmth on either side of me.

As the movie played, laughter filled the room, honest, unfiltered, genuine laughter. Carmen's loud cackling, Mom's quiet giggles, Liv's snorts, it was all so familiar, so *us*. And for a while, I let myself get lost in it. I smiled when they laughed, let the ridiculous lines and goofy scenes pull me away from everything else, if only briefly.

But even as I laughed along, something in me stayed apart. Watching them, seeing their eyes light up, hearing their joy, I felt this aching pull in my chest. Like an outsider peering in on a moment I didn't fully belong to anymore. It was beautiful. Comforting. Safe.

And it broke my heart.

Since this would be my final memory, I had already made up my mind.

I wanted to freeze it in time: Mom's soft laughter, Liv tucking her feet under the blanket and stealing popcorn from my bowl, Carmen quoting every other line with too much enthusiasm. The room smelled like vanilla from the candle burning on the coffee table. The soft glow of the TV cast a flickering light across their faces. It was peaceful, whole, *alive.*

And for a moment, I wished I could stay in it forever.

But the darkness still sat quietly in the back of my mind, patient and steady, whispering that I didn't belong in this happiness. They'd be better off without the version of me who was so broken inside.

So I laughed. I smiled. I watched them.

And I tried to memorize every detail, every sound, every smile, every second.

Because I needed it to last.

When the credits started to roll, Carmen and Liv immediately launched into negotiations over what movie to watch next. Something light, something funny, another distraction from the world's weight outside our front door. They were already looking through the options, trading opinions and playful jabs, while Mom let out a tired laugh and shook her head.

"I'm too old for a double feature," she joked, but there was already a softness in her voice, the kind that meant she'd give in if they insisted.

And, of course, they did. Liv gave her that look, the wide eyes and dramatic pout, and Carmen chimed in with, "Come on, just one more. It's a classic!" Eventually, Mom sighed and relented, curling back into her spot on the couch like she'd known from the start she wasn't going to say no.

But I didn't join in.

I couldn't.

The warmth of the blankets, the soft flicker of the TV screen, the easy comfort of being wrapped in my family's presence, it all felt slightly out of reach, like I was watching from the other side of a glass wall. I'd spent the entire evening trying to memorize every moment, etching their voices and laughter into my memory like photographs I could carry. But now... it was time.

"I'm going to go to bed," I said, my voice quiet as I slowly pushed myself up from the couch. My limbs felt heavy, like they knew what was coming.

Mom turned to look at me, her eyes kind. "Okay, honey. Sleep well."

"Night," Liv and Carmen said in unison, barely glancing away from the TV as the next DVD began to load.

I stood there for a second longer than I needed to, looking at them, really *looking*. Mom had her hand resting on Liv's shoulder, Carmen was already curled under a blanket, and Liv had the remote resting on her stomach like it belonged there. They were relaxed, smiling, whole.

I gave a small, subtle wave. Just enough to be polite. Just enough not to raise suspicion.

And then, almost inaudibly, I whispered, "Goodbye."

No one heard it.

And maybe, that was the point.

I climbed the stairs in silence, the soft hum of the TV fading behind me with every step. The hallway was dimly lit, illuminated only by the faint glow from a nightlight plugged into the wall outside the bathroom. It cast long shadows that moved as I walked past them.

When I reached my room, I closed the door gently behind me, not slamming or locking it, and just closing it, as if I might still change my mind.

I stood there momentarily, staring at the room that had held every version of me, dreams, quiet breakdowns, whispered phone calls in the dark. My posters were still on the walls, my books were stacked beside the bed, and my comforter was slightly rumpled from earlier when I'd barely had the strength to crawl out of it.

I crossed the room and sat at my desk. The chair creaked slightly beneath me. My hands moved on their own, mechanical, practiced. I pulled open the drawer, grabbed a sheet of lined notebook paper, and uncapped a black pen. I used the same one for school assignments, to-do lists, and pretending things were under control.

And then I started to write.

Dear Mom, Liv, and Carmen,

I'm sorry.

I'm so sorry to whoever finds this. Please know this wasn't something I wanted to do. It was something I felt I had to do. I've been trying to hold on. I've tried so hard, every day, to find a reason to stay. But something inside me feels broken, like a part of me got lost a long time ago, and I've never been able to find it again.

I feel like I don't belong. Not here, not anywhere.

And I know you'll say that's not true, that I'm loved, that I'm important, but those words haven't been loud enough to drown out the ones in my head. The ones that tell me I'm not enough. I'm a burden, and the world would keep turning even more smoothly without me in it.

Please believe me when I say this wasn't your fault. None of this was ever your fault. You loved me the best you could, and I felt that love, even when I couldn't hold onto it. You were my light in so much darkness. And leaving you is the hardest decision I've ever had to make.

I'm not doing this because of you, I'm doing this despite you. Because I love you so profoundly, and I hate that I've become someone who hides behind fake smiles and "I'm fine." I didn't want to keep lying. I didn't want to keep pretending I was okay.

Please forgive me. I know this will hurt. I know this will break your hearts. But I truly believe this is the only way for the pain inside me to stop.

Take care of each other, be kind to yourselves, keep laughing at dumb movies, keep holding each other close, and keep living the beautiful lives you all deserve.

I love you. I always have. I always will.

—Karina

I folded the letter carefully, lining the edges as neatly as possible. The words *"I'm sorry"* stared back at me from the front, written in trembling ink. It was quiet and straightforward but felt final, like a sealed goodbye.

I set it in the center of my desk, not bothering to weigh it down. It didn't need anything else. It was already heavy enough.

The room around me felt suddenly unfamiliar, like I was standing in someone else's space. My breath came slower, deeper, like my body was trying to prepare for something it couldn't fully comprehend.

I stepped out of my bedroom and walked down the hallway toward Mom's bathroom. The house was quiet, filled only with the muffled sounds of the movie still playing downstairs. The laughter I'd left behind now felt like it belonged to a world I was already fading from.

The bathroom door creaked as I pushed it open. I flicked on the light, and the harsh fluorescent glow stung my eyes. The mirror reflected my face, pale and tired, as if even my reflection was exhausted by the weight I'd been carrying.

I opened the medicine cabinet slowly, scanning the rows of forgotten bottles and half-used prescriptions. Cold medicine. Antibiotics. A bottle of old iron supplements. And then... There it was.

A small, orange prescription bottle, painkillers from Mom's surgery a few years ago. The label was faded, and the child-proof cap had worn smoothly for a long time. I took a glance at the contents. It was nearly half full.

I reached out and took it from the shelf, the plastic cold in my hand. My fingers tightened around it, and I just stood there for a moment, frozen.

Am I really doing this?

I unscrewed the cap. It clicked as it came off, a quiet sound that echoed loudly in the silence. I tilted the bottle, and the pills slid into my hand in a soft, controlled cascade. They felt weightless, but I knew better. I knew how heavy they really were.

I stared at them for what felt like forever. My hand trembled, the pills rolling slightly across my palm with every slight movement. My breath caught in my throat.

I didn't want to think anymore. I didn't want to feel doubt, guilt, or fear. I just wanted the noise in my head to stop. I wanted the ache to end. The emptiness. The self-loathing. The unbearable silence filled every second I spent pretending to be okay.

I clenched my jaw, raised my hand, and shoved the pills into my mouth before I could change my mind. I bent under the faucet, turned on the water, and let the stream hit my face as I drank from my cupped hands. The water was cold. It shocked my senses. I swallowed hard.

The taste was bitter. Chemical. Wrong.

I wiped my mouth with the sleeve of my sweatshirt, avoiding my own reflection, but just before I turned away, I made the mistake of looking up.

The girl in the mirror didn't look brave. She didn't look strong or free. She just looked... scared. Broken. A ghost of someone who used to be full of light.

I blinked, then backed away, leaving the light on behind me as I made my way down the hall. The walls felt longer now, like the walk back to my room stretched out purposefully. Like the house was trying to hold onto me for a few more seconds.

I opened the door to my room and stepped inside. Everything was just as I left it: the letter on the desk, the blankets pulled up on the bed, the soft glow of my lamp still casting light into the quiet. I walked over, pulled back the comforter, and climbed in like it was just another night.

I lay on my back and closed my eyes.

And I waited for the end to come.

Chapter Forty–Two

Carmen

After *Dumb and Dumber*, we settled on another comedy, *Mrs. Doubtfire*. It was one of those comfort movies we could all agree on, full of heart and ridiculous disguises. Mom had fallen asleep not long after it started, her head tilted back, mouth slightly open, a blanket draped over her legs. Liv and I stayed on the couch, the soft flicker of the television casting light over the room. Laughter filled the space, but something shifted about halfway through the movie.

At first, it was subtle. The air felt heavier. Still.

Then I felt it, an unmistakable presence.

It wasn't just anxiety or a chill from the air conditioner. No, this was something *real*. Something I knew too well. It felt like the strange static I'd experienced when Shiloh was near. But this wasn't the same. It was colder... darker. Yet oddly familiar.

I stood slowly from the couch, my body tense, every instinct on high alert. I glanced around the room, searching corners, shadows, trying to place what I was feeling.

The movie paused suddenly. Liv had grabbed the remote. "Carmen, what's up?" she asked, her voice confused but cautious.

The sudden stillness must've startled Mom, because she stirred awake with a small gasp. "What's going on?" she asked groggily.

Usually, I wouldn't say anything when this sort of thing happened. I'd learned to keep it to myself. To protect them. They didn't know the truth, and I didn't want to scare them. But this feeling, I couldn't ignore it. It gripped me by the ribs and squeezed.

"Something's wrong," I said, my voice low, shaky.

"What do you mean?" Mom asked, now fully awake.

"I don't know. I just... feel something."

I turned and looked down the hallway toward the front door, but saw nothing. Just silence. But that eerie feeling hadn't moved. I slowly turned to face the other direction, toward the stairs. And that's when I saw her.

Karina.

She was standing at the top of the staircase.

"Karina?" I called out. My voice cracked, confused. "What are you doing up there?"

But she didn't answer.

She just looked at me. Silent. Still.

There was something wrong with her face, her entire body, really. She didn't look solid. She looked *faded*, translucent… almost like Shiloh appeared to me. My heart sank. I took an instinctive step back as realization hit me like a freight train.

No.

No, no, no.

"Mom!" I screamed, panic crashing through me as I took off toward the stairs.

Liv and Mom jumped from the couch, startled, and followed me up, their feet pounding behind mine. I ran to Karina's door and yanked it open with trembling hands.

She was on her bed. Still. Too still.

Her skin was pale. Her lips slightly parted. The color had drained from her face.

"No!" I cried, stumbling to her side. I grabbed her shoulders, shaking her gently at first, then harder. "Karina! Wake up!"

She didn't move.

"Mom!" I shouted again, my voice cracking from the strain, the fear surging through my chest like a tidal wave.

They burst into the room a moment later. Mom froze for a split second at the doorway, then rushed to the bed, her hands flying into motion.

"Oh my God," she gasped, voice breaking. "No! My baby!"

"Mom, what's wrong with her?" Liv cried, standing frozen by the door.

"I'm not sure," Mom said, breathless as she knelt beside Karina and placed two fingers gently against her neck. Her face went pale. "Oh no. No pulse."

She ripped Karina's pillow away and climbed onto the bed, straddling her daughter's lifeless body. With practiced precision, she locked her hands over Karina's chest and began compressions.

"Liv!" she barked between counts, "Get my phone! It's in my room, charging. Call 911!"

Liv snapped out of her panic and bolted out of the room, her footsteps thunderous on the hardwood floors. I backed against the wall, hands shaking, tears pouring from my eyes. I couldn't move. Couldn't breathe. Everything was happening too fast.

Mom's hands pumped against Karina's chest, her face soaked with tears, lips moving in silent pleas. "Stay with me, baby. Come on. Please stay with me."

Liv came rushing back, phone pressed to her ear and something clutched in her other hand. She stopped short at the doorway, eyes wide with horror.

"Mom," she said, voice shaking. "This was in your bathroom." She held up a familiar orange pill bottle. "Hydrocodone. It's almost empty."

Mom's face crumbled for a moment, but didn't stop. "Tell the dispatcher! Tell them she overdosed on opioids. Tell them we need an ambulance *now*!"

Liv relayed the information in a frantic voice as Mom leaned over Karina again and began rescue breaths, pinching her nose, breathing into her mouth, then returning to compressions with desperate, shaking arms.

I dropped to my knees. I couldn't stop crying. I couldn't stop *seeing* that version of Karina at the top of the stairs. That ghostly image burned into my mind.

Minutes stretched like hours.

Then suddenly, Karina *gasped*.

Her body jerked, and her eyes opened, just a sliver.

"Oh my God," Mom sobbed, collapsing onto her daughter's chest. "Oh, honey... oh, thank God."

We were all crying now. Tears streamed down Liv's cheeks. I covered my mouth with both hands, overcome with relief and disbelief.

Karina blinked slowly, her gaze distant and unfocused.

She was back.

Barely, but back.

I looked at my mom, watching her stay focused, even though her heartbreak. Her training as a nurse had taken over. She'd saved Karina's life.

And in that moment, I realized none of us were ever going to be the same again.

Chapter Forty-Three

Liv

I stood there, frozen, my hands trembling at my sides as two paramedics carefully wheeled my little sister out of the house on a stretcher. The sight knocked the breath from my lungs. Karina's body looked so small, so still, swallowed by the white sheets and the humming of machines I didn't understand.

Her face was pale, her lips tinged with blue, and though the oxygen mask covered most of her features, I could still see how lifeless she looked. It was like the soul had been drained from her, and she was just... drifting somewhere we couldn't reach.

Carmen stood pressed against the hallway wall like she couldn't move, like she'd become a part of the house itself. Her face was blank, her eyes glassy. Not crying and not talking. Just staring, caught in a loop of shock she couldn't escape from.

Mom wasn't frozen, though. She was spiraling.

She clung to the nearest paramedic, firing off every medical question she could think of through sobs and gasps: "What's her oxygen level? What's her heart rate? What about organ failure? What are her chances?"

They were kind. Gentle. Calm.

But nothing they said seemed to make it through the panic that had swallowed her whole.

We followed them down the stairs, each of us moving like ghosts. The sound of Karina's stretcher wheels bumping softly against each step made my stomach twist. This moment felt eerily familiar, like déjà vu, but even more so. Much worse.

A few months ago, it was Carmen being taken away, curled up and unresponsive after her panic attack. That had been terrifying.

But this?

This was something else entirely.

This was Karina choosing not to wake up.

And I hadn't seen it. I hadn't noticed. I hadn't asked the right questions or said the right things. I didn't even realize she was in pain. I kept thinking she was just tired, distant, and in one of her quiet moods. I let her fade into the background without ever really stopping to look at her.

What kind of sister am I?

Outside, the night air hit me like a slap, tremendous and heavy. The paramedics lifted the stretcher into the back of the ambulance, locking it into place. Karina didn't stir. Not even a flinch.

Mom climbed in after her without hesitation, her hands already fumbling for her phone to call our aunt or someone else. I couldn't tell. Her voice was shaking too much.

Carmen and I didn't speak. We just moved. I unlocked my car, and we both slid inside. The silence between us was crushing.

I gripped the steering wheel with white knuckles and focused on the road as I pulled out behind the ambulance, its flashing lights painting streaks of red and blue across the road. Carmen sat stiffly beside me, her arms hugged around herself as she stared out the window in a daze. Her lips were slightly parted, like she wanted to say something, but the words just wouldn't come.

I wanted to cry. Scream. Hit the dashboard. Anything.

Instead, I just drove.

And the entire time, guilt sat in my chest like a lead weight, making breathing hard.

How could I have missed this?

How did I not notice her breaking down? All the late mornings, the skipped meals, the way she'd zone out during conversations. The way she started faking smiles that didn't reach her eyes.

How did I miss all of that?

But as those thoughts echoed louder and louder in my head, another question slowly crept in, quieter, but sharper.

How did Carmen know?

She *felt* something was wrong before any of us did.

She saw something at the top of the stairs that sent her running.

And she saved her.

While I just sat there, oblivious.

I didn't know whether to be grateful or ashamed.

Maybe both.

~~~~~~~~~~

September 27th, 1998

We arrived at the hospital just after midnight. The parking lot was nearly empty except for a few scattered cars and the bright glow of security lights overhead. I pulled into a space in the visitors' section, barely throwing the car into park before Carmen and I jumped out and sprinted toward the entrance.

The automatic doors whooshed open, and the cold air of the emergency room lobby hit me like a slap. It smelled
~~~~~~~~~~

like antiseptic and anxiety, bleach, plastic, and too many sleepless nights. Everything was too bright, too quiet, except for the distant buzz of machines and the occasional murmur of voices behind closed doors.

I ran up to the front desk, breathless and frantic. A woman with short brown hair tucked under her chin sat behind the counter, flipping through a clipboard. She wore clunky red glasses that didn't suit her face and clicked her gum as if she weren't sitting in the middle of people's worst nights.

"Karina Woodlen?" I blurted out. "She was just brought in; she overdosed. She was in an ambulance, please—"

"Okay, calm down," she said, her voice too slow for my panic. "Let me look her up."

She scrolled through the screen on her computer and rifled through a stack of intake papers like she was searching for a misplaced grocery list instead of life-or-death information. My fingers dug into the counter.

After a tense moment, she nodded. "She's being treated right now in Trauma Bay Three. You can't go back there yet. There's a waiting area down the hall to your left. You can wait there until someone comes to update you."

"Okay, thank you," I said quickly, though the words felt hollow. I grabbed Carmen by the wrist, and we rushed down the hall without waiting for anything else.

The waiting room felt like a strange kind of purgatory. Pale green walls, uncomfortable blue chairs in stiff rows, and a silent TV mounted in the corner playing some old black-and-white sitcom with the volume muted. But what stopped me cold wasn't the room; it was Mom.

She was in the center of it, pacing like a caged animal. Her hands wrung together, and her eyes were wide and red-rimmed, mascara smudged from crying. Her whole body looked tense, as if she stopped moving, she'd fall apart.

"Mom," I said softly, my voice cracking.

She spun around. The moment she saw us, her whole face collapsed. "Oh, honey. My girls." She wrapped her arms around us, pulling Carmen and me into a tight hug. We just stood there like that for a second, three broken pieces holding each other together.

"Mom," I whispered, trying to keep my voice steady. "What's happening? Is she, will she be okay?"

Mom pulled back just slightly to look me in the eyes. "They're working on her," she said. "They're giving her something to reverse the effects. That bottle of pills she took... it wasn't full. That's something, at least." Her voice wavered, thin and shaking. "She's going to be fine. She has to be fine. *She'll be fine.*"

She repeated those three words like a mantra, as if saying it enough would make the universe listen. I didn't know what to believe.

We sat down in silence. Carmen was beside me, Mom was across from us, her knees bouncing restlessly. The minutes passed slowly, each one pressing heavier on my chest. The sterile air, the humming of lights above us, and the flicker of the silent TV all blurred together as my mind spiraled.

I looked at Carmen. She hadn't spoken since we left the house. Her face was blank, but her eyes weren't. They were alive with fear, and something else, something I couldn't quite name. Guilt, maybe. Or grief.

"Carmen?" I said quietly, finally breaking the thick silence around us like fog. My voice was soft and hesitant, as if I was afraid speaking would shatter the fragile calm we barely held onto.

She turned slowly, her eyes meeting mine with a tired, unreadable expression.

"How did you know... that something was wrong?" I asked. My voice cracked on the last word.

Carmen's eyes flicked away, back down to her lap, where her hands were tangled tightly together, her knuckles pale. She didn't answer right away.

"Please, honey," Mom added gently, her voice laced with worry and curiosity. "You saw something tonight... Something the rest of us didn't."

Carmen took a deep breath and exhaled slowly, as if trying to let go of something heavy on her chest. "I'll tell you both the truth," she said quietly. "But... not right now. This isn't the time or the place. I promise I'll explain later. I will."

We didn't argue. We didn't push. I just gave her a slight nod and leaned back against my seat, trying to respect her boundaries even as the questions circled like vultures in my head.

A few more minutes passed, filled only with the soft sounds of the hospital, distant voices, footsteps echoing in the hall, and the hum of fluorescent lights overhead.

Then the door opened, and a nurse stepped inside, holding a clipboard. "Karina Woodlen?" she called out.

We all stood instantly, our bodies tense and ready.

"How's my baby?" Mom asked, her voice strained and trembling.

"She's stable," the nurse said with a reassuring smile. "We pumped her stomach, and we're monitoring her vitals. She's awake now. If you want to see her, I can take you back."

"Yes, of course," Mom said quickly, already stepping forward.

We followed the nurse through double doors and down a long corridor. Each step felt heavier than the last. My heart thudded in my chest, louder with every footfall. I didn't know what I was expecting, to see Karina alert and okay, or to find her pale and barely hanging on. I wasn't sure what would hurt more.

When the nurse finally pulled aside the curtain, my breath caught.

Karina was lying in the hospital bed, propped up slightly by pillows. Her skin looked pale, her eyes sunken and rimmed with red. Dark circles were under her eyes, and her whole body looked exhausted, like life had been drained out of her. Wires and tubes connected her to machines that beeped softly, a cruel contrast to the stillness of her frame.

"I'll give you some privacy," the nurse said softly, then stepped out and pulled the curtain closed behind her.

We rushed to her side. Mom dragged a chair next to the bed and immediately took Karina's hand, brushing the hair gently from her face.

"Sweetheart?" she whispered. "Baby, can you hear me?"

Karina's eyes fluttered open slowly. When she saw us, tears welled up and spilled down her cheeks. Her face crumpled, and she began to sob, her voice broken and desperate.

"I'm so sorry, Mom," she cried. "I'm sorry. I just... I didn't know what else to do. I didn't want to hurt you, I swear. I just... I couldn't take it anymore."

"Shh, baby, it's okay. It's okay now," Mom said, pulling Karina into her arms as best she could with the IV lines still in place. She held her close, rocking her gently, just as she had when we were little. "I'm not mad at you. I could never be mad at you. I'm so sorry I didn't see how badly you were hurting. I should've known. I should've asked more. I should've seen the signs. I failed you."

Karina shook her head through sobs. "No... no, you didn't. This was my choice. This wasn't your fault. You didn't do anything wrong. None of you did."

Mom pressed a kiss to her forehead, then leaned back just enough to look at her. "We'll talk about this more later, okay? You need to rest right now."

She gently pulled the blanket up to Karina's chin, tucking it around her like she used to when we were kids and sick with the flu. Her movements were slow, careful, and full of love and fear.

Karina closed her eyes again, but the tears didn't stop. And neither did ours.

We stayed by her side in silence, our family shaken, cracked, but still holding on.

Together.

~~~~~~~~~~

We stayed in Karina's hospital room for several hours, barely speaking, just sitting in silence and watching her sleep. The constant beep of the heart monitor was oddly comforting, a steady rhythm reminding us she was still here and still breathing. Still alive.

Mom sat in the chair next to Karina's bed, holding her hand in both of hers. Carmen sat on the windowsill, knees pulled to her chest, staring blankly at the early morning sky just starting to lighten with the promise of dawn. I stayed curled up in the corner of a chair, exhausted but unable to close my eyes. None of us had the energy to talk, but none of us wanted to leave.

It was just a little before five in the morning when the door creaked open and a man in a white coat stepped inside. His presence was calm, deliberate, and quiet, like he had walked into scenes like this a thousand times before.

"Good morning," he said softly, careful not to speak too loudly and wake Karina. He gave us a gentle nod before walking to the machines beside her bed, checking the monitors, adjusting a few settings, and jotting notes on his clipboard.

"I see it's been a difficult night," he said, turning to face us, his expression kind but serious. "So I'll keep this brief."
~~~~~~~~~~

He looked over his notes one more time before speaking again.

"From what we can tell, Karina is going to be okay."

All three of us exhaled at once, the collective breath of a family that had been holding itself together by a thread. Mom's shoulders sagged with visible relief, and I felt tears burn behind my eyes again, not out of fear, but gratitude.

"Physically, she's stable," the doctor continued. "We've monitored her vitals through the night, and her body responds well. But as you might expect, we won't discharge her immediately."

He glanced down at his clipboard again, then back at Mom. "We'll need to keep her here for at least three to five days. That's standard protocol following a suicide attempt. We must observe her, ensure her safety, and begin coordinating a care plan."

"I understand," Mom said quietly, her voice hoarse from crying and lack of sleep.

The doctor gave her a small, understanding smile. "A nurse will be in shortly to go over the next steps. But in the meantime..." He looked at all three of us, his tone gentle but firm. "You should go home. Get some rest. You've been through a lot tonight."

"I'm not going anywhere," Mom said immediately, gripping Karina's hand more tightly. "Not until I know she's okay. Not until I see her open her eyes again."

The doctor nodded, not pushing her. "Of course," he said. "We'll make arrangements." Then he shook Mom's hand with a reassuring touch before slipping out of the room.

About twenty minutes later, a nurse stepped in. Her kind face, soft eyes, and calm presence made you feel a little steadier.

"We've got a room ready for Karina on the psychiatric floor," she said, holding a clipboard. "We'll be moving her shortly. But I need a bit of paperwork completed first."

Mom stood up and took the clipboard. Her hands trembled as she signed her name on the forms, flipping through page after page while the rest of us silently sat.

"The psychiatric unit has a strict policy," the nurse explained gently. "No visitors for the first seventy-two hours. It gives our patients time to settle in, meet with the care team, and be properly evaluated."

Mom nodded, blinking rapidly. "I understand. Whatever's best for her."

"After that initial period, depending on her progress and the psychiatrist's evaluation, she may be cleared to come home. Or," the nurse added carefully, "she may need to stay longer to continue receiving treatment. We'll keep you informed every step of the way."

Mom swallowed hard and nodded again. "Thank you. Truly."

The nurse smiled kindly before leaving to prepare for the transfer.

As soon as the door closed, Mom sat heavily in the chair beside Karina again. She brushed a strand of hair away from Karina's forehead and whispered something we couldn't hear.

None of us said anything. No more questions, explanations, or words were left to fill the space. Just waiting. Just breathing, holding on to the hope that things were finally starting to turn toward healing.

It was finally time to say goodbye, a little after eight in the morning.

The sun had risen hours ago, but it felt like time had stopped somewhere in the middle of the night. We were still trapped in the same ache, raw fear, and silence. When the door to Karina's room opened again, two male nurses stepped inside, both wearing calm expressions and the kind of quiet professionalism that came with doing something difficult, over and over again.

"Good morning," the first one said gently, directing his voice more to Karina than any of us. "We're here to take you upstairs now."

He stepped closer to her bed and spoke in a low, reassuring tone. "We're going to escort you to our psychiatric floor. Upon arrival, you'll undergo an intake interview. After that, we'll get you something to eat, if you're feeling up to it, and we'll help you settle into your room."

Karina nodded slowly, her face pale and solemn. Her eyes were rimmed with red, swollen from the night before, but something in them looked calmer now, tired but calmer.

The second nurse added, "We'll give you all a few minutes to say goodbye."

They stepped out into the hallway but remained just outside the door, giving us space while still keeping a watchful eye.

Mom turned toward Karina first, her hands already shaking. "Okay, sweetheart," she said softly, a new wave of tears rising in her throat. "You're going to be okay. In just a few days, you'll get the help you need. You'll be back home before you know it, and we'll be waiting for you every step of the way."

She bent over the bed and pulled Karina into her arms, holding her so tightly it looked like she never wanted to let go. Her tears fell into Karina's hair as she whispered, "I love you so much."

"I love you too, Mom," Karina sobbed. "I'm so sorry. I didn't mean to— I didn't know what else to do."

"I know, baby," Mom said. "We're going to get through this together."

After a long moment, Mom slowly stepped back, holding Karina's hand for as long as she could.

Then it was my turn.

I walked over, my chest heavy, and wrapped my arms around my little sister. She felt so small. So fragile. "I'm sorry I wasn't there for you when you needed me," I whispered into her shoulder. "But I'm here now. I love you so much, Karina. You're not alone, okay? I'll see you in a few days."

Karina nodded into my shoulder. I gave her one last squeeze before stepping aside.

Carmen was the last to step forward.

She didn't say much, just wrapped her arms around Karina and held her close. "I love you," she whispered, her voice steady and low. There was a kind of peace in Carmen's tone, something unspoken but deeply understood between them.

Before she pulled away, Karina leaned in and whispered something in Carmen's ear. I couldn't hear what she said, and Carmen didn't say anything after, just nodded slowly and gave Karina's hand a final squeeze.

When we stepped out into the hallway, the two nurses returned to Karina's bedside. A nearby nurse quietly detached the wires from the monitors and gathered the cords and equipment to the side. The machines that had been beeping all night went silent.

The two men gently helped Karina sit up. One stood on either side, steadying her as she slid off the bed. She looked weak, like every step took effort, but she didn't resist.

There was no fight left in her, just quiet resignation, like she knew this was something she had to do, whether she wanted to or not.

As they walked her out of the room and down the hallway, we followed behind in silence. No one said a word. The hospital felt colder and louder now. Every footstep echoed, and every breath felt too loud in my ears.

When they reached the elevator, the nurses helped Karina inside. She turned around to look at us, her family, standing just feet away, but feeling like we were already separated by something invisible and vast. Her eyes welled with tears again, and she mouthed the words as the doors began to close.

"I'm sorry."

And then she was gone.

The elevator doors slid shut, and we were left in the quiet hallway, staring at the space where she had been.

None of us moved. We just stood there, hollow and numb, wishing we could have done more, said more, anything to take away the pain that brought her to this moment.

But for now, all we could do was wait... and hope.

Chapter Forty–Four

Karina

The elevator ride was quiet, but inside, my mind was anything but. Every second felt like a countdown to something I couldn't name. My heart pounded in my chest, and I kept wringing my hands, the pads of my fingers sore from picking at my cuticles. I had no idea what would happen or how I was supposed to feel. I knew everything had shifted, and there was no going back.

But what surprised me most was what I felt when I first woke up in that hospital bed earlier: *relief.*

Real, unexpected, bone-deep relief.

It hit me like a wave. I realized I didn't actually want to die. Not really. I just wanted the pain to stop. The hopelessness, the darkness, the constant weight pressing on my chest like I was drowning in plain sight. I didn't know how to ask for help, but now, help had found me.

The elevator dinged, snapping me out of my thoughts. The doors slid open with a low groan, revealing a sterile hallway lit with cold fluorescent lights. The two male nurses, one older and one younger, stepped out with me sandwiched between them. We walked down the hall until we reached locked double doors. One pressed a buzzer, and a nurse on the other side let us in.

The moment the doors shut behind me, I felt it. I was inside now. Locked in. Like a prisoner, but also like a patient. I'd made a choice; a bad one. And now, I was here to face the consequences.

They led me into a small, simple, quiet, and clinical intake room. Two couches against one wall, a round table with four chairs in the middle, and a clock ticking way too loudly in the silence.

"Go ahead and have a seat," one of the nurses said. "A nurse will be in shortly."

One left the room, but the other stayed near the door, watching me. I guessed it was policy. I slid into one of the chairs at the table, my legs feeling like they barely worked, and immediately began picking at my nails again.

A few minutes later, a nurse entered the room carrying a food tray. Her kind face and warm voice helped my anxiety simmer just a bit.

"Hi, Karina," she said gently, setting the tray before me. "I'm Amanda. Are you feeling hungry?"

I gave her a hesitant shrug and glanced at the food: scrambled eggs, bacon, a fruit cup, and a sealed orange juice. I peeled the top off the juice and took a sip, to have something to do with my hands.

Amanda sat in the chair beside me. "I know you've had a long night, but I need to ask you a few questions. Is that okay?"

I nodded, still avoiding her eyes.

"All right, can you confirm your full name and date of birth?"

"Karina Marie Woodlen. October 2nd, 1982."

"Thank you," she said, jotting it down. "And can you confirm that you're here following a suicide attempt?"

"Yes," I whispered, my voice barely audible. I looked down at my lap, ashamed.

"Okay, are you currently taking any medications, or do you have any previous mental health diagnoses?"

"No," I replied quietly.

She wrote more on her clipboard. "Have you ever been hospitalized before? For anything mental health related?"

"No," I said again. Every answer felt heavier than the last,

Amanda gave a gentle nod and stood up. "All right, the next step is changing you into clean clothes. A privacy screen is in the corner, you can change behind there."

I stood up and strolled behind the screen, my hospital gown hanging loose on my shoulders. I untied the strings at my neck and let them fall to the floor, standing there in my underwear for a moment before Amanda handed over a set of clothes: gray sweatpants and a soft navy-blue T-shirt. I dressed quickly and handed the gown back to her. She tossed it into a laundry bin and gave me a small smile.

"Okay. Let's get you to your room."

I followed her out of the intake room, past the double doors, and into the heart of the unit. The hallway stretched in both directions, sterile and quiet, with identical doors lining the walls. We turned right, and Amanda led me several doors down before stopping in front of one on the left.

"This is your room," she said, opening the door.

I peeked inside. The room was clean but straightforward. There were two beds, each with plain white sheets and gray blankets, and two open wooden shelves on either side. A bathroom was tucked in the corner, and the door was slightly ajar, but I noticed it had neither a lock nor a handle from the inside. A window was covered with thick plastic, it let in light but didn't open.

"Your roommate's name is Jessica," Amanda explained. "She's at a group activity right now."

She handed me a folder, pulling it from beneath her clipboard. "Inside, you'll find the weekly schedule: music therapy, arts and crafts, journaling time, and group therapy. Participation isn't mandatory, but it's strongly encouraged. It really does help."

I opened the folder and looked through the schedule, trembling.

"There's also a common room across the hall," she added. "TV, coloring pages, books, and two phones in case you'd like to call home."

Amadna turned toward the door but paused before leaving. "I know this is overwhelming, but you're not alone here. I'll check on you again soon. The doctor will meet with you before lunch."

She gave me a soft smile. "Take your time settling in. You're safe now, Karina."

And then she left.

I stood alone in the doorway for a minute, unsure of what to do. Then I walked to my bed, one of the two by the wall, and slowly sat on the edge. The mattress felt stiff beneath me, but it didn't matter. I wasn't really aware of my body anymore.

I stared at the wall across from me. *Why did I do this?* The thought echoed in my mind, circling relentlessly. *What was I thinking? How could I have been so stupid?*

And yet, even in the midst of all the regret and confusion, something else began to flicker in the farthest corner of my mind.

Hope.

Small, quiet, fragile. But still there.

Chapter Forty–Five

Carmen

The drive home was a silence that felt neither peaceful nor quiet, but loaded, awkward, and suffocating, the kind of silence that rang louder than any noise.

My sister had tried to take her own life.

And I saw her ghost,

No one said anything as we rode back. Liv kept both hands on the wheel, her knuckles pale from how tightly she gripped it. Mom stared blankly out the passenger window, her body slumped and motionless except for the occasional tremble of her shoulders. I sat in the back seat, pressed against the door like I was trying to disappear, my heart pounding beneath my ribs. I was trapped in my head, trying to figure out how to explain the truth, *my truth*, to two people who had no idea what I'd been hiding.

When we finally pulled into the driveway, we moved like ghosts, quiet, tired, and haunted. The engine clicked softly as Liv turned it off. We exited the car one by one, the doors shutting with hollow thuds echoing into the early morning.

Mom walked straight to the kitchen inside the house, as if it were the only thing keeping her upright. She flipped on the stove and reached for the teapot without saying a word.

"Anyone want some tea?" she asked, her voice almost too soft to hear.

"I'll have one," Liv replied quietly, her voice hoarse.

"I'm okay," I murmured, though my throat was dry and aching.

Mom didn't respond. She stood there, her hand still resting on the teapot's handle, her gaze fixed as if it held answers she couldn't find anywhere else. Silent tears rolled down her cheeks, dripping onto the counter. She didn't wipe them away.

Liv sat at the kitchen table, her head buried in her hands, mumbling something under her breath, prayers maybe, or just fractured thoughts trying to make sense of the night. I stood near the wall, unsure what to do with myself, afraid that if I moved, I'd collapse under the weight of what I knew I had to say.

The teapot eventually whistled, loud and shrill, breaking the thick silence like glass shattering on tile. Mom moved mechanically slowly, grabbing two mugs from the cabinet and dropping a teabag into each. She poured the hot water with shaky hands, the steam curling up like smoke from a fire we didn't know how to put out.

She carried the mugs to the table and sat down, wordlessly pushing one toward Liv. I stayed standing, my back pressed against the wall like I needed its support to hold me up.

Then Mom looked up at me with red-rimmed eyes. "Sit down, Carmen."

Her soft but firm voice made it clear this wasn't a suggestion.

I moved to the table and sat beside Liv, who hadn't looked up.

For a long time, none of us spoke. The only sounds were the soft sips of tea, the hum of the refrigerator, and the occasional sniffle from one of us trying not to cry.

Then Mom broke the silence. "What's going on, Carmen?"

I looked at her, startled, and then quickly away. My fingers tightened around the hem of my sweatshirt.

"Maybe we should get some sleep first," I tried, desperate for a few more hours to figure out how to say the unsayable. "We're all exhausted—"

"No," she interrupted, her voice stronger now. "Something is going on, and you need to tell us. I saw you on those stairs last night, Carmen. You knew something was wrong before we did. You saw something."

Liv finally looked up at me then, her eyes wide with pain and confusion. "How *did* you know?" she asked. "Why did you run upstairs like that before we even realized?"

I swallowed hard, the air thick and heavy in my throat. My hands were shaking now, and I pressed them between my knees to hide it.

This was it.

I couldn't keep it in anymore.

They deserved the truth, even if it made them look at me like I was crazy, even if it changed everything.

"I saw Karina," I started, my voice shaking. "I felt something before I saw her. Like a presence. Cold, heavy... familiar. And when I looked up the stairs, there she was."

Liv blinked slowly, confusion painting her face. "I don't understand. What do you mean, you *saw* her?"

"I saw her ghost," I said softly. "At the top of the stairs."

A heavy silence dropped over the room like a curtain. No one moved. No one spoke. Only the distant hum of the refrigerator filled the air.

Finally, I took a shaky breath and added, "It wasn't the first time something like this has happened."

Mom sat up a little straighter. "What do you mean?" she asked carefully.

"Ever since we moved into this house... things have been happening," I explained. "Things I didn't want to believe at first. However, I've learned a great deal about myself. About what I can do."

Mom furrowed her brow. "Learned what, honey?"

"The voices I hear... the things I see..." I paused, swallowing hard. "They're not hallucinations. I don't have schizophrenia or anything like that. I—" I hesitated, searching their faces for a sign of belief. "I have a gift; an ability. I don't understand it completely yet, but I can see spirits. I can communicate with them."

Mom's hand twitched slightly as she reached for her tea, her face straining to remain calm. But I could see the worry behind her eyes, the panic just under the surface.

She drew in a slow, tight breath. "Carmen... have you been taking your medication?"

"No," I said, more forcefully than I intended. "Because they never worked. Not once. I've still heard the voices, still seen things. The meds just made me feel numb. Empty. But this is something real."

Mom's voice trembled as she placed her hand on mine. "Oh, sweetheart, you need help. You're not well. This is breaking my heart."

I pulled my hand away and stood up, my chair scraping against the floor. "No, Mom. I'm not sick. I know how it sounds, but this isn't some episode or delusion. It's real, and if you don't believe me, you can ask Rhea."

"Rhea?" Liv said, eyebrows knitting together. "The neighbor?"

"Yes. Rhea has known for a while. Since moving in, I've seen a little girl named Shiloh. She died decades ago. And Rhea was her best friend when they were kids. She confirmed everything."

Mom covered her mouth, her face turning pale. "Oh my God," she whispered.

"The things that happened here, the cabinet doors slamming, the strange noises, the shadows, weren't my imagination. That was a demon. It was tied to this house, but we dealt with it. Viola helped. And Shiloh, she was scared. She just wants someone to help her move on."

"No," Mom said suddenly, standing up and crying. "No, this can't be happening. I can't lose another daughter. We need to get you help. Right now."

Her voice cracked on the last word. She was spiraling.

"Mom, please, listen to me. I'm telling you the truth. You *have* to believe me."

"Liv," Mom said, ignoring me now, "grab your car keys. We need to go. She needs to see someone. She needs treatment."

Liv hesitated for a second, glancing between us, clearly torn. Then she got up and grabbed her keys from the hook near the door.

"Come on, sweetie," Mom said gently as she walked toward me, tears streaking her cheeks. "It's going to be okay. I'll be with you every step of the way. We'll get through this."

"No," I whispered, backing away. "Please. Please just trust me."

I could see it in her face; she couldn't. She loved me, but she didn't believe me.

Mom reached out to grab my arm. "Carmen, please. Don't make this harder."

"I'm not going to the hospital!" I shouted. "I'm *not* crazy!"

Then, without thinking, I turned and bolted.

"Carmen!" Mom screamed at me.

I threw the front door open and ran into the cool morning air.

I ran as fast as I could toward Rhea's house, my lungs burning with cold morning air and panic. My shoes slapped the gravel road with every frantic step. It was Sunday, I was sure she'd be home. She had to be.

When I reached her porch, I didn't hesitate. I banged on the door with both hands, breathless and desperate. Within seconds, the door creaked open.

Rhea stood in a loose sweater and jeans, her expression immediately tightening with concern.

"Carmen?" she said, scanning me. "What's wrong?"

"I told my mom," I gasped. "About the spirits. About the house. She thinks I'm losing my mind. She's trying to take me to the hospital."

Before she could respond, Brett appeared behind her, drawn by the noise. His face shifted from confusion to immediate concern when he saw me.

"Hey," he said, stepping forward and wrapping his arms around me. I collapsed into him, the adrenaline wearing off, replaced by exhaustion and dread.

"Rhea, please," I said, turning back to her. "You have to come. You have to help me explain. Make her understand I'm not crazy."

Rhea didn't hesitate. She grabbed a thick coat from a hook near the door and shrugged it on. "Let's go," she said firmly.

"I'm coming too," Brett added. There was no question in his tone; just certainty.

I didn't argue. I was too relieved; the more people who knew the truth, the more voices that backed me, the better.

We piled into Rhea's car. The drive back to my house felt longer than the sprint to hers, like the silence was heavier with every passing minute. My hands trembled in my lap, and my stomach twisted in knots. I didn't know what would happen when we got back. I just hoped it wouldn't be more screaming or, worse, more disbelief.

Mom and Liv were outside when we pulled into the driveway, pacing near the car. They both looked up at the sound of tires crunching the gravel. My mother's face crumpled in relief the moment she saw me.

"Oh, thank God," she breathed, rushing toward the car. "Sweetheart, you scared me so badly. It's okay now. Everything's going to be okay. We just need to get you help."

"She doesn't need help," Rhea said gently but firmly as she stepped out of the car. "She's not sick. She's telling the truth."

Mom stopped in her tracks, her expression snapping from relief to disbelief.

"I don't believe this," she said, eyes darting between us. "Rhea, don't enable this delusion. She needs a doctor, not stories."

"Mom," I said, trembling but strong, "Look."

I turned and slowly lifted the back of my shirt, revealing the jagged, faint scars that had never fully healed, those marks the demon left on me. The air turned still.

My mother's breath hitched. "Oh my god... Carmen, what did you do to yourself?" Her voice cracked, and her eyes welled up with tears again.

"She didn't do that to herself," Brett said, stepping beside me.

"It was a demon," I whispered. "One who lived in this house. One we got rid of. But not before it left a mark."

"I was there," Rhea said. "I've seen it, too. I've known about this house's history since I was a child. That little girl, Shiloh, she isn't just some figment of Carmen's imagination. I played with her when I was younger. She's real. And Carmen has a gift, not a sickness."

Mom stood frozen, eyes wide, processing it all like she couldn't decide which way was up anymore. Liv looked just as stunned, her hands clasped together like she was trying to hold herself still.

"Let's all go inside," Rhea said gently. "Please. We'll explain everything. From the beginning."

No one protested. Silently, we all turned toward the front door and stepped inside.

The living room was exactly as we had left it the night before, blankets tangled on the couch, empty popcorn bowls on the coffee table, and the faint echo of laughter still haunting the space.

Only now, it felt different. Heavier. Like the walls themselves were waiting for what came next.

We all took seats, Mom and Liv on the couch, Brett beside me, Rhea across from us in the armchair.

And in the silence that followed, I realized something: this was the moment I had feared for so long. But I wasn't alone anymore. I had people beside me. People who believed. People who knew the truth.

Now it was time to help my family believe it, too.

"The second I stepped into this house the day we moved in, I knew something was wrong," I began, my voice low but steady. "It was like... like there was an invisible veil. The outside world and the inside of the house didn't belong to the same reality. The air felt heavy, as if it were pushing in on me. It made me physically sick."

"I remember that," Mom said softly, nodding. "You threw up when we brought in the first box."

I nodded. "Yeah. And that wasn't the end of it. The closet, remember when the door slammed shut on me and I couldn't get out?"

Liv's eyes widened a little. "You said it got stuck."

"No," I said, shaking my head. "It didn't get stuck. Something shut it. And while I was in there, I heard voices. Not just in my head, I felt them around me. Whispering. Watching. I was trapped and terrified. Like, I was never going to get out. And those voices... they didn't stop. Not then, and not after."

I paused for a breath, watching Mom process what I was saying.

"Later, I saw her," I said. "Shiloh. She came out of my closet. A little girl, maybe twelve, wearing an old-fashioned green dress. Her skin was pale, almost translucent. She looked at me, and she spoke. She wasn't just a dream. She was real."

I glanced at Rhea, who gave me a gentle nod of encouragement. "Then, when I went to Brett's house for the first time, I saw a photo in the hallway. It was her, Shiloh. I asked Rhea about it later, and she told me she knew Shiloh when she was a little girl. That Shiloh had died here, in the woods."

Mom gasped softly and covered her mouth, her hand trembling.

"I asked Rhea to take me to her shop," I continued. "There's someone who works there, Viola. She's a psychic, like me. Everything started to make sense when I told her everything that had been happening. For the first time in my life, I felt understood. I realized the medication never worked because I wasn't sick. I wasn't hallucinating. The voices I heard, the things I saw, they were real. And they always have been."

Liv stared at me with wide eyes, her tea forgotten in her hands. "You mentioned something about a demon," she said quietly.

I nodded, my throat tightening. "Shiloh wasn't the only presence in this house. There was something else, something darker. It fed off fear. It stalked me for weeks. At first, I thought I was losing my mind again. I was terrified to go to sleep. Then one night, it attacked me."

"What do you mean?" Mom whispered.

"It left marks on me. Deep ones. The scratches across my back, burns that didn't make sense. Viola and her husband are part of a paranormal investigation team. Together, we confronted it. We forced it out."

I looked down at my hands. "But it wasn't easy. It almost killed me."

Silence fell over the room like a thick fog. The only sound was the refrigerator's hum and the occasional creak of the floorboards as the house settled, as if it were listening.

"I know this sounds unbelievable," I said finally, "but I swear to you, every word is true. We got rid of the demon. But Shiloh... she's still here. And she needs my help. She's been trapped in this house for decades, and I think she's finally waiting for something, maybe for someone to help her move on."

I looked at both of them, pleading with my eyes.

"I know it's a lot to take in. But I'm not crazy. I don't need a hospital. I need you to believe me."

"I believe you," Liv said suddenly, her voice quiet but firm. She looked at me with wide, glassy eyes, her fingers curled tightly around her tea mug. "I've noticed things, too.

The cabinet doors. They open on their own. I thought maybe it was just the house settling or drafts, but... it always felt weird. Like there was something more."

Relief swelled in my chest like air after drowning. She believed me.

Mom sat back slowly in her chair, her expression unreadable, still trying to absorb it all. Her eyes flicked from Liv to me, then finally to Rhea. "What do we do now?" she asked, her voice shaky and uncertain. "How can we help her? How do we... protect her from this?"

Rhea leaned forward, elbows on her knees, speaking gently but with conviction. "Right now? Nothing. There's no immediate danger anymore. Whatever dark force was here or haunting this house has been taken care of. Carmen helped drive it out. She's safe, for now."

Mom's lip trembled. "But this thing, this... gift? This ability? You're saying it's real?"

Rhea nodded. "It's as real as anything else in this world. Carmen's not sick. She never was. The voices, the visions, they weren't symptoms of an illness. They're part of her. A part most people will never understand, but that doesn't make it any less true."

Mom looked down at her hands in her lap, silent tears rolling down her cheeks. "I've spent years trying to fix her. Doctors, specialists, pills... all of it. And I treated something that didn't need to be fixed the whole time."

"She's not broken," Rhea said softly. "She's different. And yeah, it's not going to be easy. Living with this kind of sensitivity, it's intense. It can be overwhelming. But it's not a curse. It's a connection. Carmen can see and feel things others can't. That comes with a burden, but also with a purpose."

Liv leaned forward, glancing between all of us. "So what happens now? I mean, Shiloh's still here, right? What does she want? Why is she still around?"

"I don't know yet," I admitted. "But I feel her. I know she's waiting. And I think she needs help crossing over. That's why she showed herself to me... why she's still here after all these years."

Rhea nodded in agreement. "When spirits linger, it's usually because something unfinished is holding them back, fear, trauma, guilt. Carmen may be the only one who can help her move on. But there's no rush. Shiloh isn't a threat."

Mom looked at me again, eyes red but softer now. "And you... You believe this is who you are?"

I met her gaze and nodded. "I do. For the first time in my life, I have come to understand myself. And I'm not afraid anymore."

Silence hung in the air for a long moment, thick, but no longer tense. Just full. Full of everything we'd never said before. Years of confusion, fear, and longing for clarity.

Finally, Mom reached across the table and took my hand in hers. "Okay," she whispered. "Then we'll figure this out together."

Chapter Forty–Six

Karina

September 30th, 1998

After three long days in the hospital, I was finally allowed to go home.

Strangely enough, those three days were more comforting than I ever imagined they could be. I didn't feel pressure to smile or pretend. No expectations. No hiding. Just space to breathe and process everything that had led me there. The nurses were kind. My roommate, Jessica, was quiet but warm in a distant way. We didn't talk much, but understood each other without saying a word.

Every day, I met with a doctor who didn't make me feel broken. I told him things I hadn't told anyone, not even myself, about how I'd slowly stopped enjoying the things I used to love, how every day started to feel heavier, darker.

Like I'd been living under a storm cloud that never moved, and I couldn't find the sun no matter how hard I tried.

He listened and then told me something I hadn't expected to hear: "This isn't your fault." He explained I had depression. A real condition, not a weakness or a flaw. And he said it could get better. Not overnight, but slowly, with time, effort, and help.

I was prescribed Prozac and given a referral for a therapist. I felt the slightest flicker of hope for the first time in months, maybe even longer. Perhaps I wouldn't have to feel this way forever.

I was discharged on Wednesday, just after 3:00 p.m. I gathered my few things, hugged Jessica goodbye, and followed a nurse through the familiar, locked doors. My stomach twisted in knots. I hadn't spoken directly to my family since I was admitted; the doctor had kept them informed, but still, I was scared. Scared to see them. Frightened, they'd look at me differently. Afraid I'd see in their eyes the pain I'd caused.

But when I stepped into the lobby and saw them, my mom, Liv, Carmen, all waiting there for me, something inside me cracked open.

Mom rushed forward and wrapped me in a hug so tight, it felt like she was trying to hold all my broken pieces together with her arms. Her tears soaked into my hair.

"I'm sorry, Mom," I whispered.

"It's okay, honey. I'm just so glad you're okay," she whispered, her voice trembling.

Liv hugged me next, wrapping me in warmth. Then Carmen stepped forward and embraced me. Her hug lingered a little longer, and I felt her fingers grip tighter like she didn't want to let go.

After a few moments, I pulled away, wiped my eyes, and asked, "Can I go home now?"

Mom smiled through her tears. "Absolutely, sweetheart."

We walked out to the car together. I sat in the front seat beside Mom, while Liv and Carmen climbed back in. The ride was quiet at first, full of that heavy silence that isn't awkward but sacred, like everyone is trying to find their footing again after something earth-shattering.

After a few minutes, I turned around to look at Carmen. "Thank you," I said softly.

Carmen glanced up, surprised. "For what?"

Liv looked confused. "Yeah... what are you thanking her for?"

I glanced between them, then back at Carmen. "The other day... when I was still at the hospital, before they took me upstairs... You were the last person I saw. And I remembered something. I remembered seeing you at the bottom of the stairs. It was like a dream, as if I were floating outside of myself, but I knew it was real. You saw me. And that's when you got Mom and Liv. That's when you saved me."

Mom turned slightly in her seat, her eyes meeting Carmen's in the rearview mirror. "Is that true?"

"Can I tell her, Mom?" Carmen asked cautiously.

Mom hesitated. "I don't know, honey. Maybe we should get home and talk later. We've had enough for one day."

"I'm fine," I said. "Please, just tell me. I want to understand." "She's going to find out eventually, Mom," Liv added gently. Mom sighed and nodded. "Okay. Go ahead."

And that's when Carmen opened up. During the rest of the drive, she told me everything about the voices, the shadows, and the strange events she'd kept hidden. About Shiloh. About Viola. About the demon and the markings on her back. About how she could see things others couldn't. She'd thought she was sick, too, but now knew it was something different, something real, a gift.

If I hadn't experienced what I did, that strange, out-of-body moment, I might not have believed her. But I had. And I did, every word.

By the time we pulled into the driveway, my head was spinning, but not severely. It spun in a way that made space for something new, understanding.

We exited the car and started walking to the front door, but I stopped just before entering.

I turned to Carmen. My voice shook a little as I spoke. "I think there's a reason you have this gift. Because if you didn't... You wouldn't have seen me. And I wouldn't be here. You saved my life, Carmen. Thank you."

Her eyes filled with tears, and she didn't say a word; she just hugged me again. And this time, we both held on like we knew it was the beginning of something new. Something healing.

Something hopeful.

~~~~~~~~~~

I sat on my bed, staring blankly around my room. Everything looked the same, but I didn't feel the same. None of the posters on the wall, the books on the shelf, or the little collection of trinkets on my nightstand had changed. But I had. Something inside me had shifted.

My eyes drifted to the window, where sunlight poured in, soft and warm. A part of me hated how normal everything looked. The world hadn't stopped spinning just because I almost left it. It felt wrong. Like there should've been a sign or something, an earthquake, a lightning bolt, a crack in the sky. But there was nothing. Just the quiet hum of life moving forward, as if nothing had happened.

I thought about the pills. The silence that had followed. And the truth I couldn't ignore anymore: I had made the wrong choice. But in that moment, curled up on my bed,
~~~~~~~~~~

the weight of everything crushing me, it hadn't felt bad. It had felt like the only option I had left, the only way to end the pain.

But afterward, in the hours I spent alone in that hospital bed, I realized something. It wasn't my only option. I'd just forgotten that I had others. That help was still within reach. That I mattered more than I thought I did.

Everyone in the house gave me space when I got home, and I was grateful for it. I took a long, hot shower, washing the last few days off my skin, then pulled on clean clothes, soft sweatpants, and a hoodie. I grabbed one of my favorite books from the shelf, curled up on my bed, and let the quiet wrap around me like a blanket.

After a few hours, I heard Liv moving around in the kitchen. The scent of something comforting, maybe tomato sauce or garlic bread, floated up the stairs. It was starting to feel like home again, piece by piece.

A soft knock came at my doorframe.

"Can I come in?" Mom asked gently.

I looked up from my book. She stood there with her hands clasped, eyes red-rimmed but warm. I nodded.

"Yeah. Come in."

She stepped into the room and sat on the edge of my bed, her eyes studying me the way moms do when trying to see inside your soul.

"I need you to promise me something," she said, her voice low but firm. "If you ever, even for a second, feel like you want to hurt yourself again, you'll come to me. I don't care what time it is. I don't care where I am. You talk to me. Promise me, Karina."

I could see the pain in her face, the tightness around her mouth, the way her eyes shimmered with unshed tears. I hadn't just scared her, I'd broken something inside her, something sacred.

"I promise," I said, my throat tightening. "I promise, Mom. I'm so sorry. I'll never do it again."

She leaned over and pulled me into a hug. I wrapped my arms around her and held on, anchoring myself. Her arms were warm, solid, and genuine. And suddenly, I didn't feel like I was drifting anymore.

After a long moment, she pulled back slightly and brushed a strand of hair from my face.

"I need to ask you something," I said.

"Okay, but first... I need to tell you something."

I blinked, "What is it?"

She took a deep breath, then exhaled slowly. "You don't have to be okay right away. Healing isn't a straight line. It's okay to take your time."

I nodded, tears prickling at the corners of my eyes again.

"And now," she said softly, "what did you want to ask me?"

I hesitated. This was hard to admit, but I couldn't carry it alone anymore.

"I've been getting bullied at school," I said. "It started before the semester even began. This girl, Amber... we ran into her at the mall. She recognized me at school, and ever since then, she's been harassing me. Whispering things in the hallway, spreading rumors, and mocking me in front of others. She makes every day a nightmare."

Mom's jaw tightened, but she didn't interrupt.

"I tried to ignore her. I even tried standing up to her, hoping she'd back off. But it only made things worse. And I just... I didn't know how to tell you. I thought maybe if I just toughed it out, it would stop. But it didn't. And now, going back there..." I shook my head, voice breaking. "I can't. I can't face that again. I love learning. I really do. But school doesn't feel safe anymore. Is there any way... Could I finish high school from home? Just until I'm ready to try again?"

Mom looked like someone had punched her in the stomach. She reached out and took my hand, squeezing it.

"I wish you'd told me sooner," she said quietly. "But I'm glad you told me now. And yes. I'll call the school tomorrow. We'll figure something out, okay? You don't have to go back there. I won't make you."

The relief hit me so fast and hard that I almost started crying again. I nodded, grateful beyond words.

"Thank you," I whispered.

She leaned in and kissed my forehead. "I'm proud of you, Karina. Even now. Especially now."

As she stood and left the room, I lay back on my bed, feeling the first real sense of peace I'd felt in months. I didn't know what came next, but for the first time, I felt like I might be strong enough to find out.

<div align="center">~~~~~~~~~~</div>

October 2nd, 1998

It had been almost a week since I tried to end my life, and every day since, I'd woken up feeling more and more grateful that I hadn't succeeded. The pain wasn't completely gone, but it felt manageable now, like something I could hold without letting it crush me.

Mom had followed through on her promise. After a lengthy conversation with the school counselor and principal, I was enrolled in a homeschooling program. It was a huge relief. I could finally breathe again without the looming anxiety of walking those halls, without bracing myself for Amber's cruel words or sideways glances. School felt safe now. Mine again.

Most days, I followed a gentle routine. I'd wake up late, eat breakfast in my pajamas, and work on school assignments across my bed or curled into the oversized chair in the library nook. I'd read for hours sometimes, getting lost in stories that made me feel like I belonged somewhere else, somewhere simpler.

Mom returned to work a few days ago, Liv returned to her job at the coffee shop, while Carmen settled into high school rhythm again. Slowly, the house found its rhythm, too. It felt like life was beginning to stitch itself back together.

It was my birthday. Sixteen. A number that felt both ordinary and impossible. I never thought I'd make it here, and now that I had, I wasn't sure what to make of it.

There was no big party, no flashing lights or loud music; just me, my family, and a quiet comfort that, for once, felt like enough.

Liv had promised to take me out driving later this week. The thought both thrilled and terrified me. I still didn't have a car, but that didn't matter. It was something to look forward to, something that belonged to me.

I hadn't seen anyone outside my family since before the hospital. Not even Sarah. I missed her terribly, but I knew Carmen had explained everything to her and Brett. That made things easier, requiring less explanation and relief.

Around three, I heard the front door creak open and the sound of Mom's keys hitting the bowl in the foyer. I smiled softly as I heard her footsteps heading straight to the kitchen. The scent of vanilla and sugar followed as she started baking my birthday cake. Liv would be home soon, and Carmen wasn't far behind.

I was sitting in the library chair, a worn copy of *Anne of Green Gables* open on my lap, when I heard the door swing open again. The sound of laughter and muffled voices floated down the hall.

"Hey," I called, standing and peeking my head out of the doorway.

By the front door stood Carmen, flanked by Brett and Sarah.

My heart leapt. "Sarah!"

I dropped my book and ran over, wrapping my arms around her before I could even think. She hugged me just as tightly, like she'd been holding in the same breath I had.

"I missed you," she whispered.

"I missed you, too," I said, grabbing her wrist without letting go. "Come on. Let's go up to my room."

I tugged her upstairs, the two of us giggling like we used to before everything got so heavy. Once we reached my room, we sat cross-legged on my bed. The air between us felt a little thick at first, uncertain, like we were both holding words in our mouths we weren't sure how to say.

"Does anyone at school know?" I finally asked, my voice quiet.

Sarah shook her head. "No. Everyone just thinks you're out sick. Amber even asked about you yesterday."

The mention of Amber's name made something twist inside me: anger, hurt, fear, but I pushed it away. I didn't have to face her anymore. That chapter was closed.

Sarah must've noticed my change in expression, because she quickly changed the subject.

"Hey, here," she said, grabbing a pink gift bag from the floor. It was covered in a butterfly pattern and stuffed with pastel tissue paper. "Happy birthday."

A smile broke across my face. "Sarah…"

"Open it!" she said, practically bouncing.

I pulled the paper out and tossed it gently to the floor, reaching inside. The first item was wrapped in light blue paper and sealed with butterfly stickers instead of tape. It felt like a book, and I was right.

I peeled the wrapping away and gasped; *The Giver* by Lois Lowry.

"I love this book," I said, holding it to my chest. "I always wanted my own copy."

"I remembered you said that after we finished it in class," Sarah said, grinning.

"Thank you," I said, my voice thick with emotion.

Next, I pulled out a sweet and warm candle, the scent of strawberry shortcake wafting toward me the second I opened the lid. It was my favorite scent in the whole world, comforting, familiar, and safe.

And finally, I reached in and pulled out a small green journal with a gold-etched butterfly and a silver lock on the side.

"Write your own story," Sarah said softly. "You've been through a lot, Karina. Maybe writing it down will help. Or maybe you'll write something totally new. Either way, it's yours."

I looked down at the gifts in my lap, and then back at Sarah, my bestest friend, sitting across from me with hope and love in her heart.

"You're the best," I whispered, leaning over to hug her. "Thank you. For everything."

She hugged me tightly, and I knew then that no matter how much I'd been through or how much it still scared me, I wasn't alone.

Not anymore.

Chapter Forty–Seven

Liv

After helping Mom finish dinner, I stayed behind in the kitchen to help her put the final touches on Karina's birthday cake. We'd gone with her favorite, chocolate with raspberry filling and whipped cream frosting, and Mom had even added a ring of fresh raspberries around the top. It wasn't fancy, but it was beautiful in its own way, just like Karina.

I had just finished piping the last swirl of whipped cream when I heard the front door creak open.

Footsteps. Then a familiar voice.

"Hello?"

I looked up, instantly recognizing it. Nina.

I wiped my hands on the front of my apron and rushed toward the entryway, excitement fluttering in my chest. When I saw her, I smiled widely and hugged her tightly without thinking.

"I'm so glad you're here," I whispered, kissing her cheek softly.

Nina smiled but hesitated. "Are you sure I'm not intruding? It's a family thing. I don't want to overstep."

"Not at all," I said, looping my arm through hers. "It's a birthday, not a board meeting. The more, the merrier."

She chuckled and followed me into the kitchen, where Mom plated the last food.

"Girls, could you carry this into the dining room and call everyone down?" Mom asked, wiping her hands on a towel.

"You got it," I said. Nina and I each grabbed a few serving dishes, Mom's homemade mini chicken pot pies, a bowl of roasted vegetables, and a tray of fresh salad. We brought everything to the table, arranging it carefully, and then I stepped onto the stairs.

"Dinner's ready!" I called up.

A few moments later, I heard footsteps pounding down the stairs. Karina appeared first, her face glowing, followed by Sarah, then Carmen and Brett, who were mid-conversation but quieted as they entered the room.

Everyone took their seats around the dining room table, a gentle hum of conversation filling the space as we passed plates and pitchers of lemonade.

"This smells amazing," Karina said, inhaling the scent of the flaky pot pies.

"Mini chicken pot pies," Mom said with a proud smile.

"My favorite," Karina grinned, eyes lighting up. She looked healthier than she had in a while. Her cheeks were rosier, her eyes clearer, like some fog that had followed her for months had finally started to lift.

We all dug in, clinking silverware and sharing stories from the week. The pot pies were warm and creamy, filled with tender chicken, carrots, and peas in a buttery crust that melted in your mouth. They were comfort food in the truest sense.

Laughter bubbled up here and there, Karina recounting a book she was reading, Brett making one of his famously terrible puns, Sarah playfully teasing him, and it felt like the air had cleared for a while. Like we were just a normal family, gathered for a birthday, basking in the comfort of each other.

But then something shifted.

I caught it out of the corner of my eye, Carmen suddenly whipping her head toward the hallway.

Everyone at the table fell silent. The shift was so sudden and sharp that even Nina paused mid-bite. Carmen's expression darkened slightly, her eyes narrowing as if trying to listen to something the rest of us couldn't hear.

"Carmen?" I asked gently, my fork paused midway to my mouth. "Is something wrong?"

All eyes turned to her.

She turned back slowly, her expression unreadable.

We all knew. We were all thinking it. Ever since we learned the truth about her gift, her ability to see and communicate with spirits, every flicker of emotion on her face came with a silent question: *Is she hearing something again? Is there something here?*

"No," she said quickly, maybe a little too quickly. "It's nothing."

Then she leaned in toward Brett and whispered something in his ear, too quiet for anyone else to hear.

Brett nodded subtly, then returned to his food as if nothing had happened.

Mom, Karina, and I exchanged a knowing glance. We didn't press it. Carmen would tell us in her own time if it was something important. That had become our unspoken agreement: don't push or pry. Let her come to us.

The conversation resumed, hesitant at first, like we were testing the air, but soon the room was filled with warmth and laughter again.

I felt it as I looked around the table, at my sisters, at Nina beside me, at my mother, who was finally smiling again; that quiet sense of healing. Maybe, just maybe, we were going to be okay.

Even if there were things we didn't understand. Even if the shadows still lingered at the edges.

We had love. And for now, that was enough.

~~~~~~~~~~

After dinner, Nina and I stayed behind to help Mom clear the table and wash the dishes. The kitchen buzzed with running water and clinking plates while laughter drifted in from the living room where Karina, Sarah, Carmen, and Brett huddled together, trying to pick a movie. Their voices overlapped with excitement and playful arguing over what to watch, filling the house with a warmth that had been missing for a while.

Nina stood beside me at the sink, drying plates as I washed them. Now and then, our shoulders brushed, and we exchanged quiet smiles. It felt good, simple, domestic, and comforting. After everything that had happened, normalcy was a gift.

Once the kitchen was clean, I opened the drawer by the stove and pulled out a small box of birthday candles that Mom kept tucked away for special occasions. Nina took the box from my hands, carefully pressing a candle into each swirl of frosting on the cake. When she was done, she struck a match and lit the wicks, one by one. The flames danced gently, casting flickers of light across the kitchen.

Mom returned just in time, flipping off the overhead light. "Ready?" she asked with a warm smile.

"Let's do it," I said, and together, we carefully carried the cake into the living room.
~~~~~~~~~~

As we stepped inside, everyone turned toward us, their faces glowing in the soft candlelight. Carmen dimmed the floor lamp, and momentarily, the only illumination came from the tiny flames flickering atop Karina's birthday cake.

We all gathered around her as the familiar tune of *Happy Birthday* filled the room. Though a little off-key, our voices were filled with love and joy. Karina sat between Sarah and Carmen on the couch, smiling so wide it looked like her cheeks might hurt. It was a genuine smile that I hadn't seen on her face in a long time.

When the song ended, we all clapped and cheered as she leaned forward, her eyes reflecting the candlelight. She paused for a second, as if making a wish that meant more than most, then took a deep breath and blew out all the candles in one go.

Cheers and applause erupted again, and Mom took the cake back into the kitchen to cut it into generous slices.

"Chocolate with raspberry filling," Brett said with a grin. "Best cake ever."

"She knows me well," Karina said with a little laugh.

When Mom returned with plates, we all dug in, the room falling into a contented silence broken only by the sound of forks on plates and the occasional hum of satisfaction.

Once everyone had their cake, we turned our attention to the stack of presents on the coffee table. Karina leaned forward and started unwrapping them, one by one, her excitement growing with each reveal.

Carmen gave her a novel she'd just finished reading, a fantasy book about a girl with unusual powers, and a CD from a new indie band she knew Karina would love. "You've gotta listen to track six," Carmen said. "It reminded me of you."

I handed her my gifts next, a hardback copy of *The Secret Garden*, which we'd both loved as kids, and a Tamagotchi. "For when you're bored during homeschool," I teased. "Now you can have a digital pet to keep alive."

Karina laughed and hugged me. "I love it."

Mom handed her an envelope with money and a box containing a few cute outfits, a soft sweater, jeans, and a cardigan. "Something to make you feel good when you get dressed in the morning," she said with a kiss on Karina's forehead.

Nina offered her a gift bag with a vintage-style T-shirt and a delicate necklace with a tiny star charm. "The shirt reminded me of you," she said. "And the star... because you're still shining, even after everything."

Karina's eyes misted over as she thanked her softly.

Finally, Brett handed her a wrapped package that included a CD and a DVD of an old favorite coming-of-age film. "This one's a classic. You've got good taste," he said.

Karina beamed, looking at the pile of thoughtful gifts around her. "Thank you, all of you. This is the best birthday I've had in... I don't even know how long."

We smiled, each of us quietly taking in the moment. There was no extravagance, no giant party or flashy decorations. Just love. Family. Healing. And the feeling that, after everything, we were still here, together.

Chapter Forty–Eight

Carmen

October 3rd, 1998

It was Saturday morning, and the house was tranquil. I had just finished breakfast, scrambled eggs and toast with a little too much butter, the way I liked it. The smell of coffee lingered faintly in the air even though Mom had already left for her early shift at the hospital. Liv was upstairs getting ready for work, humming along faintly to music through her bedroom door. The peacefulness of the morning was comforting in a way I hadn't felt in a long time.

Karina and I rinsed our plates in the sink, and the clinking of ceramic echoed in the kitchen. We slipped on our shoes and jackets, the crisp October air already sneaking in through the thin cracks of the doorframe. I zipped up my hoodie and tugged a beanie over my ears.

"Are we ready?" Karina asked, slinging her bag over her shoulder.

"Yeah," I said, tugging open the door. "Let's go."

We walked side by side down the gravel road, our shoes crunching through the scattered leaves that had begun to blanket the ground. The trees lining the street had started to turn, flashes of amber, gold, and crimson painting the branches like fire against the gray sky. Fall had always been my favorite season. Something comforting about the chill in the air was the way the world seemed to slow down and prepare for rest.

As we neared Brett and Sarah's house, I spotted Sarah standing by her uncle's car. She was wrapped in a thick scarf, her breath visible in little puffs in the cold air.

"Hey!" Karina called out, waving as we got closer.

Sarah smiled and waved back. "You guys are right on time."

She hugged me quickly before the two of them climbed into the car. "Call me later," I told Karina as the door shut.

"Have fun!" I called as the car pulled away, its tires crunching over the gravel at the end of the driveway.

I turned toward the front door and let myself in. The warmth of the house wrapped around me immediately, and the faint scent of cinnamon and sage hung in the air, probably from one of Rhea's spell candles.

I found Brett in the kitchen, seated at the table across from Rhea, a steaming mug of coffee in his hands. He looked up and smiled when he saw me.

"Morning, babe," he said, standing up and hugging me. He kissed me softly on the cheek, and I felt some of the tension I'd been holding melt away.

"Morning," I said, and then nodded at Rhea. "Hey. How are you?"

"Good morning, Carmen," she said warmly. "How are *you* feeling today?"

"I'm okay," I replied, sliding into the chair next to Brett. "Did Brett tell you what happened?"

Rhea nodded, folding her hands on the table. "He told me you heard Shiloh again."

"Yeah," I said slowly, my fingers tracing an invisible pattern on the table's wood grain. "She said something... strange. She told me to meet her in the woods. I have no idea what that means."

Rhea leaned back slightly, thoughtful. Her brow furrowed as she considered the message. "The woods could be significant," she said eventually. "Sometimes spirits are drawn to where their connection to the world is strongest. The woods are where she died."

"Why would she want Carmen to go there, though?" Brett asked, his arm resting gently around my shoulders.

"Maybe she wants to show her something," Rhea offered. "Something Carmen needs to see. Or maybe it's where she feels safest and can speak most clearly."

I hesitated, feeling a strange mixture of curiosity and dread settle in my chest. "Should we go?" I asked. "I mean... today?"

Rhea gave me a measured look. "I have some paperwork I need to finish this morning for the shop," she said. "But after lunch? Yes. We'll go. The sooner we understand what Shiloh needs, the sooner we can help her find peace."

I nodded, the decision settling over me like a quiet weight. "Okay. After lunch."

Brett gave my hand a reassuring squeeze, and I leaned into him, grateful I wasn't facing this alone. The woods had always seemed peaceful from a distance, but now they held a mystery that called me in deeper. I didn't know what I'd find there, but I knew one thing: I couldn't ignore it.

~~~~~~~~~~

Brett and I went to his room while Rhea stayed downstairs to finish her paperwork. The house was quiet, filled only with the soft hum of wind against the windows and the occasional creak of the floorboards below. His room was warm and familiar, filled with little reminders of the boy I had grown to love: his posters, organized guitar picks, and the faint scent of his cologne lingering in the air.
~~~~~~~~~~

We climbed onto his bed and curled into each other like we'd done a dozen times before, our legs tangled beneath the blanket. His arms wrapped around me, and we lay there for a long moment, breathing each other in. When he leaned in to kiss me, it felt like everything else melted away: Shiloh, the darkness, the past. For now, it was just us.

We kissed slowly, tenderly, our hands tracing soft patterns against skin and fabric. His fingers brushed the side of my face, and I smiled against his lips.

Between kisses, he whispered, "Can I come with you? To the woods?"

I paused for a second, searching his eyes. His concern was genuine, protective, and gentle; it made my chest ache a little in the best way.

"You can," I said softly, my voice barely above a breath.

His eyes widened slightly in surprise. "Really?"

"Yeah," I nodded. "I trust Shiloh. I don't think she would ever hurt us."

He brushed his thumb across my cheek and smiled, the kind of smile that made me fall for him all over again. "Okay. Good. Thank you."

He leaned in again and kissed me, and this time it deepened, slower, more intense. I melted into him, my heart thudding gently in my chest, not from fear or anxiety, but from want. From closeness.

After a few minutes, I felt a familiar craving stir inside me, a desire to feel even closer, to remind myself that I was still alive and here.

I let my hand drift down his side, fingers teasing the edge of his shirt. "You know…" I said with a half-smile, "It's been a minute since we…"

"Yeah," he said, his voice low and husky. He pulled back just enough to look into my eyes, checking in, waiting. I nodded.

He lifted his shirt over his head and tossed it aside, then helped me out of mine. Skin to skin, we took our time, our hands exploring, memorizing. There was no rush, just warmth, trust, and a kind of gentle urgency that felt more like a promise than anything else.

He reached over to his nightstand and pulled open the drawer, grabbing a condom without breaking the moment. His other hand never left mine. Then he kissed me again, deeply, reverently, and we let ourselves fall into each other completely.

There were no words for a while, just the soft rustling of sheets, the shared rhythm of breath, and the feeling of being held, truly and completely.

Later, when we lay tangled beneath the blanket, his hand resting lightly on my hip, he whispered, "I'm with you, okay? No matter what happens in those woods."

I turned to look at him, brushing my fingers through his hair. "I know," I whispered back. "And I'm not afraid anymore."

And I wasn't. Not with him beside me.

~~~~~~~~~~

After Rhea made Brett and me lunch, grilled cheese sandwiches with perfectly crisp edges and warm tomato soup, we cleaned up, grabbed our jackets, and packed a few things before heading out the door. The sky was a soft, overcast gray that made the autumn colors pop against the horizon. The air smelled of leaves and distant chimney smoke, crisp with that familiar October bite.

We didn't head into my house, but past it, cutting across the street toward the abandoned home across from mine. Behind its weathered shell lay the tree line, overgrown, unkempt, wild, and beyond it, the railroad tracks where Shiloh had died.

As we approached the edge of the yard, the weeds grew taller, swaying like whispers in the wind. The ground dipped slightly, leading us into the forest. Here, the world was quieter. Our footsteps crunched softly over brittle leaves, twigs, and gnarled roots that twisted like sleeping snakes beneath our feet. The deeper we walked, the more the world seemed to change, less like our home, and more like something frozen in time.
~~~~~~~~~~

After a few minutes of navigating the woods, we saw the gleam of steel tracks through the thinning trees. Rhea paused at the edge of the clearing, her eyes scanning both directions. Her expression tightened, brows furrowed in memory.

"Over here," she called, her voice distant, like she wasn't present. Brett and I quickened our steps, weaving through the trees until we reached her.

An old wooden cross stood at her feet, weathered and leaning slightly as if the earth was tired of holding it. A rusted circle of wire lay before it, what must've once been a wreath. The ground around it was cleared of debris, almost like something sacred had preserved the space.

"This is where they found her," Rhea said quietly. She exhaled a shaky breath, her voice trembling. "I haven't been back here in over thirty years."

I stepped beside her and gently wrapped an arm around her shoulders. She didn't speak for a moment, just laid her hand over mine and stared at the old cross like it held all the answers she had ever needed.

After a while, she straightened her shoulders. "Enough reminiscing. Let's get to work."

Brett, kneeling beside the track, glanced up. "How are we going to talk to Shiloh? I thought you said you couldn't control it?"

"I can't," I replied honestly. "Not exactly."

"But we have ways to open the door," Rhea said, unzipping her backpack. "Tools that can help amplify her presence."

She pulled out four small white candles and a spirit board carved into smooth, polished wood. The board's letters and symbols appeared worn from use, yet remained sharp and precise. The planchette was nestled in a small black pouch.

We cleared a patch of ground and sat in a semicircle, Rhea, Brett, and I. She placed the candles at each corner of the board and lit them one by one, their flames flickering in the soft breeze. The woods felt different now, still and thick with energy, like the air was holding its breath.

"I've never done this before," I confessed, my voice barely above a whisper.

"You'll be fine," Rhea reassured me. "While you two were... upstairs, I talked to Viola. She gave me a list of questions." Rhea reached into her backpack, pulled out a folded notepad, and handed it to me.

I unfolded the paper slowly, reading the neat list of questions written in Rhea's handwriting. It felt surreal, like a dream I wasn't quite awake from.

Taking a deep breath, I placed two fingers from each hand on the planchette. Rhea did the same.

"You too, Brett," Rhea said gently, her tone focused but calm. He nodded and joined us.

I closed my eyes for a moment, centering myself, then asked the first question aloud.

"Shiloh? Are you with us?"

The board remained still. The only sound was the wind rustling through the trees.

"Shiloh," I said again, stronger this time, "I call out to you. Are you with us?"

The planchette shivered, then slowly slid toward the top-left corner of the board, hovering over "YES."

Brett let out a soft, "Whoa," but Rhea raised her finger to her lips, signaling him to stay quiet.

"Shiloh," I continued, trying to keep my voice steady, "you asked me to come here. To help you. What do you want me to do?"

For a few seconds, nothing happened. Then, the air changed. It grew colder, heavier. A breeze blew through the clearing, snuffing out one of the candles. And then the planchette began to move again.

I read the letters aloud as they were spelled out: "T-E-L-L H-E-R."

"Tell her?" I asked. "Tell who, Shiloh?"

The planchette moved again, this time more slowly and deliberately. "R-H-E-A."

I turned toward Rhea, who sat frozen in place, her breath shallow.

"What do you want me to tell her?" I asked.

Suddenly, my vision swam. A wave of nausea hit me like a punch to the stomach. I leaned back on one hand, my free hand pressing against my forehead.

"Carmen? Are you okay?" Brett asked, concern etched into every word.

I didn't answer immediately because I heard it, her. Shiloh's voice, clear as ever, not inside my head, but around me. Whispering, yet powerful. And she was crying.

"She has a message," I said slowly, my voice hollowed out with awe. "She wants Rhea to know the truth. Her truth. About what happened."

Rhea leaned forward, her eyes glistening. "Then tell me," she whispered. "Please, Carmen. I need to know."

And so, I did. Word for word, I told Shiloh's story as it poured into me, raw, heavy, and honest. The wind hushed as I spoke, like even the trees were listening.

"The day I first met you, Rhea, was the best day of my life. I remember it as clear as crystal. It was springtime, not long after my seventh birthday. The world smelled of lilacs and fresh-cut grass. You and your mama came calling on our house for the first time. I was sitting on the front steps, playing with a bit of twine, and your mama asked mine if we might be allowed to play together. Mama said yes, and from that moment on, you were my dearest friend in all the world.

You didn't look at me like other folks did. You weren't put off by the way I spoke or the way I held my head when I tried to listen. You knew I couldn't hear right, but it never once made you treat me differently. You loved me for who I was. We played pretend in the garden, made daisy chains, whispered our secrets into old tree trunks like fairy houses.

You told me about school, about the world beyond my porch, and you taught me words I'd never heard. You gave me a world, Rhea. You gave me friendship. Safety. Joy.

But there was one secret I never did tell you. I think I should have, but I was scared. You saw for yourself that my father wasn't the kindest of men, but you never knew the depths of his rage, nor the shame he carried about me.

From the day my hearing loss was discovered, Daddy said I was broken. I brought shame to the family name, and he said I wasn't fit to be seen. They never let me out much. I didn't go to school like you did. I never walked into town or rode a bicycle down Main Street. When visitors came, Daddy would lock me in the upstairs closet, the one in the guest room. I recall the scent of mothballs and aged cedar. I remember the darkness and how time seemed to bend and twist within it. I think I started losing pieces of myself in those walls. But when I was with you, Rhea... I remembered who I was. You reminded me. You gave me back to myself.

The day I died, I was waiting for you. You were due home from school any minute. I had a fresh notebook and wanted to play our game, the one where we wrote letters to fairies and left them in hollow trees. But my hearing aid had gone dead. I could hardly hear anything, not even my breath. I needed a new battery, but Daddy was on the telephone, conducting business, and Mama was out.

I was never supposed to disturb him while he was on a call. But I thought if I were quiet, he wouldn't notice. So I crept inside his office. I opened drawers, one by one, looking for batteries, but instead, I found a box. It was hidden beneath a stack of old ledgers. Inside were letters, dozens of them. They were from your mama. All addressed to my father. I couldn't read them all, but the ones I did read made my stomach twist. I didn't understand everything, but I knew it was something important. Something meant to stay hidden.

Daddy caught me. He must've heard me rustling around. He hollered at me, but I couldn't hear. He grabbed me hard by the arms and shook me. I remember crying, begging him to stop. But something in me broke loose. I yanked free and ran. I ran as fast as I could.

I didn't stop. I burst out of the front door, across the street, and through the yard. I ran into the woods, heading toward your house the quickest way I knew, along the railroad tracks.

But I couldn't hear the train.

Not until it was far too late.

I've been here ever since and tied to that place. Not because I was angry or afraid, but because you never knew. I couldn't leave without telling you the truth.

Rhea... your mama and my daddy had an affair. It started shortly after I was born. Nobody ever spoke of it. Not back then. Folks kept things behind curtains and smiles. But the truth is... You are his daughter, too. My father was your father.

You and I, we were more than just friends. We were sisters. You were my only family, the only love I ever truly had. I just wish I could've told you while I was still alive.

Now that you know, I can finally rest. I'm not afraid anymore. I love you, Rhea. I always did."

When it was over, the three of us sat in silence, our hands resting in our laps, our breaths slow and shallow. The forest around us held its breath, too, like it understood that something sacred had just happened. The towering trees stood like quiet sentinels, their leaves barely rustling in the stillness. Even the birds had fallen silent, as if nature was paying its respects to the memory of a little girl who had been silenced too soon.

A truth, buried beneath shame and sorrow for decades, had finally risen to the surface. Once locked away behind closed doors and sealed letters, a voice had been heard.

Then, I felt it.

A shift in the air. A soft hum against my skin, like the world's energy was changing.

"She's here," I whispered, my voice trembling as I turned to look deeper into the trees.

Brett and Rhea followed my gaze, but I knew they couldn't see what I did.

"Shiloh," I said softly.

There she stood, no longer the pale shadow that used to flicker in the corners of my vision. She was whole now. Her long hair flowed gently around her face, and her green dress fluttered lightly, though no wind stirred. Her eyes, bright and calm, met mine. I thought she might speak for a moment, but she didn't need to. Her smile was enough.

"She's smiling," I told them quietly. "She's facing me. She said... thank you."

And then, like the mist at dawn, she began to fade. A soft and radiant white light surrounded her, and within seconds, she was gone.

But she didn't leave emptiness behind. Instead, I felt something settle in my chest, a quiet warmth. A sense of calm. Peace.

"She's moved on," I said, my voice barely above a whisper. "She's free now."

Rhea was silent for a long time. Her eyes were glassy, the weight of the truth sitting heavy in her hands. She was trying to hold it all, grief, revelation, the tangled web of her childhood rewritten in a single afternoon.

But underneath it, I could see it in her face: relief. The ache that had lived behind her eyes for so many years, the questions that had never been asked aloud, finally had an answer.

She wiped at her cheeks with the sleeve of her sweater and then reached for me. Her arms wrapped around me in a tight hug, so full of feeling, I could hardly breathe. But I didn't pull away.

"Thank you," she whispered, her voice cracking under the weight of it all. "Thank you for giving her back to me."

I nodded against her shoulder. "She never left you. She just couldn't find her way until now."

Brett placed a gentle hand on my back, and the three of us just sat like that for a few moments longer, grounded by the quiet power of what had happened.

Eventually, Rhea exhaled and stood. "We should head back," she said softly, her voice steadier now, as if something inside her had finally clicked into place.

We packed up everything in silence. The spirit board, the candles, Rhea blew each out gently, like putting a chapter to rest.

The walk back through the woods was quiet. The sun had dipped lower in the sky, casting a golden glow through the canopy above us. Fallen leaves crunched underfoot, and a soft breeze danced through the branches, as if nature itself was exhaling along with us.

When we reached Rhea's house, we paused momentarily on the porch. No one spoke, but the silence didn't feel heavy anymore.

It felt like peace.

It felt like goodbye.

And in the soft hush of the early evening, I knew something for sure:

Shiloh was finally home.

And Rhea wasn't alone anymore.

None of us were.

~~~~~~~~~~

May 22nd, 1999

I stood in the bathroom, staring at my reflection in the mirror. The soft fabric of my graduation gown rustled around me, the cap slightly askew on my head. I adjusted it with trembling fingers, still not entirely believing that this day had come. Graduation. A word that used to feel so far away, so unreachable, especially during the darkest moments of this past year.

The girl staring back at me wasn't the same girl from a year ago. She had walked through fire, quiet, personal, invisible flames that scorched her spirit and shaped her in
~~~~~~~~~~

ways no one could see from the outside. I thought about the silence I had once lived in, the secrets I carried, the pain that nearly broke me. But I also thought about everything that came after, the uncovered truth, the souls that found peace, the love I was given, and the strength I saw in myself.

So much had changed.

And yet, standing here in my cap and gown, I didn't feel heavy anymore. I felt light. Not because the pain was gone, but because I had made peace with it. I had turned it into something more. Something meaningful.

I glanced down at my hands, remembering how they shook with fear and doubt. Now, they were steady and confident. They had written goodbye letters, but held on to people they loved, comforted those in need, and helped guide a lost soul home.

The memories of that year lived inside me: the haunting whispers, the tearful nights, the joy of healing, the shock of secrets revealed, and the serenity of knowing I'd made a difference.

I smiled.

Without everything that had happened, every terrifying, beautiful, life-altering moment, I wouldn't be the person I am now. Not even close. And while I wouldn't have chosen the pain, I wouldn't trade the growth for anything.

Today, I wasn't just graduating from high school.

I was graduating from who I used to be.

A year ago, I never could have imagined this would be my life. If someone had told me I'd be speaking with spirits, uncovering buried truths, and helping souls find peace, I would've laughed, or maybe cried. Back then, everything felt heavy. I was drowning in confusion, fear, and a constant ache that I couldn't explain. I thought something was wrong with me. I thought I was broken.

But now... now, I know the truth.

And for once, I'm grateful.

Truly, deeply grateful.

Because of the fear, the nights I spent questioning my sanity, and the moments I wished I could be anyone else, they led me here, to a place of understanding, acceptance, and purpose.

I've made peace with my gift. What once felt like a curse, like a weight pressing down on my chest, now feels like a calling. A responsibility. A quiet, powerful light inside me. I know now that I was never meant to ignore it. I was meant to embrace it. To use it.

To help.

Even through all the darkness and agony, even through the moments when it felt like the world might crack open beneath me, none of it compared to the feeling I had when Shiloh found peace. That moment, when her spirit finally let go of the pain and crossed into the light, it was unlike anything I'd ever known.

It was pure. It was powerful.

It was joy.

Not the fleeting kind you get from laughter or a good day. But the kind that fills your soul and makes you feel part of something bigger than yourself. Knowing that I helped someone find closure, that I gave voice to a truth silenced for decades, felt like standing at the center of something sacred, as if I had touched something eternal.

It felt... euphoric.

And in that moment, I knew something with absolute certainty: I would do anything to feel that again. To help another soul speak. To uncover another hidden truth. To walk alongside the lost and help them find their way home.

This is my life now.

Not one I planned, not one I ever would have chosen, but the one I was meant for.

And I'm okay with that.

More than okay.

I'm finally free. I'm finally whole. And for the first time in a long time, I'm exactly where I'm supposed to be.

And as I took one last look in the mirror, straightened my cap, and stepped out of the bathroom, I knew one thing for sure: this wasn't the end.

It was only the beginning.

Epilogue

In the near future, the unfolding saga of Carmen's destiny continues in Whispers Between Worlds: *The Second Shadow.*

Though this chapter closes on a hard-won peace, a quiet dawn after a long and arduous struggle, Carmen's true journey has only just begun. The echoes of past battles may fade, but the future, ever-unfolding, promises new horizons and formidable challenges. This peace, so dearly bought, isn't an endpoint, but a brief respite, a moment to gather strength before the path ahead reveals its true complexities.

This next chapter will plunge Carmen into a maelstrom of rediscovered dangers and profound self-discovery. The echoes of her past battles will resonate anew, demanding more from her than she ever thought possible. The quiet triumph of today will serve as both a foundation and a stark contrast to the tempests that lie ahead, pushing her beyond the boundaries of her current understanding and into the heart of a world teeming with both wonder and peril.

Barely five years after embracing her extraordinary gift, a power she's only just beginning to comprehend and control, a chilling shadow from her past resurfaces. It's an enemy she believed vanquished, a darkness thought defeated, now re-emerging from the depths to threaten not just her burgeoning peace, but her very existence. Attacked and shattered, Carmen finds herself fighting not merely for her life, but for the very essence of her soul, for the light she has painstakingly cultivated within herself. The tapestry of her destiny is still being woven, and indeed, the most perilous battle still awaits.